Angel Beneath The Maple

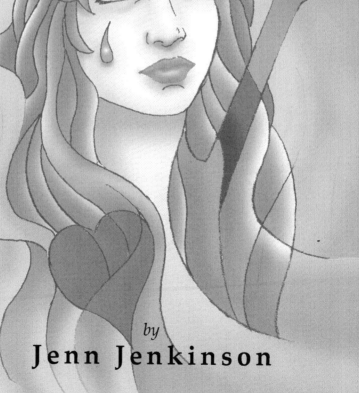

by

Jenn Jenkinson

Angel Awakens

A continuous rain murmured its discontent against the windows in the late night darkness. The fresh clean smell of it permeated even into the snug little house nestled amidst the lilac and honeysuckle hedges which almost completely hid it from the street. Hedges which were welcoming and sweet smelling in the warmth of the daytime sunshine now sagged and brooded eerily under the weight of the rain. A warm yellow glow came from the porch light left burning for the one not yet home. Another light came from a window towards the back of the house.

It was an inconsistent glow with a modern bluish tint from a flickering computer screen. The light cast eerie shadows across the face of the woman sitting before the screen. Her fingers played across the keyboard and almost gently eased the mouse around its pad as she surfed. Her shy face, framed by long dark wavy hair had a doe like quality about it; the look of an innocent creature. Her blue grey eyes scanned the screen before her as she traveled the world with her mouse as a guide.

Down the hall, the children were tucked safely in their beds. She always made sure of her babies' safe trips to dreamland before beginning her nightly escape into the world of the internet. And she could just make out their soft breathing from her seat in the small den, such a reassuring sound in the otherwise quiet house.

Angela had discovered what she now viewed as her own private world in the cyber-pathways of the internet. Here she could pick a topic and search even obscure references, finding pictures of places and things she might never otherwise see, uncovering information about topics that her narrow life at home with her children would probably not have exposed her to before. Angela had also discovered chat rooms and people she could "talk" to all over the world. She had, after her first tentative experimentation on the net, decided not to reveal to anyone her newly expanded horizons. So she surfed here late at night when her husband, Lucas, was out at work and the children were safe in dreamland.

She heard the car pulling up outside, the sound of his booted footsteps up the sidewalk deadened a little by the falling rain. Next came the turn of his key in the lock and, as he entered the side door of the house, she quickly clicked and closed the browser window leaving only the flyer she was supposed to be designing for a local hardware store visible on her screen.

Lucas flipped on the kitchen light as he closed the door behind him. His piercing hazel-green eyes made a quick survey of the living room in the light that spilled from the kitchen doorway. Finding it empty, he crossed the kitchen, without removing the wet boots, and leaned the electric guitar in its case against the wall by the table. He brushed a hand across his damp coal black closely cropped hair then wiped it across his jeans.

Lucas was a handsome man in his early thirties, tall and lean, but certainly muscular. He had what women liked to call a "bad boy" look about him and certainly attracted a lot of attention when he played in the evening. He had almost jet black perfect hair and green eyes which sparkled with a light of their own whenever he chose to bless those around him with a smile. He was a rock guitarist for a house band in one of the clubs in the large metropolitan area which he and Angela called home. But his first musical love was the blues and it sometimes galled him that he could not make a living at the genre he loved.

Angela heard him coming down the hall and murmured a "Hi Lucas, how'd it go tonight?" He walked into the den flipping the overhead light on. Angela's eyes took a second to adjust to the sudden wash of light.

"What'd you say?" He asked roughly.

"How did it go tonight?" She repeated the question in very soft tones. She had turned her chair a little towards him, but did not look up or meet Lucas's gaze.

"Same as always." The reply was flat, resigned. "Stupid morons got no damn musical taste. Playing shit for the masses." Lucas had crossed the tiny room in two quick strides and placed one strong hand on Angela's shoulder, gripping almost tightly enough to make her wince. "Come on, leave this crap for tonight," he said, head nodding towards the computer, "And make me a cup of tea."

She closed her file and shut down the PC, sighing very quietly to herself. 'Why couldn't he be content' she mused. 'Or at least not act like it's my fault no one likes the blues.' She pushed her chair away from the desk and followed Lucas back down the hall to the kitchen.

He picked up his guitar case and went down the basement stairs, where he had built himself a small but well insulated room to use as a studio. Five of his six guitars, two electrics, two acoustics and, the prized possession, a National Steel were lined up neatly along one wall. He put the Stratocaster back in its place in the lineup and shrugged ruefully. Sometimes he just got so angry that the music he loved music that had spawned so many popular genres, was so sadly misunderstood. He'd even tried with Angela and she listened politely, made the appropriate positive comments but continued to play her Rod Stewart or, infinitely worse, old disco crap from the early 80's when they were both teenagers.

At least when he was a teen he was already focused on what good music was all about and was drinking in all the Robert Johnson, Howlin' Wolf, Muddy Waters and their contemporaries he could find. Lucas loved playing, lived and breathed just for the feel of a guitar making beautiful sounds beneath his hands. He ran one hand over the case of the National Steel, then shook off his thoughts and turned to climb back to the kitchen.

Angela had her back to him as he walked back into the room and he stared almost angrily at her. 'Damn woman never looks at me no more!' he thought and then like a black flash, 'Wonder if she's looking at someone else?' He said nothing and slumped at the table, finally reaching to take off the ankle high boots he was wearing.

Angela finished wiping countertops that really didn't need wiping and reached for mugs from the cupboard. Making tea was one thing she was good at, making sure the mix of milk and tea was just right; the tea allowed to brew just the perfect length of time. They had been having tea like this when he got in from his gigs ever since she'd first moved in with him seven years ago. Sometimes Angela thought tea time was their best time.

Except for the bubbling hum of the kettle the kitchen was silent. Neither Lucas nor Angela seemed ready to break the quiet peace between them. Then Lucas arose after taking off the boots which he had kicked under the table and closed the distance between himself and his wife. He leaned hard against her pressing her slim body tight against the counter. One hand came round and caught her chin pulling her face round towards him. The other grasped her rather too tightly around her shoulders.

"You'd better be ready when I am tomorrow, woman." his voice growled, "I can't be late for a gig just 'cause you're putting on your face or something." He chuckled and let her go just as the kettle started to whistle its need for her attention. "You're lucky I decided to take you to a gig to see the new band", he finished flatly.

"Yes Lucas, I promise I'll be ready on time." she murmured, as she mechanically poured the tea. "Thank you for letting me come, it's been so long since I've seen you play." She turned towards him with the tea mug in her hand.

Lucas took the proffered mug and went through into the living room, flipping the TV on to a late night talk show and sprawling on the couch. Angela followed him and took a seat on the edge of a high back easy chair. She sipped her tea and watched her husband more than the images on the TV screen.

Sometimes, when he was quiet like this, Angela could almost see the man she'd met seven years before; the man who had swept her off her feet. He had been so handsome, so worldly and so streetwise that she had been somewhat in awe of him. Lucas had impressed the rather innocent small town girl then and now he still had a certain power over her.

When Angela finished her cup of tea she was ready for bed, relaxed and mellowed by the hot beverage. She first made Lucas a second mug and then said a soft goodnight. He barely acknowledged her departure. She went along the hall, checking in on the children one last time before crawling exhausted into the king size bed covered in cozy old fashioned quilts. She snuggled down and was asleep almost immediately.

Lucas channel surfed through late night television fare for another half an hour and then as the clock in the kitchen turned to 2:00 am he went down the stairs to his little homemade studio, and picked up one of the acoustic guitars. His hands gently caressed the instrument, pulling beautiful yet haunting sounds from it.

When Lucas finally came up to bed it was starting to get light outside. Angela stirred, instantly alert, as he slid in beside her, but he merely turned his back and closed his eyes. She stared at the wall on her side of the bed watching as the morning light slowly crept in and defined the shadows around her. She was still lying awake and thoughtful when her daughter, five year old Melissa, burst into the room.

"Mommy, Mommy, the rain has stopped." The child's words came excitedly, "Can we go to the park now?"

Lucas stirred in his sleep and rolled over towards his wife. In one quick move Angela slid out of bed and scooped up her daughter.

"Hush sweetie, Daddy's sleeping still" she whispered to the girl as she carried her quickly from the room. She gently pulled the bedroom door closed behind her and then turned back to the child. "Your Daddy works way late at night time Melissa. We can't be waking him so early." After giving her a quick hug, Angela deposited the child back on the floor. "Go wake your brother and Mommy will make you some breakfast."

Melissa, dark and green eyed like her daddy, skipped off down the hall, singing merrily, "We're going to the park; we're going to the park." Angela made her way resignedly to the kitchen, knowing that even with not enough sleep she must be up with her babies.

After breakfast, Angela dressed both her children and herself as quietly as possible to avoid disturbing her sleeping husband. She put jackets on both children and got out a stroller for two year old Tyson. Locking the door of the little house behind her, she took Melissa by the hand and pushed the stroller before her down the front walk. Just on the corner, a half block from the house there was a small playground shaded beautifully by five magnificent maple trees. Angela loved these trees because they reminded her so much of the stately old maple in the backyard of the home she had known as a girl.

Angela was keeping one eye on Melissa as she rode on a small spring horse nearby and was pushing Ty in the baby swing. She knew from experience that her son would not be content with this very static form of play very long. Like his father, Tyson was very active and into everything. Sure enough, it wasn't long before Tyson was making his needs known with loud cries of "Down" and "Ball". Angela smiled and lifted her son from the swing. She retrieved a brightly coloured ball from the rack beneath the stroller's seat and rolled it to Ty. He giggled excitedly and kicked it, managing to connect quite well as the ball rolled across the grass.

Five year old Melissa quickly quit her tiny playground steed and joined her Mom and brother in this new game. Angela was gratified with the way her daughter was helpful and kind with Tyson. She seemed to embrace the role of being a "little mother" to the boy. The three of them laughed together as they tossed and kicked the ball all around the tiny park. Eventually they wound up beneath one of the big maple trees and Angela wrapped her arms around both her babies. Her mind's eye had a sudden vision of her own Mom sitting with her under the maple tree very much like this one. As she cuddled the children and they were both blessedly quiet, she let her mind take a walk down memory lane.

"Mommy how did this tree get so big?" the six year old Angela asked innocently as she cuddled snugly in her Mom's arms.

"It started as just a tiny seed Angie, and just grew and grew, till it was the very biggest tree in the yard."

"I feel safe here under the tree," the child stated, "Just like I feel safe when Daddy is home and tucks me in. He is as safe and strong as our beautiful maple tree."

Angela's Mom gazed in surprise at the little girl in her arms. It made her very happy that her daughter was content and secure but she was most surprised at the insightful comparison the child made of her steadfast protective father and the beautiful maple which seemed to stand watch over the little family.

Angela nervously put finishing touches on her blush and looked worriedly in the mirror. She didn't get an opportunity to dress up and go out much these days and was uncomfortable in a dress and heels. But she was excited that Lucas had agreed to her coming to see him play. He'd only been with this band for a few short weeks. After filling in a couple of times for an ailing guitar player, he had at last been offered the gig permanently. Angela had been thrilled for him. His hours at the music store were being cut back to part-time only and the regular income with this house band couldn't have come at a better time for the little family.

Lucas paced across the kitchen impatiently. Behind him, sitting at the table was his brother Kurt with his nephew in his arms and niece, Melissa, standing beside him impatiently tugging on his sleeve. Kurt had come over at Lucas's request to watch the kids so that Angela could go to the gig. Two years older than Lucas, Kurt had dark hair but not so perfectly black as his little brother and his eyes were more hazel than the almost unreal emerald that sparkled for Lucas Reeves. He had felt some joy when Lucas had called him about looking out for his niece and nephew, not only did he love the kids but he was pleased for Angie that she was going to have an evening out of the house.

Little Melissa was continuing to tug at his sleeve. "Uncle Kurt, Uncle Kurt, you gotta come see my pony, my little pony." The child demanded.

Kurt shifted Tyson onto his lap, held safe there in his strong right arm and put his other arm round Melissa's waist. He scooped the child in one smooth motion and sat her on his left knee. Two year old Tyson had Kurt's big hand in his two tiny ones examining the calluses and tiny scars. These were workman's hands; Kurt was a carpenter and cabinet maker. His business was booming in the thriving economy here on the coast where there were plenty of folks building beautiful and expensive homes with plenty of hand wrought woodwork within and without.

"I will look at your pony in a minute, young lady." he told the child. "First I am going to finish talking to your Daddy."

Lucas wheeled around from the counter then, just as Angela walked into the kitchen. His jaw slacked as he gazed at his wife. He was so accustomed to seeing her in jeans and shirts that he found himself almost surprised when he realized how very pretty she was in her dress and high heeled shoes. Kurt looked from one to the other of them and finally broke the silence.

"You look great Angie!" He said with open admiration. "She's a knockout Lucas."

Lucas cast a black look at his brother then turned back to Angela. "Come on, let's get going." He picked up the guitar case, pulled open the side door and was gone. Angela planted hurried kisses on her children's foreheads, smiled shyly at Kurt and hurried after her husband. Kurt watched as the door closed behind her and wondered if his younger brother ever realized what a wonderful woman he had married.

The Stardust Room was a very popular dance spot for the city's younger set, catering mainly to young professionals; the single office crowd. Lucas led Angela past the few people milling around outside the neon lit entrance. He nodded curtly to the bouncer there.

"Hey Lucas, is this your gal?" the bouncer asked, trying to make conversation. Lucas barely glanced at him and didn't break stride.

"Yeah man, my wife!" Lucas snapped at him. Angela gave the young man a quick smile but hurried after Lucas.

The club was similar to others like it that Angela had been in. Deep burgundy upholstery and dark wood contrasted with a light grey colour on the marbleized table tops. The band stand was at one end of the room with a fairly good sized dance floor also in the light grey marble pattern. On either side of the dance floor there were three large booth seating areas which were up one step from floor level. It was to one of these that Lucas led Angela. Three men and two women were already seated there.

"Sit down Angela" Lucas told her and she slid into the side of the booth which faced the stage. "This is my wife, Angela" he said briefly. He wheeled around then and headed straight to the small stage. Angela stared after him, watching him bend to open the guitar case before she realized that the man to her left had been speaking to her.

"I'm sorry, I didn't catch that." She said softly.

"I'm Vic, Angela," the blonde, blue eyed man repeated, smiling warmly at her. "I manage Stardust Room."

Angela was grateful for his smile. She was feeling rather out of place all of a sudden. "Pleased to meet you, Vic."

"You know everyone else I expect?" He said, nodding towards their table mates.

"Umm, actually no; Lucas just started with the band and I haven't been out to see them till now."

"Well then, this is Lenny, drummer. Need I say more?" Vic said with a wink, indicating the tall slim man to his left. "Next to him is Roxanne, she sings up a storm" The very petite and redheaded Roxanne smiled a warm welcome to Angela. "Then we have Don, the keyboard genius." Don was another blonde man with glasses that hid deep brown eyes. He raised his beer glass in a toasting gesture to the introduction. "And Don's better half," Vic finished with a chuckle, "This is Sherry, Don's wife."

"Nice to meet you all." Angela said quietly. Vic looked after ordering Angela a vodka and seven-up. After the two players had finished their beer, they excused themselves and joined Lucas and the bass player already on stage. Both women stayed with Vic and Angela.

"Do you play, Angela" the question came from Sherry.

"No. I guess one player in a family is enough." Angie replied.

"Your husband is awesome on that axe, girl!!" Roxanne spoke up. "He absolutely burns up those frets!"

"He lives for playing guitar." Angela agreed, feeling more at ease talking about Lucas than herself. "When I first met him he was playing and I couldn't believe how great he was. I hope our kids inherit some of his talent."

"You two have kids?" Sherry asked, "Wow that's hard when he's a player and out nights a lot."

"It's okay," Angela replied. "We have two, Melissa is five and my son Ty is almost two."

Roxanne excused herself now and went to join the rest on stage. Angela realized she was shaking with anticipation. She hadn't seen Lucas playing a gig for a long time now and every time she saw him in a club like this, she remembered all over again the man she had fallen in love with. He was so at ease and happy when he played. Angela finished the last swallow of her drink and wondered how it had gone down so smoothly and quickly. Vic noticed her empty glass too and was quick to gesture to the waitress to bring a fresh one.

Another man with a guitar had joined the band on stage and Angela knew this must be Jason the rhythm player and singer. Then, with no introductions and little fanfare, the band got to work. They opened with a couple of Top Forty tunes that Angela could tell Lucas did not have his heart in at all, though he played them proficiently enough. The third song into the set was an old classic rock song Sunshine of Your Love which gave Lucas a chance to really shine. The Cream tune was directly drawn from the blues roots that Lucas lived and breathed. She smiled with pride as he stole the show with his blistering guitar work. At the end of the number she came close to standing to applaud but held back and instead took another long swallow from her second drink. Vic, always observant in his job, did not miss the private struggle that waged behind the soft eyes of the young woman beside him.

Roxanne took over lead vocals next and did a powerful job of Aretha Franklin's Respect, following it with a lighter hearted arrangement of All I Wanna Do by Sheryl Crowe. Lucas's guitar complimented and accented Roxanne's voice very well and the two artists maintained an eye contact between them as they played.

By the time the band had finished six songs in the first set, Angela had finished her second drink and was tapping her feet, dancing in her seat and telling Vic enthusiastically about what a wonderful talent her husband possessed.

The second last song in the first set had just been added by the band to give Lucas a chance to sing one and to stretch himself into the more familiar blues genre he so loved. At the opening sounds, Angela knew Stevie Ray Vaughan's The Sky is Crying and she felt a shudder go through her as Lucas stepped up to the microphone. She was held transfixed and completely focused on her husband as he played and sang. Lucas, however, didn't really see anyone in the room as his eyes were half shut and the music was all he felt or saw in his mind's eye.

After the applause had faded the band went immediately into the final song of the set a cover of Creedence Clearwater Revival's Sweet Hitchhiker. Angela sat back with her hands, now a little sore from applauding Lucas's performance folded together on the table. Vic placed one of his large hands over both of hers and caught her attention.

"He really is a great player Angie. All I can say is Wow." He said.

She smiled up gratefully at the big blonde man beside her. Vic self-consciously withdrew his hand from hers just as the waitress deposited yet another highball in front of Angela. This time Angela picked up the drink with an almost devilish look in her eyes and quickly gulped nearly half of it. On stage, her husband had just glanced her way wondering if his wife was enjoying the show.

When the band finished the set, Lucas carefully placed the Stratocaster in the guitar stand by his amplifier and then headed off the stage towards the back of the club and the kitchen door. Angela was somewhat surprised that he hadn't come straight back to their table. Roxanne rejoined them and so did both Don and Jason. Angela was quickly laughing with the merry little group and didn't notice, till he was standing over her, that Lucas had returned.

Vic got up to let Lucas slide in next to his wife. But instead of doing so, Lucas took Angela quite firmly by the wrist and pulled her towards him. She slid hurriedly out of the bench seat and stood in front of her husband as he glared down at her.

"Lucas you were awesome," she started, but the look in his eyes stopped her abruptly. He had not loosened the iron grip on her wrist though he had brought his own hand down by his side out of sight of the rest at the table. Angela was trying very hard not to let the tears that were welling up in her eyes fall in front of these nice people. He leaned very close to her now as though to give her a kiss but instead whispered angrily in her ear.

"I've called you a cab. Get in and get home. You've already drank too much, damn it!" The words hurt perhaps far more than his iron grip and she nodded her acquiescence. He released his grip and she stepped back from him, head bowed.

She mumbled quick goodbyes claiming a headache and made for the door. Lucas wheeled and went back to the stage and picked up the guitar.

When Angela's key turned in the lock of the front door, Kurt looked up from the TV in surprise. She paused just inside the door to slip out of her heels. The business of removing the shoes allowed her to talk without meeting her brother-in-law's gaze.

"The kids both in bed?" she asked.

"Yep." he replied, the question really on his mind, however, he was loath to ask. "Melissa made me read her three stories before she finally settled down. It's so cool that she loves books."

"Yes it is." Angela had crossed the living room now and stood in the entry to the kitchen, her shoes still in her hand. "Can I get you a cup of tea or anything, Kurt?"

"What....oh no Angie that's okay." Kurt was still puzzled why Angela was home so early. "What's up, aren't you home kind of early?"

She stepped out of sight into the kitchen before she answered. "I had a headache," she told him. "Better if I just come home."

Kurt rose from his chair and stood in the kitchen doorway, leaning one shoulder up against the doorframe. Angela was standing with her back to him at the kitchen sink. Her shoulders were hunched over as though she were much older than her thirty years. A strange emotion crept through Kurt then and he had a sudden desire to run from the house.

"Well maybe you should take some Tylenol and lie down." he told her. Then he asked a question that he already anticipated the answer to, "Do you want me to stay till Lucas gets home?"

Angela's hands had a near death grip on the edge of the counter before her as she sought to control her tears and the fear that came with them. "No Kurt, just go, please." She said, her voice tiny and cracking.

"Okay Angie," Kurt replied. He was still confused by the strange emotional knot in his stomach as he pulled on his work boots and grabbed his jacket. Angela did not turn from the sink but had reached in the cupboard to retrieve a glass. She was running water as Kurt opened the side door. She merely nodded as he spoke a quick goodnight and gently pulled the door shut behind him.

Angela let the tears come after Kurt had disappeared through the door. She stood hunched over the kitchen sink, glass still in hand and sobbed till she couldn't find tears anymore. Exhausted, she finally turned away from the counter and shuffled towards the bedrooms.

She went into the bedroom first and stripped herself naked, shivering in the cold but eager to be rid of her dressed up clothing. She pulled on a mid-calf length flannel nightie and wrapped her arms around herself taking comfort in the fabric's soft warmth. A pair of light blue bedroom slippers in a fluffy fabric kept her feet warm.

She went next and checked on each of her children, gently tucking blankets back around Melissa, and then pulling the doors to both their rooms shut behind her as she left.

Angela washed her face in the bathroom sink without turning on the light. The drinks she had had earlier at the club did not seem to be affecting her at all. She flipped the light on in the den and turned on her computer. She needed time to compose herself and going online for a while would change her focus. Perhaps Lucas would have calmed down by the time he was home and things would be okay, she thought.

She logged on and quickly entered the bookmarked site of a music fans online chat. She had found this place a couple of weeks before and had discovered some friendly people online with both a common interest in the music and a sense of family amongst them. These were unconditional friends to whom she could choose to tell as little or as much as she wanted about herself; people to whom she could talk without Lucas interfering and controlling her contact .

Everyone here used nicknames to identify themselves and Angie had followed that practice. She was known here as Lucas-girl, and had at least let her new friends know she was the wife of a guitar player. They were a merry group of people, some of whom were musicians themselves, and they always made her smile. She had told them last night how excited she had been to be going to see her husband play.

When she logged in this night she got the inevitable question, how had the gig gone? She replied that Lucas had played great. Then one of the chatters, realizing the time difference in their locales asked a question she had not really been prepared for, "How come you're home so early, Lucas-girl?" Perhaps because the question caught her off guard, Angela answered without thinking. "Because I got a little tipsy and Lucas sent me home." She stared at the words on the screen before her and wondered what they thought of her now.

A nickname that was new to her was first to make a comment in reply and the words stunned her, bringing a lump to her throat. "Sent you home? I hope Lucas is your father and I hope you're underage, Lucas-girl..." he typed. Angela stared at his words and her own. "No," she typed with shaking hands, "Lucas is my husband." A sudden flush of embarrassment came over her and her right hand drew her mouse to set the curser over the close button. But something held her to the screen.

The new nickname typed again. "And he SENT you home? How old are you?"

Angela felt a little defensive now and replied "I'm thirty. Lucas was playing and I was drinking way too fast. He sent me home is all. He was looking out for me."

The other typed again. "He SENT you home?" Angela did not reply. She stared long and hard at the screen as the words continued to flow across it. How many of the others in the chat had read this exchange? A nickname that she did know, Musicguy typed in a message to the new nickname, "Lay off, man." was all it said. Angela was grateful for those three words. She watched the chat for another half hour rather than taking part. Then she logged off and turned off the computer. The clock was turned 1:00 am and Lucas would be home soon.

Angela was snuggled down in bed when she heard Lucas's key turn in the side door lock. The door was kicked shut behind him and a crashing sound followed. Under the covers, Angela started to shake uncontrollably.

Lucas had thrown his keys across the room where they had hit a vase on the kitchen table and brought it crashing to the ground. He stomped across the kitchen and put his guitar down, amazingly gently, considering the rage which was boiling in him. In his jeans and leather jacket he made a menacing sight as he stormed through the hallway towards the bedroom, his eyes flashing angrily.

He did not turn on the bedroom light but could see Angela's huddled form in the light spilling in from the hallway. He crossed to the bed in two short steps and pulled back the covers. Lucas grabbed hold of her by both shoulders and pulled her up and off the bed in one motion. Angela's legs buckled beneath her and she wound up on her knees at her husband's feet.

"You stupid little bitch!" he yelled, biting off each word with a sharp staccato edge. "How the hell do you think it looks, you sitting there getting pissed with Vic?"

"Lucas I'm sorry." She whimpered. He grabbed her again, one hand on her upper arm his fingers digging in and bruising, the other grabbed a fistful of her long dark hair and he literally pulled her to her feet. "Oh God Lucas, please don't." She cried, tears already streaming down her cheeks.

"Damn you!" he yelled. His hand released her hair and he swung it open but forcefully across the side of her skull. Angela reeled, her head swimming with pain, but did not fall because of the near death grip in which Lucas's other hand held her. Lucas hit her twice more and then pushed her back to her knees. His voice, still menacing, came very quietly now.

"Stupid bitch sucking back drinks like that. Did Vic turn you on or something?" As he spoke he was unbuckling his belt and unzipping his fly. "I'll give you something to suck on you little slut!!" Lucas took another firm grip on Angela's head by way of a fistful of her hair at the back of her neck and with the other hand forced her lips open and rammed his cock into her mouth. Choking and sobbing with shame, Angela knelt before him and submitted to his will.

When Lucas climaxed it was all Angela could do not to choke and start to retch. She slumped to the floor; tear stained, head pounding and hoping that Lucas was done with her. He stood over her for a moment in the dark, then turned and was gone.

Lucas finally came up to bed two hours later and she was still on the floor where he'd left her, asleep. He gently picked his wife up and placed her under the covers. Then he undressed and slid in next to her, placing a protective arm around her before he too slept.

Sunshine, which had climbed high enough in the sky to find its way in through the curtains, warmed Angela's face and roused her from sleep. Her head hurt terribly still and her right arm felt numb and sore. She came awake slowly at first, then suddenly sat bolt upright when she became aware of how eerily quiet the house sounded. Head swimming she slid quickly out of bed and ran first to her children's rooms. Finding them empty she made her way to the kitchen still fighting off dizziness with every step.

The kitchen was spotless, not a dish on the counter or in the sink and the table wiped clean. There was also no evidence of the broken vase from the previous night. Instead, on the center of the table, was a bud vase with two red roses in it. A small card was leaning against the vase with one word across it in Lucas's neat script. "Ange"

She fumbled with the card, tears stinging her eyes and making it hard to read the words inside. "I love you. Took the kids out with Kurt. Be back later." She slumped onto the closest chair shaking with relief edged with pain. She used a corner of her nightie to staunch the flow of tears. Then she sat, still crumpling the edge of her gown in her fists, as she took several long deep breaths and fought to control her emotions.

After a few moments, she had regained composure and quietly reread the note. Angela sighed softly, calmer now, knowing in her heart that Lucas would not harm her children. She had to pull herself together before they came home. He wouldn't want to see her like this. Placing the note gently amongst the greenery in the bud vase, she rose and crossed to the kitchen sink. She filled a glass with cold water and gulped it down as she padded barefoot down the hall to the bathroom. She bent and turned the taps on for a shower.

Angela pulled the nightgown over her head and caught a glimpse of her form in the mirror. The black bruised finger print marks were plainly visible on her upper right arm and her left cheek and ear were both somewhat swollen and still reddened from the blows Lucas had delivered there. She closed her eyes against the sight and stepped gingerly into the shower. The warm water sluicing over her body seemed to ease some of the physical hurts she had been feeling. The other pains she was unsure what to do with and so relegated them to that dark place in her mind where such nightmares belonged.

A thick towel wrapped snugly round her form, Angela stood at the sink and brushed her teeth for what seemed an eternity. Then she turned to her hair and brushed her long dark tresses until they were thoroughly dry. Still wrapped in the towel, she went back to her bedroom and made the bed before choosing a pretty blouse, her blue jeans, a bra and panties to dress in. The clock by the bedside said 3:00 pm.

Angela first made sure that something was planned and waiting in the kitchen for dinner, before she went into the den and turned on the computer. Just like the previous evening, after the housekeeping chores of checking email, she logged into her bookmarked Music Chat site. Several people were online this afternoon, some of whom she had chatted with before.

In this chat room, nearly everyone always said hello, even to the newcomers. So Angela spent the first few moments exchanging hellos with her "friends". A week or so before, she had started to chat one-on-one in "private message" with a keyboard player from clear across the continent, whose nickname was WhyDoThat. He had caught her eye on the general chat because of his great sense of humour which never failed to make her smile. But he wasn't online this afternoon and usually chatted mainly late at night after his gigs. Some of the women she knew though were on line and she was glad of the company.

The "girls" were chatting about men, their foibles and women's ways of dealing with the other sex. Angela mainly listened but found she had an increasing urge to reach out and make a real friend of one of these women. She was just trying to decide how to approach a "private message" with MelodyBlue when her head was struck by sharp blinding pains from the headache which had been brewing there. The few people in the chat were mainly people Angela had chatted with before and she impulsively typed in "Oh man I have such a headache, anyone know what's good to take for it?"

"Tylenol" "Advil" all the usual suggestions came back at her. MelodyBlue had a bit more to say. "You sick hon?" she typed. "Why the headache?"

"Well I got a little tipsy last night" Angela replied, trying to be at least half way truthful. "And then I banged up my head real good"

"Dang girl" MelodyBlue typed again.

"Well it's just I'm kinda dizzy now" Angela added.

"Dizzy. That's not good hon!" As Angela was reading these words, her Private Message screen beeped for her attention, causing her to jump with surprise. It was MelodyBlue messaging her.

"Hon, what did you bang your head on?" she asked.

"Oh nothing much." Angela realized the minute she typed those words that it was a giveaway answer.

"Hey girl, did Lucas hit you?" this time Angela jumped just because of the words on the screen. 'How could MelodyBlue know', she wondered.

"It's no big deal." She tried to brush it off. But MelodyBlue persisted.

"Hon if he hit you it's a very big deal." she typed. "You don't have to tell me, but you do HAVE to tell someone!!"

"It doesn't happen often." Angela was still trying to deflect the conversation that now seemed unstoppable.

"Hon, is there someone you can talk to there? Someone you trust?"

"I have no one Melody. And besides I love Lucas."

"That don't give him the right to abuse you. Girl you need to talk to someone about this. An abuse hotline or someone."

"My only friends are you guys in the music chat." She replied. "WhyDoThat and I have been talking a bit about me and Lucas fighting, but...." Angela couldn't finish the sentence.

"WHY is an awesome guy. I've shared a lot of my troubles with him. He won't lie to you and he won't ever break your confidence. Talk to him girl" MelodyBlue's words were the encouragement that Angela had been looking for. But now she heard Lucas's car in the driveway.

"I gotta go, Melody" she typed hurriedly. "Tell WhyDoThat I'm looking for him? Later." Without waiting for the reply, she quickly logged off the chat, just as the side door opened and her children's voices could be heard in the kitchen. She hurriedly turned off the computer and met her daughter part way down the hall to the kitchen. The girl flew into her mother's arms and Angela winced a little when the child's hands wrapped round her bruised upper arm.

"Mommy!" Melissa squealed, "Daddy and Uncle Kurt took us down by the ocean. I gots some shells! You gotta see!"

Angela gave Melissa a big hug, automatically reaching to brush the child's hair from her face then allowed the girl to take her by the hand and lead her through to the kitchen. Lucas had already retrieved a can of beer from the fridge and was sitting at the table with his son on his lap and a messy mix of shells and bright rocks before them. He glanced up when Angela and Melissa came in.

"I took them out so you could rest, Ange." He said quietly. Angela merely nodded in mute response. She spent a few minutes with both her children examining their treasures from the beach. Then she crossed to the sink, washed her hands and started to prepare dinner. Lucas toyed with a couple of the rocks in front of him, tapping a syncopated rhythm on the beer can and casting tentative glances at his wife's back. Finally he put the rocks back down and in three long legged strides came to stand directly behind her where she stood in the ninety degree corner where one counter surface met the other.

He reached round to her right shoulder with his left hand and quite gently spun her around to face him. His arms now went round both hers and he planted his hands on the counter behind her. Angela was shaking a tiny bit, but she saw that his eyes were clear, bright and smiling, so her tension was somewhat abated. He bent his head towards her and kissed her gently on each eyebrow, at the same time stepping just a bit closer so she was literally pinned in the corner of the room, countertop at her back.

"I want you Ange. Makes me crazy watching you." He half crooned, half growled the words in her ear. Angela was still trembling but it was fear mixed with excitement. She looked up into her husband's intense face and he pressed himself hard against her now, bringing one of his legs to force hers apart, his thigh coming into contact with the crotch of her jeans. Her hands went round him at the waist, fingertips caressing the small of his back. He brought his mouth down over hers and kissed her very deeply and thoroughly. She reacted to him instantly and he chuckled at the immediate arousal he was able to elicit. Even with his children in the room, Lucas pressed her again and slid one of his hands down to rub her clitoris through the jeans she wore, the other hand slid into her blouse and gave her right breast and nipple a sudden and unexpected pinch. Angela moaned with both surprise and arousal at once and Lucas kissed her hard again, triumphant as he felt her shudder with a small climax. The encounter ended abruptly and Lucas turned back to his children, taking them through to the living room while Angela finished preparing the supper.

Kurt had been a bit surprised when Lucas had turned up with the kids that morning but he had no other plans and happily agreed to spend the day with them. He asked how Angie's head was and instantly regretted the question. Lucas had snapped back at him that his wife's health was no concern of Kurt's. Like so many times before, Kurt let the issue drop. Even when they were kids Lucas's black moods were something to be avoided at all costs.

The brothers had a great day with the kids. Kurt reveled in playing with his niece and nephew in the sand, helping them to create a somewhat lopsided but lovable sand castle. Young Melissa was such a "mother" sometimes for her brother Ty and, as he watched her, Kurt couldn't help but think about Angie.

Lucas dropped Kurt at his house and headed home with his children. Kurt walked thoughtfully up the path to the front door, stooping to pick up a small stack of the inevitable flyers on the porch. He unlocked the door and went in kicking off his sneakers as he went. The house was not overly large and only had two bedrooms, but it was comfortable and all that the confirmed bachelor really needed. He went through to the kitchen and opened the fridge. A bottle of imported European beer caught his eye and he casually took it out while contemplating the rest of his meager larder.

Half an hour later he carried a plate with a pork chop and some macaroni and cheese on it through to the living room and turned on the TV. He surfed through the stations as he toyed with his dinner, seemingly with no real appetite for either. He finally settled on one of those true-life ride-a-long shows featuring a day in the life of a police patrol. These things were either hopelessly funny or a bit depressing but either way it was better than most of the soap-opera type fare on the other stations.

The segments this night included a naked and inebriated man wandering the streets of a residential neighbourhood and a young daredevil who had decided to skateboard down a long steep hill on a busy highway. Kurt, on his second beer, was laughing out loud. After a commercial break, the show returned with a segment about drug busts. Kurt surfed on; he had no stomach for that right now.

His mind was only half on the television and he still kept seeing his sister-in-law as he had last seen her the previous evening: slumped over the sink valiantly trying to hold back her tears and, he realized her fear. His mind flashed back to a scene from two years before.

Lucas and Kurt had been out for the night. The brothers had known, even as Lucas backed the car out of the driveway that they were going to get drunk. Lucas had said it was a "boy's night out" and had given the eight months pregnant Angela a quick kiss telling her not to wait up.

Kurt had been closer to sober when it came time to go home, so he drove. The lights were all off in the little house when the car pulled in by the side door. Lucas stumbled from the passenger seat almost before Kurt stopped the car and stamped noisily up the steps. "Damn bitch went to bed." He mumbled.

Kurt locked the car and followed his brother up the steps. "It's okay man." he said, "We had a blast. Damn that blonde was gorgeous!" Both men laughed coarsely as Lucas fumbled with his keys.

"Yeah well Kurt, you should a made a move on her." Lucas told him with a cruel chuckle. "Then you wouldn't be sleeping on my fucking couch tonight!"

"Maybe Angie'll make you sleep in the doghouse when she sees the shape you're in little brother." Kurt told him as they practically fell into the kitchen.

"That'll be the day, Kurt!" Lucas told him, his eyes flashing angrily even in the dim light from the street. Kurt knew when to back off and without another word stumbled through to the living room and flopped onto the couch. Kurt sat there staring blankly at the shadows. The anger in Lucas's voice had taken the edge off the evening rather abruptly.

He wasn't sure how long he had been half sitting half laying there when he heard Lucas's voice raised from down the hall.

"Damn it bitch!" He was yelling. "Get the fuck up!" What Kurt heard next brought a chill to his heart and fear raced up and down his spine. Angela screamed, but the scream was muffled and cut off abruptly. Kurt heard the sickening thud of what could only be a fist being smashed against flesh; then came several sharper sounds, unmistakable as open handed smacks delivered in rapid succession. He could hear the soft plaintive sound of Angela's sobs and he started to get up off the couch. When Kurt reached the doorway between the kitchen and the hallway he stopped in his tracks. He could still hear Angela sobbing but he also could hear his brother speaking in a voice that almost sounded like an animal growl.

"Ange you are my fucking wife!" He was telling her, "Don't ever tell me no, bitch." Kurt stood transfixed by the horror of what he was hearing, knowing full well how angry his brother could get. He heard, and almost physically felt, three more blows rain down from Lucas's hand then almost started to retch right there as he heard the tearing of fabric of what must have been Angie's nightgown as it was torn from her. He turned away, the bile already rising in his throat and raced to the bathroom. Even the sounds he made as he vomited repeatedly did not erase the terrible screams of pain and fear that came from the master bedroom as Lucas sodomized his pregnant wife brutally.

Kurt was pulled back to the present by the sound of a car horn on the street outside. He stared at the beer in his hand and suddenly had no stomach for it.

Images of Angie's face again assaulted his mind and he knew his cowardice for what it was and loathed the man he had become.

Angela made sure that her little ones were safe and snug in their beds: sea shells stowed and stories were read; hugs and kisses given and prayers all said. Then she went to the den, because even the friendly words across the chat screen were better than being so alone. She wasn't sure why she was drawn back to the chat again and again but her need to reach out was becoming stronger each day. Only her fear that Lucas would somehow take even this away from her stopped Angela from excitedly telling anyone about the music chat and the secret friends she now had found.

Lucas would not be home from his gig for hours so Angela went surfing for a while, chasing the fears out of her mind by looking at websites for faraway places she would probably never visit. Two hours later she logged in to the music chat room. WhyDoThat was not online when she logged on but she expected that he would be anytime now. The three hour time difference in their locations allowed her to chat with him after a gig while Lucas was still away. She made shy small talk with the others online until Why logged in. She said her greetings to him in the main chat room with all the others. Why was a popular figure on the chat and it always took him some time to get through all the pleasantries. Angela watched and wondered if Melody had passed on her message.

Suddenly her Private Message screen beeped for her attention and she started a little in her chair. It was WhyDoThat with the simple words, "Hi Angela" She had told him her real name about a week before when they had been talking about the kids and Lucas.

"Hi Brian." She responded.

"Melody said you wanted to talk. You ok Angela?" The question surprised her a little. She wondered just what Melody had told him.

"I'm okay," she typed. "Had a headache earlier but it's not so bad now."

"Did you and Lucas have another fight?" Brian persisted.

"Yeah kind of. He was mad at me about drinking so much when I went to his gig."

"Angela you are a grown up. He's treating you like a child."

"No, he had a right to be mad. I did drink way too fast. He works there Brian, it doesn't look very good if I'm getting all tipsy."

"Maybe it doesn't but Angela you're only human. And Lucas should have asked you to slow down, not SENT you home." Angela remembered then that

WhyDoThat had been on the chat the other night when she'd said Lucas had sent her home.

"He was looking out for me." She explained.

"And was he looking out for you later on Angela?" Brian asked. She felt her heart race at the question, remembering Lucas coming home in a rage.

"What do you mean?" She asked.

"Angela you don't have to tell me anything. But I do know you are reaching out. I will listen. And I will be honest when I give you my opinions. Sometimes I might say things that hurt you, but I'll always tell you the truth. Now, you tell me something, does Lucas hit you?"

Angela stared at her message window for a long time, rereading Brian's words. She was shaking and her heart was pounding in her chest. Finally she typed very slowly and deliberately. "Yes he does, sometimes."

Brian was quick to reply, "Did he beat you last night?" Angela was weeping now but compelled to continue.

"He was angry; he hit me a few times."

"Angela no matter how angry he is HE SHOULD NEVER HIT YOU!!"

Angela jumped as though Brian had actually shouted at her. She didn't answer, between the tears and her shaking she couldn't type. He continued. "Angela, you need to tell him that you will not tolerate that kind of thing anymore. He needs to understand he can't do that to you."

"I can't tell him that Brian. He would just get angry." She finally typed.

"He better learn to control his anger or someday it's gonna bite him right in the ass!! But Angela you need to look after yourself and the kids. You need to tell him you won't put up with it no more."

"He's not always like that Brian; he's really sweet with the kids. He was wonderful when we met. Always looked out for me." Angela was starting to feel defensive about Lucas, her urge to protect him overruling her fear of him.

"Angela even once is too many times. Why are you talking to me right now?" That brought Angela up short. She wasn't even really sure. She knew that Lucas would be furious if he knew she was discussing their business with anyone at all.

"I'm not sure Brian." she typed honestly. "Sometimes it's bad, you know? But sometimes we have tea and talk, like we used to." As she waited for Brian's reply, her mind wandered back to the Lucas she used to know.

A young Angela, barely twenty three, walked at the side of a tall, lean, good looking young man. He had one muscular arm draped around her shoulders protectively. Lucas was in blue jeans, a muscle shirt and a black leather jacket. His face was quite youthful but the shadow of hair growth on his chin masked that somewhat and gave him a dangerous hoodlum look. Angela kept stealing glances at this man by her side, surprised that such a handsome and talented man wanted anything to do with a shy wallflower like her. Lucas led her down the street and turned in to a little dress shop. Angela was taken aback. She'd never even really dated before but the thought of a man wanting to go dress shopping seemed totally foreign.

"Let's get you something new and pretty to wear." he told her. Angela looked quizzically up at Lucas. Did he mean that what she was wearing wasn't good enough, she wondered. She didn't voice her question, but followed him as he led her by the hand to a rack of rather flashy clothing. Lucas pulled several different garments off the rack in rapid succession. Each was far shorter, more revealing and flashier than the conservative clothing Angela was used to wearing. He finally selected a silver mini-dress with only spaghetti straps above a plain empire line dress and a black leather mini skirt with a royal blue top that was cut like a man's shirt but was sleeveless and open at the neck to well below her cleavage.

"Go try these two on for starters." he told her. "And come out and let me see you." he finished with that sexy chuckle that she was very attracted to from the first time she heard it. She went into the fitting room and stared at herself in the mirror. Ever since she'd met Lucas six months previously, she had remained baffled as to what such a good looking man, who attracted nearly every girl who saw him play, saw in plain-Jane Angela. She looked at the clothes he'd given her with a mixture of amazement and trepidation. She was always very comfortably and conservatively dressed; though, ever since she'd started seeing her "guitar player", she'd been trying to be a little bolder in her choices. But these outfits were something else again.

She put the silver dress on first and then, feeling very self-conscious, she took a deep breath and pulled open the fitting room door. Lucas turned towards her as she stepped shyly into the space in front of the fitting rooms where the big three-sided mirror threw multiple images of her everywhere. Lucas stared at her so intently that she lowered her eyes to the floor to avoid that avid gaze.

"Turn around Ange, let me see the back. And smile, you look great!" She turned around and felt the corners of her mouth turn up despite how nervous and uncomfortable she was feeling in this short and sexy outfit. Her head came up a little with her back to Lucas and then she saw herself in the mirror and his reflection as he moved closely behind her. One of his hands came up and pulled loose the tie she had holding her long hair in a ponytail. Her dark wavy hair cascaded all over her shoulders and contrasted beautifully with the silver dress. She stared in amazement as she started to see herself through his eyes and became aware of what a handsome couple they really made.

"Lucas, I...." she faltered, unsure even what she had wanted to say. He stood close behind her and ran his fingers from the nape of her neck down across her skin and the satiny soft fabric of the dress to the small of her back. There he tapped a rhythm out with his fingers and grinned at her in the mirror over her shoulder.

"You're perfect, Ange." He told her huskily, leaning close to her ear. "You're going to turn heads for sure in this one. But none of them jerks can have you, 'cause your all mine!"

She laughed at him and he hugged her warmly from behind. Then he chased her back to try the other outfit on. She hadn't felt this much attention and love from a man since her Dad had died when she was barely fourteen.

Brian's next words brought her back from her thoughts of the past. "Like you used to." he typed. "Why do you think that changed?"

"I don't know, well, it didn't, we still do that sometimes. We just don't talk much anymore."

"You gotta get him talking Angela. You have to tell him he can't be hurting you anymore. Is there anyone there you can go to?"

"Go to?" She was taken aback. "You mean tell someone about this?"

"You're telling me, hon" he reminded her, then continued. "Angela, think of your kids, they shouldn't grow up with this going on."

"Lucas would never hurt the kids, he loves them." Angela was shaking now and she wasn't sure if she was fearful of how far this conversation was going or angry at Brian for his seeming ability to know how to get to her.

"Maybe so Angela. But they will be affected by what he is doing to their mother. Think about it." Just as Angela was reading this last, she heard Lucas's car in the driveway.

"I gotta go, he's home." She typed hurriedly.

"Okay Angela, but we will talk some more, okay?" he replied.

"Yes Brian when I can. Good night." She rapidly closed the chat screen and was gone.

By the time Angela had logged off her computer and gone through the hall to the kitchen, Lucas was already in the house. He had kicked his boots off under the table and she heard him going down the basement stairs to put away his guitar. She crossed to the counter and filled a kettle to make some tea. She stretched to reach cups out of the cupboard and winced a little from the bruising on her upper arm. Lucas had padded unheard back up the basement stairs with his Gibson six-string in one hand.

"Hey Ange, you're up." He said. Angela jumped, startled by his voice, and almost dropped one of the cups in her hand.

"Yes Lucas." She said softly. She placed the cups carefully on to the counter and turned towards him, surprised when she saw the guitar in his hand. He reached his other hand out to her and spoke equally softly.

"Come on girl; let's go sit in the living room till the kettle boils." He took her hand and led her through the doorway. He guided her to take a seat on the couch and settled next to her with the guitar across his lap. She wasn't sure what to make of his mood this night but at least the black anger of the previous evening seemed to have passed. Her discomfort was apparent as she toyed with a corner of the cushion beside her with one hand and chewed nervously on her finger nail of the other hand, keeping her eyes down so as not to meet his intent gaze.

Lucas appeared not to notice his wife's nervousness as he took a more business-like grip of the guitar and started to play. He merely toyed with the instrument at first; getting the feel of the acoustic again after playing electric all evening. He repeated a series of chords and scales, the finger exercises that had drove his Dad to anger at their repetitiveness when he practiced them for hours as a child. Just as Angela was starting to relax a little, the kettle started to whistle and she jumped nearly out of her skin. Lucas put the guitar aside and put one hand on his wife's knee.

"Girl you sure are jumpy tonight." He said. He stood as he spoke. "I'll make the tea this time, okay?"

She was completely taken aback but nodded her mute acknowledgement. She heard him in the kitchen as he made their tea but she also was sure that she was hearing the sound of her own heart pounding loudly in her ears. Her hope was soaring that her strong and wonderful Lucas was back to look after her once again like things used to be. She looked up at him as he came back into the room a cup in each hand.

"Thank you Lucas, this is so wonderful." she told him, voice ever soft. He smiled but said nothing. After taking one drink from his tea, he had the guitar back in hand and started to play. Angela relaxed back into the cushions of the couch and listened as her husband talked to her the way he knew best with slow acoustic blues. Lucas managed to drink his tea between songs and Angela smiled as she remembered many nights just like this one when they'd first found one another.

After about an hour of playing, Lucas put the instrument aside and reached for the now sleepy Angela. She came quite willingly into his arms. His strength was very apparent as he effortlessly slid one arm under her and lifted her onto his lap as though she were just a child.

"Come here Ange." he said, with the husky growl that always aroused her almost instantly. He took her head gently in both his hands and pulled her mouth onto his. Angela's lips were already parted, ready for him and his tongue quickly probed into her and danced with hers as she trembled excitedly.

"You're still the hottest girl I've ever had." He told her, when their kiss finally ended. He stood, gathering her in his arms as he did so. Still kissing her deeply, he carried her through the house to their bed. Angela's arousal matched her husband's and she was already pulling at the buttons of his shirt as he placed her gently on the edge of the bed. He put one hand round both hers and whispered huskily, "Not yet."

Lucas undressed her with the gentle hands that had coaxed such beautiful tones from the guitar in the living room. As he did so, Angela was moaning with each caress and it was like her husband's hands could coax music from her too; like she was his instrument. He rained gentle little kisses all over her as he went. Only after she was fully naked before him, would he allow her to touch him again. Angela undressed Lucas with the same care and caresses that he had given her, but it was she who continued to moan with passion as he stroked her nakedness with knowing hands.

Later, as she lay almost spent across his chest, she tried to focus on his eyes in the dark. She loved him when he was gentle, that much she knew, but could she tell him what was in her heart? She searched the darkness for an answer and found none.

"Lucas, I love you." Was all she murmured before sleep overtook them.

Angela stirred in her husband's arms and he was instantly awake and aware. His grip tightened round her and she yielded allowing herself to be drawn closer. Her back was to him now so she couldn't read his expression but his grip, though firm, was not unduly harsh. Lucas's lips brushed the back of her neck with soft little kisses and with each touch Angela relaxed more. She felt his body tense and harden against her back.

"Morning baby," he murmured softly. His hand, which hand been gently stroking her breasts now slid up taking a hold of her shoulder and pulling her round to face him. She looked up into his intense green eyes, seeing herself reflected in his passion before he bent to kiss her deeply and her own eyes closed as her mouth parted to welcome him. The long passionate kiss was all they managed as Angela heard the voices of both her children coming down the hall.

Lucas rolled away from her and grabbed his jeans, sliding them on quickly as he moved to the closed bedroom door. He threw Angela his shirt and her panties as he opened the door and squatted down to hug both children at once. Angela scrambled into her panties and pulled Lucas's shirt round her just before her daughter clambered up on the bed. Lucas and Ty went off down the hallway hand in hand.

Angela giggled and cuddled with her daughter, all the time keeping one ear tuned down the hall, listening to Lucas and his son. Lucas had helped Tyson with getting dressed and then they had gone looking for breakfast. Angela chased Melissa to her room to find clothes and finally sat up in bed herself. She wrapped her arms round herself and pulled the fabric of Lucas's shirt close to her face where she could clearly smell his aroma. Brian was wrong, she thought, she only had to learn how not to get her husband angry then things would be all right.

Angela left Lucas's shirt on and pulled her own jeans on with it, then with Melissa skipping down the hall ahead of her, she followed the aroma of coffee towards the kitchen. Lucas had Tyson at the table with a bowl of porridge and a glass of apple juice and was helping him to eat with much laughter, tickles and mess. Angela smiled ruefully. She'd be cleaning the mess when her two boys were done, but didn't really mind. She crossed to the coffee maker and, taking the full pot, filled the empty mugs waiting there. She added cream to Lucas's mug and carried it to the table with her own, careful to place it well out of reach of her baby son.

"Thanks Ange." Lucas said, as he "flew" another spoonful of porridge into his son's mouth. Angela helped Melissa to get a bowl of cheerio's and a sliced banana. Once the child was settled, she took a quick gulp of her coffee and put some bread in the toaster for Lucas and herself. While it was toasting, she leaned her back against the counter and watched Lucas with Tyson.

He and the boy couldn't be anything but father and son, they looked so much alike. The dark hair and intense green eyes that made Lucas so popular with the ladies had been passed down to his boy in full strength. Lucas glanced up at Angela and winked as Tyson gleefully took the last mouthful of porridge. She smiled back at him.

"Wish you could be up to feed him every time." She said, turning back as the toast popped. "He'll eat for you, he gets cranky for me."

Tyson started shouting to be down from his high chair then and Lucas's reply went unheard. Angela finished putting peanut butter and bananas on two slices of toast for her husband and brought them to the table. She lifted Tyson out and he toddled happily round the room. She spread peanut butter on her own toast and finally sat down.

Lucas had turned his attention to Melissa and they were making faces at one another across the table. 'He is terrific with the kids, so I guess the Other is my fault.' she thought, even in her own mind refusing to give the abuse its real name as though not to speak it made it less real somehow. Her coffee, nearly cold now, still tasted pretty good and the caffeine was at least making her feel a bit more awake.

"I would love to go back to bed." she said quietly. Lucas glanced across at her with a rather smug look.

"You just can't get enough of me, can ya girl?" He chuckled, totally misunderstanding her intent. Angela didn't bother to correct the mistaken impression but just smiled shyly at him. He reached under the corner of the table, out of sight of his young daughter's eyes and ran a hand up the inside of Angela's thigh. "Maybe tonight. If you're a very good girl." he laughed. "I'm working at the store today 12 till 7, so I'm gonna stay downtown, catch some supper and go straight to the gig."

"Alright Lucas." Then, just as she spoke, another sound came from the living room. It was the unmistakable twang of the Gibson's strings as young Tyson had found Daddy's guitar leaning against the couch where Lucas had left it the previous night. Angela's heart raced a little, already anticipating her husband's displeasure that no one, meaning herself, had paid attention to Tyson and kept him away from the instrument. But the expected explosion did not come.

"Oh man!" Lucas exclaimed, getting up from the table and heading towards the sound. "He wants to play, Angie. That's so awesome!"

Lucas took the instrument up from its place against the couch and sat with it on his knees. Tyson had at first whimpered because his new toy was being taken from him but Lucas beckoned the boy over and started showing him the guitar and patiently naming the various components as Tyson's little fingers pointed to them. Angela stood in the doorway and watched them, amazed at her husband's gentle patient manner.

Lucas was in a place which he had thought that he would never attain. His own son, at just two, was showing the same unswerving interest and aptitude for music that Lucas himself had felt as a child. The elation that Lucas felt was overwhelming as he played with his son and the beautiful six stringed instrument. All his life he had looked for some approval for what he felt was as natural and necessary an act as breathing. He lived to play his guitars. His memories of home and his father, usually submerged, came flooding to the surface in the little living room where his son was playing with the strings delighting in the sounds he produced.

Lucas had been barely nine years old when he had first picked up a guitar at a friend's house. He had shown a natural aptitude for the instrument and his pal's father, who played himself, had quickly gifted the young Lucas with a modest six string acoustic which he had but rarely played. He had shown Lucas a few rudiments but soon realized that the boy was such a natural musician that he would need little guidance or encouragement to become a most gifted player.

When Lucas brought the instrument home his father's reaction had been instant and quite brutal. He had demanded to know where the boy had found the money for the guitar and when Lucas told him that the instrument had been a gift his father flew into a rage.

"Don't ever take no gifts from nobody boy, damn you!" He had shouted as Lucas stood near to tears in front of the big man. His father, Karl, was a longshoreman and true to the profession was a giant of a man who was loud even when just speaking. When angered, he was a most imposing sight indeed. Lucas was much more like his mother, though tall for his age; he had almost delicate features and was what his father laughingly referred to as a little pansy momma's boy. "And what the hell do you want with a damn gittar anyways! It's a waste of time." The big man raised his hand as though he was going to smack the boy and then, seeing Lucas burst into tears, he dropped his arm and laughed. "Go on get outta here ya little wimp!"

Kurt, at eleven years old, was standing in the doorway as Lucas fled from their father. He saw the tears across his little brother's cheeks and wondered what he had done this time to incur Karl's wrath. He shrugged off the thought and spoke to his father.

"Hey Dad, we still gonna take a look at the truck engine? Ya promised." Karl grinned at his older son. 'Now that boy's got the makings of a real man.' he thought with pride

"Yeah Kurt, let's get to it and leave the damn women in the house."

His words were lost on young Lucas Reeves who had gone out the kitchen door and back gate. He walked down the lane behind the houses in their street till he came to the road and turned down the hill towards the water of the inlet. Once on the rocky strand, he found a perch on a comfortably sized rock and took the guitar in both hands. Lucas played to sooth the fear, shame and hate in his heart. And, though the young boy didn't know it then, he played his very first blues that day.

Tyson was fascinated by the sounds the guitar made. He watched as Lucas took a firmer grip on the instrument and started to play that haunting melody from childhood. Angela heard the guitar as she stood cleaning the few dishes from breakfast and was moved at once by how beautiful and yet intensely lonely it sounded. She dried her hands as she crossed to the living room doorway to watch him play.

Her son had sat on the floor at his father's feet prompting Angela to wish she had a camera at hand instead of a tea towel. Lucas was playing with his whole body, moving as the music moved him. The plaintive sound from the strings beneath his fingers caused a shiver of mixed emotions, grief edged with fear, to race up Angela's spine. Even young Melissa, who had been dressing a doll on the chair opposite her father, stopped what she was doing, clutched the doll tightly against her and listened.

As Lucas's song ended, Angela took one step into the room and opened her mouth to speak. She was silenced by one look at her husband's face. He had been weeping as he played and tear stains streaked his handsome but boyish features. Lucas, realizing for the first time that she was there, took an ineffectual swipe at the tears with the back of his hand. Melissa, still clutching her doll, was the first to break the silence in the room.

"Daddy's crying." The child murmured with surprise.

It was as though the child's words had broken a spell under which Lucas had played. He stood suddenly, a black angry light starting to glint in his green eyes still swimming in tears. In two strides he crossed the distance between himself and Angela. He pushed roughly past her and she stumbled against the doorjamb banging her shoulder and forehead.

"Damn it to hell, I'm going to be late." Lucas growled. Guitar in hand he disappeared downstairs to his music room. Behind him in the living room, his little family took a collective deep breath; Melissa's big eyes seeking her mother's face across the room.

A few minutes later, Lucas came back up the stairs with the Stratocaster and the Gretsch in their cases. He sat and pulled on his boots as Angela stood by the counter watching, still grasping the tea towel in a near death grip. He took his leather jacket off the rack near the door and, without a backward glance or a single word; he stamped out of the side door. Angela sighed heavily and turned back to her children.

Since Lucas would not be coming home for dinner, Angela saw the whole day stretching gloriously ahead of her. She brushed her long hair free of night time tangles, washed up and made the beds. She left Lucas's shirt on because somehow it comforted her. Tyson followed her everywhere as she went about the house. Angela kept up a steady stream of chatter with the bright eyed two years old and Tyson, for his part, seemed to study Mom's every move with great interest. Melissa was playing with her doll and was mimicking Mom's actions.

She went back to the kitchen and got bread and sandwich fixings out of the cupboard. She made simple processed cheese slice sandwiches for herself and Melissa and packed them in a plastic container along with a couple of apples. She opened another cupboard and pulled out two jars of processed baby food for Tyson and retrieved a plastic spoon from the cutlery drawer. Angela carefully packed all of these things into the bottom a small day pack that she had pulled from the hallway cupboard.

On top of all that, she put jackets for her children, a few diapers and supplies for Tyson, a tube of sunscreen and a couple of towels. Melissa stood quietly by watching her Mom with interest. Finally the girl could contain her curiosity no more.

"Where we going Mommy?" she asked.

"What makes you think we're going somewhere, sweetie?" Angela teased the girl.

"You're putting lunch and things in the bag." The child said, with an exasperated tone. "So we must be."

"I thought we'd take the bus down to the big park by the beach where the zoo is." Angie told her.

"Yippee!" Melissa shrieked happily. She started dancing around the kitchen with glee. Tyson, who had been industriously driving a toy truck across the floor, got caught up in his sister's enthusiasm and joined her dance.

While both children were dancing and singing "The zoo, the zoo" over and over, Angie reached for the recipe box that sat in the very back corner of the kitchen counter. She reached behind the last of the cards in the small file box and pulled out a twenty dollar bill which she slid in her pocket. 'That should cover zoo admission and drinks for us all, maybe even ice creams.' she thought hopefully. The piggy bank supplied her enough change to take the bus both ways. Angela glanced quickly round the house, put the pack on her back and taking Tyson by one hand and carrying his folding stroller in the other, she led them out the door.

Angela and her children all enjoyed the bus ride. The harbour city they called home was built largely on the delta and the downtown core with its monolithic office towers stood on reasonably flat land. But Angela and Lucas lived on the north shore of the inlet where the land was mountainous and the houses, businesses and schools were all built into hillsides and half hidden amidst stands of dark green forest. The ride down the hill on the bus afforded several spectacular views of the harbour below.

The children were both excited by the adventure of riding the bus. Angela didn't take them out like this often because Lucas didn't approve much of her going too far with them without him driving the family in the car. When they went past one large park with a playground visible from the road, Melissa was sure they had missed their destination.

"Mommy there it is!" She cried, "That's the park right there!" But the bus kept moving. Angela reached for Melissa's pointing hand and gave it a squeeze of reassurance.

"That's not the right park, sweetie." Angela smiled indulgently. "The park we're going to a very much bigger than that and all the way down near the beach. Look!" She pointed out of the window of the bus which had stopped for a traffic light. From this vantage, one could see the waters of the inlet and spread out along one shore there was a broad area of green, with trees and grass. The park took in about forty acres of property along the inlet and had a beach, several playgrounds and a small zoo.

When the bus started to move again both children were happily playing pat-a-cake. It seemed to suit Melissa's childlike sense of motherhood to entertain her little brother and Angela was always surprised by how much patience the little girl seemed to have.

It was somewhat cooler down here near the water than it had been up the hill near where they lived. So the first thing Angela did, after they were all safely off the bus, was get both children's jackets out. Melissa contentedly put hers on 'all by myself'. Tyson, on the other hand, saw a jacket as an inconvenience and was already pulling the sleeves off again as quickly as Angela had managed to put them on. She chuckled to herself, "Little boy, you're just as stubborn as your father." As soon as the words were out of her mouth, Angela was taken by a sense of fear and it was a fear she was unable to name.

The park and zoo were not as busy as they would have been if they had waited till Sunday when Lucas could take them all. Angela felt relaxed and, strangely free, walking the pathways of the little zoo with her children. Both children kept taking her hand to drag her to see one animal or another. The big hit with both of them was the monkeys. Tyson was giggling and dancing as the little primates scrambled through their habitat putting on a very unorthodox but amusing acrobatic display. Melissa was making faces at one chimpanzee who was imitating the girl's expressions to her unending delight.

The little family had their modest picnic lunch spread on the two big beach towels under the sheltering boughs of another big maple tree much like that beautiful specimen in the park close to home. Tyson's eyes were drooping after he'd eaten and Angela stretched the boy out on a towel in the shade with her jacket over him and let him sleep. From one pocket of the little pack, she pulled a child's fairy tale book. She leaned her back against the trunk of the big maple and Melissa settled right between her outstretched legs. She read almost all of Puss-in-Boots to the girl before her eyes drooped too. Angela smiled to herself; both her children were so content, at least no one could say she wasn't a good mother.

She threw her head back and looked up through the boughs of the grand old tree. Just like before, memories of the maple from her childhood home flooded back to her.

By the time Angela was ten years old, she had climbed nearly every climbable tree in the neighbourhood, rode her bicycle down every big hill she could find, become an expert at skipping stones across the river, in short, she was a confirmed tomboy. Sister Pamela, older than her by three years, looked disdainfully at Angela whenever she raced into the house with tales of trying out skateboards, shooting baskets and other equally horrid and unladylike pursuits. The sisters could not have been less alike.

Pamela's animosity towards Angela grew not just out of their differences but because the older girl knew in her heart that Angela would always be their father's favourite. The tomboy in Angela appealed to her father, who would have liked a son. So for Angela's eleventh birthday, Paul Griffen had brought home sufficient lumber to help her build a tree house in the maple in the back yard. Angela had been thrilled.

Father and daughter spent hours together making the project. Angela had scavenged some leftover bits of carpeting from a construction site nearby and precariously carried them home on her bicycle. They used them to cover the floor and part way up the walls of the interior of the tree house, making it snug indeed. When finished, and Paul had taken pains to ensure this, the little sanctuary was both sturdy and safe. He had little or no fear that his beloved Angie would come to any harm in her tree house perch.

Angela practically lived in the tree house over the next three years. She would come racing in from school and, with only a short pause in the kitchen to grab a snack; she would climb the ladder and settle down to do her homework in the fresh air away from big sister and her giggly friends. Angela couldn't understand Pamela's need to chatter endlessly with all her equally annoying girlfriends about boys, clothes and makeup. For the younger girl, nothing mattered much except the pretty dancing shadows cast by sunlight filtered through the big tree's leaves.

By the time Angela had reached fourteen, she still had no interest in the trivial world of boys and fashion. Her favourite clothes were blue jeans and t-shirts or even a "borrowed" one of her father's flannel casual shirts. She would slide them out of the laundry basket and sometimes got away with wearing them for a day or two before her mom noticed and recovered the goods. She loved them because they were warm, soft and smelled of Dad, his cologne and the more pungent but comforting odor of his sweat.

She came home one afternoon to a house which seemed overly quiet. But she shrugged off the strange foreboding that she had at first felt and, backpack stuffed with text books and potato chips, she made the climb to the tree house. Usually she would have about two hours of solitude until dinner at six o'clock. Then Mom would call from the back door and she'd run in to join the family.

Just five minutes after entering her little eerie in the tree, Angela sensed that her peace was not to be. She rolled slightly to one side and looked out into the yard through a small square window which faced the house. Her mother and Pamela were just crossing the patio and making their way across the grass to Angie's hideaway. A sudden chill went through the girl and she knew, without knowing why, that she did not want to come down from the tree this afternoon.

Her Mom called up to her as she stopped beneath the tree. "Angela, sweetheart, please come down, we need to talk to you."

Something in her voice didn't feel right and Angela became terrified. Why were they here? Why did both of them come to get her? She could see that her Mom had placed one arm round her older daughter's shoulders and Pamela was practically hiding her face against her mother shoulder. Something was terribly wrong here, but Angela simply couldn't conceive of what it may be.

"Angela please." Her Mom's voice was cracking with emotion. "Please come down."

Angela moved finally, but she moved like a puppet. There was a deep dread feeling coming over her and in the face of her nameless fright it took much strength for the girl to climb back down the ladder from her sanctuary, obedient to her mother's summons.

Angela stood before her Mom, fists balled up tightly and feet shifting nervously in the grass.

"Angie something awful has happened." Her Mom began. The rest of Mom's words pounded at her like physical blows as she already felt the unknown fears grow into something very real and very terrible. "Your father has been in an accident. His car missed a curve on the road. Angela, daddy's dead."

Angela stood speechless for a few timeless and tense seconds. Then, instead of seeking comfort with her mother and sister, she turned and fled. With a practiced and unconscious ease she vaulted the back gate and disappeared into the woods behind the house.

Angela's mother looked from her older daughter to the gate where her younger one had vanished and started to weep again. She took Pamela into a warm embrace and comforted herself by comforting her child.

"Don't worry," she told her, "Your sister will come home. She just needs a little time."

The shouts and laughter of a group of teenagers passing close by brought Angela back from her reverie. Tyson was stretching and yawning and would soon be awake from his nap. Melissa still lay comfortable and safe with her head on one of Mom's legs. As Angela shifted her weight though the little girl woke quite suddenly. She sat bolt upright and stared, with a worried little expression, at her mother.

"Mom, you're crying." The child said, amazed. "Are you sad?"

Angela reached up to her face and felt the tears on her cheeks. She used the sleeve of Lucas's shirt to wipe at the tears as she spoke to the child.

"I was a bit sad, Melissa. I was thinking about your grandpa and how much he would have loved you guys." Even as she spoke, Angela felt a lump rise in her throat. If only her father could have been around to share in her life, to walk her down the aisle, to see his grandchildren, would he have been proud of her? The though came with very mixed feelings.

"Where is grandpa, Mommy?" Melissa asked, innocently enough. Her brother had now sat up and come to give Angela a big hug, his little arms squeezing round her neck. Angela hugged the boy back warmly.

"He's in heaven sweetie. He's watching over us all."

Both children were refreshed from their lunch and short nap. They ran gleefully a few steps ahead of Angela to the playground. After playing and a final visit to the beloved monkeys, she led both children to the bus stop to go back up the hill to home.

When they got to their bus stop, Tyson had again fallen asleep. Angela was faced with the dilemma of carrying him, the backpack and the stroller all at once and also helping her daughter down from the big vehicle. A young man near the front of the bus took the stroller from her gently and helped them onto the street.

"Thank you so much," Angela said shyly.

The young man smiled reassuringly. "You're welcome. You sure you're gonna manage all this? I can walk you home if you like?"

"No, no," Angela replied, suddenly nervous. "We'll be fine. I can put him in the stroller now."

"Okay then." He replied, lightly. "Have a good day." He turned away and crossed the road away from Angela's street much to her relief. Something about the encounter made her uneasy.

Angela was glad to be back in the quiet house with the door secured. She put away all that she had carried with them to the zoo and by the time she was done the napping Tyson was back up demanding her attention. She took both children through to the living room and settled down with some Winnie the Pooh videos. Angela loved these tales nearly as much as the kids did and Lucas was too impatient most of the time to sit through them.

Angela cooked them a little supper of pork sausages, mashed potatoes and mixed vegetables with gravy. She pureed some of the vegetables in the blender and gave them to Tyson along with mashed potato and gravy. He was a little young for the spicy sausage meat.

After dinner the kids played in the yard for a little while. Angela sat on a cheap plastic lawn chair and kept a close eye on them while trying to read a little of a paperback novel that she'd bought with a little of the leftover money from last week's groceries.

Later, once the kids were bathed and down to dreamland, Angela turned on the computer and completed a couple of flyers that she'd been doing for the local florists shop, adding some very pretty graphics to them and printing copies to go to the owner for her approval. Angela didn't make a lot of money from this desktop publishing but she enjoyed the little bit of creativity, she felt good about the extra money and not having to ask Lucas when she needed a little to treat the kids.

Angela checked her email. Then her hand hovered over the bookmark which would take her straight to the music chat room. She stared at the screen, thinking about her last talk with Brian. She must have said something that made him think the very worst of Lucas. He couldn't see that mostly her life was okay. Her husband wasn't a monster, like Brian had tried to insinuate. Perhaps she should just stay away from the chat for a while.

She shut off the machine and crossed the hall to fill the tub. Angela was still soaking in a tub of hot bubbles when the phone suddenly rang. She wrapped a towel hastily around herself and made the short dash to the phone by the bed.

"Hello." She answered in her soft-spoken tone.

"Angie," Lucas was raising his voice over the background noise but to Angela it sounded like he was shouting at her. "What took you so long to answer the phone?"

"I was in the bathtub." She explained.

"You on the bedroom phone right now?" He shouted again.

"Yeah I am." She said simply.

"Well well," He said, with a lusty chuckle in his voice. "I'd better be finishing this last set and getting home huh?" Angela was starting to shiver from standing in the dark with just a small towel wrapped round her dripping form.

"Sure Lucas. I'll be here." She quietly told him.

"Damn well better be, girl!" He snapped back at her. She jumped at his words and the almost threatening tone they carried. "Did you wear that shirt of mine all day?"

The question caught her unawares but all the same she smiled to know he was sentimental about things sometimes. Her foot reached out and slid under the fabric of the shirt where it lay on the floor beside the bed.

"Yeah Lucas, I did. You were close to me all day."

"I'll be home in about an hour and half." He told her, still with that almost animal chuckle in his voice. "Go finish your bath now."

"I love you, Lucas." She urgently whispered into the phone but got only the buzz of a line gone dead. He had already hung up on his end.

Angela returned to the bathroom and settled back into her bubbles. She was tired from her day in the fresh air and sunshine, but if she bathed and was all pretty for Lucas when he got home perhaps they could be more romantic for a change and, she dared to hope, she may find him in a mood to talk.

Fresh out of the tub, Angela did feel wider awake and happily sprayed on some of Lucas's favourite scent and put on a pretty blue blouse and a cream coloured mini skirt she knew he really liked. She carefully applied just a small amount of makeup then sat and brushed her long dark hair until it was dried and shining.

Angela went through to the kitchen and put a bottle of cola in the fridge. If Lucas felt like having a drink instead of tea, she would like to have some vodka with the cola instead of a beer. She went into the living room and lit two candles at each end of the low coffee table. As their soft scent started to fill the room, Angela curled herself onto the big armchair to wait for her husband.

She heard the car pull in to the driveway and a strange shiver of anticipation ran up her spine. Lucas would be so pleased she had dressed up for him. Angela started to get up from the chair then stopped in her tracks. Several car doors opened almost at once and more than one voice was heard outside. She realized instantly that he had brought others home with him.

Angela was standing just inside the doorway from the kitchen to the living room when Lucas opened the side door and ushered two men and a woman through it and into the kitchen. They were all talking merrily but Lucas stopped mid-sentence when he saw his wife. He stood the strat case in hand; staring at her with his eyes flashing angrily.

"Geez Angie, you just get in from a date?" He asked, glaring at her with undisguised annoyance. The rest of the party went suddenly quiet on hearing Lucas's angry outburst. He seemed not to notice and turned to one of the men, Angela remembered him as Lenny the drummer, and took the Gretsch case from him. He turned back towards Angie and spoke again, "Don't just stand there, dammit! Get these folks some drinks."

Angela's heart had sunk with his first words to her and all she had really wanted to do was flee. But she nodded mutely at him and turned to their guests.

"Please come in everyone." She said, trying hard to hide the quaver in her voice. She motioned them through to the living room. Meanwhile, Lucas had taken the two electric guitars and stomped off down the basement stairs.

"What can I get for you to drink?" She asked when everyone was seated. The two men, Lenny and the rhythm player, Jason, both asked for a beer. Roxanne, the petite singer from the band, gave Angela a very long and appraising look, then asked if she might have some wine in the house. Angela smiled at Roxanne and said, "Actually I do happen to have a bottle of white wine in the fridge."

"Thanks hon, I sure appreciate it." Roxanne said, smiling warmly back at Angela.

Angela went back into the kitchen to get the drinks just as Lucas came back up the stairs. He crossed to where she stood at the fridge just out of sight of the living room. He grabbed her arm and spun her to face him. She bit down on her lip to avoid crying out as his grip closed on her upper arm. His other hand came up and took a fistful of her hair pulling her to him. She could smell beer on his breath and knew that they had been drinking a bit during the night's gig, even though Lucas was far from drunk. He kissed her very hard, forcing his tongue into her mouth and pulling her head back by the hair. Tears welled up in her eyes but she did not fight him.

Lucas took his mouth from hers and whispered harshly "You'll get more of that later. Gonna dress like a two bit hooker, then what do you expect? Gimme a beer." He pushed her away from him, but before he turned away himself, he put one hand under her miniskirt and roughly rubbed at her crotch through her panties. Angela turned back to the fridge to get the beers, her shame bringing a crimson shade to her face.

She gave the men each a beer and then went back to open the wine for Roxanne. As she was struggling with the corkscrew, she sensed rather than saw someone watching her. She glanced over her shoulder into the smiling open face of red-headed Roxanne.

"Sorry we descended on you like this, hon." Roxanne said.

"It's okay," Angela replied, "Lucas brings people home sometimes like this. I'm used to it now"

"Still," Roxanne pressed her, "I think I'd be safe in guessing you weren't expecting us tonight and you sure weren't out on any date."

Angela felt a lump rise in her throat and her reply seemed like that of a child, her voice was so shaky. "No, I guess not. But it's okay." She had just removed the cork from the bottle and triumphantly turned to Roxanne with a glass of white wine in hand.

"Thanks Angie. Is it okay if I call you Angie?" Roxanne asked as she took the proffered wine.

"Sure." Angela said quietly.

Roxanne motioned to the kitchen table. "Why don't we girls sit here and talk?" She suggested. "Go on pour yourself some wine too, it's okay."

Angela hesitated, looking through the doorway towards Lucas. He wasn't looking her way but was engrossed in deep conversation with the other two men. She was still a little reluctant but took another glass from the cupboard and poured herself some of the wine too.

Both women sat at the table in silence for a few moments. Angela took a sip of the wine then glanced nervously towards the living room again. The motion did not escape Roxanne's attention, but she did not comment on it. Instead she put her glass down and stretched both arms way above her head. After the stretch, she grinned at Angela and winked, "Now that felt better. It's been a long day." She told her. "How 'bout you?"

"Well it wasn't too bad." Angela said shyly. "Took the kids to the zoo and just did the housewife and mom thing mostly."

"That's so cool though Angie." Roxanne told her warmly. "I envy you, because I would really like to have kids, but you sort of need a man in your life first, you know?" She finished with a chuckle.

Angela took a long slow sip of her wine before she answered the other woman. "Roxanne, I'm sure you'll meet a nice man and have children when the time is right."

Roxanne's laughter at that was contagious and Angela found herself giggling too. She took another drink from her wine, then sat back more relaxed than before. Roxanne studied her companion with a practiced eye, and noted the slightly darker bruising over her left cheekbone. She glanced over Angela's shoulder to where she could see Lucas Reeves sitting in an easy chair in the living room. The two seemed an unlikely pair in some respects. He was so self-assured, ever aggressive in his approach to both guitars and people, she by contrast was so shy and soft-spoken. Angela was reaching for her wine glass again when Lucas shouted from the living room.

"Bring me another beer Angie. Geez girl what the hell you doing out there?" Angela rose quickly from the table and opened the fridge. She went through to the living room and passed the full can to her husband, then bent to retrieve his empty one from the coffee table. She paused a moment, empty can in hand, and spoke in her ever timid voice, "Are you guys ready for another?"

No thanks Angie." Both men said almost together. She nodded, turned and fled the room. At least from Roxanne's vantage point it seemed like she fled. Angela placed the empty can in a box by the fridge which already held other bottles and cans. Then she flopped tiredly back down at the table.

"Hey hon," Roxanne said, a worried note creeping into her voice. "You okay? You look real tired."

Angela picked up her wine glass and stared at the golden liquid silently for a few moments. Just when Roxanne thought she wasn't going to answer, she spoke in a voice barely louder than a whisper and choked with emotion that she was trying to control. "I'm just real tired. It's been a long day with the kids and all. And they'll be up early tomorrow and so will I... and, well I....," Angela couldn't find the words to finish her thought and, instead, she tipped back her glass and emptied it. Roxanne fought the urge to put soothing arms around the other woman and comfort her.

"Angie, you don't have to stay up for us. Go to bed." The redheaded woman told her. "I'll get these boys outta here pretty quick. Trust me."

Angela stared at Roxanne through tear filled eyes and shook her head mutely 'No'. She looked into the living room again as if seeking her comfort there. Roxanne felt helpless and baffled by this quiet nervous woman.

"I think I should go and join Lucas and the others." Angela said. "I'm being a terrible hostess. Please Roxanne; come back to the living room." Roxanne allowed herself to be ushered back to the front room where the men were talking about various blues artists that they all admired. Roxanne settled on the couch next to the drummer, Lenny, and Angela curled up on the floor at Lucas's feet with her head resting against his knee. Though she was listening to the conversation, she did not contribute anything herself. Lucas absentmindedly combed his fingers through his wife's long dark hair.

Roxanne leaned over to Lenny and whispered to him that they should go soon. He gave her a quizzical look and she nodded surreptitiously at the exhausted Angela. Roxanne almost giggled at the situation which was starting to feel like charades. Lenny knew the petite redhead had great common sense and excellent people sense so was quick to follow her lead.

A very few minutes later Lenny, Roxanne and Jason were on their feet and awaiting a cab to take them home. Lucas and Angela, arm in arm, saw them out the front door. When the cab pulled away Lucas closed the door and turned the deadbolt, then he spun round to face his wife.

"What the hell are you all dressed up like a whore for?" He shouted.

"Lucas when you called from the club and I was in the bath and naked and ....," She faltered, not sure how to explain.

She saw the blow coming but didn't even try to avoid it. His open hand caught her forcefully across the left cheek and she staggered with the momentum of it. He took her by both shoulders and shook her. When Angela focused once again on Lucas's face she could see his eyes had that angry black look she'd come to know so well.

"Lucas, please don't." She whimpered.

"Please don't what?" he bellowed and his raised voice hit her almost as hard as his hand. "You stand there in front of my friends looking like a fucking hooker and expect me to treat you like a lady!"

"Lucas I didn't know you were bringing any one home." She faltered again.

He pushed her hard backwards and she fell straight onto the easy chair he had been sitting in. Lucas roughly pushed her skirt up around her waist and pulled her panties off her, tearing them as he did so. He slapped her hard a couple of times with one hand as he unbuckled his belt and pulled open his fly.

"You want to dress like a fucking whore; I'm gonna fuck you like a god damned whore." He told her, in a low angry growl. Angela's head was dangling backwards over the arm of the chair and she felt quite dizzy. She screamed when Lucas roughly entered her but his hand came up and jammed something soft into her mouth effectively gagging her. Her head was swimming, tears streamed down her cheeks as her husband assaulted her.

Lucas reached climax quite quickly and pulled his cock out of her. He stood menacingly over her for a moment and delivered a parting shot. "How does it feel to be fucked like a slut? Don't ever do that to me again, you hear me bitch?"

He left her there and went to bed. Angela shifted her weight only enough at first to get her head some support on the arm of the chair, then reached up and pulled the gag out of her mouth. She almost vomited in revulsion right then as realization struck her that he had gagged her with her own torn panties. She sat in the darkness of the living room for a long time, shivering and frightened.

Hours later, it was only her concern for her children's wellbeing that allowed her to overcome her fear and creep into the bedroom. As she slid into bed beside him, Lucas rolled towards her. She cried out in a muted voice but he merely wrapped a strong protective arm around her and slept on.

Angela stirred in her sleep and the gentle strumming of an acoustic guitar weaved its way into her consciousness. Lucas was sitting on the bed beside her, Gibson in hand, watching her sleep and doing endless scales, chords and finger exercises. Outside it was still mostly dark though a tiny hint of daylight was starting to colour the eastern sky. She turned onto her back, still not fully awake, and a barely audible moan escaped her lips as one of her bruises reminded her of its presence. The sleep that fogged her mind and the pain that dulled her senses did nothing to obscure the frightening visions of her semi-dream state and the events of late last night.

Lucas saw the shadow of pain and fear pass over his wife's face and his fingers faltered on the strings. He looked away from her and started to play in earnest, a wrenching blues riff that tore through the remaining shreds of Angela's sleep state. Her eyes came open already filled to overflowing with tears. She saw Lucas through the kaleidoscope of her tears, his form all broken into myriad parts. The image shifted as she blinked and as he moved with the music. Angela felt a sudden deep sadness for him as his pained and shattered heart seemed to be floating before her.

He turned towards her as the last notes of his lament faded. The guitar was placed gently on the floor beside the bed and he bent to kiss her cheek. She winced in pain as his lips touched the bruised surface of her cheekbone. Lucas pulled back from her and seemed to notice for the first time the tears which were flooding from her eyes.

"Baby, I'm so sorry!" He crooned. One of his hands brushed back the hair which had fallen across her face as he bent to kiss her again. Angela turned away from him on her side and, almost without conscious thought, drew her legs up till she was in a fetal curl. She waited for the blows to fall, knowing that even her mute rejection would probably rekindle his rage. Lucas stared, slack jawed, at the childlike form before him but did not move.

Long moments later he arose and taking the guitar with him left the room. Angela remained where she was, sobbing uncontrollably till sleep took her once more.

Hours later, Angela woke again, this time to the sound of children's voices. Melissa and Tyson were standing beside the bed studying their mother earnestly. As soon as she opened her eyes, Melissa turned and scampered to the door, calling,

"Daddy, daddy! Mommy's awake now!"

Tyson toddled closer to the edge of the bed and stretched his little hand towards his mother's face. Angela slid her own hand from beneath the covers to intercept his small one.

"Momma got boo-boo." He stated simplistically.

"Yeah sweetie. But it's okay." just as Angela was reassuring him, the door swung fully open. Lucas and Melissa came in, the child just ahead of her father proudly carrying a small tray with toast spread with peanut butter and jelly. Lucas carried a mug of steaming tea.

"Daddy and I made you breakfast in bed." The girl told her.

"Thank you, my darlings." Angela said. "This looks lovely." Angela sat up carefully, biting her lip to avoid grimacing in pain in front of either the children or Lucas. The children, as though sensing the tension between their parents, were quick to disappear searching out other toys or games. Lucas had deposited her tea on the night table beside her and now stood uneasily beside the bed.

"Angie, I...." He began then faltered.

"Lucas, I love you, you know I do." Her voice, though cracking with the strain, had a note of resolve that usually wasn't there. "But, I need some time alone. You really hurt me last night." She was struggling valiantly to hold back yet another flood of tears. He was clenching and unclenching his fists as she spoke and the fear crept up her spine. But still she continued. "I want you to go stay at Kurt's for a while. We need some time to think, both of us do. I love you."

Lucas took one step towards her. Angela automatically brought her arms up and bent herself against the expected attack. But nothing happened. She ventured a glance up at her husband and saw his eyes had gone angry black, but something more, they were swimming in tears. His anger had arisen only to cover his fear and sadness.

"I will go." He told her, biting each word off angrily. "Just because I need a break from your pitiful whining. I'll be back when you come to your senses, baby!" Angela watched in silence as he threw some of his things from the closet and drawers in a bag and stormed from the room. She got up then and went through the hall only as far as Melissa's room where her children were playing. Closing the bedroom door she sat on the floor with them and listened as Lucas made a couple of trips to the car, taking clothes and several of his guitars with him. Angela did not move from her place on the floor even after she heard the car back noisily out of the driveway. She gathered both children on her lap and held them, singing softly, The Mockingbird Song, and wondered just what she had done.

Beneath The Maples

Summertime was the best time in Angela's mind. Even when it did rain in the summer, it was a gentle warm rain just right for walking. She loved the walk from home to work, twenty blocks through tree lined streets which were mainly residential. Modest small town houses with the usual bright assortment of flower beds littered with lawn ornaments, bird feeders and other decoration that their owners used to lay claim to their own small tract of paradise.

Though technically classified as a city, Angela's home town was just that a small town some seventy miles up the great river delta from the sea. The river valley here, surrounded by coastal mountains was littered with small towns and junior cities that had grown up round the local industries of fishing, farming and logging. Where the river actually met the sea, a large port city had grown up to become a major metropolis with huge office structures, the largest port in the country and a big city's sophistication and squalor.

Angela had been there a few times in her life, but the bustle and the myriads of people everywhere had been rather overwhelming. She had enjoyed the beautiful large parks, many of which were at the water's edge with wonderful beaches and glorious gardens. The maritime climate seemed to be ideal for innumerable different flowers and shrubs to abound. Her father had made numerous trips there when she was a child. In fact, he had been returning home from the "big city" when the accident happened that had taken him from them. Angela sometimes thought her discomfort with visiting "the city" was tied closely to the loss of her cherished father.

The walk to work was a wonderful time of solitude for the young woman. At twenty two, she was still living with her mother, the two of them sharing the family home after older sister Pamela had married two years before. Sometimes she thought about getting a little apartment of her own, but she liked her mother's company well enough as long as she wasn't being pestered about getting out and finding a man, like her sister Pam had done. Angela was still a tom-boy at heart and, though she sometimes dreamed of a nice young man coming in to her life, she was shy enough that the few dates she had ventured on had been awkward and uncomfortable evenings which she would rather forget.

Angela worked at a small mortgage and loan company, doing various clerical duties. There were three young women in the office and a matronly office manager who oversaw the three girls as though she were a mother hen with her chicks. Mrs. Bradshaw, who no one would dare to call by her Christian name Margery, was always punctual and precise and expected her employees to be the same. The other two girls who worked with Angela were close to her own age, just marking time in office jobs while on the proverbial search for Mr. Right. Christie was tall, blonde and gorgeous. Angela always thought she should be a model. Her laughter was infectious and she often came in on Monday's with wild tales of weekend trips down to "the city". She seemed to go through a stunning line up of boyfriends with more frequency than most women went through pairs of shoes. The third in their little trio was Rebecca, but everyone called her Becky. She was about Angela's height, five feet six. Unlike Angela's slim boyish frame though, Becky was somewhat heavier and would probably age into a matronly figure much like Mrs. Bradshaw. She was also much more daring than the shy Angela. Christie and Becky often went out together after work; they were a popular pair in the dance halls and cabarets that the young singles flocked to in the long hot summer evenings. Both girls would frequently try to convince Angela to join them, but more often than not Angela would beg off with excuses of things to do for her mother or babysitting for her little nephew.

This particular Thursday morning, as soon as Angela walked in the door of the office, both her young co-workers were eager to tell her about their previous evening's adventures. Mrs. Bradshaw did not come in until 8:30, so Christie and Becky both pulled their chairs round to Angela's desk, faces alight and bursting to share their news with her. Christie spoke first.

"Hey Angela you should have come with us for sure last night girl!" She said. "We went down to Rock City Cabaret! What a blast!!" Angela smiled indulgently at her friend as she stirred the coffee on the desk in front of her. Becky, grinned somewhat mischievously, then said, "Christie maybe we can convince Angie to go back with us tonight?" Christie and Becky both exchanged nods and then Becky continued. "Angie, you know how you love good music?" Angela looked from one woman to the other, and wondered just what they thought might make tonight any different than any other.

"I do like good music, of course." She said cautiously, not wanting to give them too much encouragement. "But going to those big cabarets, well, it's so noisy and the guys are really crass and rude sometimes."

Christie spoke again. "I'm telling you Angie, you've got to come back there with us tonight. Becky and I will protect you from the guys, I promise." She giggled.

"Okay," Angela replied, "I'm not saying that I'm going. But I have to know what is so all fired important that I have to go with you for? You two will do much better without me trailing along." Becky shook her head in mock exasperation at her shy friend.

"Angie you can't just live alone with your Mom forever. And besides, like I said, you like good music, don't you?"

Angela had to laugh. "Yes Becky," she agreed through her giggles. "But what's that got to do with it? You said yourself that most of those bands that play the cabaret circuits are just okay."

"Well I was wrong." the vivacious blue-eyed Becky admitted. "We danced all night to these guys. They are called Immortal Beat and they really rock! You would love them."

The office entrance door swung open and Mrs. Bradshaw stepped through. She sized up the scene before her rather quickly.

"Ladies, I trust your coffee club meeting is about to adjourn." She said sternly. Angela couldn't help but smile. "This is a place of business, let's get to work."

"Yes Mrs. Bradshaw." Both Christie and Becky answered. They scooted their chairs back to their own desks but cast conspiratorial glances at Angela as they went. Mrs. Bradshaw gave all three girls an appraising look, assuring herself that they were, in fact, getting down to the work at hand. Then she turned and marched off to her own more private office.

The three younger women were quiet for a time, each focusing on their own tasks. Angela was concentrating as she tried to do some calculations on a file and didn't see Becky until she was right beside the desk. Angela jumped a little in surprise as Becky dropped a file folder in front of her. She looked up quizzically at her friend.

"What's this?" Becky put a finger to her lips to shush the question then spoke barely above a whisper.

"It's a picture of Immortal Beat. Check out the guy second from the left. He's the guitar player and he's absolutely gorgeous. Christie and I have to see him again and you, Angela, are coming too. No wimping out this time!"

Angela stared at the cover of the folder without attempting to open it. Becky went back to her desk but kept glancing over at her friend. Christie, having watched the surreptitious delivery of the file folder, was grinning from behind her computer screen. She picked up a thick black marker and on a plain piece of paper wrote, "LOOK AT THE PICTURE ANGIE" in large letters. She held the sign up as soon as she caught Angela's eye.

Angela chuckled to herself as the whole scene, like many others the three women had played in, reminded her of high school. At least her childhood memories of what high school had been like for sister Pamela. Angela's own high school experience had been much different. She had been unable to shake off the grief of losing her father and had been nearly invisible to her fellow classmates. They would, if they recalled her at all, remember her as the shy girl who rarely spoke and who never attended any of the social functions that most students took delight in.

Angela glanced over her shoulder towards Mrs. Bradshaw's office and assured herself that the older woman was safely preoccupied at her tasks. Then she slid the file folder directly in front of her and opened the cover. The photo inside was printed on a standard 8 1/2 by 11 sheet of paper and was obviously intended to be a promo flyer for the band. They were comprised of four members, but Angela's eyes were drawn instantly to the young man second from the left. He was, as Becky had indicated, extremely handsome. He looked to be about the same age as Angela herself, early twenties. He had black hair, cut short very much like a James Dean style. It was difficult to say for sure how tall he may be from this photograph as there was no real frame of reference. But Angela could certainly tell he was well built and strong. He was wearing blue jeans and a black leather vest open at the front which contributed to a mysteriously dangerous look. His chest and upper arms showed the strength and development of a man who obviously kept in very good shape. But his eyes were the feature that truly drew Angela to him. Even in just a photograph, those eyes seemed to reach out and "see" right into her. Their brilliant green colour looked almost unreal.

Angela looked up from the picture to realize both her young friends were watching her with undisguised anticipation. She smiled at both of them and held her hand up, thumb raised to signal her approval. Then she hurriedly slid the file folder discreetly under another on her desk, because Mrs. Bradshaw emerged from her office at just that moment.

The face of the young guitar player kept superimposing itself on Angela's thoughts all morning. Later in the day she had gone back to the file and looked again more closely and discovered his name in the caption beneath the picture. Lucas Reeves, she rolled it over on her tongue. Somehow he fit the name to a tee and she wondered if it was his real name or a stage name that had been adopted.

By lunchtime, Christie and Becky found there was little left to do to convince Angela to accompany them that evening. The timorous young woman had become so curious about the young guitar player that she eagerly agreed to go with them to Rock City that evening.

Angela sat with her mother at the little table tucked in one corner of the kitchen. The two women were sharing their days activities over a modest dinner. Angela's mom had started working only after her husband's car crash had left her a widow with two teenage girls to support. She worked for a department store in their business office. Summer season was very slack and, as usual, the office had been full of rumours of layoffs. Angela listened politely to her mom and made appropriate sympathetic comments, but was still very much distracted by her own plans for the evening. Finally her mom asked, "How was your day, Angie?"

"Well, it was okay." Angie tried to sound noncommittal and low key. "Just another day at the office. Oh by the way, I'm gonna go out tonight." It was like an afterthought. Angela intended it that way because she didn't want her mom to make a big deal of it.

"Going out!" Her mom said, jumping on the words immediately. "On a date?" Her mother's words were so laden with hopeful intonation that Angela almost felt sad and guilty about getting her hopes up.

"Not a date, mom." The young woman replied, and watched her mother's face fall a little. "Just going to go out with Christie and Becky down to Rock City. They tell me there's a very good band playing there right now."

"It's a week night," her mother cautioned. "Don't stay out too late."

"Mom, I'm twenty two. I am a big girl now." Angela laughed. "But thank you so much for caring about me. I love you."

Her mother laughed too, it was a standing joke between them. But she inwardly worried that Angela was not as big a girl as she should be. Her daughter was still such an innocent child at twenty two. If only Paul had still been alive, perhaps Angie would have grown up better under his guidance. They had always been so close.

A short time later, Angela stood in the middle of her bedroom wrapped in a toweling bathrobe after showering and feeling very frustrated. She was at a loss to know what she should wear for the evening. Unlike Christie and Becky, she didn't go dancing all the time and had no real idea what was appropriate attire. Maybe she should have asked the girls before they all left the office. She looked at her closet again but was still no further ahead.

"I'll brush my hair first," she told herself, "and then decide."

She took pains to brush her almost waist length mane of black wavy hair till it shone. And as she brushed, a vision of the young guitar player came to her. His eyes were far too green to be real she decided; the picture must have been altered. By the time her hair was brushed to her satisfaction, she had decided to wear her black jeans but was still uncertain about a blouse. Every one that she owned suddenly looked far too prim and proper for the atmosphere of a cabaret. She heard the doorbell ring.

"Oh no," she thought. "They're here."

Moments later, Christie tapped lightly on Angela's bedroom door.

"May I come in Angie?" She asked.

"Come on in, Christie." Angela replied, pulling open the door. Christie stepped past her into the room with a broad grin on her face and a shopping bag in her hand.

"We thought you might be having difficulty deciding what to wear, so I brought some help!" She told her friend holding up the shopping bag proudly. Christie looked Angela up and down with a critical air. "Okay," she said, "The jeans aren't too bad, but how about blue and way faded and funky looking?" Angela was ready for any help and allowed her friend to take over wardrobe without much protest.

In ten minutes, Christie had Angela in form fitting blue denims and a white halter top that Angela truly thought should be only worn as underwear. Christie tried in vain to convince Angela that it looked just fine. Finally they compromised and Angela chose a contrasting red shirt to be worn over the halter like a jacket. Before she changed her mind again, Christie helped Angela to apply a little make up and hustled her out to the waiting Becky in her car.

The three women were laughing merrily by the time they arrived at Rock City. Angela was a bit more relaxed but her nervousness was renewed when the man at the door insisted on seeing her identification before he allowed her to enter the club. Being put on the spot like that made her feel very awkward.

They chose a table on one side of the room right next to the dance floor and the stage too. The band had not started yet, but Christie assured Angela that they would be on very soon. When the waitress came over to take a drink order, Angela was again at a loss to know what to order. She didn't drink often and usually just a social glass of wine at holidays. Becky was quick to help this time.

"Angela, I think we should have Margaritas. They're great tasty cool treats in the summer time." Becky told her, and Christie nodded her agreement. "Besides we can order them by the pitcher." The girls all agreed on a pitcher of Margaritas and Angela sat back trying hard to look like she fit in here. She was sure everyone was staring at her and really felt self-conscious so close to the front of the room. The Margaritas arrived and Christie poured each girl a glassful. Angela sipped hers tentatively at first, but certainly had to agree with Becky that they were very tasty indeed.

The band came on without much fanfare. A young man, obviously from the club, stepped up to one of the microphones on the stage and gave them a very brief introduction and they started to play. Their first song was an oldie but a standard of many so-called bar bands, Long Cool Woman, by the Hollies. Angela watched Lucas Reeves intently as his hands brought the guitar to life. A young man approached the table the women were at and asked Christie to dance. She quickly agreed and disappeared with him into the crowd on the floor. Becky leaned closer to Angela and almost shouted to be heard over the music.

"See, we told you." She said triumphantly. "Isn't he gorgeous?" Angela glanced briefly at her friend, barely able to take her eyes away from the intense young man on the stage.

"You were right." Was all Angela could say. Becky looked at her friend and was quite surprised at the intensity on the usually timid face. She seemed unable to tear her eyes away from the handsome young guitar player. Even as the thought went through her head, a hand touched her arm and Becky looked up into the smiling face of a young man whom she'd danced with the previous evening. Without a word, she smiled her acceptance of the unspoken invitation and stepped on to the dance floor with him.

Angela barely noticed the departure of her friends from the table. Only a very few bars into the opening number, Lucas had looked Angela's way and graced her with a broad grin. The startlingly green eyes, which she had suspected were touched in the photograph, she could now honestly confirm were really that beautiful an emerald green. She took another small sip from her drink, concentrating on holding the glass in both hands as though that distraction would take her focus away from the man on the stage. It unnerved her that even his casual glance at her had caused such a shiver to run down her spine. When the first number ended, Lucas Reeves leaned in to the microphone and spoke in a low and very masculine voice, "Thank you very much. That first one, Long Cool Woman, well," he paused dramatically, "I'd like to send that out to the very beautiful Long Cool Woman with the incredible long black hair right up front here." He motioned with one arm indicating Angela. Christie had just returned to the table as Lucas spoke and Angela heard her friend's muted shriek. Angela herself sat in stunned and uncomfortable silence sensing a lot of eyes turning towards her.

The band were as good as Christie and Becky had told her and played a wide variety of well know rock and roll music which kept most of the crowd on their feet and dancing. Two different men had approached Angela to ask her to dance by the third or fourth song in the set but she had politely turned them down. She was focused on the music and, unless his eyes turned her way, she followed Lucas's every move. Whenever he did look her way, she dropped her eyes demurely but she couldn't help but unconsciously move in her seat to the primal rock rhythms and Lucas, for his part, couldn't help but notice her swaying with his every move. The second last tune in the set gave Lucas a chance to shine at what he loved best as they slowed right down and did an Otis Redding blues tune called These Arms of Mine. He sang with conviction and played with every ounce of his being and Angela was moved to see the emotion in the intense young face. By the time the last notes faded, she was leaning way forward in her seat, clasping her hands tightly together as though in prayer and tiny tears of emotion were forming at the corners of her eyes. The band flowed immediately into the very upbeat "When the House is a Rocking" to end the set on a high note. Becky and Christie both convinced Angela to get up for this one and the three women danced together joyously.

For Angela, that dance was a welcome relief to the strange and unaccustomed emotional stress that had built up in her during the slow blues number. She loved music but really couldn't ever remember being that deeply touched by a live performance before. The friends hugged each other and giggled their way back to the table as Lucas Reeves took the microphone once more and said, "Thank you all. We're Immortal Beat and we're gonna play some more for ya, after a short break."

Christie and Becky, bolstered by Margaritas, were almost like teenage girls talking excitedly with Angela about the handsome guitar player. Angela listened to their talk but cast surreptitious glances at the stage where Lucas was carefully placing his guitar on a stand next to the amplifier. Lucas turned, spoke briefly with the drummer and then swung back and came off the stage in the direction of their table. Christie caught sight of him too and poked Becky in the ribs as discreetly as possible. Angela barely had time to react and was unconsciously holding her breath.

Lucas, in the same black leather vest as the promo picture and almost skin tight black denim jeans, stopped directly in front of her. He inclined his head and placed both hands together in a very slight but respectful bow. When his head came up, Angela found herself staring speechless into those vivid green pools, her head was swimming. Lucas spoke, "Good evening. Thank you so much for being here." He said, innocently enough. "It's easy to tell you really love good music." He glanced around at all three ladies. "Mind if I join you ladies?"

Becky quickly answered for them all as she could certainly see that poor Angela was dumbstruck.

"Sure please do." She said. "I'm Becky; these are my friends Christie and Angela." She motioned to each woman in turn. Lucas solemnly took first Becky's hand in a gentle handshake, and then Christie's.

"I'm Lucas Reeves, pleased to meet you all." Then he turned his smile on Angela and proffered the same open hand to her. When Angela placed her hand into his however, he took it, gently inclined his head and kissed it. "Especially you my lovely angel with the Long Cool Black hair." Angela felt herself flush with embarrassment, but the feeling came with a strange new rush of emotion that crept magically up her spine and left her breathless.

Lucas chatted with the three women for a few minutes, though Angela said very little, suddenly finding the drinking straw in her hands very fascinating, she was most disquieted by the presence of this self-assured young man. Christie and Becky both could see the electric chemistry developing between their shy friend and the handsome Lucas Reeves. Both girls made excuses, and together, headed off towards the ladies room.

Lucas now turned his full attention on Angela. She shifted nervously in her chair and reached for her glass. His hand covered her smaller one before she had attained her goal and she was stopped short and breathless once again. She was sure she felt an electric charge race into her from his hand and it seemed to shoot to some place very deep in her soul. Her eyes met his and for a brief moment the rest of the room faded away. He broke the spell when he grinned and winked at her.

"Hey Angie," he said softly, "I'd like to thank you, especially for getting into These Arms of Mine." Angela's mind reeled at the vision those words brought to her senses and it took her a second to realize Lucas was referring to the slow blues tune he had played. Lucas continued his voice still in soft tones that made her feel like the two of them were sharing some special secret. "I can tell you really like blues, that's awesome. I live to play blues, you know?"

Angela nodded then finally found her voice, though it sounded very distant and tiny even to her, "You play beautifully Lucas," she told him. "I can see your heart when you play like that." A tiny shadow passed across Lucas Reeves' eyes at her words, but Angela did not notice. She had again dropped her gaze shyly away from his as she spoke. Lucas reached his other hand to her chin and gently brought her eyes back to him. She looked directly into the green expanse of his eyes for the first time and saw herself mirrored in a pool of passion so intense that she drew in a surprised breath.

Lucas let the moment pass. He patted her hand in almost brotherly fashion and stretched back in his chair, glancing round the room. Angela's breath was coming in a ragged rhythm which was trying to match her racing heart. She slowly calmed down and felt some of the heat start to fade from her flushed cheeks. Her mind was jumbled in a combination of fear and excitement. 'What was it about this man that so disarmed her.' She wondered. Lucas glanced at the watch on his left wrist.

"Well, time I went back to work." He announced, standing up with almost cat-like grace. "It was a pleasure meeting you Angie. With your permission, I'd like to talk more on the next break?" He towered over her now and Angela suddenly thought of the great big maple tree in the backyard at home.

"I would enjoy that Lucas, very much." She told him. Lucas winked boldly at her, this time bringing a smile to her lips, and turned back to the stage.

Angela let the noise and bustle of the room wash over her as she tried to catch her breath from the brief meeting with Lucas Reeves. She was most confused by the strange and unaccustomed sensations that his presence seemed to have awakened in her. Only once previously had one of her so-called dates tried to kiss her good night and it had been a clumsy effort that left her feeling nothing. But merely sitting with Lucas and staring into his eyes, woke feelings inside of Angela that she had never before experienced.

Christie and Becky returned to the table just before the band got started again. They suddenly reminded Angela of big sister, Pamela, and her friends from school. They were all giggles and questions about Lucas and what he and Angela had talked about. She tried to remain aloof, though inside she was trembling, and told them it was nothing, just small talk. Before they had a chance to press their friend further, the band kicked into the opening number of the second set and it became too difficult to converse.

The second set was more of the same great classic rock tunes that had dominated the first. The dance floor was quickly filled to capacity. Christie and Becky came and went frequently from the table dancing with a number of different young men. Angela remained where she was, watching Lucas. She had consumed just enough of the Margarita mix to be somewhat more relaxed and allowed herself more and more to move with the music. Lucas was all business when it came to playing but still if he caught her eye he would nod or wink his approval of her attention. In this set too there was another of the gut wrenching slow blues tunes that Lucas excelled at and that Angela was only now experiencing for the first time. She had never known that music could so completely touch one's emotions.

As soon as the set ended, before Lucas could come off the stage, Angela excused herself to go to the ladies room. While there she caught a glimpse of herself in the mirror and was brought up short. Her face was quite flushed as though she had been dancing up the same storm that her two companions had been. 'It must be really hot in here.' she thought to herself. She turned on the cold tap and brought handfuls of cooling water to her face. That seemed to help some but took off the little bit of makeup that Christie had helped her apply.

When she returned to the table, Lucas was already waiting for her. He graciously stood up and pulled out her chair, taking a gentle grip on her elbow to help her to her seat. He had a glass of beer in front of him and when she raised her glass to drink, he offered a toast.

"Here's to new blues friends, lovely lady." He said with a wink. He touched his glass to hers and then took a long swallow of the beer. Angela smiled shyly at him and sipped a tiny bit of her Margarita. She could already feel the heat rising in her cheeks again so became surer than ever that the Margaritas were to blame.

Lucas had turned his chair slightly to face her but had kept the table between them.

"So Angie, do you live here in town?" He asked. He found himself wondering how he could win over this shy but beautiful woman. 'Did she truly not understand how drop-dead gorgeous she was?' he wondered.

"Yes, all my life." She replied timidly, thinking to herself how lame it must sound to have been in this tiny town all her life. He must have travelled many places and seen many more things than she could imagine.

"That's cool." He told her. "I sometimes wished that I could settle down. But we moved a lot when I was a kid," He shrugged and shook his head sadly, "and doing this, well, I move where the gigs are, ya know?"

"That's hard," Angela said, genuinely feeling badly for him. "Don't you miss your family?"

"Not much. I've only got a bro and my mother. Haven't seen her in a couple of years and then she just pissed me off. I generally live at Kurt's, that's my bro, when I'm home." Lucas shrugged his shoulders and took another gulp of his beer. Angela sensed some sort of hurt behind the offhanded comments and wanted to reach out to him. He set the beer glass down again and ran the fingers of both hands through his short black hair in a frustrated motion.

"I'm sorry," Angela told him. "I should not have pried." He looked at her appraisingly.

"It's okay." He assured her. "That's life, ya know? What about you? You see your family?"

Angela cringed a little, suddenly feeling uncomfortable. She was sure Lucas would think she was a Mommy's girl, still living with her mother when he was so sophisticated and worldly.

"I live with my Mom, just the two of us." She said softly.

"That's cool. No sister's or brothers?" Lucas sounded casual, but he was very interested in Angela's situation. He couldn't possibly imagine that a beauty like her didn't already have a boyfriend. But then again, he thought, she sure seemed mighty shy and innocent.

"My sister got married a couple of years ago, so it's just Mom and I." Angela didn't want to tell Lucas more than that, but she knew she would if he only asked. Lucas pressed her no further as he saw the discomfort in her pretty blue eyes. He finished what was left of his beer and pushed back his chair.

"Time I went to work again." He told her, then chuckled low and suggestively. "I'll play a few just for you this time, pretty lady."

He winked, and then turned back to the stage once again. His last remark brought a shiver of anticipation racing down Angela's spine. She watched his retreating form with a longing that she could neither explain nor understand.

Christie and Becky had been visiting with some of their many acquaintances around the room while Lucas and Angela had talked. But they now reappeared, ready once again to hear what their friend had learned about the handsome musician. Angela remained quite tight-lipped, determined to keep Lucas's confidence, though she wasn't sure why it was so important to her.

The band opened their final set of the evening with the Jimi Hendrix tune, Crosstown Traffic. Lucas did not so much as glance Angela's way during the song. She reached across the little table and picked up the fresh pitcher of Margaritas that the waitress had just delivered and refilled her glass. Suddenly the fruity frothy mix was going down very smoothly. Christie exchanged a somewhat worried look with Becky. Becky leaned closer to Angela and shouted to be heard above the band.

"You okay, hon?" She asked. Angela looked at her, then across at Christie and started to giggle.

"I'm fine silly." She told Becky. "This was the greatest idea, coming here." She took a long gulp of the drink and turned her attention back to the band. Lucas had just played the last chords of the Hendrix number with an energetic flourish. The dancer's on the floor and most of the seated crowd applauded and hollered.

The band seemed to feed off the energy of their audience. Lucas counted them into the next number, a classic tune from Led Zepplin, Whole Lotta Love. He caught Angela's eye as he played the opening riff and mouthed the words "This one's for you, babe!" Angela felt an intense rush of excitement realizing he was playing with just her in mind.

The primitive and sensual rhythms of the song took hold of Angela and she started to move in her seat, rocking with the insistent beat. Deep inside her, feelings stirred unbidden and she had a flood of images half-formed flashing through her mind: Lucas kissing her deeply, the kind of kiss she'd only seen in the movies, then the image of his eyes staring lustfully down at her and finally her awareness of wanting to be looked at in just that way.

"Way Way down inside, honey you need it, Gonna give you my love...." Lucas's voice weaved an unfamiliar but wholly arousing spell around the inexperienced Angela. She felt sudden longing for something that she could not define. As the music rose to an exciting guitar solo, Lucas came down to the edge of the stage as close as he could get to her. His green eyes locked with her soft blue ones and she felt a massive shudder run through the length of her body. Just as his soaring guitar cried its climax, Angela moaned and felt a sudden release of a tension that had been building since she first laid eyes on Lucas Reeves.

Angela was barely aware of the next few songs the band played. Though her eyes still followed Lucas's every movement on the stage. Despite his distracting fascination with her, Lucas had watched Angela quite dispassionately as he played. When she moaned during his solo, he chuckled approvingly. 'You're mine, sweetheart.' He thought smugly.

This third and final set of the evening was filled with a lot more blues and rocking blues music than the previous two and Angela did not recognize the individual numbers as well as she had the classic rock tunes of the earlier sets. But the words and Lucas's guitar seemed to weave an almost hypnotic spell round her. 'Woke up this mornin' feeling round for my shoes....' 'Early in the mornin', anytime at night, I can feel your tender lips, makin' me feel alright.' It was all wonderfully simple and the rhythm of each tune seemed to find a rhythm in her body as she tapped feet, clapped hands and swayed in time. That Lucas loved to play the blues became more than apparent, as he put every ounce of his energy and emotions into each song. She was at once, wholly impressed by his dedication to the music and somewhat jealous that the same music could steal his attention from her so completely.

The last song of the evening was a Stevie Ray Vaughan favourite, The Sky is Cryin' and by its end Angela's makeup was completely beyond repair. Her tears had come unbidden and she was barely aware of them herself. Christie and Becky decided it was time they got their naive friend home to bed. Becky handed Angela a tissue.

"Here Angie, dry your tears." She said gently. "We should get going soon." Angela looked up at her friend quizzically and her fingers went to her cheek to discover the tears there. She took the tissue mechanically and clutched it in her hand, unused. Lucas had already put his guitar down and excused himself rather abruptly from the crowd of young people gathered round the small stage.

He strode across to where Angela was sitting and squatted down in front of her, placing his hands on either arm of the chair and taking pains not to touch or alarm her at all.

"Angie?" He asked, "You okay, why the tears?" Angela stared at him a moment and he saw her clouded eyes slowly come back into focus. She wanted to simply fall forward out of her chair and into his arms but was desperately frightened by the feeling. Becky took a protective step closer to Angela's side and behind Lucas; Christie got to her feet and gathered both hers and Angela's purses. Angela took a deep breath and shifted a little in her seat.

"I'm fine, Lucas." She assured him. "Just a little tipsy and got so into that 'Crying' song. I'm sorry."

Lucas smiled broadly at her answer. "Don't ever be sorry for getting into the blues, girl. I was just worried about my new friend is all." Becky put one hand on Angela's shoulder and both Lucas and Angie looked up her.

"Don't worry Lucas." she stated flatly. "Christie, Angie and I look out for one another. C'mon Angie, we gotta work tomorrow."

Lucas stood up and took one step towards Becky. He was quite a bit taller than her and she was somewhat taken aback staring up at him. Lucas smiled down at her warmly however.

"It's so great to know a nice lady like Angie has good friends like you." He told her then nodded at Christie too. "And Christie thanks for looking out for her." Both women couldn't help but beam at him as he complimented their loyalty. Angela stood up from her chair and reached for her purse from Christie. She slung the bag on her shoulder and turned to her friends.

"Wait a minute for me before we go?" She requested, suddenly seeming surer of herself. The two women looked from her to Lucas and back again. Then Christie nodded and pulled Becky towards the door. Angela turned back to Lucas Reeves.

"I want to stay with you, get to know you more." She told him with conviction. Lucas was speechless for a second. He had been ready for nearly anything from the shy, inexperienced beauty but had not expected her emphatic statement. He reached out and gently took her tiny hand in his. Like earlier in the evening, his lips sought the back of her hand and softly brushed it. Angela felt a shudder of delight go through her body and there was no doubt that Lucas had felt it too.

"Come here Angie." He told her gently and led her up on the stage. He dropped her hand and picked up his guitar from the stand. Turning to face her, he offered the instrument to her with both hands. She shook her head in confusion but took the guitar anyway, surprised by how heavy it felt. "There she is then." Lucas told her matter-of-factly. When she merely looked from him to the guitar and back again, baffled, he spoke again, "This Angela, is my mistress. I live to play her and make her sing. We lead a very strange kinda life, her and me. Like right now, we're sleeping in my car. You are a very beautiful and special person, Angela. Come back tomorrow, please, I want to know you better. But tonight go home with your friends. Be safe and sweet dreams."

She stared wordlessly at him and he gently took the guitar from her grasp. He placed the instrument back on its stand then took Angela tenderly by one arm.

"Come on beautiful. I'll walk you to the door." He saw her safely back into the company of Christie and Becky, then without another word, he pivoted and strode back across the room.

Angela had not said anything about Lucas to either of her friends on the way home despite their urgings to tell them all about her talks with the guitar player. She went straight to bed, once she was safely in the door at home, avoiding the inevitable chat with Mom about her evening out.

Once in bed however she was not able to close her eyes nor could she escape the flood of images of Lucas from parading through her mind. He was handsome, there was no doubt about that, but it was the passion with which he played, the striking green of his eyes and the fact that he had paid attention to her at all that had Angela completed spellbound. She did sleep eventually, but fitfully at best. She woke several times during the night with that same overwhelming sensation that she had felt as Lucas had played. Angela found herself hugging her blankets and pillows to her slim form and wishing that they were Lucas.

Angela had neatly avoided her Mom again in the morning, showering as soon as she got up then hiding in her room until Mom had gone to use the shower. She grabbed a muffin from the kitchen counter and headed out the door, munching as she walked. Foremost in her mind was going back that evening to see Lucas again; going alone to such a place seemed the most overwhelming and daunting idea. But going with Christie and Becky, as well intentioned as they were, was no solution either. Perhaps if just sensible Becky could go with her, Angela thought maybe the level headed girl would understand her desire to see Lucas again.

Both her friends were eager to get her impressions of Lucas and were still quite excited that the young guitar player had seemed so interested in Angela. For her part, Angela was still baffled by Lucas's attention. She was a very beautiful young woman but she herself seemed barely to realize it. She was lost in a reverie of thoughts about Lucas when Becky spoke and she only heard the last few words. "...........going to see him again?" Becky finished.

"Pardon me?" Angela asked, shaking her head. She looked at her friend and suddenly knew the question from her expression alone. Christie's phone had rung and she turned away from the conversation, missing Angela's reply. "He wants me to go back tonight."

"Are you going?" Becky asked her, quite matter-of-factly.

"I want to, very much." Angela told her friend timidly. "But to go all alone...." She didn't finish her thought.

"Angie," Becky told her with a wink, "I think I have a solution for you. Remember that guy I was dancing with a lot?" Angela didn't really, but nodded at her friend. Becky continued, "Well he asked me to meet him there too, tonight. And it's Friday. Christie's going down to the city. So it will be four of us, 'cept that Lucas will be working."

Angela stared at Becky for a moment then started to smile broadly. Things seemed to be working just the way she wanted them to, she thought.

"Then I can go." She said, the relief and excitement mingled in her expression and her tone.

"Yes, of course you can silly." Becky told her.

Christie was almost jealous that she would not be able to join her friends that evening when she found out about their plans. Becky and Angela promised faithfully to fill her in on all the details on Monday. The three friends went shopping at lunch time and found Angela a satiny black shirt with a modestly high collar which would look great with the faded blue jeans and still satisfy Angela's somewhat reserved outlook on fashion. Angela could barely concentrate on her work all afternoon, as her mind kept slipping back to visions of Lucas Reeves.

Becky and her date, Don, picked Angela up nearly half an hour earlier than the girl's had the evening before. Angela was polite, as always, when greeting Becky's date, but it was easy to see her mind was elsewhere. When they arrived at Rock City the stage was in darkness, they would have to wait for a while for the band to start. Angela, feeling more confident her second time in the club, led the three of them to the same small table right by the corner of the stage.

A waitress strolled over from the bar to take their drink order. Becky and Don decided to drink beer and ordered a pitcher between them. Angela wrinkled her nose at them in distaste when they said she should join them.

"Yuck," she laughed, "I don't like beer." Behind her, unseen, Lucas had walked across from where he had been sitting with the rest of his band mates in a dark corner of the room. She jumped in surprise when he spoke.

"Beer will grow hair on yer chest." He said with a chuckle. She spun her head round to face him and he smiled broadly. "Glad you're here Angel. Why don't you drink what you like best?" He suggested.

She struggled with that notion because she really had very little experience with drinking. Lucas had slid gracefully into the chair alongside hers and put his hand out towards Don. "Nice to see you again too, Becky. Hi man, I'm Lucas."

Don took the proffered handshake and the two men grinned at each other in greeting. Angela had no idea what she should drink and was increasingly aware of the impatient look on the waitress's face. She turned to Lucas.

"Lucas, I don't know what to drink?" she said. He looked appraisingly at her and rubbed his chin with a thumb and forefinger as though deep in thought. Then he grinned at her and spoke softly, "Angela, I think you'd make a great vodka drinker." He told her confidently and then he looked up at the waitress.

"Bring her a vodka and seven-up and I'll have another beer, thanks." Angela was grateful that he'd taken her lead and ordered her something. He was dressed in light blue jeans tonight with a white muscle shirt and he still had a dangerous rogue look about him.

When the drinks arrived, Lucas took a long swallow of his beer then, leaving the glass on the table, rose from his seat. He held a hand out to Angela.

"Do you want to learn how to tune a guitar?" He asked, taking her quite by surprise. She placed her hand in his and, smiling happily, allowed him to lead her up onto the stage. He guided her to a hard and uncomfortable perch on the guitar's amplifier, then picked the guitar up and squatted down in front of her. He whispered almost conspiratorially.

"It doesn't really need to be tuned." He confessed. "Just thought we could talk here easier, ya know?"

Angela looked shyly at him, feeling somewhat conspicuous perched on the corner of the amplifier. He ran practiced hands across the strings of the guitar, making very soft tones that only the two of them could really make out with the amp turned off. She concentrated on those hands, studying the calloused finger-tips which moved lightly across the fingerboard as he idly played soft riffs. Too timid suddenly to meet the intense gaze of those emerald eyes, she spoke softly to his hands.

"You play so beautifully. Where did you learn how?" She asked.

"I just kinda picked it up," he answered, "When I was a kid, you know? There was this neighbour who taught me some stuff, gave me a guitar. Then I just like played all the time and got better some."

Angela saw, in her mind's eye, a vision of a young Lucas sitting alone in his room playing endlessly to become so good. 'He must have been a lonely boy.' she thought. That somehow reassured her, seeing a connection between them even when they were young.

"While you were focused on your music, I was perfecting the skills of a tom-boy." she told him. "I was kinda shy when I was a kid."

Lucas looked up at her then, his eyes sparkling mischievously.

"No, really?" He laughed, his voice all mock-shock. "I would never have guessed. You're so outgoing now."

She felt herself get all hot as she blushed with his words. But he smiled reassuringly at her and winked.

"It's okay, I'm only teasing you." He said softly. "Besides I'm very attracted to quiet gals."

His words brought a new flush to her face and her hands gripped the edges of the amplifier tightly. Lucas was observing her closely and realized just how off balance his remark had made her. 'Damn' he thought, 'she's so beautiful and so innocent.' He played a couple of strident chords which effectively changed the mood.

"So Angie, any requests tonight?" He asked her. Angela was still trying to catch her breath from the realization that the handsome talented young musician had openly admitted an interest in her. She nervously brushed her long hair back from her face and spoke hesitantly.

"Well, I liked that Arms of Mine song." She told him.

"Great tune, by Otis Redding. We do it in the first set." He stated. "So that one's yours okay?" As he was speaking the drummer came onto the stage and Lucas replaced the guitar on its stand. "We're going to get started soon. Come on." He rose and held out his hand. She timidly placed her hand in his and allowed him to lead her back to the table.

Angela took a drink of her vodka and seven when she sat down, rolling the fizzy liquid round her mouth before swallowing. It was a great taste; sweet, bubbly and the alcohol was barely discernible. She took another quick swallow then turned to Becky.

"He's really very nice, Becky." She told her friend. "He's going to play a song just for me in the first set."

Becky grinned at her friend, shaking her head in mock amazement.

"We finally get you out of your mother's house and starting to live, and look at you!" She laughed, "You pick up the cutest guy to come along in this town in recent history!"

Angela flushed with embarrassment, remembering Lucas's recent admission of his interest in her. Don raised his beer glass in a toasting gesture towards Angela and announced, "It's only right Becky. Look at Angela, this gal is gorgeous! She certainly deserves the best!" Becky gave him a teasing smack on the forearm but also raised her glass. Angela, still flushed, raised her glass too and the three young people drank together.

Like the previous evening, the band opened with Long Cool Woman and again Lucas made a point of singling Angela out at the end of the song. The set proceeded with the usual list of classic rock tunes. Angela was content to watch Lucas as Becky and Don came and went from the dance floor. When Lucas was introducing These Arms of Mine, he moved his microphone across the stage to his right, placing it as close as the cord would allow to where Angela was sitting.

She sat spellbound as he sang the very passionate lyrics and several times during the tune their eyes locked for long moments till she modestly dropped hers. Every time that he looked at her now, she was assaulted by her own mixed up emotions and a dim awareness of his growing lust for her. Angela had never felt such sensations before and the intensity was frightening to her.

Immortal Beat finished the set again with the upbeat, When the House is A Rockin', and Don, Becky, Angela and a guy friend of Don's, whose name Angela had missed in the sound of the band, all danced together. When the song ended, Don's friend had leaned close to Angela, given her a peck on the cheek and whispered thanks for the dance. She smiled at him, excused herself and quickly made her way to the table. Lucas was already off the stage but she couldn't see him anywhere. She sat and took a drink from her second vodka, wondering just where Lucas had disappeared.

Across the room, Lucas had come off the stage on the left side and gracefully made his way swiftly through the dancers still on the floor till he stood face to face with the young man who had danced with Angela. The young man looked quizzically at the intense guitar player.

"Hey man," Lucas said, a low dangerous note in his voice, "Angela is my girl, so back off." His prospective competition raised his hands in a gesture of surrender to the angry figure before him.

"Sorry man, it was only a dance." He said, trying to make peace. "She was sitting all alone and...." His voice trailed off when he saw the angry look pass over Lucas's face.

"Just back off!" Lucas repeated, biting off every word.

By the time Lucas had joined Angela, the anger had passed and he was again clear eyed and grinning. He ordered a beer and then slouched back in his chair, stretching long legs under the table. His right leg brushed against Angela's calf and even that contact was enough to bring a shudder of electricity rushing up her spine. She took another drink of her vodka, trying to calm herself.

"Tomorrow's Saturday," Lucas stated, "Do you work on Saturdays?"

"No." Angela told him. "Just Monday to Friday."

"Well, maybe we can do something?" he asked. "How 'bout lunch, ya know, and then maybe go for a walk or something? You can show me 'round."

"That would be really nice Lucas." She answered her heart jumping.

"Then it's a date." He said, chuckling. His beer had arrived and he raised his glass. She smiled and brought her vodka glass to meet his with a satisfying clink. Both of them drank and Angela took as long a drink of hers as he did. He watched her out of the corner of his eye, wondering if she realized how fast she was drinking.

"Better slow down a little there, girl." He cautioned. "I don't want you to be getting too tipsy to talk later."

She smiled at his concern, but put the drink down all the same. Becky and Don rejoined them and for a while Lucas was distracted, talking guitars with Don. Angela listened to every word, learning for the first time that the beautiful instrument that she'd held the night before was a Fender Stratocaster, somewhat of a favourite among guitar players. She loved how animated Lucas was when he was able to talk music and guitars and wished she knew more so she could share his love of music more.

The second set was much like the previous evening had been. Angela, now on her third vodka, was feeling more and more relaxed, knowing that Lucas was genuinely interested in her. She was still spellbound by his intensity when playing and that intensity was pulling her into the music more fully than ever before. She moved in her seat with every beat and her whole body drank in the primitive rhythms with a new found excitement. When Lucas played a blues number in this set it was Willie Dixon's Bring it On Home. Angela was still amazed by the depth of emotions that came through in blues music, when he played it was something that Lucas was sharing with her and she felt so thankful for that. When his half-closed eyes did occasionally focus as he sang, it was on Angela that he focused.

She had ordered another drink for herself and a beer for Lucas just before the blues number had started and the waitress delivered them just as the band was playing the closing number of the set. By the time Lucas had replaced his guitar on its stand and rejoined her, she had drunk nearly a third of the drink. He noticed, but didn't comment.

They had the table to themselves for the whole break as Don and Becky were across the room visiting with friends. Lucas had drawn his chair a little closer to hers but still remained aloof, keeping a respectful distance between them. Angela wanted to somehow close that gap but was unsure of herself and so fiddled nervously with her drinking straw. Under the table, she crossed and uncrossed her legs, fighting with an unfamiliar urge that was seemingly trying to take her over.

Lucas talked more about the music and she willingly listened as he enthusiastically told her that the background of a lot of the rock she listened to was the blues that he loved. He was able to name many old blues masters that she had never heard of, whose tunes had gone on to become well know hits of rock and rollers. His knowledge impressed her, but his enthusiasm and admiration touched her more.

Just before Lucas was ready to go back to the stage, Don and Becky came back to the table and announced that they had all been invited to a house party. They said they had to leave now and, if Angela was coming too, she'd better drink up. Angela's eyes widened in surprise and she looked from Becky to Lucas and back again.

"Becky, I want to stay." She told her friend. "There's still another set." She was looking plaintively at Becky, silently begging her to understand that she couldn't go and leave Lucas here. Lucas put one hand out on her forearm and she instantly turned towards him.

"It's okay," He reassured her. He looked up at Becky and Don, his hand still resting on Angela's forearm. "I'll drive Angie home. She'll be fine with me." Becky looked at Angela, long and hard, searching her shy friend's face.

"You okay with that, hon?" she asked at last.

"Yes, oh yes..." Angela breathed. "Thank you Lucas." Her relief and excitement at Lucas's offer to see her home was written all over her flushed and smiling face.

The three young people said their goodbyes. The two women promised to talk the next day. Then Don and Becky departed. Angela turned to Lucas and tentatively patted his hand where it still lay on her arm.

"Thank you." She told him softly.

Lucas squeezed her arm with his hand then rotated his wrist grasping her hand in his. He held her hand and leaned closer to her, gently brushing her cheek with his lips. She shuddered with arousal. He squeezed her hand again, then broke the contact and drained his beer. He rose, winked at her and headed back to work.

The hard rocking blues of the third set was an insistent beat which Angela found she could no longer possibly ignore. She rocked right along with Lucas and the band, dancing excitedly in her chair. Lucas was soaring, enjoying himself immensely and looking forward to some private time with the timid beauty that had arrived so recently in his life. He caught her eye several times during the set and was thrilled to see that her soft blue eyes had a new light in them, a passion that had been previously submerged. Her very shyness attracted him, innocence which none of the girls he usually met had possessed.

Angela had to be patient when the set ended. Lucas talked for some time with his band mates. Then she sat on the edge of the stage and watched as he went through the ritual of putting the Strat into its case. Finally, he turned to her and grinned.

"Ready beautiful?" He asked.

"I'm ready," She told him. He held his free hand out to her and she fell into step beside him across the dance floor and out into the now almost empty parking lot. He led her to a large older Buick in a far corner of the lot. He released her hand and turned the key in the passenger door. He reached in and took the lock off the back door too and opened it, putting the guitar in. He turned to Angela with a somewhat sheepish look.

"Please excuse the mess," He told her, indicating the fast food debris and clothing that littered the back seat. "I'm kind of living outta the car when I'm on the road and I wasn't expecting company, ya know?" Normally quite fastidious, somehow the mess didn't bother Angela at all.

"It's fine, Lucas." He helped her in then went around to the other side. Once he had started the car he turned to her expectantly. She was nervously clasping and unclasping her hands in front of her, suddenly extremely uncomfortable in such private and close quarters with him.

"Angela," he spoke softly but with a chuckle, "You need to tell me where we're going." She flushed once again, thinking how foolish she must appear. She gave him some directions and he put the car in gear and moved off. He tuned the radio to a late night soft rock station, quite a contrast from the harder bluesier material he had been playing. She settled back trying to calm her racing heart.

When they pulled into her street, she finally thought she had her emotions under control again. He pulled up to the curb in front of the house and put the car into park. Lucas turned towards her and as soon as his passion filled green eyes met hers she realized that her emotions were nowhere close to controlled. He reached his right arm across the back of the seat and spoke huskily, "Come here, baby."

She slid across towards him shaking almost uncontrollably. As soon as his arm came around her, he felt her trembling. His left hand found her chin and he raised her face to his. Angela's blue eyes, filled with both passion and terror, looked back at his green ones. He brushed the hair from her face and traced her cheek with his fingertips. She continued to tremble and he spoke softly, trying to reassure.

"It's okay, Angie, it's okay." He crooned. "I won't do anything that you don't want. It's okay. You do like me, don't you?"

She had trouble at first even finding her voice and when she spoke the words came all in a rush. "Lucas, I'm so... scared. I've never felt like this, I've never... Oh God, I'm sorry, I've never." Her tears came then and he gently touched them with his fingertips. Lucas had been stunned with the realization of the truth of her absolute innocence. He held her, gently patting her back as she sobbed into his shoulder.

As her crying subsided, he again put a hand under her chin and raised her now tear stained face to his. He waited till he could see in her eyes that she was seeing him and not her fears, and then he spoke again.

"Angela, I won't hurt you." He told her. "I will walk you to the door right now, say good night and be on my way. If you say that is what you want. Okay?" Her eyes blinked in surprise at him. She fought an inner battle, realizing that of all the things she wanted, she did not want Lucas to leave. He watched with detached interest as she fought her inner fears. Finally, she looked back at his lustful green eyes and in mute acquiescence she brought her lips to his.

She was still trembling with a mix of excitement and fear but her decision was made. Her fear actually increased his ardour, her innocence made his passion for her more insistent. He kissed her back gently at first but then his tongue started to probe against her closed lips. His arms had encircled her now and his hands were running over her back and sides, gently caressing and playing with her body as though it were yet another instrument. His insistent tongue finally won and Angela parted her lips allowing him to taste her more fully. She moaned softly as his tongue entered her.

Lucas brought one hand to her chest and started to rub his fingertips across her nipples through her satiny shirt. She moaned again but tensed a little. He withdrew his tongue from her mouth and planted soft kisses on her cheeks and forehead, but his hand continued to caress her breasts. Angela went quite tense beneath his hands and he suddenly realized with astonishment that she was about to climax. His mouth found hers again and his tongue plunged into her. This time her own tongue started to dance timidly with his and her hips started to move rhythmically. Lucas heard her moan again and held her close as she shook with the force of her orgasm. When her trembling subsided, he gently kissed her cheeks again and whispered softly,

"Angie, you're beautiful. I want you so bad." He kissed her more firmly, and then leaned back a little from her. "I want this to be right, baby. Not here in the car. Ssshh now," He crooned as she started to speak. He had seen the porch light come on and realized that Angela's Mom was probably watching from the house. "You need to go in now, get some sleep. Tomorrow is soon enough my angel."

Angela realized at that moment too that the light had come on and she seemed to suddenly alter back to the shy girl Lucas had met the previous evening. She smiled at him, still flushed with arousal and tried to smooth her hair and blouse. He turned the key and pocketed it as the engine died. He then slid from behind the wheel and went round to open her door. He walked her to the door and gave her a quick almost brotherly peck on the cheek. She turned her key in the lock then looked over her shoulder at him, "Lucas, thank you," She softly whispered.

He inclined his head in a respectful gesture, hands pressed prayer like together, then turned abruptly, walking briskly back to the car. Angela opened the door and stepped into the front hall.

Though the porch light was on, the rest of the house was in darkness except for the glow of the small lamp over the stove in the kitchen. Angela slipped out of her

shoes and padded softly through the living room towards that light. Her Mom was sitting at the kitchen table with both hands wrapped round a mug of tea. She looked up at her daughter with a smile.

"You're home a little late." She said, matter-of-factly. "Who was that driving you home?"

"A little late I guess, Mom, but tomorrow is Saturday." She agreed, not willing to argue. "He was just a friend of Becky's and mine." She added, thinking that the lie was only a little white lie, after all Lucas did know Becky.

"Well," Her mother told, I'm glad you're home safe." She was studying Angela's face, which was still somewhat flushed, searching for some clue as to the change in her usually shy daughter. Angela had been out now two nights in a row and that was quite out of character for her. Mrs. Griffen was baffled.

"I've just made tea," Her mother said. "Would you like some?"

"That'd be great, Mom." Angela replied, and crossed to the counter herself, reaching for a mug. "I'll just take it with me to bed though. I'm really tired."

Angela's Mom nodded but said nothing more. Angela poured her tea, kissed her Mom on the forehead and padded towards the door.

"Night Mom." She called softly over her shoulder.

Angela closed the door to her room and set the mug of tea down on the night table. She gazed round the room in the light which came through the gossamer curtains from the street lamp outside. Suddenly the room seemed foreign to her, though it had been home all her life. She stripped off her shirt and jeans and stretched out full length across the top of the comforter. Visions of Lucas Reeves seemed to assault her from the shadows.

She tossed restlessly and her hands came up, almost unconsciously, to her breasts. He had fondled her there, she thought, no man had touched her like that before. She tried to replicate his touch and did feel her nipples grow hard beneath her fingertips. She moved her hips restlessly, with a new longing that she barely comprehended. Angela moaned softly and cried out Lucas's name. Then, as if suddenly aware of herself once again, she rolled up to a sitting position. She drank the tea quickly as it was now lukewarm, then slid demurely under the covers and slept.

Angela had been in somewhat of a panic since she had woken up. She wanted to look nice for Lucas but was unsure what he was apt to wear or where he may be taking her. Finally she settled on a pale blue sundress, full skirted and buttoned through the front. She added cream-coloured low heeled sandals and a matching cream jacket to cover her bare shoulders. When she went through to the kitchen, her Mom looked up in surprise.

"You look nice Angela. Where are you off to?" She asked.

"Ummm...." She faltered, knowing that this inevitable question would come and not sure why she was reluctant to answer it. "I am going out with a friend for lunch." She admitted finally.

Her mother studied her for a moment unsure why Angela seemed so evasive lately. The girl was an adult but Mrs. Griffen still had motherly concerns. She was still very curious about the young man who had seen Angela home the previous evening.

"Anyone I know?" She asked; a leading question. Angela shrugged, and smiled coyly at her mom from behind a glass of orange juice which she had just brought to her lips. After a long sip from the glass she answered.

"No Mom, you haven't met him yet." She explained. "His name is Lucas. He drove me home last night." Her mother's face remained impassive, but underneath she was actually quite excited that Angela may at least be starting to come out of her shell.

Lucas pulled up in front of the house just as the mother and daughter were having this exchange. He had put on a t-shirt instead of his usual shoulder baring vests, hoping this would at least give Angela's Mom a fairly favourable image of him. He had tidied the car since the previous evening and the Stratocaster was safely stored in the trunk. He went up the short walk to the neat little bungalow and rang the bell.

Angela jumped a little, startled by the sound but also by her own anticipation. She crossed to the door picking up her little shoulder bag purse on the way. Mrs. Griffen followed a step or two behind her. When Angela opened the door and Lucas first saw her, his jaw dropped in surprise. The sundress made her seem more childlike than her real age of twenty-two and he almost felt like he was back in high school with what could only be her mother standing right behind her.

"Lucas," Angela said softly. Lucas nervously played with the car keys in his right hand and glanced past Angela at her mother before he spoke.

"Hi Angie." He inclined his head very politely to Mrs. Griffen, "You must be Angela's Mom. I'm Lucas Reeves. Pleased to meet you ma'am." He put out a hand and gave the older woman a strong handshake.

Mrs. Griffen smiled back at him, thinking that at least he was as polite as he was handsome. Angela had stepped through the door and now stood half facing her mother.

"I'll be back later Mom; we're going for a walk after lunch so maybe by sup-per time." Lucas looped his arm through the crook of Angela's elbow and started to lead her away.

Then he paused, and speaking to both women, he said, "Actually Angie, I thought we'd just catch dinner too, and then you can just tag along to the gig and make a day of it." Angela looked up at him in surprise but nodded her agreement immediately. Mrs. Griffen was taken aback more by the remark than her daugh-ter. 'So he was a musician?' she wondered. She smiled and waved goodbye, but turned back into her house feeling somewhat uncomfortable.

Lucas took her to a nice little cafe for lunch where they were able to laugh and talk about all sorts of thing that Angela never thought she'd dare share with any-one, let alone a man. Lucas managed to put her at ease and always seemed inter-ested in the silliest of her stories. She told him about the tree house and how it had been her second home. He asked politely if it was still there and she, giggling, had to admit that not only was it still there but she still climbed up to it now and then.

Lucas never mentioned their romantic interlude in the car from the previous evening and seemed to take pains to be the perfect gentleman with her. She won-dered self-consciously if he had been disappointed at her lack of experience and skill at such things.

There was a tearful moment when Angela told Lucas about losing her fa-ther, but he was very sympathetic to her and told her he was sure her father still watched over her from heaven. She was deeply touched at how gentle and sensi-tive he was to her feelings. She asked him about his parents and briefly wished she had not broached the subject.

A very sad look crossed his face, which he consciously scowled to cover up. He told her that his father had left the family when he was barely fourteen and that his going had actually been a good thing. Lucas surprised himself by admitting to Angela that his father had been a very harsh man indeed and had regularly beaten the young boy in order to "toughen him up." Angela nearly cried again as such betrayal from a parent seemed incomprehensible to her.

They walked, for what seemed to be miles. Angela had first shown Lucas the small office building where she worked and then they had cut through several blocks of commercial streets till they reached the banks of the lazy little river that meandered through the center of town. There was a beautiful wide pathway which followed its banks and the young couple was content to stroll hand in hand under the dark cool of the trees along its way.

Lucas did most of the talking as they walked. Telling her earnestly about the blues music he loved so much. Seldom had the young guitar player had a more receptive audience. Angela was willing to listen and learn from him and to open her ears and her mind to the beauty he saw in the music.

They occasionally paused; once to watch a mother duck and her ducklings march single file across the path ahead, another time to throw stones into the dark green water. Angela was beginning to feel she had known Lucas forever. As they neared a bend in the stream and were about to follow the path around the corner, she tugged a little on his hand and grinned mischievously.

"Come on, I want to show you something." She told him, in childlike fashion. She led him to a large tree by the edge of the path and stepped carefully behind it. Hidden by the tree itself was a narrow track which led through the trees away from the river. It was along this track, in dappled sunlight that she guided Lucas till they arrived at a gate which barred their way. Just over the gate was a big yard with a bungalow beyond. To the left of the gate in the yard was a huge old maple tree.

Angela reached over the gate and slipped the latch with knowing fingers. She turned back to Lucas and put her finger to her lips in a gesture of shushing. Then the young couple went through the gate and stood beneath the massive maple. She pointed triumphantly up at it and whispered, "See, there it is, my tree house."

Lucas studied the house perched in the crook of two great boughs of the tree. The child's hideaway had been very sturdily constructed. He smiled at Angela and nodded his approval, but quietly pulled her back out of the yard, closing the gate behind him. Once they had started back down the path to the river, he spoke.

"Thank you so much for showing me your sanctuary." He told her solemnly. "It's getting late; we'd best get back and grab dinner. I have a gig."

She thrilled inwardly when he called it a sanctuary, knowing he understood her so well. They made their way silently back the way they had come. When they had nearly reached the car he let go of her hand and slid his arm around her shoulders. Her own arm went naturally around his waist and she hooked a finger into his belt loop. Spending so many hours one-on-one with him had finally allowed Angela to relax more in his presence.

When they got to the car, Lucas leaned up against the front fender and pulled her in to him. Both his arms encircled her slim form in a warm hug. She threw her head back to look up at him and he met her timid gaze with sparkling green laughing eyes. He gently brushed back some of her hair from her face. With her body pressed against his, he could already feel her trembling excitement. It was all that Lucas could do to restrain his ardour at least for the moment. He bent his lips to hers and gave her a gentle reassuring caress, with none of the urgent passion of their open mouthed kiss in the car the previous evening. He hugged her again and Angela melted against him, feeling safe in his arms.

"Well, Angie," He said with a chuckle, "Time you checked out the normal dinner of the travelling musician."

She looked up at him, puzzled. But he said nothing more. He pulled the car keys out of his pocket and opened her door, helping her to get seated before moving round to the driver's side. Angela thought at first that they were headed straight to Rock City without a stop for dinner, but a couple of streets away Lucas turned off into a fast food drive-in parking lot.

"Welcome to Gourmet Road Food, Angie." He announced. She giggled and remembered all the fast food debris that had been in the car the first time she'd been in it.

"This is fun, Lucas." She smiled then added. "But you just cleaned house." He laughed heartily at that. They went in, ordered burgers, fries and pop to go and then took their feast back to the car. He drove the rest of the way to Rock City and parked in the far corner of the lot again.

They picnicked on the front seat of the big car, laughing at each other like a couple of teens; each feeding the other French fries. Even Angie delighted in tossing her food wrappers into the back seat as she was done with them.

Dinner done, Lucas became more serious. He retrieved the guitar from the trunk, locked his own door and went round to the passenger side. Angela had already scrambled out. Lucas insured her door was locked too, took her by the hand and headed across the parking lot to work.

They were arriving at Rock City a good hour prior to the public opening and the doorman was surprised to see Angela with Lucas.

"Evening man." He said to them both, casting a questioning but approving look at Angela, in her pretty sundress.

"Hi," replied Lucas, "This is my girl, Angie." His tone, though not aggressive, was so matter-of-fact that it brooked no argument. The doorman smiled and let them both pass. Angela was still reeling from hearing Lucas call her "his girl".

He led her across the room to the 'regular' table. Then Angela watched as Lucas, the drummer and the bass guitar player held an impromptu rehearsal. She was unable to follow most of their talk of chords, riffs and lead-ins but she did gather from what was said that they had decided to try a couple of different tunes in the playlist that evening. None of the little snippets of music that they played seemed familiar to Angela but she was amazed at how the three men seemed to follow each other with their instruments making words almost unnecessary.

About thirty five minutes later the keyboard player strolled into the club. Lucas spent a few minutes briefing him on the changes to the line-up. Then he joined Angela at the table. The other three men retired to a table in the back corner to relax until it was time to start.

As soon as Lucas sat down, a waitress came over from the bar and asked if they would like a drink. Lucas ordered a beer for himself and vodka and seven for Angela. After the girl had departed, he leaned forward, elbows on the table, his chin in his hands and studied her for a long moment. Finally he spoke, "So, pretty boring stuff, huh?" He asked. She smiled at him and shook her head.

"No, actually it was kinda neat. It was like you were all talking but through the music." She told him, voicing the thought that had struck her as she watched. He dropped his head on one side as though to see a different facet of her that he'd missed before, a broad grin that reached right into his eyes spread its light on her.

"You're awesome, baby." He said quietly.

The waitress returned with the drinks and both of them were quiet for a moment. When she was gone, Lucas reached out and tapped his forefinger on the rim of her glass.

"You take it easy on this stuff tonight, okay?" He told her, and she smiled at his concern. "Only one per set, promise?"

"I promise." she told him easily. "Your music keeps me high anyway."

Lucas beamed at her and Angela felt that now familiar tingling sensation up her spine. They chatted quietly until it was time for him to start, noncommittally reviewing their day, neither of them seeming to want to get into a serious discussion for the moment.

Once the band had opened the first set, Angela became a little uncomfortable seated alone at the table with a roomful of young people around her in couples and groups. Lucas had taken the two other chairs that had been at the table away, leaving only Angela's and his. He made a point of leaving a full beer at his place. Also he had stripped off the t-shirt, replacing it with his black leather vest, and leaving the shirt draped over his chair. These signs of his presence should discourage anyone who thought that Angela may be all alone and in need of company.

The first set was exactly the same right up until after he had done the slow blues tune, These Arms of Mine. When the last chords of that number had faded Lucas had stepped up to the microphone.

"Thanks," he started, "We're gonna do a new one we've been working on for ya. See I'm a player and I don't get to dance with my gal so much, like you all can." Quite a few of the crowd giggled or applauded at that point and Lucas paused a moment then continued. "First of all though, if I'm going to dance, I need my gal by my side. Angie, can you please come up here, darlin'."

Angela was dumbstruck. Her first reaction was how could they have planned this in front of her and she never even knew. Then she comprehended fully what he was saying and her shyness left her almost immobile. But he smiled reassuringly at her and held out his right hand. She stepped on to the stage amidst a smattering of puzzled applause from the young people on the dance floor. Lucas guided her round to his left side and motioned for her to put her arm round his slim waist. She did so and found herself tucked practically in between him and the guitar. His left arm draped somewhat round her as his hand gripped the fret board. Lucas chuckled low and sexy, and said, "There ya go, now ain't that nice?

Now we're gonna do a Stevie Ray Vaughan tune for you, Close to You." The band led into the song and Angela couldn't help but sway with Lucas's rhythms. He gently bumped hips with her as he sang, "I wanna be close to you baby as the hair on your head, Close to you babe you better believe what I said." It only took a few bars and she was comfortable with his rhythm. Towards the end she slipped her other arm round him, just above the guitar and rested her head against his chest and shoulder. At the close of the song, Lucas released the guitar strap and took hold of the Fender by its neck alone. His right arm came round her shoulders and, guitar still in hand; he bent his mouth to hers and kissed her very thoroughly his tongue probing into her half open mouth. Angela's knees felt almost like they were going to buckle and she moaned very softly, a sound only he heard.

Without releasing his grip on her, Lucas put the guitar back on to its stand then led her off the stage. He ordered them a fresh round of drinks and then went in search of the men's room. Angela was still trying to catch her breath. She glanced around the room shyly, sure that nearly every eye in the place must still be on her and spotted Becky making her way towards the table. Her friend's familiar face seemed to help Angela to find some emotional solid ground again.

"Hi Becky." She said.

"Hi?" replied Becky, with a look of puzzled amazement. "What was that? You're 'his girl' now? I tried to call you earlier. Your Mom said you were out but I never guessed that you'd be with him."

Angela dropped her eyes shyly for a moment and then looked up at her friend. "He really surprised me with that. I had no idea he was going to get me up on stage. God Becky I was so embarrassed." Her friend giggled merrily at that.

"Well you looked great together. In fact, you looked like you were both very much in love!" she said. Angela reeled at her words. The thought had dared to cross her mind earlier in the day but she had dismissed it. 'This was a crush, nothing more.' she thought. But now hearing the words from her friend, she wondered.

Lucas arrived back at the table then and Becky hastily slid out of his seat.

"I gotta run, Angie. See you at work, Monday." Barely waiting for a response, Becky headed away from them. Angela called a polite goodbye after her but was already focused back on Lucas. He picked up his beer glass and took a long thirsty swallow. Then he winked at her.

"Hope you're not mad at me or nothing." He said, with a chuckle. "I couldn't resist having you up there for that one." She mutely shook her head "no". After all, she wasn't really mad, just embarrassed and totally surprised. She took a tiny sip of her own drink before finding her voice.

"I'm not used to it, is all." she told him, "The attention I mean…"

He reached across the table and gently covered her hand with his own. "Get used to it, Angie. You are the most gorgeous creature I've ever met. Maybe you don't realize it, but you turn heads everywhere you go. I watched it today when we were walking, ya know?" She was very flattered, but was modestly inclined to believe that it was the handsome man whose arm she was on who had 'turned the heads'.

Neither of them spoke for the rest of Lucas's break but instead they were content to sit quietly watching the people around them. He seemed to be quite distant from her but also never broke the contact of his hand with hers; his fingers drumming rhythms on it or lightly caressing the inside of her wrist. Angela was lonely for even that light casual contact, when Lucas returned to the stage for the next set.

The last two sets were much the same playlist that Angela was now famil-iar with and she happily even started to sing along with some of the songs. Lucas would wink at her whenever he saw her singing, which would result in her starting to giggle with embarrassment, but it wasn't long before she would start to sing again. The only change that the band had made to the playlist in the final set was to add a song to the end, right after The Sky is Cryin'. Lucas played and sang this one more or less solo with just a little backing from the bass player. "The nighttime is the right time to be with the one you love…" he crooned. Angela could not take her eyes from him and could not stop shivering as the guitar and voice seemed to go straight to her heart.

Lucas came off the stage as soon as they had finished and gave Angela a soft kiss on the forehead. "I have a couple of real quick things to take care of first, Angie, and then I can take you home."

She nodded mutely at him, while inside her heart fell; home was not where she wanted to be taken. Her naive innocence would not allow her to give her hunger a name, even in her deepest thoughts, but her body was betraying her true desires with the electric trembling gripping her spine and the sudden flush in her cheeks. When Lucas came back to the table, he had a paper bag in the crook of one arm though Angela could not guess what might be in it. He put it down on his chair and went to retrieve his guitar. With the paper bag in one arm and the guitar in the other hand, he instructed Angela to grasp his arm and they headed for the car.

Lucas put the guitar and the bag both into the trunk and then helped Angela into the passenger seat. He slid in behind the wheel, started the big car and cruised off towards her home. He seemed strangely quiet and Angela, deep in her own thoughts, was entirely silent. When they turned into the end of her street, Lucas finally broke the silence between them.

"I want you so bad, Angie." He said, very soft and low. She felt her heart jump as it seemed to skip a beat and she felt a sudden, unaccustomed aching which she was unable to fathom. Before she had a chance to respond, he continued. "I want us to be together tonight but," he paused and her fear took the upper hand to her passion. 'But what?' she wondered, panic stricken? "I don't want your Mom to worry, Ange. I'm going to take you home, but I need to know first, can you leave again without her worrying or knowing?" Angela had trouble at first understanding his words, but then she almost wanted to laugh from a combination of nervousness and the picture which rose in her mind of herself, not many years before, climbing out of her ground floor bedroom window in the wee hours of a summer's eve like this to watch the stars in the vast black sky. All she replied was, "Yes Lucas, I can."

He reached across the seat and found her hand and gave it a reassuring squeeze, as he pulled the car to a stop in front of the house. He was out of the driver's seat immediately and opened her door. He walked her up to the house with one arm protectively round her shoulder. Before Angela turned her key in the lock, he took her in his arms and held her against him. Through his jeans she could feel a hardness and the realization of what she was feeling caused her to whimper with a mixture of desire and fear.

"Twenty minutes, my love." He whispered, "At your back gate."

Even in the dark Lucas had an excellent sense of direction and had no trouble, once he'd parked the car well away from Angela's street, in finding his way along the river bank to the little path which led to her back gate. When he got there, he noted there were no lights on in the house at all. He waited silently, the paper bag clutched under one arm, along with a blanket from the car. In just a minute or two, he saw a movement by the back corner of the house.

As she moved away from the house and towards the gate, he noticed she had changed to jeans and sweatshirt. He smiled to himself, seeing the tomboy for the first time and knowing that the stunning but innocent beauty was only masked for a time. She opened the gate and slipped through. He caught up her right hand in his free left one and set off back towards the river. As they had walked the river path that afternoon, he had seen several small glades which were mostly sheltered by bushes from the public walkway. It was to one of these he led her.

He put the paper bag down carefully and together they spread the blanket out across the turf. He sat down and patted the blanket beside him. She sat down keeping a few inches of space between them and immediately gazing up at the stars above them. They both kicked off their shoes.

"Stars are awesome, don't you think?" she asked. He had reached for the bag and was lifting a pair of wine glasses out of it.

"Yeah they are. I used to play guitar, sometimes all night long, in a clearing like this. Only mine was next to the sea; a cove close to our house." He had produced a bottle of champagne and rapidly set about popping the cork. When she saw it, she was almost childlike in her excitement, clapping her hands and giggling. He chuckled along with her. The cork popped with a satisfying sound and he poured them each a glass of the bubbly liquid.

"A toast." He said, "To tomboys, the stars and you, my love." They drank together and she sought his eyes out over the rim of her glass. His eyes were halfway closed, almost like they were when he sang slow and beautiful blues. He quickly drained his glass and put it aside. He kneeled up beside her and smoothly took her glass too. Then he put a hand on each of her shoulders and gently pressed her down to a prone position on the blanket. Still kneeling beside her, he bent from the waist and brought his mouth to hers. Her hands at first came to his shoulders as though to push him away, but then she gave in and slid them round his neck. That first kiss was very tender and he pulled back and looked into her eyes after it, seeing only desire there he moved on.

He planted soft little kisses all over her face and in between the kisses assured her in a low husky tone that she was all he desired. Angela's head started to swim with the new passions that he was awakening. He felt her hands start to caress the back of his neck and he thrilled to her touch. "Oh baby!" he crooned, "That feels so good."

She froze for a moment in fear when she felt his hands go to her sweatshirt, but she tremblingly let him slide it over her head. He folded the shirt and gently lifted her head, slipping it under to become a pillow. He gazed down at her with passion filled eyes.

"My God you're beautiful." He breathed. He kissed her again but this time more insistently and she opened her mouth to his probing tongue. Her own tongue danced timidly with his and he felt her body tense a little as her hips started to move in a slow lazy rhythm.

When he removed her bra, she again froze beneath his touch and whimpered with fear. He kissed her again very softly until he could feel her relax beneath him. The cool night air caused her nipples to become immediately erect and sensitive so that when his fingers caressed them she cried out in surprise.

"Sshhh my love, it's okay." He was highly aroused by watching her strange combination of fear and ecstasy as she discovered such intimacy for the first time.

But he restrained his lust for the moment, knowing that to rush her may be to lose her.

Angela was experiencing so many sensations all at once her head was swimming. She felt her taut nipples and his fingers as they caressed her. She became suddenly very aware of an aching sensation which was emanating from her loins. Her legs were pressed firmly together and she was feeling a hot wetness between them.

Lucas brought his mouth to one of her nipples and she cried out in surprise. His free hand came up to her mouth and he slid his forefinger in gently caressing her lips. She let her tongue dance with his fingertip like it had danced with his tongue, and then she started to suck on his finger. When Lucas felt her mouth reach for and hold his finger, suckling it, he chuckled low in his throat.

"Good girl," he crooned, "That feels nice."

He let her suck the finger for a while then brought his mouth back to hers; this time plunging his tongue into her quite insistently. Angela's hips started to gyrate a little harder now and she started to caress his chest and flat stomach through his t-shirt. He reached down with one hand and pulled the t-shirt loose from his jeans. With a little urging, she slid her hands under his shirt and felt his skin for the first time. He bent to concentrate with his mouth on one of her nipples again. Her breath was becoming ragged laced with soft moans and whimpers.

Lucas allowed her to take his shirt off and he sat back momentarily as she caught her breath. In the moonlight, she was a vision lying half naked before him. He looked down at her through eyes heavy with lust. Angela looked back at him and reached one hand out which grasped his belt.

"Please Lucas." She begged. He looked questioningly down at her, with his hands resting on his thighs.

"Please what, my love?" He asked, wanting her to say it. She still held tight to his belt with one hand but the other slid unbidden to her breasts. She caressed herself as he watched her and waited. Finally she moaned and the moan became words.

"Lucas, I want you." She breathed, barely above a whisper. He reached for her then at her own slim waist and unbuttoned her jeans. His mouth found her nipple again as one of his hands slid into her jeans and panties in one fluid motion. His other hand had guided her smaller one to find the hardness of his cock beneath his jeans.

As soon as his fingers slid into her panties, Angela suddenly spread her once tightly pressed legs. Lucas felt a wash of lust and satisfaction when his hand encountered the dampness already there between her legs. As she caressed his cock through his jeans, his hand took possession of her womanhood, finding and rubbing her clitoris and gently inserting a tentative finger into her. He bent to kiss her again and she reached for him and sucked his tongue into her. Angela's hips bucked madly as she felt his fingers explore and fondle her most private parts. She moaned with pleasure and suddenly tensed as she started to climax. He continued to play with her as she moved her hips faster and pushed herself hard against his hand.

As her orgasm started to subside, Lucas withdrew his hands from her body but only long enough to grasp her jeans and panties together and in one smooth motion slide them from her. He sat back on his heels and unbuckled his belt, sliding off his own jeans.

Now he straddled her naked form, placing one knee on either side of her. This time when he took her hand, he placed it round his hardness. Her eyes opened very wide in some surprise and he smiled down at her, bending to kiss her sweetly on each cheek.

Angela felt his hardness and was aroused but frightened by it. 'Lucas was so worldly, so experienced, how could she please him?' She wondered. He looked down at her again, questioningly.

"Do you want that, baby?" There was no doubt in her mind what he was referring to. She looked up at his face, framed by stars and the night sky and reached up with her free hand caressing his chest. Her hand on his cock was gently exploring the length and hardness of it. Lucas was almost overwhelmed by lust once again but waited for her reply.

She took in a ragged breath, seemed to steel herself and murmured, "Yes Lucas, I want that." He needed nothing more.

One of his knees slid between her legs and eased them apart. He gently caressed the insides of her thighs till she spread herself even wider for him. Her head was thrown way back, her back arched and her hips were once again starting to move. Lucas could hold back no longer. He took his cock from her gentle grasp and brought it to her entrance still wet from her first climax.

He entered her gently, but still she cried out a little, and his feeling of love mixed with a certain triumph was complete. As he started to move inside of her, she brought her arms around him and her hips again gyrated in a near frenzy. When she started to scream he placed two fingers in her mouth and growled, "Suck them babe." She complied and he moved harder and faster, demanding now his own satisfaction. Wide eyed and sucking hard on his fingers, Angela watched Lucas's animal passion just as she felt his cock pounding into her. She was on the brink of her own second orgasm when he released his seed into her and she felt the warm gush flowing through her.

Lucas rolled away from her but left his fingers in her mouth. Sensing her orgasm was near again. with his other hand he rubbed her clitoris and plunged two fingers into her, watching with satisfaction as she climaxed under his hands once again. He then relaxed beside her and took her into his arms. Angela was sobbing very softly. He caressed her hair and cheeks.

"It's okay, my love." He murmured, "You're a woman now, is all. It's okay."

Angela curled against his chest, hiding her face and feeling safer wrapped in his man-smell. She wasn't even sure why she was crying.

"Lucas, I love you." She said.

He pulled the blanket up round them both and Angela slept there in his arms.

Angela awoke shivering with cold and it took her a moment to adjust to her surroundings. Lucas was a couple of feet from her, dressed in his jeans again and sitting with his back to her. He raised the wine glass in his hand and drank some more of the champagne that had been all but forgotten to their passion. As soon as he heard her stir, he turned towards her.

"Hey beautiful," he said softly. He slid back closer to her and offered her the glass in his hand. At first she shook her head, refusing more. But he wrapped one arm around her and then held the glass to her lips anyway. "Drink some, love. It'll make you feel better."

Finally she took the glass from him and he turned and reached for her sweatshirt. He helped her put the shirt on and her shivering subsided a little. Angela drained the last of the champagne from the glass and looked up at him with a question in her soft blue eyes. He answered her tentative look with a question of his own.

"You okay, baby?" He smoothed her long black hair away from her face. She pulled the blanket up round herself more and leaned against him.

"Lucas?" She ventured timidly. He remained silent, holding her close while she sorted her thoughts out. Finally she continued, "Is it always like that?"

"Oh baby, you still have so much to discover." he told her. "But tonight, my love was magic." His words, even more than his enfolding arms seemed to warm her and chase her shivers away. Her arms came out of the blanket and found a comfortable resting place wrapped round him.

They sat quietly together for several minutes, until finally Lucas stirred against her. He reached down and around her, gathering the blanket as well and gently placing her on his lap. Her arms now encircled his neck and shoulders and she leaned forward to kiss him.

Lucas responded to her kiss and brought one hand up to tangle in her hair. He held her then by her hair and she winced a little at the pain but did not protest. Her mouth opened to his tongue and he kissed her deeply. He could feel her start to tremble with excitement again which only served to reawaken his own ardour. But Lucas broke off the kiss, not eager to push her too far. She looked quizzically into his eyes and saw there a strange mixture of lust and frustration. He shook his head as if trying to shake off a dream, then looked up at the night sky.

"It's starting to get light, my love." He told her gently. "We must get you home." He slid her down off his lap and reached for her jeans. She started to pull the jeans on and Lucas, who had stood up to pull on his t-shirt closed in behind her and reached round with both arms to pull them into place and fasten the fly. Then he hugged her warmly from behind and showered tiny kisses across her neck where her hair had fallen away baring it.

He folded the blanket up and put the bottle and glasses back into the paper bag. He carried them as far as the path back towards her back gate, leaving them at the base of a tree to be retrieved on his way back to the car. Putting a protective arm around her, he led her back through the woods towards home. At the gate they parted, after a long sweet kiss. Lucas told her in a hushed voice that he would see her tomorrow after lunch. He stayed, unmoving by the gate, until she rounded the corner of the house, then he turned and disappeared into the darkness.

Angela slept late that Sunday morning and didn't hear when her mother tapped on the door about ten o'clock to see if she would go out for breakfast. When she did awaken after eleven thirty, the house was silent. She lay amid her little girl quilts and looked around the room like it was a stranger's. Whenever she closed her eyes she saw Lucas and in her mind she kept hearing his voice low and gentle but demanding in his lust. She arose, pulled a robe around her nakedness and walked through to the kitchen.

There was a note on the table. Mom had gone to meet Pamela, her husband and son for breakfast and would return later. Angela made a cup of steaming hot coffee and carried it back down the hall to the bathroom. She ran a tub full of bubbles and stepped in. She felt a twinge of pain when the warm water went between her legs and she remembered how forceful Lucas had been as he climaxed in her. 'I'm just not used to it,' she reasoned to herself, 'He would never hurt me.'

By the time her bath and coffee were done and she'd dressed in jeans and soft turquoise shirt, the front doorbell was ringing. She glanced at the clock on her night table with surprise and raced for the door.

Lucas stood there, leaning nonchalantly against the doorjamb. He grinned at her as soon as he saw her.

"Good morning, Angie." He laughed.

"Morning?" she asked, "But it's one twenty!"

He laughed out loud at that. "I know silly," he told her, "But I'm guessing you haven't been awake very long."

She dropped her eyes shyly and he approvingly smiled as she blushed with some embarrassment.

"I'm not quite ready to go out." she explained, "My hair's not dry, and..."

"That's okay." He stated simply. "Why don't we just stay here? Got more of that coffee I'm smelling?"

Angela moved aside a bit as Lucas stepped through the doorway. He slid his feet out of his boots and placed them neatly side by side on the floor. He straightened up, looking round with interest at the cozy living room. Finally focusing back on Angela, he held out his arms to her and she stepped into a warm hug. He stood quietly for a moment, stroking the soft but damp length of her hair. Her arms wrapped round his waist, head nestled against his chest where she could hear his heart beating a steady strong rhythm.

"I'd like to stay here safe for always, Lucas." she murmured softly. He responded in gesture, putting a hand under her chin and bringing her face up to his. He inclined his head and kissed her tenderly, without urgency. Then he stepped back a pace, chuckling softly.

"If you did, then I'd never get that coffee." He held out one hand to her and added, "Lead on, woman."

She took his hand and led him through to the kitchen. He took a chair at the table and she turned to the counter to pour a mug of coffee for him.

"Nice house, Angie." He told her. She turned towards him, mug and spoon in hand. He was gazing out the big bright windows which looked onto the backyard. One could see the maple tree and the back gate from here. She followed his gaze and her mind turned instantly back to the previous night. He looked round at her, to see her face flush a little with the thought. 'God she is beautiful' he thought.

"What you thinking about?" he asked, though he had already guessed. She blushed even more at his words and had trouble putting the mug down without spilling its contents. Lucas took the spoon out of her hand trailing a fingertip down the inside of her forearm as he did so. She shivered with delight at the sensation it brought her.

"I was thinking about last night." she finally answered in a tiny voice. He stirred some sugar into the black coffee, watching it dissolve in the hot liquid. She sat down opposite him.

"Good thoughts, I hope." He said as lightly as possible. "I want us to have more 'last nights', my love, many more."

"Yes Lucas, good thoughts." She told him, her eyes sparkling with excitement, her heart leaping. 'He does still want me.' she thought with relief.

Lucas took a couple of long swallows out of the coffee then pushed back his chair.

"Why don't you show me the rest of your house?" He asked. She led him on a brief tour of the tiny bungalow, finishing at her own bedroom. She put her hand on the knob to open the door and suddenly froze. It was such a frilly little-girl place, she was sure he'd laugh at her. Lucas was standing behind her in the hall and took a step closer till he had her almost pinned between him and the door. He reached one hand round and covered hers on the doorknob. The other arm he snaked tightly round her slim waist.

"And last but not least," He chuckled, "We have Angela's bedroom!" He turned the knob and pushed open the door. They stood together on the threshold for a moment then he half pushed, half walked her in. She started to tremble and wasn't sure if it was embarrassment, fear or arousal, or perhaps all three. Lucas gazed around the room with an appraising look in his eye. Finally he took her shoulders and spun her round to face him.

"It's exactly what I thought it would be." he said with a wink, "Just as pretty as you are." He stepped in much closer to her and gathered her into his arms. His head inclined to kiss her and she responded kissing him back. As they continued kissing, he gently moved forward so that she was forced to back away inch by inch till she felt the bed at the back of her legs. He gently applied a little more pressure both in the kiss and on her shoulders with both his hands and she fell backwards onto the bed. He stood over her with hands clenched tightly at his sides.

Lucas looked at her sprawled before him and became instantly aroused; her innocent look among the frilly pillows and flowery patterns on the bedspread seemed to spur his lust.

"Angie, I want you, right here, right now." he stated, then asked in a voice laden with emotion, "May I?" Angela was at once excited and frightened, but her fear this time was more that her mother would arrive home.

"My mother, Lucas..." she started to say. He reached behind him and pushed the bedroom door shut, hearing it latch with a satisfying clunk. Then he turned back to her, waiting no longer for her permission, and started unfastening her jeans. Angela tried to roll away from him, but he sat on the edge of the bed and stopped her with one arm.

"It's okay, my love." he told her softly but firmly. "You're a big girl Angie; this is your choice, not your Mom's."

At his words she went quite limp under him and he finished undoing her jeans and quickly slid them and her panties from her. He bent and kissed her very deeply, their tongues doing a dance that Angela now took full part in. Then he turned his attention elsewhere, first his hands explored her thoroughly till she was moaning with delight and then he started to gently kiss her from her belly button slowly down across her flat stomach. Angela's eyes flew wide open when she realized what he intended and her legs suddenly tensed and came together tightly in fear once more. Lucas drew in a breath of frustration when she froze.

He sat up a little and looked at her face; her eyes were full of fear. "Angie, open your legs, now!" He said, in a tone no longer gentle or tolerant. He put one hand down and forced it in between her legs. She gave in to him and let her legs spread once again. He smiled triumphantly. "You're gonna love this baby." He told her. Lucas lowered his head and started to lick the length of her labia and tease her clitoris with his tongue. He never looked back at her face to see the tears in her eyes. She moaned and responded with her hips to his tongue and lips and felt terribly ashamed.

After she had climaxed, he stood and dropped his own jeans to the floor with hers. His mouth, tasting of her, came back to kiss her once again. He moved over her amidst the feminine trappings of her little girl bed and started to pump his erect cock into her. Angela couldn't help but move with him as she started to feel yet another climax building in her. Even her deep shame at the realization that he had licked and sucked her 'there' brought more arousal with it.

When they lay quietly, both spent from exertion, she finally dared put a voice to her hesitation.

"Lucas," She started, tentatively. He turned his face towards her and she continued with her eyes downcast. "When you licked me 'there', well... I mean... do you like it?" Lucas was struck again by how innocent she was of such things.

"Oh baby, sometimes it's the best." He told her. Angela contented herself with that. She snuggled against him, taking comfort from his strength and confidence.

After a few minutes, Lucas rolled away from her.

"We should get dressed before your Mom comes home." He told her. "And we need to talk." This last was thrown in like an afterthought, but it brought her heart into her mouth just the same. They both put their clothing back on and returned to the kitchen. Lucas turned his chair sufficiently so they were face to face, and then took both her hands in his.

"I'm driving home to the city tonight for a few days." He stated simply.

"But..." She stammered, her mind was thinking many terrible things, 'he's not coming back, he's got a girlfriend there.' He squeezed her hands reassuringly.

"Ssshh, it's only till Wednesday. We're back at Rock City next Wednesday till Saturday again." he assured her. "I have a couple of days that I can go in and work for my brother. And I need the bucks. You're going to hafta get used to it Angie if you're going to be my girl. There just ain't enough cash when you're gigging."

She stared at him dumbstruck. She'd heard every word but somewhere along the line had become hopelessly hung up on one phrase which she kept rolling over in her mind. 'If you're gonna be my girl.' Finally she found her voice.

"I understand, Lucas." She said quietly and shyly met his eyes. As she felt herself falling into his green eyes which seemed full of kindness, she spoke from her heart. "I love you, Lucas Reeves."

He released her hands and took her face into his palms. He gently kissed her forehead and each cheek before he spoke again.

"I love you too, Angela." He told her. "Wednesday will be here quickly, I promise."

He released her, stretched and stood up.

"I have to get on the road if I'm gonna make it home by suppertime."

She followed him silently to the door, watching as he pulled on his boots. He straightened up and took her in his arms again, kissing her long and deeply. Then he stepped to the door. As he put his hand on the knob, she felt the tears sting her eyes. He pulled open the door, leaned back to her and kissed her again this time his tongue sliding into her mouth and taking her breath away.

"That should keep us both till Wednesday, my love. Be safe."

She stood holding on with both hands to the door jamb until he got to his car. He unlocked the car door, then stopped and raised one arm to her. She waved back and kept on waving until the car had disappeared.

Angela found it fairly easy to keep her own counsel about her relationship with Lucas when it came to her mother. When Mom had come home that afternoon she had been rather sarcastic about how late Angela had slept and about her impression that this new young man in her life was the problem. After she heard that, Angela became determined to keep her thoughts and feelings about Lucas to herself, reasoning that her mother wouldn't understand anyway. The two women had become somewhat closer since Pamela had moved from the house but there had always been a barrier between them. Angela had been her Daddy's little girl and Mrs. Griffen had never been able to get that close to her daughter.

Monday morning however, when Angela returned to the office, things were not so easy. Christie and Becky were both after her for more details of the "date" with Lucas. The three young women were again gathered around Angela's desk and their questions were beginning to cause Angela some embarrassment.

"Come on Angie." Christie was saying. "Tell us what's going on." Christie was almost mad with herself for being away in the city when Angie finally 'broke out of her shell' as she had put it.

"Yeah Angie, what exactly did Lucas mean the other night, when he had you up on stage and called you his gal." Becky giggled, "And gawd girl, that kiss!"

Angela felt herself flush with modesty and Christie was quick to notice.

"He must be an awesome kisser, he's just soooo gorgeous!" She sighed. "Angela, you'd better tell us all girl!"

"We're friends okay!" Angela said, sounding somewhat exasperated.

"So you're seeing him again?" Becky asked.

"Yes, he'll be back to play Wednesday till Saturday at Rock City." She told them.

"Be back?" Christie asked. "Where's he from?"

"He lives down in the city with his brother." Angela explained, "He goes down and works for his brother whenever he has a couple of days to do it. Gigging alone doesn't pay the bills."

"Wow, listen to her!" Becky laughed. "She's talking like she's in the biz. 'Gigging'!"

All three girls laughed at that. But Angela was surprised herself by how much she seemed to have changed in three short days. Their chat was broken up as usual by the arrival of Mrs. Bradshaw, but Angela knew her friends hadn't given up on the topic just yet.

Lunchtime came and sure enough the girls were right back to their interrogation. They had all taken their sandwiches and cans of soda to a nearby park a block or so from the office. Angela tried to evade their questions about her and Lucas Reeves but was it was becoming increasingly difficult. She was somewhat relieved when an old friend of Christie's came along and pulled her away from the conversation. She and Becky drank their sodas in silence for a while. As Angela watched people passing by, Becky was studying her friend's face, trying to fathom the change which was there in her eyes. Finally she spoke,

"Angie, how serious is this getting, with you and Lucas?" Angela froze; her soda can halfway to her mouth. She took a deep breath and, before she spoke, her eyes dropped to the ground.

"Becky, he's so wonderful. He really cares for me." She told her friend. Something in the way she said it and the look in her eyes caused Becky to wonder even more how serious things were between her shy friend and the young guitar player.

"Angie, have you two....?" Becky hesitated, not wanting to upset Angela by saying what was on her mind. Angela looked confused, but slowly a certain light came into her eyes and Becky knew before Angela spoke.

"If you're asking what I think you're asking," Angela almost whispered, "Yes, he's made love to me." Angela blushed at her own words, amazed she had admitted it, even to Becky.

"Angie!" Becky wasn't sure what to say, she was certainly no prude but her friend was such an innocent and had always vowed she'd stay a virgin till she married. "Why girl? He's a musician; he'll be gone in a week."

Angela regretted telling Becky the moment she'd opened her mouth and her friend's words burned across her mind and heart leaving her nearly in tears.

"He's not like that Becky. He said he loves me." She stated, "He'll be back on Wednesday and you'll see."

"Angela, I just don't want to see you get hurt is all." Becky said softly, "He's used to travelling and seeing different towns all the time, you know?" Angela shook her head trying to shake the growing fear that Becky's words were bringing.

"Lucas is in love with me, Becky. I saw it in his eyes." she told her friend flatly and something in her tone told Becky the conversation was over. Both women said nothing and the looks on their faces were enough to silence even the effervescent Christie when she rejoined them.

When they returned to the office after lunch, Angela's fears melted in seconds. There on her desk was a huge vase filled with two dozen long stemmed roses, twelve white and twelve red. A card with them read simply, "I love you, my angel, Lucas" Angela looked triumphantly at both her friends' stunned expressions.

"He loves me." She told them quietly.

The big Buick pulled up in front of the house just before supper. Kurt Reeves glanced out the window and grinned to himself. Lucas's timing for things like meals was always impeccable. 'Well,' he thought, 'He's here in time to mow the damn lawn after dinner. Might as well work for your meal, little bro."

Lucas pulled both his amplifier and the Stratocaster out of the car and carried them to the door. He was about to kick on it to let Kurt know he was there, when his brother opened it for him.

"Hey man," Kurt said by way of greeting.

"Yah Kurt thanks." Lucas passed him by and hauled his burdens down the hall to his room. He put them down then returned to the car to grab the duffel that carried his clothing. Everything in the bag was deposited into the washing machine the minute he walked in, along with the clothes he was wearing. He grabbed a clean pair of jeans from the bookshelf in his room which doubled as a dresser and went through to the kitchen, shirtless.

Kurt turned round from the steaks he was marinating on the counter when Lucas walked in.

"So Lucas how was the gig?" he asked. Kurt often had the feeling he should hold his breath whenever he asked this question when Lucas got home, because one could never tell just how he may react. If the gig had gone pretty well then Lucas would be ready to say so, but if it had been a bad show, bad crowd or something, Kurt's little brother would show undisguised annoyance and almost unreasoning anger. But today was good. Lucas grinned at Kurt and crossed to the fridge to grab a beer, as he answered.

"Great gig man! I'm gonna love going' back there for four more days." Lucas told him.

"That's great." Kurt answered.

The two men were silent for a while. Lucas went out back to the small deck and lit the barbeque, then stood for a while deep in thought and sipping his beer. Kurt brought the steaks out and laid them sizzling on the grill.

"So we got a contract up in the Uplands," Kurt announced. The Uplands was a rather upscale neighbourhood that Kurt loved getting work in. It usually involved nothing but the best materials and fanciest plans that the well-to-do denizens could afford and a two day contract building new cabinetry would often pay two weeks or more worth of expenses with a tidy profit as well. "Probably take us two days, but big bucks."

Lucas turned to his brother. "Cool man. I could use the cash. Hey do you know of a florist 'round here?"

Kurt looked up from the barbeque to Lucas with a quizzical expression, wondering if he'd heard correctly.

"What? Why would you need a florist?" He said finally.

Lucas grinned and answered with the obvious. "'Cause I wanna send some flowers."

Kurt's curiosity was now fully aroused. He turned away from the barbeque and stepped over to the railing Lucas was leaning against. Lucas glanced sidelong at his older sibling, enjoying immensely the feeling of one-upmanship this topic was giving him. Throughout their youth, Kurt had been the favoured child in their father's eyes and Lucas still resented his older brother.

"Yeah Lucas, flowers." Kurt said, a note of exasperation creeping into his voice. "So what's the deal? Did somebody die or did you find a girlfriend?"

Lucas laughed at that. "Nobody kicked it, man." he said, none too kindly. "But I found me an angel. She's the sweetest thing I've ever tasted! Damn she's hot and mine man, all mine!" He lifted the beer can to his lips and drained what was left, then threw the can across the lawn towards the shed. Kurt stared at him for a moment before he finally reacted.

"This angel of yours got a name?" He asked, "And if you think she's so hot, how'd you know she hasn't got a whole line up of guys sniffing after her?"

Lucas looked at Kurt with triumph in his eyes.

"Because, big brother." He bragged, "She was a virgin till last night!"

"Holy shit, Lucas!" Kurt exploded. Lucas looked at Kurt's shocked expression with smug satisfaction. Kurt may be older and every bit the steady hard working man's man that their father had always told Lucas he was too much of a pansy to ever become, but he doubted very much if Kurt had ever captured a hot virgin like his Angela. Kurt took a deep breath before he said anything further, then he said quietly, "Well at least you're sending her flowers."

Lucas went back into the kitchen and grabbed two more beers. He handed one to Kurt, who was back at the barbeque. After an lengthy uncomfortable silence between the two men, Lucas finally spoke quietly.

"Look Kurt," he explained, "It ain't like you're thinking man. I'm gonna do more than send flowers. Angela's my gal; I'm going to have her by me. She is gonna be my wife."

Kurt lifted the steaks onto a plate and motioned Lucas to follow him into the kitchen, where he grabbed a bowl of Caesar salad and a tub of potato salad out of the fridge. Kurt put everything on the table and sat down before he finally answered.

"Oh man, are you serious?" He asked. "You love her? Wow Lucas, she must really be something else! Congratulations man!"

Lucas looked at his brother for a long moment, amazed that Kurt seemed genuinely happy for him. The idea that anyone in this so-called family really cared about each other had never occurred to him.

"Yeah man, she's perfect. I love her." He told his brother and then shrugged and focused on his supper.

Wednesday was one of those stiflingly hot July days in the delta valley. Angela had put on a soft cream sundress with a scarlet sash for work and to keep the sun from her head and eyes she had worn a creamy straw hat with matching scarlet ribbon for walking.   Her long black hair was an attractive and eye-catching contrast to the soft cream fabric.

When she walked in the door at the office Becky and Christie both stared openly at her. Christie finally broke the silence.

"Good morning Angie!" She said brightly, "Wow, you look totally awesome! Like a southern belle or something!"

Angela laughed at her pretty blonde friend and carefully removed the straw hat. She was feeling just a little bit more radiant than usual because today Lucas would be back. She placed the hat on top of the file cabinet behind her desk right next to her still beautiful roses. Then she turned back to her friends.

"Well I only wanted to dress cool, you know?" she explained. "It's supposed to get real hot today!"

Becky grinned mischievously at that.

"Real hot Ange?" She asked, casting a knowing look at Christie who grinned back. "Your guitar player's coming back today, isn't he?   Could that be why it'll be so hot?"

Angela blushed nearly as red as her scarlet sash and turned hastily towards the coffee pot. Behind her, the girl's exchanged a look of awareness mixed with concern for their friend, but neither of them spoke.

Angela turned back with coffee in hand.

"Yes, Lucas will be here today." She said flatly. She crossed to her desk, sat and started shuffling through the files in her basket. Her friends said nothing further but took her cue and got down to work.

Angela tried very hard to concentrate on her work but no matter how hard she tried her thoughts kept straying back unbidden to Lucas. 'When would he be here? Would he call her?' She had decided he would probably just call her when he got in to town and make plans then. Once that thought was in her mind, she would jump every time the phone rang. Becky, watching her reach almost frantically for the phone once more, was beginning to get anxious herself. The sensible and stalwart girl was quietly saying silent prayers that Lucas Reeves was for real and would be back soon, for Angela's peace of mind. For Angela, the day seemed to drag interminably.

When four o'clock rolled round and the girls started to pack up their desks, Angela was near to tears. She was frightened now as Becky's words from days before were like hammers in her mind and heart. 'Why girl? He's a musician; he'll be gone in a week.' Just as they were about to go out the door, the phone rang one last time and Angela dove for it.

Behind her, Christie said, "I gotta go, see you all tomorrow." But Becky stayed and waited as Angela, with a disappointed look on her face, dealt with a late customer call.

The two women walked out the door together. Becky was about to say something which she hoped was helpful or reassuring to her devastated friend, when Angela stopped dead in her tracks as though she'd seen a ghost. Becky followed her gaze and almost most burst out laughing from relief. Parked at the curb, directly in front of the building was Lucas Reeve's big old Buick. Lucas himself was leaning nonchalantly on the front fender, looking handsome and dangerous as usual in his black denims and a black leather studded vest.

Angela recovered from her initial surprise at seeing him there and quite literally flew into his arms. He was laughing at her but all the same his arms wrapped warmly around her and swept her clear off her feet. He found her mouth with his and kissed her deeply, dislodging the pretty straw hat.

"Hey baby," he said, placing her back gently on her feet on the sidewalk. "I missed you."

Angela was all smiles and tears at once. She had barely noticed that the hat had fallen.

"Lucas, you're here!" She said, wonderingly. Lucas bent to pick up the hat and replaced it gently on her head. His hands traced her cheeks and down her neck and bare shoulders. Angela shivered with excitement and delight.

"Of course I'm here, silly girl." He told her. Becky, standing silently a few paces away from them, couldn't help but think that perhaps she had made too hasty a judgment of the musician. Lucas turned as though noticing Becky for the first time.

"Nice to see you again Becky." he said politely with a respectful nod of his head.

"You too, Lucas." Becky answered then turned to Angela. "Umm, well, Angie I'll see you tomorrow okay?"

"Sure Becky." Angela replied; now all smiles but quite focused on Lucas and nothing else. Becky turned, waved briefly over her shoulder and headed off down the street.

Lucas once again wrapped Angela in his arms. Her arms slipped naturally round his waist and she stood breathing in the scent of him and hearing his heart beating in his chest. She nuzzled against his chest where the vest was open at the front and impulsively began to bestow tiny kisses on his skin. Lucas drew in breath suddenly at the feel of her lips on him. He reached down and put a hand under her chin raising her face to his once again. She looked up at him and waited, breath held, as he carefully studied her face. Her eyes were clear, bright with unshed tears of emotion and met his gaze only hesitantly. He chuckled, low and sensually.

"Oh baby," He breathed. "You have no idea what that does to me, do you?"

"Lucas?" She asked innocently. He bent and kissed her again, this time opening her mouth with his tongue and for a few brief moments the street and the people in it faded from their awareness. He broke the contact first and smiled warmly at her.

"You are my angel, for always, okay?" He asked. She nodded at him mutely and he led her to the car.

Lucas climbed in, started the car and pulled in to what almost laughingly passed for rush hour traffic. Angela was a little surprised when he passed by the road which would have taken them towards her house. She glanced that way briefly but said nothing. Lucas spoke as though answering her thoughts alone.

"I've got a surprise for you." He told her, but would say nothing more.

They drove until they reached the service road which paralleled the main highway past town. Here there were gas stations, cafes and small motels which serviced travelers from the highway. This was also only a few minutes' drive from Rock City. Angela assumed Lucas was going to take her out dinner and she thought 'I'll have to call Mom and let her know not to hold supper.'

Lucas pulled in to the parking lot of one of the little motels, a fairly modern and cozy looking little spot. He parked in front of the last unit on the row, number 25. Angela looked quizzically at him. He grinned, said nothing, got out of the car and opened her door for her. He had pocketed his car keys and was waving a motel room key at her and chuckling.

"Kurt had a great contract for us. I made big bucks." He told her. "No living in my car this week, baby. We've got our own place."

Angela was speechless. She was happy for him that he wouldn't be sleeping in the car. She had thought a lot about that lately, how hard and lonely it was for him when he was playing and away from home. But his words 'our own place' were echoing in her mind and that brought a thrill of excitement edged with something else that she couldn't quite grasp.

Lucas seemed not to notice that she hadn't answered. He wrapped one arm around her shoulders and led her to the door. After unlocking and pushing the door open, without warning he swept her into his arms and carried her through the door like a groom would carry his bride. Angela shrieked in surprise. He set her gently onto the edge of the bed then stepped back, put both hands up in a palms first gesture and said, "Don't move, I'll be right back."

He disappeared out the open door and she heard the trunk open. She glanced around the room and noted that his duffel bag and some of his other personal things were already in the room. When he reappeared he had a large paper bag from a local submarine shop in one hand and a guitar case that she'd never seen before, much wider and deeper than the Stratocaster's case, in the other hand. He put the bag down beside her.

"More gourmet road food, Angie." He explained. "Dinner is served and now for some dinner music." He laid the guitar case on the bed and flipped the four catches which held it closed. Then he very gently lifted out a Gibson acoustic six string. "I never bring this baby on the road with me. But I wanted to play some soft stuff, just for you."

"Lucas this is wonderful." She beamed at him. "But I should call my mother. She'll be wondering where I'm at."

He nodded behind her to where the phone sat on the small night table beside the bed. She slid along the bed and started to make her call, behind her, Lucas was idly strumming the guitar. Her mother did not sound very pleased, but all the same she said nothing when Angela left her message.

Lucas and Angela ate submarine sandwiches and sipped on sodas as he played soft tunes for her. Mostly they were songs without words but she was struck by how much the music spoke to her and what wonderful but sometimes sad emotions it filled her with. He mainly played with his eyes almost closed so it was sometimes hard to tell what he was feeling, but the feelings were quite transparent in the sounds he lovingly coaxed from the instrument.

Angela had almost lost track of time as she listened to him play. So she was surprised when he laid the Gibson aside and leaned forward, giving her one long deep kiss. His hand cupped her cheek for a moment and he stared into her blue eyes. Then, as if shaking away a dream, he shook his head and stood up.

"Time to go to work." He announced.

Lucas had packed up real quickly after the last set. They had left Rock City and driven straight back to the motel. Once there however, he slowed their pace by getting the Gibson out and playing her another melody. She sat cross-legged in the middle of the bed, her full skirted sundress billowing all round her. The melody he played was straight from his heart and as soft and beautiful as the vision before him.

They made love gently, with no urgency. She lay almost floating in his arms feeling safer there than she had felt in years.

But it was over too soon. They dressed and Lucas drove her back to her mother's. Angela had not wanted to go home but her sense of duty to her mother and her job responsibilities left her no alternative. Lucas understood that and gently encouraged her.

"It's okay, my angel. We have tomorrow and many more." He whispered as he kissed her goodnight at the front door. She searched his handsome face, earnestly.

"Do we, Lucas?" She asked timidly.

"Yes love, many more." Lucas confirmed softly. "Now go, till tomorrow." He kissed her forehead and walked quickly away as though, if he stayed, he would be unable to let her go.

Thursday morning came way too early for Angela, after her late night with Lucas. She showered hurriedly, glad that the water sluicing over her seemed to be waking her up and washing away exhaustion. She was wrapped in a big bath towel, sitting on the edge of her bed with a hair dryer in one hand and a brush in the other when her mother put her head in the door.

"Morning Angie." She said cheerfully. "You were in rather late last night."

"Mom, I'm not sixteen." Angela replied and her mother was somewhat taken aback at the edge in her daughter's voice.

"Sorry," She said, "I was just surprised, it's not like you. I've put coffee on, come get some, okay?"

"Sure Mom. I'll be there in a couple of minutes." Angela hurriedly finished drying her hair and tied it back in a ponytail. She pulled on underwear and another of her summer dresses. As she went down the hall to the kitchen, she promised herself to hold her tongue with her mother. 'After all,' she reasoned, 'she's only looking out for me. If she knew Lucas, she'd know it was ok.'

Her mother was at the counter for her second cup of the morning and so poured Angela's too.

"Thanks Mom." Angela said softly, then added, "And thanks for being concerned, I know you love me."

"I do love you, Angie." Her mother agreed. "You never stop being a Mom, even after your kids are grown up. You seem really interested in this Lucas and I just worry is all. Perhaps if he was a local boy and I knew his folks, you know, like Pamela." Angela almost broke her own promise when she heard that, but she took a deep breath and pictured Lucas's handsome face in her mind, before she replied.

"I'm not Pamela, Mom," she answered quietly. "And Lucas is a very nice and very talented man."

Belle Griffen looked at her daughter searchingly for a moment, then seemed to think the better of speaking her mind. Instead she said lightly,

"Well maybe I should meet this talented young man of yours? Do you think that the two of you would like to come home for dinner on Friday evening? Before he has to go and play, of course."

Angela was taken by surprise by her mother's suggestion, but was suddenly eager to bring Lucas to meet her, and then her mother wouldn't have to worry so much. She just hoped Lucas would agree.

"Umm, yeah, sure Mom." She said tentatively, "I'll have to ask Lucas first, of course, but I'm sure he'd like that." She gulped down what was left of her coffee, glancing at the clock. "I've got to run, gonna be late. I won't be home for dinner."

"I know, I know." Her mother chuckled, "You're eating with Lucas and watching the show. Have a good day, Angela."

"You too, Mom. I love you." Angela called over her shoulder on her way out the door.

Lucas picked her up right after work again and they went straight to the motel with the obligatory stop at a drive-in to get burgers and sodas for dinner. Angela was more comfortable with their little haven in the motel room now and when she'd finished eating, she lay back on the bed and closed her eyes, listening to the soft tones of the Gibson.

Lucas played on even though she very quickly fell asleep; he did not feel slighted at all. He sang softly so as not to disturb her, but the words of longing and passion he crooned were for her alone.

Fifteen minutes before it was time to go to Rock City, he shook her gently awake.

"Hey Angel. It's time to go." He whispered, kissing her softly on the cheek. She woke all smiles. The little catnap had clearly done her good.

On the way to Rock City she told Lucas about her mother's invitation to dinner. He was silent for a while and she began to wonder if he might be unhappy that she had said yes. Finally, he reached across the seat and squeezed her hand.

"That's a great idea, Angela." he said with a smile. "Tell your Mom we'll be there and thanks very much. I don't get home cooked very often, 'cept what Kurt and I cook."

Angela and Lucas repeated the previous evening's routine, going back to the motel after the gig. But Angela still looked so tired, Lucas merely held her and cuddled for a while, telling her more tales of the life of a player. After a very short time, he stretched, yawned and claimed to be sleepy too. He drove her home and made sure she was safely inside.

Next afternoon, Lucas left the motel a couple of hours earlier than necessary to meet Angela after work. He parked the car quite close to her office and went for a walk around the small downtown shopping district. It was cooler today than the last couple of days had been. Lucas had put on a pale blue t-shirt and his black leather jacket instead of the usual vest.

He picked up a coffee to go from a coffee shop and found an empty bench in the same little park that Angela and her friends liked to come to at lunch sometimes. A few yards away, a couple of young women watched Lucas with great interest, whispering between themselves. He was studying the row of small shops across the street from the park and didn't notice that one of the women had approached him, till she was standing nearly right in front of him. He looked up startled.

"Umm, hi." the woman started, tentatively, "Aren't you from that band, ummm, Immortal Beat? Playing at Rock City?"

"Yeah." was all he answered. Seemingly bolstered by even that small encouragement, the woman continued.

"I just think you guys are so great." she gushed at him. "What a cool name for a band! Hey do you mind if I join you?"

Lucas didn't answer immediately. He quite boldly stared at her from head to toe and shrugged inwardly. 'You're nice,' he thought, 'but my Angel's got you beat all to hell!' Aloud, he said, "Sorry, I'm meeting my wife in a little bit. Just killing time." She blushed scarlet, mumbled an almost incoherent apology and fled back to her friend. Lucas chuckled inwardly.

He drained his coffee and strolled across the street to a small jewelry shop that he'd seen there. There were no other customers in the shop, but all the same the clerk, a fiftyish looking woman, did not seem overly pleased to see him. 'She probably thinks I'm here to rob the joint.' Thought Lucas.

"May I help you?" she asked in a tremulous voice.

"Well yeah," He told her softly. "I'm looking for a gift for my gal."

"A ring perhaps, Sir?" She said, a little more comfortable now on hearing his soft voice.

"No, not a ring, at least not yet." He chuckled. "But something special, to let her know I think she's special."

The clerk smiled at him, then gestured to a display case in front of her. "How about a locket? There are many different ones and they open to hold a picture or other keepsake."

Lucas studied the lockets she'd pointed out carefully. Some were very ornate some were simpler. Most were either oval or heart shaped. His attention centered on a heart shaped piece about an inch wide and an inch and a half long. It was silver and totally unadorned, simple polished surfaces almost mirror like and it hung on an equally simple fine silver chain. He pointed it out to the clerk.

"I'd like to see that one, please." He asked. The clerk fumbled with her keys to the display and retrieved the locket for him.

Lucas held it in his palm feeling the weight and the cool smoothness of it. He gently worked the clasp and opened it. He smiled to himself, thinking, 'it's perfect, simple and pure just like Angie.' To the clerk he said, "This is the one, I'll take it."

She beamed at him, "May I gift wrap it for you, Sir?"

"No," he said, reaching for his wallet, "I have something at home that I want to put inside first. Thanks anyway."

She took the locket from him and placed it into a slim box, sale concluded, she handed it back and he slid it into the inside pocket of his jacket.

Back on the street, he glanced at his watch. It was almost time to meet Angela, but first he turned into a flower shop on the way. He picked up a big bouquet of brightly coloured blossoms for Angie's Mom. 'Couldn't hurt.' he thought, though he was pretty sure that Mrs. Griffen didn't like him much already.

Angela had put on a pretty mint green suit, skirt and jacket, for work with the satiny black shirt that Becky and Christie had helped her pick out the week before. Lucas immediately thought how great the silver locket would look against the black shirt, but mentally checked himself. 'Two nights left,' he thought, 'the surprise would wait till the perfect moment.'

"Hi Angel," He said, his arms automatically enfolding her. She hugged him back, tilting her face up to his. He bent and gave her a peck on the cheek.

"Hi Lucas," she murmured, and then a questioning look came into her eyes. "Flowers?" He smiled almost sheepishly and explained.

"They're for your Mom. I thought maybe it'd help."

"She'll like you, Lucas." Angela told him. "Just like I do."

Lucas chuckled at that. He wrapped one arm round her and walked her to the car.

When they arrived at the house, Angela's mother was already in the kitchen preparing something that was starting to fill the house with a delicious aroma. Lucas removed his boots and followed Angela through to the kitchen.

"Mom?" She ventured. Her mother turned from the counter where she had been busy, smiling in welcome.

"Hi honey." She replied then turned to Lucas wiping her hands on a towel and offering one for a handshake. "Welcome to our home Lucas. It's nice to really meet one of Angela's friends."

Lucas returned the handshake firmly, but couldn't help but notice that Mrs. Griffen's smile did not reach into her eyes at all. "Thanks for inviting me, ma'am." He told her formally. "It's a privilege to be invited to a home-cooked meal for sure." He offered the flowers to her with a respectful bow of his head, "These are for you, Mrs. Griffen."

"Thank you, Lucas. They're very pretty." She took the flowers and laid them on an open space on the counter.

Angela satisfied that everything was peaceful so far, excused herself to go and change to jeans. Belle Griffen turned back to what she was doing but casually glanced around at the handsome young man standing nervously across the room. 'He is very striking to look at,' she thought, starting to understand better Angela's preoccupation with him. Finally she broke the silence between them.

"Angela's a very special girl, Lucas." She told him, an almost angry light in her eyes. "I sincerely hope you know that."

Lucas was at first taken aback by the woman's sudden show of bravado and was tempted to put her in her place right then and there. But he checked his anger, knowing that Angela could walk back in at any moment. Nonetheless, Mrs. Griffen saw the black look which had briefly come into his eyes and, without being quite sure why, she felt a sudden twinge of fear.

"You're right, Mrs. Griffen." He replied neutrally. "She's very special indeed."

Angela came back into the kitchen, still sporting the satiny black shirt but now casually comfortable in jeans. She looked back and forth between Lucas and her mother as if trying to guess at their conversation. Belle turned to her daughter.

"Angie, why don't you take Lucas on a tour of the house, dear?" She suggested. "Dinner will still be about twenty minutes."

"Sure Mom." Angela replied, blushingly remembering the afternoon she'd done just that. Lucas was instantly aware of the irony too and winked boldly at her. The exchange between them did not go unnoticed by Mrs. Griffen.

They made a whirlwind tour of the house, though Lucas couldn't resist pinning Angela against her bedroom wall, with a mischievous grin and giving her a deep wholly arousing kiss. She giggled nervously when he finally released her and led him back towards the kitchen.

"Come on," she said. "Let's go out back and I'll show you the inside of my tree house." He put his hand in hers and allowed her to lead him through the hall, past Belle Griffen and out into the yard.

Mrs. Griffen watched the young couple cross the yard and was somewhat surprised when she saw her daughter lead the way up the ladder to the tree house. Angela crawled into the tree house and moved across the floor a little to give

Lucas enough room to join her. He slid alongside of her and wrapped one of his arms round her instantly. They sat comfortably, backs against one wall, looking through the sun dappled leafy views that the little hideaway provided.

"This is so cool Angie." Lucas told her. "Your dad loved you very much, baby."

"Yeah Lucas, he did." she answered, in a voice barely audible. He glanced down at her, seeing the tear starting to form at the corner of her eye.

"Oh baby, I never meant to make you cry." Lucas crooned, "It's just I can see his love all 'round you up here. I wanna love you that much. You're so very special." Angela looked up at him in amazement. 'How could he know her daddy was here, in this place?' She always climbed to the tree house now when she wanted to talk to Paul Griffen; his presence was here for her.

"I love you Lucas Reeves." She whispered.

"And I love you Angela." He said in a voice choked with passion. "I want you by my side always." They hugged and he showered small kisses all over her face.

Belle Griffen called from the back door that dinner was ready. Lucas and Angela exchanged longing looks and then both burst out giggling like children. They climbed back out of the tree and went in to eat.

Belle Griffen had prepared teriyaki beef short ribs with roasted potatoes and a Caesar salad. The three of them were mostly silent through dinner as though they'd each decided that conversation was best not attempted. Angela's Mom did study both her daughter and the dangerously handsome guitar player quite closely though somewhat surreptitiously.

"That was a fantastic meal, Mrs. Griffen." Lucas finally said, pushing back his chair just a little.

"Thank you Lucas." the older woman said. "I'm glad you enjoyed it."

"I did indeed." He agreed, and then he turned to Angela. "We're going to have to get going, Angie. First set waits for no one."

"Ok Lucas." She answered. She slid her chair back and stepped over to her mom. She placed both arms round the older woman's neck and gave her a quick peck on the cheek. "See you later, Mom. Don't wait up, ok?"

"Have fun, Angela." Said her mother, then cautioned, "But be careful."

"Don't worry so Mom," Angela laughed, as she followed Lucas towards the door. "Lucas will look after me."

Her mother laughed and called a quick goodnight after them. When the door closed behind them, Belle Griffen spoke out loud to the empty kitchen. "That's exactly what I am worried about Angie."

Lucas was having a great night on stage on that Friday night. He seemed to just soar higher and further on each guitar solo. Angela was excited for him too, seeing the rapture in his face. He came off the stage after the second set and literally picked her up and spun her round. She laughed joyfully at his exuberance.

"You are absolutely awesome, Angel." He told her, when he'd put her back on her feet.

She looked at him with sparkling eyes. "Me?" She questioned. "Lucas, you're the one up there playing so beautifully!"

"You are my inspiration, my love!" He said emphatically.

The third set started out with the same high that the second set had ended on and then the unthinkable happened. Suddenly, Lucas's amp went dead. He turned, bent over and fiddled with the knobs. He then checked the lead wires, jiggling them to make sure that everything was plugged in. Angela sat tensely in her chair, not knowing quite what had happened but seeing the stress start to grow in Lucas's movements, even from behind. He turned every knob and jiggled every switch possible and still nothing. The bass player put his instrument down and joined Lucas, they had a brief conversation during which Lucas said no more than about four words and those, though under his breath, Angela could see were short, sharp and extremely angry.

The bass player made a quick apology to the crowd telling them there would be a brief delay, and then headed off the stage. Lucas put the Stratocaster down and strode over to their table. He picked up the full beer sitting there and drained the glass immediately. Angela looked up at him with concern in her eyes.

"Lucas?"

"What?" He snapped at her. "Damn it, Angie!! Get me another fucking beer. This damn piece of shit has gotta work!!" He slammed his glass down on the table so hard that Angie was surprised it didn't shatter, then turned and went back to the stage. She had cowered a little when he yelled at her, as though the words had been physical blows. But she found their waitress and ordered the beer. She sat there reasoning to herself that he was such a perfectionist it was no wonder he was angry. Moments later, everything was okay. Whatever the bass player had brought in from his car had been jury-rigged and the amp again worked.

Lucas was very quiet on their way back to the motel room that night. He glanced sidelong at Angela and seemed to soften a little at the sight of her.

As soon as the door closed to the motel room, she was in his strong arms. He didn't go slowly at all this night, the urgency of his need for her seemed dictate the pace. Lucas had her naked almost before she knew it and very quickly brought her to climax with his hands and tongue. Angela lay panting with her own passion and remembering his words the first time, that she would love this. She was laying on her back across the bed, her head right on the edge. Lucas, still in his jeans, came to that edge and bent down and kissed her, his mouth still tasting of her juice.

Her eyes had closed as he had started to kiss her. He withdrew for a moment then she heard his fly open and the jeans fall to the floor. She was expecting him to crawl onto the bed bedside her, but instead she felt his hardness press against her cheek. Her eyes flew open in surprise.

"Take it Angie." he told her, offering his hard cock to her mouth.

"Lucas, I...." She started to whisper. He reached down and took a handful of her hair and though he didn't pull on it, he made it clear that he would.

"Angie, I want you to taste me." His voice was calm, words soft and she relaxed a little. "I've tasted you, baby. This would give me so much pleasure. You want to please me, don't you?" She nodded very slightly, not wanting to pull her own hair. He put a finger into her mouth and she sucked on it like she had the first night with him. "There, see." he said. "Now take it, babe." He withdrew the finger and pushed his cock into her mouth. At first she thought she would choke but she closed her eyes tight, picturing the sun dappled platform of the tree house as he moved in her mouth and then she sucked at his erection as he crooned, "There's my good baby. That's so nice, Angie."

He withdrew from her mouth before reaching climax and entered her still wet pussy. His mouth bent to hers again and between kisses, as they both moved together, he whispered huskily, "I love you Angel, thank you." Their urgency now seemed to be equal and she frantically writhed beneath him, seeking her own climax with his.

Later, she lay in his arms and he stroked her long dark hair. Her fingertips were idly tracing circles and whirls on his chest but otherwise she lay quite still. He spoke in the darkness.

"Angie, thank you, my love." He said softly.

"For what?" She asked.

"For taking me into your mouth." He answered. "You're so beautiful and it turns me on so to have you taste me and suck me like that."

She was trembling just a little, but he definitely could feel her emotion. He smiled to himself, 'makes me want you more, baby.' he thought.

"I'm not sure about it, Lucas." She told him. Not even daring to say the words.

"You were awesome, baby. Very gentle." He told her. "You're the most beautiful, sexy angel in the whole world. And you're mine. This makes me the luckiest man."

It was close the three in the morning when he drove her home and walked her up to the door. The house was in darkness. Angela put her key in the lock then turned to him as he pulled her in for a kiss.

"I don't want to bring you home tomorrow night, Angie." he stated, as he held her against him. "I want you to stay with me all night. I wanna be able to reach for you and you'll be there."

Angela, hearing his words which echoed her own longing, didn't know what to say at first. She held a little tighter to his waist and buried her head against his chest. "I want that too, Lucas. I want to be with you."

"Then stay with me tomorrow night. Just stay." he told her, his mouth speaking the words against her cheek, his hot breath making her giddy with desire again.

"But...." She hesitated.

"Ange, you're a grown up." Impatience was now creeping into his tone. "Tomorrow's gotta last a while for both of us. Stay the night with me. Promise me?" Though it sounded like a question, for Angela there was only one answer.

"Yes Lucas, I will stay all night." She whispered. He kissed her again then, as she opened the door, he moved swiftly back to the car.

Angela slipped off her shoes just inside the door and then tiptoed across the living room. As she reached the doorway to the hall, her mother's voice came out of the darkness and she wheeled back to the living room in sudden fright.

"Angela, where can you possibly be till this hour of the night? Everything's closed." Belle Griffen asked harshly.

"Mom, you scared me to death, sitting there in the dark." Angela said, ignoring her mother's question.

"How well do you know this man?" her mother continued, leaning over as she spoke to turn on a single lamp by the couch.

"Mom!" Angela protested. "I'm grown. I don't think it's any of your business."

Mrs. Griffen stared at her daughter in disbelief. Angela had never spoken to her in that tone before. She decided to try a different approach.

"I know you're grown, Angie." She said more softly, patting the couch beside her. Angela came closer but did not sit. "I love you sweetheart. And I'm not sure I trust this Lucas character."

Angela clenched and unclenched her fists, trying to be calm. "I know him! Doesn't that matter?" she said quietly but angrily. "He loves me, Mom. He'd never hurt me." Her mother wondered at that last comment but decided that it was too late at night for them to argue further. She spoke tiredly, when she finally replied.

"It's late, we're both tired. I love you, honey." she told her daughter, as she stood and put one arm around the young woman's shoulders. She could feel Angela tense up beneath her touch and was very surprised by that but did not comment. "Let's just go to bed and talk in the morning."

Angela curled into a tight ball almost completely under her covers, but she could still hear her mother's voice and her knuckles tapping on the door. She had no clear idea what time it might be, but hesitated to turn over and look at her alarm clock. If her mother heard her stirring, she'd never leave her alone. Though Angela had never been very close with her Mom, she'd never quite thought of her as the enemy when she was a teen, perhaps because she wasn't at all rebellious. They had merely lived in the same house and shared little else. But now, all Angela could see was that her mother didn't like Lucas, who she loved more than she'd ever thought possible. Her timid character would simply not allow her to face the showdown that she sensed her mother was planning.

Eventually Belle Griffen moved away from Angela's door. She could hear the girl breathing, so she knew she was still in the house. She would just let her sleep awhile longer and try again. She went into the kitchen, poured another mug of coffee and slumped tiredly at her kitchen table. She'd thought all this kind of trouble and worry would be long over when the girls got to be adults. But though the years had passed Angela by, she had never somehow grown beyond the shy fourteen year old who had run to the woods and hidden her grief when her daddy had died. 'And now,' Belle thought, angrily. 'This young stud with a guitar thinks he can just take her over.' Belle's frustration only deepened when she realized that she knew no clear way to stop Lucas, if that truly was his intent. She put her head on her arms and prayed that the guitar player would be gone tomorrow and never return. The short term hurt that would cause her daughter was probably the best bargain available.

Angela heard her mother sobbing even from under the covers and was sorely tempted to go to her. Instead, she slipped out of bed, pulled on her jeans and a shirt and brushed her hair only enough to tie it back into a pony tail. She laced on a pair of running shoes and, as quietly as possible, slid up her window. Angela slipped out through the bedroom window landing lightly on the grass of the front lawn. She did not pause or look back, but moved at a brisk walk away from the house. Running, she reasoned, may draw too much attention to her. She just wanted to get away for a while, to think.

She made her way to the riverbank and, with her always good sense of direction, went straight to the clearing where Lucas had taken her only one week before. She sat in the grass in the middle of the circle of trees, gazing up at the blue sky dotted with fluffy summer clouds. Angela watched the clouds and wished that she could race with them to wherever they were bound, especially if Lucas would be there too. She remembered his words when he brought her home, 'Tomorrow's gotta last a while for both of us.' How long? She had wanted to ask. It was then that she had decided to let go of her fears and do what was in her heart. She would stay with Lucas Reeves, tonight and for as long as he wanted her.

When she walked back into the house through the back door, her mother was no longer in the kitchen. In fact, Angela discovered, Belle Griffen had left the house. There was a note on the kitchen table which read;

"Angela, honey I love you. There's some lunch on the counter. I'll be back by suppertime."

Angela read and reread the short note. She shrugged and retrieved the sandwich her mother had left on the counter for her. She poured a mug of coffee and took both to her bedroom. She kicked off her running shoes and crawled back under the quilt. She was still there when Lucas beeped the car horn about four o'clock. Her eyes flew open in shock, realizing in an instant that she had fallen asleep and what the sound was that had awoken her. By the time she had grabbed her purse and shoes, Lucas was ringing the front door bell.

Angela ran to answer it and, when it swung open, he was surprised by the frazzled looking woman he beheld. He held out his arms to her instantly.

"Baby, what's wrong?" He crooned. She let him enfold her in his arms and quickly buried her face against his chest. "Tell me, Angie." He said quietly.

"Lucas, it's all crazy," she told him and he could even hear her voice tremble. "Mom and I fought about you last night. I just need to....." She stopped then almost in tears and not quite sure what she had intended to say.

"You need to go wash your face," He told her, giving her a strong and reassuring hug. He put one finger under her chin and brought her face up towards his. He smiled down at her, green eyes sparkling. When she met his calm gaze, he continued. "Wash up, you'll feel better. Don't forget to put some extra clothes for tomorrow and your toothbrush in a bag. Is Mom here somewhere, Angie?"

"No," she replied timidly, "Least I don't think so, I fell asleep."

"Okay then, go do as I told you. I'll wait right here."

She went and washed up; the cool cloth restoring some vigor to her. Then she put a few things into a canvas bag as Lucas had told her. She looked around the bedroom as though not expecting to be back at all. As she went back down the hall, she thought perhaps she should leave her mom a note. She stopped dead at the doorway to the living room, Lucas was gone.

Her head swiveled round in a panic and she was about to run towards the front door when she caught a movement in the kitchen. Lucas was standing at the table reading her mother's note. He turned towards her when she walked in.

"You ready?" He asked. She nodded then suddenly shook her head 'no'.

"I just have to..." she started.

"Write a note for your Mom, baby." He finished for her. "We don't want her to worry."

Angela took the paper from her mother's note, turned it over and quickly scrawled a few short sentences. She put the note neatly back on the table, propped against the vase holding the flowers which Lucas had brought the day before.

"Mom, love you too. I've gone to see Lucas's gig. We'll be eating late, after the show. I won't be home tonight. Don't worry, I will see you tomorrow. Angela"

Lucas and Angela walked out the door arm in arm, him carrying her canvas bag. Angela was still shaking with emotion and Lucas found himself angry at Belle Griffen as though this was somehow her fault.

By the time they had picked up dinner and driven to the motel, Angela was more her calm smiling self. And when Lucas picked up the Gibson and started to play for her, he could see the tension start to drain out of her. By the time that they had to leave for Rock City, she was back to being Angela, quiet and smiling shyly as he bent to kiss her long and slow.

"Welcome home, baby." He told her. "You'll always have a 'home' with me."

His words echoed in her mind all the way on the short drive to Rock City.

Becky and Christie were both out dancing too that night and were happy to sit and keep Angela company between their trips round the dance floor. They got her up to dance with them a couple of times and Lucas was pleased that she was having fun with the girls. For the first time since the previous weekend, he did a repeat performance of the song "Close to You", having Angela once again join him on stage. This time when they kissed, she laced her arms round his neck and pulled his mouth to hers. He grinned at her sudden boldness.

As they came off the stage together, he whispered in her ear, "Did you forget all those people were watching you, Angel?" She flushed with sudden embarrassment and he chuckled with delight.

To Angela, it was at first strange to make love to Lucas and then fall asleep in his arms; only to wake, feel his arousal again and want him once more. Dawn was coming over the eastern mountains when they both finally fell into a deeper sleep, she curled with her back against his chest, his one strong arm resting across her breasts, hand curled around her shoulder. Their legs were tangled and snaked together. The warmth and smell of him surrounded her with an unaccustomed contentment.

When Angela finally opened her eyes, the sun was already high in the sky. She stretched and rolled from her side onto her back. The soft sounds of Lucas strumming the Gibson penetrated her senses and she twisted up a little to find him. He smiled at her from the end of the bed and continued playing.

"Hi sleepyhead." He said softly. She sat up a little more and the blankets fell away from her. She modestly grasped the sheet and pulled it round her to hide her nakedness. Lucas chuckled, not unkindly, and laid the guitar aside. He crawled across the bed, bringing his mouth to hers and they kissed long and passionately. She allowed him to push her gently back onto the pillows. He caressed her through the flimsy sheet fabric and she giggled softly as his fingers tickled her ribs.

"I'm hungry, Lucas." she told him, almost pouting like a child. He grinned down at her and covered her face and neck with tiny kisses.

"Me too," He agreed, mischievously. "Hungry for you!"

They were both content to play and, for the first time, she was tickling and exploring him as much as he was her. Lucas was surer than ever that this night had been right for them. His Angel was radiant. He bent and kissed her again. This time their hungry mouths devoured each other, tongues probing and dancing together. He felt her move against him, her body asking for what her shy heart and mind could not allow her to vocalize. He slid under the sheet with her and they moved together towards ecstasy.

Afterwards, she lay quiet in his arms, head on his chest, listening to his heartbeat. Lucas stroked her long dark hair from her face and gently traced her face with his fingers.

"You are what I have waited and hoped for all my life, sweet angel." he told her. Angela nearly cried when she heard his words. Her fingertips stretched up to his lips and traced round them then continued cross his face as if trying to memorize each part of him. Lucas caught one of her fingers between his lips and sucked on its tip. Then he suddenly sat up much straighter and the mood was shattered.

"I have a present for you." He told her. He slid out from under her and crossed to where his jacket lay across the chair. He reached into the inside left pocket and pulled out a long slim jewellery box. Her eyes widened in surprise.

Lucas came back to the bedside, then dropped to one knee and presented the box to her. Angela looked from him to the box and back again, then finally took a deep breath and lifted the lid. The heart shaped locket gleamed up at her and she could see her own face, though distorted, reflected in its mirror-like surface. She looked back up at Lucas with tears welling in her blue eyes.

"It's so perfectly beautiful Lucas." She murmured.

"Wait," he whispered, "There's more." He bent down and picked up the Gibson from the bedside. He carefully loosened the tuning peg on one of the strings. As he worked he explained to her. "This little tiny string here is the bottom E string, but for you and I it's going to be my heartstring." He removed what she knew must be a perfectly good string from the guitar then curled it until it became a tiny coil.

"Open the locket, my love." He instructed. Her fingers found the tiny catch and she opened the heart. He placed the string inside and together their fingers reclosed the heart. He took the chain and, while she held her hair up off her neck he clasped it round her. The heart slid on the chain to a comfortable resting place just above her breasts. "There now, you will always have my heartstrings to tug on." He told her. "I love you, Angela."

"I love you, Lucas," she said with sudden conviction. "So very much."

He took her out for an early afternoon breakfast at one of the little diners along the service road. He'd already checked out of the motel and the car was loaded for his return trip to the city. Neither of them had mentioned his going back all night or morning, but now the inevitable faced them.

Lucas explained his plan to her as they ate.

"You see all my gigs for the next five weekends are close by, not more than fifty miles the furthest." he outlined. "So what I'm gonna do is meet you after work Friday. You got to be ready to travel, like with weekend stuff, ya know?" She nodded and he grinned. "It'll be like an adventure. I'll pick you up and bring you with me for Friday and Saturday night gigs. Then drive you home on Sunday, before I head back."

"Oh Lucas," she breathed, tears welling up again. "You're so wonderful. I thought you'd go and forget me."

He reached across the table and wiped a tear that had rolled across her cheek. She took his one hand in both hers and, still crying, managed to kiss all his fingers one by one. Finally she took his index finger into her mouth and started to suck gently. He beamed at her.

"I could never forget you, my love. I want you by my side." He told her. "Angela you complete me."

The next few weeks became a whirlwind for Angela. She worked hard all week, really throwing herself into her tasks to keep her mind from wandering to Lucas. The silver heart was her only jewelry now and she never was without it.

Becky and Christie were happy for their friend. In their view, since Lucas had gone out of his way to adjust his schedule to be with her, driving sometimes many miles out of his way to bring her with him on weekends, he must really care for her. They found the whole thing quite romantic and Becky, usually so sensible, confessed some jealousy of Angie and her handsome musician.

Things weren't so easy at home. Belle Griffen was devastated from the moment that Angela had stayed out all night with Lucas. When mother and daughter did talk, it was in short words and phrases. Mostly though, Angela tried to avoid her mother, retiring to her room as soon as possible after the dinner dishes were done and waiting till the last possible moment to emerge in the mornings. She spent her time alone reading books from the library about the blues and the early years of rock and roll, fascinating stories that somehow made her feel closer to Lucas.

Belle had talked to her older daughter Pamela about her fears and, in an effort to somehow break through to Angela; she invited Pam and her husband and son to dinner one evening. Brent Johnson had been an honour student in high school and captain of the basketball team. He and Pamela had been two of the most popular kids in their high school class; even then Angela had looked at them with a mixture of awe and envy. Popularity came easy to Pamela and she never quite understood her shy, awkward tomboy sister.

After dinner, Angela slipped away to her room and her books as usual. A short time later, there was a light tap on the door and Pam's voice, "Hey Angie, can I talk to you a minute?" She asked and without waiting for an answer she pushed open the door.

Angela was taken aback by her sister's bold entrance into her room. They had barely talked as girls and certainly were not close now. She swung her legs off the edge of the bed where she'd been lying with her book and motioned Pamela to take the little easy chair in the corner by the window. Pamela sat down and glanced at the cover of Angela's book, "Blues Guitar: The Men Who Made the Music"

"Reading lots, Ange?" She asked.

"What?" Angela replied, not quite ready for the turn Pamela's conversation took. "Oh yeah. It's kind of interesting stuff."

"Angie, we're all rather worried about you." Her older sister told her.

"Who are we?" Angela asked, though she could already guess.

"Well Mom and I, and Brent too really." Pamela explained. "You know you don't have much experience with men. And this guy, this guitar guy, he's really not your type." Angela couldn't believe her ears.

"How would you know what 'my type' is Pam?" she asked, a slightly sarcastic note in her voice. "You've hardly talked to me since we were kids. You have no idea who I am."

"And you have no idea who this guy is?" Pamela snapped back, her voice rising. She had only come to talk to Angela at her mother's request. 'How dare her little sister talk to her like that.' she thought.

"He has a name Pamela." Angela stated and, though she was shaking underneath, her voice did not show much of her emotions for a change. "His name is Lucas. And I know him far better than you or my mother do. Did she put you up to this little talk?"

"Mom's worried about you Angela." Pamela admitted.

"You and Mom have been on my case for years to go out and meet a nice young man. And when I do, you're still not happy for me." Angela sadly told her.

"Ange, why couldn't you go out with someone from here at home, like Brent?" Pamela asked, truly baffled.

"Because I'm not you Pam," Angela answered. "Brent's very nice, for you. Not for me. Now please go, I don't want to fight with you."

Pamela nodded and without a word she left the room, closing the door on her way out. She had no stomach for a fight either and if Angie was determined to ruin her life, who was she to stop her after all, she wondered. Angela turned on her side, hugging a pillow to her, and wept.

After a Saturday night gig, in a town some forty miles west of Angela's home, she and Lucas went for a late night drive. He knew the roads very well all over the huge expanse of the delta valley from driving to so many different places to play. Not far out of town the road they were on climbed and wound its way up a tree covered hill, the highest spot of land around. It was so completely dark that even the trees by the road side were hard to pick out. As they neared the top of the rise however, Angela could see a strange almost unworldly glow from the far side.

Lucas brought the big car to a stop in a pull off where the road flattened out on the brow of the hill and Angela drew in her breath in surprise. The slope fell away very steeply to the west and the reason for the glow in the sky was now plainly spread before her. From this vantage point they had an unobstructed view all the way across the thirty or so miles to the coast and the big city that Lucas called home. He turned off the engine and the effect of the darkness and the glowing city before them in the silence was, to Angela, strangely beautiful.

"Lucas this is amazing." She said quietly.

"Come on, baby." He prompted, opening his door and sliding out of the car. She joined him at the front of the vehicle and they both stood, arms wrapped around one another, looking out over the land. Slowly, Angela's ears became aware of the night noises of small animals rustling through the grass, the wind in the trees, an owl calling in the distance and Lucas's heart beating as her head was pillowed against his chest.

"Angela that's home." He told her simply. "It's not so far off, huh?" She thought about her own home when he said the word and wondered if it would ever feel like home again.

"Your home Lucas," She corrected softly. "I have none."

Lucas froze when he heard her words. Then he quickly recovered and turned a little towards her, his hand turning her face up to his. He searched her eyes and her expression trying to understand her meaning. He wasn't sure what she may be trying to tell him. There was a low stone wall in front of them and he took a step towards it, bringing her with him. He sat, pulling her down beside him, placing one strong arm securely around her shoulders and again turning her face gently around to him.

"What do you mean, Angie?" He asked finally.

She was hesitant at first to speak, but he gently questioned and finally her discomfort with her mother and the whole story of her talk with sister, Pamela, poured out of her along with the tears which had been hidden for days. Lucas listened quietly, rubbing her back and trying to comfort her. Inside he was seething. 'How dare they try to take his angel?' He thought; his anger seething at the idea.

When Angela had no more words she still had tears left and Lucas pulled her against him and let her weep. When her sobbing finally subsided, he bent to her and kissed her tear stained cheeks. Then he started to rock her gently, rhythmically as he sang a quiet lullaby. She listened to only his voice then, all other night noises seemed to fade away. Her hand came up and clasped the silver heart where it lay against her skin. Finally he spoke again.

"Angela, they don't understand you, baby." He told her. "From what you've told me, I don't think they ever have. You're the black sheep of your family, just like me. You have a home, always, with me. Don't ever forget that, my angel. I love you."

She turned her face up to his and her eyes, still red from weeping, held a new hope and light. He bent to her and they kissed deeply. Feeling his strong arms round her, his lips on hers, she suddenly thought 'this is where I want to be, for always.' She moved her body against his and he felt her arousal.

"Not here," he whispered. He led her back to the car and drove them back towards the little town they had come from. She slid across the seat and wrapped her arm around him as he drove. She was sleepy and her head had nodded against him before they arrived at the little room that was their weekend home. Her arm had slipped down from his waist and her hand was gently resting on his pants, arousing him more. He parked the car and started to slide from behind the wheel; she stirred and clung to him. He smiled, lifting her with him from the car and using a foot to kick the door shut. He kissed her deeply again and she put her arms round his neck, opening her mouth to him.

"We're home, baby." He told her. "As long as we're together, we're always home."

In the week before that fifth weekend, Angela became increasingly withdrawn. Even her friends at work noticed that she barely joined in their chatter at all. Lucas would be going back to the city and he confessed he did not know how long it may be before the band once again got a gig which brought them east towards her home town. She could not imagine losing him now but had not the courage to consider what a move all alone to the big city may entail.

Her only hope lay in his words, which she repeated over and over in her head like mantras, 'There now you will always have my heartstrings to tug on.' 'As long as we're together, we're always home.' She must find a way to be with him.

Angela ate in silence on Wednesday evening. Belle had grown used to the long silences between them and no longer even tried to speak to her daughter about Lucas. The few attempts had been most unpleasant for both women. She wondered though, as she studied her daughter, if something between her and her young guitar player may have changed. There was barely detectable air of sadness over Angela where in previous weeks there had only been quiet resolve.

"Angie?" Belle ventured.

"Yes, Mom?" Angela responded softly.

"You seem kind of sad tonight." Her mother told her. "Did something happen? Can I help?" Angela looked puzzled for a moment and her hand briefly rubbed the silver heart locket dangling round her neck as though drawing strength from the amulet.

"Nothing is wrong, Mom. I was just wishing it was the weekend again." She said flatly. Angela pushed her chair back and took her plate to the sink. "Dinner was great, thanks Mom." She told Belle as cheerily as she could manage.

Before her mother could answer, Angela crossed to the hallway and slipped into her running shoes. Belle Griffen followed her; surprised that she had not gone straight to her room as that had been her routine so much these past few weeks.

"Going out?" She asked.

"Just for a walk." Angela replied noncommittally. "I'll be back in a little while." Angela turned the door handle, slipped out and was gone.

She walked down the front street the turned down a curving boulevard which was lined with beautiful stately old oak trees. Just a few blocks down the road, she turned in through large wrought iron gate posts and walked with a sense of reverence among the gravestones in the city's lone cemetery. Angela made her way to a particular grave under the boughs of another beautiful maple tree much like her tree at home. A stone, not fancy or shaped by cutter's tools but brought off the granite mountains to the east, marked the site of Paul Griffen's grave. A simple plaque read 'Paul Griffen 1943 - 1984 Beloved Husband & Father'. Angela knelt in the grass by the stone.

"Daddy, I love you." She whispered. "You came from a different place before you lived here. You moved to provide a home to your wife and later to us girls. All creatures leave their nests, dens, burrows and such, that's how you explained it to me, I remember. Daddy, I love him. I need to be with him. Please help Mom to understand, because I still can't talk to her. I will miss you and the maple tree, but Lucas will help me to find my own sturdy maple. He understands, Daddy. I love him. Goodnight Daddy, I'll miss you."

She ran her hand very lightly over the surface of the grass before the stone as if to briefly touch the spirit who had guided her childhood. Then, quite dry eyed and calm, she turned and walked back the way she had come.

Angela's feet next took her back to the clearing where Lucas and her had begun their journey together. Once again she was able to sit in the grassy circle and almost sense his presence with her. Summer was waning and the air was chillier than the hot July night they had first come to this place together. Angela thought about that. Watching the seasons change throughout her life had been a delight. Paul Griffen had made a game of it. Who would spot the first robin in the spring? Who could find the perfect fall leaf in shades of red and gold? Who could make more snow angels? Her Dad had shown her the magic of the changing seasons and taught her to enjoy those changes. 'Was this just another change?' Angela wasn't sure, but she was sure that somehow Lucas was her summer, fall, winter and spring all in one. A stray leaf fell into her lap and broke her reverie. She arose and quietly went on.

Belle Griffen saw her daughter come in through the back gate by the maple tree. She was about to get up and put the kettle on hoping that a cup of tea shared may help them find each other, but she stopped surprised, when Angela climbed up the ladder and disappeared into her tree house.

It was starting to get dark when Angela climbed into the tree house. Memories of building it came flooding back to her along with the more recent memory of climbing here with Lucas and how he had understood her father's presence here. She wondered at that. How Lucas, who had not had a 'real' father in his life, could understand so readily what Angela's daddy had meant to her. She believed somehow the two men had touched one another, perhaps here in this place and Lucas now knew her father's love. The thought comforted her.

When she finally returned to the house, her mother had retired to her own room to read. Belle Griffen heard Angela come in and contented herself that at least the girl was home and safe, for now.

Wednesday evening in Kurt's living room found the brothers watching the TV and drinking beer. Both men looked tired. They had worked twelve hour days for the last three to get Kurt's latest contract done before Lucas returned to the road.

"Man I am whipped!" Kurt said. "But we got it done little bro." Lucas raised his beer can in salute to his brother and grinned.

"Big bucks, huh?" He chuckled. "It was worth it, man. Hey you going to pick up the cheque tomorrow?"

"Yeah man, about noon probably." Kurt replied. "What time you leaving for your gig?"

"Not till about three, it ain't that far and I don't pick up Angie till Friday." Lucas told him. "So maybe I can get some of my portion and still make the bank?"

"Yeah sure or I can bank it for you." Kurt said agreeably, then added, "What you gonna do 'bout Angie, man? How are you going to see her now that the band's back in town?" Lucas took a long swallow of his beer before he answered his brother.

"I'm bringing her home with me, Kurt." The statement fell like a bombshell between the men. Kurt stared at Lucas for a long moment, not sure he'd heard right.

"You mean like for a visit, right?" He asked finally.

"No man, I mean I'm bringing my girl home. She's going to live here with me, well with us." Lucas stated flatly.

"Damn Lucas!" Kurt exploded, "She's hardly had a chance to know you yet man, watching you gig, it ain't the same as real dating!"

Lucas drained his beer and slammed the can on to the coffee table. Kurt felt sudden regret at his outburst and remained impassive as Lucas stood and strode across directly in front of his older brother. Kurt watched as Lucas's normally emerald green eyes seemed to go dark for a moment with the younger man's rage. Lucas brought his face to within about two inches of his brother's and spoke through clenched teeth.

"She knows me, damn it! And I know what's best for her." He snapped, "And it ain't sitting out there in small townville being Mommy's little housemate! I'm bringing her home!" His anger seemed to pass for the moment and he turned abruptly and left the room. Only a minute or so later Kurt heard the buzz of the amplifier followed by the wail of Lucas's guitar coming from down the hall. 'Let him wail.' he thought.

Kurt watched the TV through eyes that were not really seeing the picture. As Lucas played on, Kurt Reeves mind took him back to when the brothers had been teens; he nineteen and Lucas just turned seventeen.

They had gone to a party on the beach close by home. One of those summer gatherings of teens who wanted to cut loose, maybe break the rules and drink a few beers. This group was all guys and there was a lot of arm wrestling and tough talk as the young adults challenged each other in the age old rituals of manhood. Lucas was keeping out of most of that as usual. He had been sitting on a driftwood log just outside of the main ring of young men around the bonfire. One of the boys noticed him as he was staring, almost dreamy eyed, out across the moonlit water.

"Damn, look at little Lucas!" The young man taunted. "He's mooning over some poetry or summthin'!"

At first Lucas ignored the other boy completely. But the boy simply couldn't leave it alone. A couple of the other young men in the ring had turned to see what was happening. Kurt turned too.

"Yer a pansy-ass, Lucas Reeves!" The young man jeered. "Geez even Lucas is a pansy-ass name."

Lucas turned towards his tormentor then and Kurt saw in the flickering light from the bonfire that Lucas's eyes had gone an angry black. Before anyone could have reacted, Lucas sprang from his seat on the log and lunged at the young man who had taunted him. The tormentor, taken by surprise, was bowled over instantly by the force of Lucas's charge. Lucas was on him immediately and started rained blows down from both fists. The young man could do nothing in the face of the younger Reeves' fury but to raise his arms in defense against the blows.

Kurt and another of the older boys reacted by then and both of them reached in and pulled Lucas from his victim. Lucas fought against both older boys with a certain mindless furor that was, for his brother, frightening to behold. It took both boys several minutes to calm the younger one down. Then Lucas glared at his brother, with a look of pure hatred that chilled Kurt to the bone, turned and sped off into the darkness. There was no doubt in Kurt Reeves mind that night that Lucas would have killed him had not the horrible storm of his anger abated.

The last weekend was bitter sweet for Angela. She enjoyed watching Lucas play and sing, as always, letting herself go with the music and feeding directly from his energy. But she felt haunted by the fact that this may be their last interval spent together for an indefinable time. She was unsure how to tell Lucas of her fears and so kept them to herself. Lucas seemed exceptionally upbeat too, which only added to Angela's apprehension. She began to wonder if perhaps she was indeed just a 'summer fling' like her mother had suggested.

After the gig on Saturday evening, Lucas was on a natural high driven mainly by how well the band had played and how great the audience reaction had been. The place had been jumping and no one had gone home before closing. He hugged Angela happily at the close of the show.

"Baby, this is what makes it the best!" He told her excitedly. There were a number of people, women mostly, crowded round them waiting to talk to Lucas. He answered a spate of questions about where the band was from, when they'd be playing next and where. Angela, who had been standing beside him, slipped quietly out of his grasp and took a seat back at the table. She watched as Lucas animatedly chatted with the merry group. One woman seemed to be pressing him with more personal than musical questions. She was taller than Angela and blonde like her friend Christie. Lucas was laughing merrily at something she had said, when the woman leaned towards him and kissed him on the cheek. He put an arm around her and gave her a brief squeeze. Angela, looking on, felt all her fears realized in a flash.

A few minutes later, the little group broke up and Lucas finished packing up his things. He came across to the table and handed the car keys to Angela. Then, packing amp and guitar, he made his way towards the door. Angela followed behind, watching his retreating back and wondering whether this was a portent of things to come for them. When they got to the car she unlocked the trunk so he could stow his equipment, then turned and unlocked her door. She slid into the front seat and reached across to unlock his side. Lucas slid behind the wheel and reached for the keys from her.

"Wasn't that the greatest, babe?" He asked, still excited.

"Yeah Lucas, it was real nice for you." She said softly, her voice unmistakably carrying a hint of regret.

He turned towards her, examining her with his piercingly green eyes.

"What's wrong?" He demanded. She cringed inwardly at his words. 'How could he not understand that she felt frightened and the fear was of losing him?'

"I'm tired is all." She said softly.

He responded, in a voice which was low and almost menacing, "Angie, if you're upset about that chic in there, don't be! She was just a chic, ya know? I'm with you here, now. Get it?" Angela trembled a little at the tone of his voice.

"Lucas, I'm sorry." She whispered.

He started the car and they drove back to the motel in silence. Once there his mood seemed to have changed completely and they made love gently and lovingly for hours. Angela found herself wanting him more and more and it was she who would reinitiate their passion after each long cuddle session. As dawn was greying the sky, she finally relented, letting him sleep.

Angela slept only fitfully herself and finally gave up the effort entirely. She sat cross-legged on the bed with one of the discarded blankets wrapped round her to ward off the morning chill. At first she merely watched him sleep, amazed at how childlike and innocent he seemed in repose. That made her think of the young boy that Lucas had been, who had given up trying to ever live up to his father's vision of manhood. He must have been far lonelier that she herself had been. 'At least,' Angela thought, 'I had the unconditional and ever-present love of my father while I was young.'

Her eyes roamed round the room, coming to rest on the Gibson's case standing in one corner. It still amazed her that he brought the instrument along on weekends just for her entertainment. That he chose to serenade her with his first love, music, was very moving to Angela. He shared music each night from the stage but it never quite held the amazing intimacy that just he and she and the guitar shared. "I was foolish to be worried about that girl at the bar,' she thought. ' He does truly love me, I can't doubt that now.'

She reached forward and placed one soft and tentative hand on his shoulder, just wanting to touch him not wake him. She whispered softly; hardly aware herself that her words and thoughts were now audible.

"I love you, Lucas Reeves." She told him and herself. "I will give you all the unconditional love that any man would ever need. Just stay with me, for always."

Angela barely realized that her tears had started to flow but, whether Lucas sensed her unrest, heard her words or felt her hand, he stirred and opened his eyes. His focus on the sad eyed face of his beautiful Angela was instant. He rolled himself up till he was sitting beside her with strong arms pulling her sobbing form against him.

"Angie, what's wrong?" He crooned. "Baby, talk to me." It took her a few moments to compose herself and even then her sobbing continued through her words.

"Lucas, I love you." she managed to say.

"I love you too, my Angel." He whispered, head bending close to hers. "But why the tears? Tell me." She leaned against him, taking some comfort from his warmth but turned her head away, focusing on the Gibson in the corner rather than speaking to him.

"You're going back home now." She explained. "It's like a beautiful dream that I'm just waking from. But Lucas, I don't want to wake up." as she said this her tears started anew. He held her, almost like she was a baby and rocked her till she calmed again. Finally, when she was still in his arms, he spoke again.

"Angie, look at me." He said quietly but compellingly. When she didn't turn her head towards him immediately, he took her chin and gently pulled her to face him, saying once again, "Angie, look at me."

He continued once he had her full attention. "Baby, this isn't a dream. And it isn't going to end, not if you don't want it to. Sshhh," he admonished, noticing that she was about to speak again, "I want you to come home with me today. Come to the city and live with me, well with me and Kurt least till we get our own place."

Her eyes widened in disbelief. Lucas smiled at the almost childlike response his words brought. "We can go up to your place so you can pack some things and talk to your mom, then we'll both go today, together. I'm going to take you home, Angela."

She had a brief moment of apprehension when Lucas mentioned her mother, but one look in his liquid soft eyes, seeing herself reflected there and knowing he truly loved her allayed her fears. Lucas looked down at her and, even with her tear stained face and exhausted circles beneath her eyes, thought she was the most beautiful creature in the world. He bent and kissed her softly, then pulled her down with him under the blankets.

"Sleep, my love." He whispered. "We'll go home soon." They both drifted back to sleep this time, Angela held close in his arms.

It was only about a forty five minute drive to her house from the motel they had called home for the weekend. But the trip seemed interminable as Angela rehearsed over and over the way she might tell her mother that she was leaving. Her heart was glad that Lucas would be there with her for strength, but her head told her his presence may make the situation infinitely harder. Her mother had not made any secret of the fact that she both mistrusted and disliked Lucas intensely.

They pulled up in front of her house and Lucas reached across the seat and squeezed her hand reassuringly. She looked up at him with a weak smile.

"It'll be okay, Angie." He said. "Do you want me to come in too?"

"I want you with me, but..." she hesitated, and he merely waited for her to continue. "I'm scared that seeing you will make Mom feel worse." He almost smiled at her last words, remembering wryly that he'd been thinking the same thing.

"We'll go in together, my love." He said with sudden certainty. "After all, we're starting our life together today."

She managed a grateful smile and waited till he got out and opened her door for her.

They walked in the front door of the house together and Angela kicked off her running shoes. Lucas was bending to remove his boots when Belle Griffen walked in to the room. She looked dubiously at Lucas, wondering what this may be all about.

"Hi Angela," she said, focusing on her daughter alone.

"Hi Mom." Angela said softly. "Mom, I need to tell you something."

Belle's pulse began to race and she felt that clichéd feeling of her heart in the back of her throat. But she swallowed once and gestured in the direction of the living room chairs.

"Maybe we'd better sit down." She suggested.

"Thank you Mrs. Griffen," Lucas said respectfully. "That's an excellent idea."

All three of them stepped from the hall into the living room and Belle Griffen took a seat in what had been her husband's favourite easy chair. Angela raised one eyebrow slightly but otherwise made no sign that she'd noticed the significance of her mother's choice. Lucas sat right next to Angela on a small sofa facing the easy chair directly. He put one relaxed but reassuring arm around Angela's shoulders. Belle looked at her daughter expectantly.

"Well Angela, what's this all about?"

Angela hesitated only a moment, then bolstered by Lucas's closeness she came straight to the point.

"Mom, I'm moving out." She rushed on not willing yet to give her mother a chance to argue. "I'm going to take some things with me today and when I decide what else I will need, we'll drive out for a weekend to get my other things."

"You're doing what?" Belle had somehow prepared herself that the two young people may have decided on a sudden engagement after a whirlwind courtship, but she was not even close to being prepared for the very sudden loss of her youngest daughter.

"I'm moving to the city to live with Lucas." Angela said, her voice starting to crack with emotion. Her hand went to Lucas's leg, seeking strength from touching him alone. He covered her hand with his and she grabbed on and held it as if for dear life.

"Angela," Belle almost shouted, "How could you do something this rash and sudden? You barely know this man!"

"I know him, Mom," she said, starting to weep softly, but biting her lip with resolve and continuing. "And I love him. And Lucas loves me." She paused then added, like an afterthought, "It's you that hardly knows me."

Belle came out of her chair then; anger as well as fear crept into her raised voice.

"And how was I to get to know you? You have shut yourself away from everyone in this family since your father died. I have tried all ways to get to know you, to be your friend, your mother, and you never let me in!" Belle was shaking with frustration but she took a breath and continued, "Angela, I can't just stand by and let you ruin your life with this man! I love you."

At her mother's last words, Angela started to cry openly. Lucas squeezed her hand, and then spoke to her, ignoring Belle Griffen. "Angie go and pack your things. Your mother and I need to talk." Lucas did not speak harshly at all but Belle's jaw dropped a little at his words and her eyes widened as her daughter quietly left the room.

Mother started to follow her daughter towards the hall then, as though she'd thought the better of her action, she instead rounded on Lucas, who was still sitting impassively on the couch.

"Talk?" She shouted at him, "We have nothing to say to one another, Mr. Reeves!"

Lucas actually chuckled at that. The last time someone had said Mr. Reeves in Lucas's memory had been on one of those rare occasions when Karl Reeves had visited the boys' school. Lucas looked up at Mrs. Griffen, his face unreadable.

"I believe we have plenty to talk about, Mrs. Griffen." He said with a slight smile. "After all, we both love her. At least we have that much in common to start with."

"Love her?" Belle asked, trying to make a conscious effort to lower her voice. "I have loved her since the moment she was born. I am her mother. I think I know what's best for my daughter!"

Lucas stood up and crossed to the front window, his back to Angela's mother. When he spoke, his voice was still quite low, but had taken on an unmistakably menacing tone.

"I don't think you have a clue who Angela is, Mrs. Griffen." He said, "She's a grown woman, very nearly twenty three years old. She's the one now who decides what's best for Angela, not you."

"And you're the best for her?" Belle questioned querulously. "You're a sometimes employed guitar player who probably has a woman in every town!"

Lucas rounded on Mrs. Griffen then and she stepped backwards a pace then fell back into the easy chair that she had vacated. He took two long strides and stood over her, eyes flashing black in the afternoon light.

"I am in love with your daughter. And she with me." He said, his voice no longer low and infinitely more dangerous. "I make more money in a month than you and Angela put together. I'm sure she's told you, I work for my brother in his business whenever I'm not playing. Guitars are expensive and I do what I have to do! Just as I will do whatever I have to do to make sure that Angela is looked after! Including taking her away from this place which is practically holding her hostage! If you do love your daughter, and I believe you do, then let her go! Do I make myself clear?" He stood unflinching waiting for a response.

Belle, shaking with a combination of fear and anger, nodded wordlessly. Lucas backed off a pace, then turned and went down the hall to Angela's room.

When Lucas and Angela came back out of her room, Belle Griffen was still sitting in the easy chair. She glanced up at the young couple now laden with a duffle bag, one of Angela's old high school back packs and a canvas bag. She also noticed that Angela carried the dolphin stuffed toy that her father had brought her home two weeks before his death and Lucas was toting the flowery bedspread that she herself had sewn for her daughter.

"Mom?" Angela almost whispered.

Belle Griffen stood up and put her arms around her daughter and Angela returned the hug despite her burdens.

"I love you, Angela. Please take care." Her mother managed while holding back her tears, then she added, "Honey, Tuesday is your birthday, please call me. I want to share a bit of it with you."

"I will Mom." Angela promised. "I love you; it's time for me to fly now, is all."

Belle released her hold on Angela and stepped back. She glanced very briefly at Lucas, but said nothing.

"Good night, Mrs. Griffen." he uttered, respectful once again. "I will look after Angela. I do love her."

Lucas and Angela walked back to the big Buick and he stowed her things in the back seat. He helped her into the car, and then went round to the driver's side to climb in. He glanced briefly at the house; Belle Griffin was looking out the front window. Lucas waved but got no response. He climbed in and started the car. Just two blocks from the house, he pulled over to the curb and stopped. He pulled Angela in against him and held her till she had cried herself out. Then, with one arm around his sleeping beauty, he put the car in gear and made for the highway.

Kurt had just finished a beer as the football game reached halftime. He went through to the kitchen, not really sure when Lucas might get back, but he had decided none-the-less to put the roast beef in to start slow cooking. As soon as his brother crossed his mind, he wondered if indeed he would be bringing Angela home with him today. Kurt chuckled wryly to himself, if anyone could bring this apparently perfect woman home, it would be his little brother, he thought.

He had just slid the pan into the oven and reached for a fresh beer when he heard Lucas's car pull up out front. He glanced out the window and his jaw dropped. Lucas had just opened the passenger door on the big car and Angela had stepped out. She was wearing jeans and a baggy sweat shirt, but even dressed down she was simply breathtaking. She had a soft unsophisticated look that combined with her natural beauty to give her a uniquely attractive aura. Looking at his brother standing beside this petite dark haired beauty, he had to admit to himself they made a handsome couple.

Lucas had handed a couple of bags to Angela from the back seat of the car, and then moved to the back of the vehicle to open the trunk. As he was pulling guitars and the amplifier from the trunk, Angela looked around as though trying to get her bearings. Kurt noticed that one of her burdens was a dolphin stuffed toy and he shook his head in wonder, "My God, Lucas, she's like a little girl." He said aloud. He shook his head clear of the image, put his beer can on the counter and went to give them a hand.

"Hey Lucas, welcome home man." He called from the front step. By the time he had crossed the lawn to join them; Lucas had completed the unloading of the car, now the edge of the lawn was littered with duffel bags, an amplifier and two guitars in cases.

"Hey Kurt, glad we are home, for sure." Lucas chuckled, "Right Angie?"

"Yeah Lucas, very glad." she said softly and Kurt couldn't help but notice that her eyes remained downcast where they'd been since he had walked out the front door.

Kurt bent to pick up some of the gear on the lawn. "Let's get this stuff inside, okay." he said. Lucas also grabbed the strat case and the amplifier and both men moved towards the house. Lucas called over his shoulder to Angela.

"Come on, my love. Let's give you the grand tour." Angela followed them inside, giggling nervously. Once inside, Kurt put down the things he'd brought in and wiped his hands on his jeans. He then stuck a hand out towards Angela tentatively.

"Hi," he said, "I'm Kurt. It's nice to meet you, Angie. It's great to have you here."

Angela looked up at Kurt for the first time since her arrival and he was struck again by how very young and innocent she seemed. She shyly put her tiny soft hand into his big rough one and he shook it gravely. Angela managed a very tentative smile as she looked at the big man in front of her. 'It's easy to tell Lucas and Kurt are brothers,' she thought, 'But Kurt is rougher somehow, his features not as chiseled and defined as Lucas.' Though not much taller at all than Lucas, he somehow seemed much bigger.

"Thank you, Kurt," was all Angela managed to say. Her soft tones echoed the shy innocence that Kurt felt surrounded her. Lucas winked at his brother.

"Didn't I tell you, I'd found me an angel?" He asked, grinning broadly.

Kurt shook his head, with an almost identical broad grin. "You sure did Lucas and you sure weren't kidding!" Angela blushed with his words.

Lucas leaned closer to her, giving her a kiss on the cheek and, at the same time, relieving her of some of her burdens. "Come on baby; let's get some of this stuff put away. I should warn you; Sunday's are usually my laundry day round here."

Kurt headed back into the kitchen but called over his shoulder, "I'm getting a beer; what can I get for you two?"

Lucas answered for them both. "I'll have a beer man, thanks. Angie will have a little bit of vodka with some cola."

Angela was still emotionally exhausted from the confrontation with her mother and she followed Lucas through the laundry routine in a bit of a daze. He helped her hang and store her clothing in their room, thinking how wonderful it was to call it 'their room' now. Then, with everything stowed, he kicked the door shut and took her by the hand. They sat side by side on the edge of the bed and he wrapped both arms around her.

"Welcome home baby." He whispered. She cuddled closely to him, but her eyes sought out his and when he saw her apprehension, he stroked her dark hair and started to gently kiss her forehead. "Angie, it is okay baby. You're home with me. It's different than what you're used to but it's gonna be fine. I love you baby." He assured her.

He felt some of the tension start to melt away from her as her caressed her and suddenly he became very aroused wanting her with an unusual sense of urgency. He bent down to her mouth and kissed her deeply. Angela responded to him immediately and Lucas pressed her back onto the bed. She realized, even as she became more aroused by Lucas undressing her, that she could hear the television quite plainly from the other room. Somehow, knowing that Kurt was right within earshot was embarrassing to the point of fear for Angela. Lucas was turned on by the look of passion mixed with a trace of fear in her eyes as he entered her. Their lovemaking was brief but intense.

Afterwards, as they lay comfortably entwined still, he whispered softly in her ear. "Baby, now it's official. Welcome home."

Kurt had cooked them all a wonderful meal and the three of them sat down with big appetites. Angela's spirit was bolstered by the feast of roast beef, roasted potatoes and vegetables all swimming in thick rich gravy. She felt a little out of her league in this bachelor pad and the familiarity of good simple cooking reassured and relaxed her.

Lucas and Kurt talked about the contract Kurt had for them this week. Angela was silent, content to listen to the two men. She sensed that Kurt was very proud of his work and workmanship. That pride showed around the house with a lot of extra touches of woodwork that he had added around doors and windows and also in the cabinet and table that were the main furnishings in the dining room they ate in.

He was softer spoken than Lucas, and his eyes were more hazel than the striking green of his little brother's. Whenever he turned towards Angela, with a comment or question, he noticed she always shyly dropped her eyes before replying. How on earth his little brother had managed to seduce such a timid beauty was beyond him. But he found himself liking her very much. It was clear that she was kind, considerate and very polite. In another time or place, one would have described her as genteel.

"So Angie, what you going to do tomorrow?" Kurt asked. Angela froze, her fork part way to her mouth. She glanced at Lucas and then dropped her eyes to her plate.

"I dunno." she admitted. She hadn't really thought past moving her things out of her mother's house. And now, many thoughts assailed her at once. There was her job she must do something about, where would Lucas be, she knew the men had to go to work, should she look for work; too many things came in at her at once. Lucas took a long swallow of his beer, and then he spoke.

"Take it easy tomorrow baby, sleep in. Then call your boss, with the bad news," at that Lucas chuckled. "Just pamper yourself. Sit on the deck in the sun and read or something."

"Sounds great." Kurt said. "Geez and we gotta work all day!"

Angela blushed and fleetingly met Kurt's eyes. He saw the innocence there mixed with a passion for life and began to understand why Lucas had fallen for this girl in a big way. Angela turned her eyes back to Lucas and smiled at him.

"I will relax for one day, Lucas. But maybe I should be getting a job, paying my way." She told him. "I have some money saved up, but......"

Lucas put a hand out and caressed her arm. "There's plenty of time for that, angel. Kurt and I make good money and the band will be gigging again soon. We'll talk about you working later."

"Alright Lucas." She agreed.

Those first days were very lonely for Angela. The bachelor household was so simple and efficient that there was little for her to do during the day. She read a little and watched TV. Mostly she waited, for the end of the day when Lucas would be home and he would get out the Gibson and play for her. She got used to Kurt being part of their lives but still avoided being alone with him. Kurt wondered at times if the girl was frightened of him.

On Tuesday, Lucas and Kurt had brought a cake home and a bottle of champagne to celebrate her birthday. She made the promised call to her mother which brought a few tears with it. But the enthusiasm of the men was catching and she was soon laughing merrily. Kurt and Lucas both had beer, so Angela ended up drinking nearly the whole bottle of the bubbly liquor by herself. Unused to drinking, she became quite giddy and sat crossed legged on the sofa giggling at nearly everything the men said. Finally, Lucas got up, went to her and practically picked her up bodily. She stumbled into him and put her arms round his neck for support. She was still giggling as he kissed her deeply then swept her up into his arms. He carried her, almost as though she weighed no more than a baby. She clung to his neck, but raised one small hand to wave to Kurt as Lucas went through the doorway towards their room.

Giggling like a schoolgirl, she softly said, "Night Night Kurt."

"G'nite, Angie, Lucas." Kurt replied.

"Night man." Lucas said, laughing deep in his throat, aroused by Angela in her drunken and giddy state.

Behind them, Kurt turned up the television and shut out other sounds.

Three weeks later, Lucas came in one night and dropped an ad for a temporary office service company on the counter in front of her as she stood cutting up vegetables for a salad. She looked at him questioningly.

"I saw that today, babe." He explained. 'It's perfect, you can work just a few days a week, whenever you want. And if I go on the road sometimes, you're free to come along."

She put down the knife carefully and put her arms round his waist. She kissed him lightly on the corner of his mouth.

"You're wonderful." She told him. "I'm getting so bored here in the day time." He hugged her back, stepping close and pressing her back against the counter. He nuzzled her ear with his lips, then found her mouth and kissed her really hard. She opened her mouth for his insistent tongue and he took her breath away. She started to suck on his tongue, knowing he liked that. But she was nervous, worrying that Kurt would walk in at any second. Lucas didn't seem concerned and boldly started to caress her breasts through her t-shirt. He finally broke the kiss but kept her pinned against the counter.

"Bored, hmm?" he laughed lustfully, "I've got a little something to cure your boredom babe." One of his hands had slid down and was caressing her through her jeans and he held her by the back of the neck as he brought his mouth back to hers again. At that moment, the back door opened and Kurt walked into the kitchen. Lucas did release her then, but slowly and Angela had no doubt that Kurt had seen an eyeful. Lucas smiled approvingly as he watched her blush with embarrassment. Perhaps, with some extra money coming in from her working for the temporary service, they should get a place by themselves, she thought.

Kurt was very quiet during dinner that night, but he did give Angela some enthusiastic encouragement about the office temp job. Angela gave him a rare gift of a smile and Kurt felt blessed that this sweet young lady had come to live with them. He just wondered if his little brother knew just what a treasure he'd found in Angela.

The band was back gigging again, but this time in town. Lucas told Angela since she was working during the day most days that she should just stay home while he went to work and maybe come out on a Saturday night to see the show. That seemed to make good sense to Angela but she wasn't sure about being in the house alone with Kurt. The first night as Lucas left, he kissed her long and deep as he was opening the front door.

"Be good, baby," he told her, "I'll be home soon." His words, though lightly spoken seemed to carry a warning for her.

"I'm always good." she said innocently.

"Yah," he laughed suggestively. "You sure are, Angel."

As soon as he was gone, Angela excused herself politely and went to their bedroom. Kurt was a little surprised and disappointed. He felt like it was some- how his doing that Angela was so nervous around him, though he couldn't quite understand why.

Around ten o'clock, Kurt tapped on the bedroom door lightly.

"Angie?" He called softly.

"Yes Kurt?"

"I was just going to make a cup of tea. Would you like some?" he offered.

"No thank you." She answered, "I'm just going to wait for Lucas to get in and make him some tea then. But thank you for asking, Kurt."

He turned back to the kitchen, shaking his head. 'She was always so won- derfully polite and gentle', he thought, 'How would this soft innocent creature survive in the big city?'

That first night established a pattern for Angela. Whenever Lucas was out at night, she spent the evening in their room. She had plenty of books to read and kept herself busy with a little mending and sewing too.

Sometimes, when Lucas got in from a gig, she'd be already asleep curled up under the pretty quilt brought from home. And he came in some nights still high with the adrenalin of sexual energy drawn from the music and the performance. On those nights, he would not be denied. He would wake her, sometimes quite roughly and, growling his love for her, take his satisfaction. He would gently kiss and caress her afterwards, explaining that sometimes it was just the music that got him all riled up. She reasoned that at least he did always come home to her and he never really hurt her, just didn't give her time to enjoy their lovemaking. It seemed a small price to pay for his adoration.

Kurt and Lucas were late home again. Angela paced around the little house, pausing occasionally to glance out the windows. She would get in from wherever her temporary assignment had taken her usually not later than six o'clock and that had ordinarily meant that they were all home about the same time. For the last two weeks now they had been working later each evening. Kurt had said that they had booked too many jobs with short time guarantees and needed extra hours each day to get everything done on schedule. But Angela was worried about how the hours would take a toll on Lucas. Some nights he went straight to his gig without pausing to eat a little dinner.

His stress showed in other ways too. Two nights previously the two of them had been home alone for a change as Kurt had gone to the movies with a friend. She had made him a cup of tea and inadvertently forgot to add sugar. He had hurled the mug across the kitchen where it had smashed against the wall, the shattered pieces went everywhere and tea puddled on the floor.

"Damn it, Angie!" he cursed, "You know I take sugar! What the fuck is that shit?"

She was frozen in shock at the table where she sat and he reached across with one hand and grabbed her wrist, gripping and twisting it so she cried out in pain.

"Pour me another one, don't forget the fucking sugar." he told her, "And you'd better clean up this mess before Kurt gets in or he'll get pissed too."

Angela made him another mug of the tea and cleaned up the shards of broken mug and spilt tea. Lucas had taken his mug through to the living room and picked up the Gibson. When she finished cleaning up, she paused in the doorway and softly told him she was going to bed. He didn't acknowledge her and, tears welling in her eyes, she sought out the comfort of their bed alone.

As she lay there in the dark, she wondered if he was falling out of love with her. That thought led to many fears which assailed her: he had another lover, he thought she was unfaithful, he no longer wanted her. All of these dark thoughts left her feeling trapped and alone. She couldn't go home, not now. Her mother would never take her back. 'Besides,' she thought, 'Even if he doesn't love me anymore, I love him, I always will.'

When Lucas came to bed, he caressed her and kissed her softly, gently, all over, telling her again and again that he loved her and he was so sorry, he'd never meant to get so mad.

"Just bear with me, babe." He begged. "Kurt says we're almost done."

Angela took comfort in the warmth of his strong body next to her and forgave him, secure for the moment in his love once again.

Two weeks after Christmas, the two men finally came home at a reasonable hour from work. Angela was surprised but elated. Both men were strangely buoyant of spirit and kept exchanging winks and knowing looks throughout dinner. Angela looked from one to the other trying to puzzle out the meaning of this new mood. Finally, as they stretched back after eating she could stand the suspense no longer.

"Lucas?" she asked tentatively. "What's going on?"

"Going on, Angie?" he laughed, "What do you mean?" Across the table, Kurt was chuckling too.

"Something's up," she stated simply, then tried again, "Please tell me what you two are up to?"

Both men laughed then. But Lucas also stretched and got up lazily from the table. He trailed a hand up Angie's arm as he stepped round behind her chair. She looked up at him and he was grinning down at her.

"We've got a little surprise for you." He told her, green eyes sparkling. "But first we need to take a little ride in the car."

Angela was puzzled but excited all the same. She immediately got up and made for the closet for shoes and a jacket. Kurt and Lucas were not far behind, but Lucas reached past her and grabbed a scarf from the closet shelf. He waved it in front of her face and told her, "I need to blindfold you, baby. I want you to be completely surprised." She looked at him with a mix of curiosity and fear in her eyes.

"Lucas...." she started. Kurt interjected at that point.

"It's okay, Angie." he said, smiling reassuringly. "We just want you to be surprised. You'll be safe with us, we promise."

"Yeah baby, it's okay." Lucas agreed.

She allowed Lucas to tie the scarf securely around her eyes and then lead her to the car. She heard the back door open behind her as Kurt got in. Lucas slid into the driver's seat and they were off. They didn't drive very far, not more than seven or eight blocks, Angela thought. Lucas pulled over and turned off the engine. He helped her out and, with Kurt bringing up the rear, led her along what was obviously a concrete sidewalk.

"Careful now," he told her, moving very slowly, "There are three steps." Her foot contacted the first step and with his assistance she negotiated them fairly easily. He stopped her there and fumbled in his pocket till she heard some keys rattle. He unlocked and opened a door in front of them, then led her through.

"Are you ready, Angie?" He asked.

"I think so." She replied.

He took off the scarf over her eyes with a flourish and stood back to watch her reaction. The three of them were standing in the living room of a house which was somewhat similar in design to Kurt's, though looking around it seemed a bit bigger. The woodwork in the house was very obviously Kurt Reeves' handiwork. She looked around impressed but still puzzled. Lucas took her hand and led her throughout the house. It was bigger by far; three bedrooms and a small room which Lucas said would make a great office, a large airy kitchen which looked out onto a driveway at the side of the house. Every room bore evidence of the brothers' work, with new kitchen cabinets, built in units in the bedrooms and an exquisite four poster bed in the master suite.

"It's beautiful!" She told them. But was still puzzled why they brought her here. Lucas grinned at Kurt knowingly.

"She doesn't get it yet, man." he said with glee. "Come on, Angel, I have one last room to show you."

He led her down the basement stairs from the kitchen. At the bottom there was a fairly heavy wooden door. When Lucas swung it open, it revealed an interior which had been carefully lined and insulated to be as soundproof as possible. Lucas's two amplifiers and two of his guitars were already in the room. Angela's eyes widened when she saw his gear.

Lucas took both her hands in his, turning to face her directly. Kurt, still behind them leaned up against the doorframe smiling.

"Angela, my love," Lucas said gravely, "Welcome home."

Angela stood speechless for a moment, and then shook her head in disbelief.

"Our home, Lucas?" she asked, and then continued, "But when, how?"

"All ours baby. Kurt and I have been working on fixing it up for a while now. That's why we were late so much." He took her in his arms then and kissed her, slowly waltzing her round him as though listening to a soft slow blues tune. She moved with him, tears of joy in her eyes. Kurt turned and quietly padded back up the stairs to wait for them there.

When they re-emerged from the basement, Angela let go of Lucas's hand and ran to hug Kurt. He returned the embrace with gentlemanly deference and respect.

"Kurt, thank you, thank you." Angela bubbled at him. "I'm so happy, this is so awesome."

"We'll move over here on the weekend, baby." Lucas told her. She was reluctant to leave, as though leaving may make it all disappear. But Lucas grinned and said, "I have one more surprise back at Kurt's, so you'd better come on back."

Angela couldn't imagine what else Lucas could possibly surprise her with after giving them a house of their own. She was quivering with excitement as they made the short trip back. When they got back inside the house, Lucas went into their room and grabbed the Gibson case. He brought the guitar through to the living room and gently lifted it from the case. He took a seat on the edge of an easy chair and Angela sat expectantly on the couch. He fiddled about with the guitar for a moment or two then cursed softly under his breath.

"What's wrong, Lucas?" She asked. He grinned somewhat sheepishly at her.

"I need a pick for this song." He said, "Can you pass me one from in the case there?"

She nodded and reached for the cover which hinged back from the little compartment where she knew he kept picks. When she opened it, she was brought up short. Inside she spied a neat black velvet covered ring box. Lucas, still holding the guitar, was smiling broadly at her.

"You'd best open that girl, it's for you." He whispered.

As she took the box out of the guitar case and started to lift the lid, he put the guitar aside and came over to kneel on the floor beside her. She opened the box and gasped when she saw the beautiful solitaire diamond winking up at her. Lucas gently slid the ring out of the box and took her hand in his.

"Angela, I love you." he told her. "Will you marry me?" His hand holding the ring hovered near her finger, but trembled slightly as he waited for her response.

Angela was already overwhelmed by emotion after the huge surprise of the house and now this seemed to completely dismay her. She started to weep overcome with passion and Lucas wasn't quite sure for once how to cope with her. He got up from the floor and sat next to her, cuddling her in to him.

"Baby, are you okay?" he asked softly. She nodded, despite her tears and somehow managed to get her shaking under control. Finally she was able to speak.

"Yes Lucas, I'm fine." She stated simply. "And yes Lucas Reeves, I will marry you. I love you so very much."

He smiled with a combination of elation and relief. He held her hand gently and slid the ring onto her finger. Angela stared at it for a moment, and then Lucas cupped her chin in his hand and turned her face up to his. Her blue eyes met his green ones briefly before both of them closed their eyes in the rapture of a long and passionate kiss.

Angela cut back on her hours at the temporary service as soon as they got moved over to the new house. She concentrated her efforts on nest building. She sewed pretty new curtains for all the rooms. Lucas and Kurt moved some living room furniture in and Kurt promised that their own dining room furniture would be done very soon. Angela added her own personal touches to each room except the music room/studio downstairs, that was Lucas's sanctuary and she rarely set foot in the door.

Lucas seemed happier and more relaxed now too. Angela thought that it may be because the long hours no longer haunted him, but Lucas told her he was just so relieved that she had said yes when he proposed to her.

Now that he had his little studio, Lucas had some of the guys from Immortal Beat over sometimes to jam and learn new tunes. Angela thought it was fun to listen to them and make sure they all had plenty to eat and drink as they worked. Instead of just watching Lucas play, she finally felt like she was somehow helping and being part of his world.

The only dark spot for Angela had come when two days after she and Lucas had become engaged she had phoned her mother. The two women had spoken only rarely since Angela had come to live with Lucas and those conversations had been consistently uncomfortable. Belle Griffen was still hopeful, each time Angela called, that her daughter had come to her senses and was going to return home. She made no effort to hide her disappointment when Angela told her how wonderfully things were going and she seized every opportunity to make unpleasant comments about Lucas.

So when Angela called to tell her that she was engaged, Belle Griffen was quite cold. Lucas, sitting across the room from Angela, heard only her half of the conversation, but what he did hear made him very angry. Angela's voice sounded almost pleading as she said, "But Mom, I love him." And then, "Mom, please I want you at our wedding." Lucas kept his head down, looking over the tabs for a new song he was working on, but his ears were tuned only to his soon-to-be bride. Angela finished the conversation with a choked sounding, "Goodbye Mom. I love you." She gently hung up the phone and, without a word, picked up the sewing she had put down to place the call.

Lucas wondered, but decided not to press her on what her mother had said. He'd heard enough to know only that Angela had been upset by it and in his mind that was unacceptable. But for now he'd give things time. Angela's mom may just come around. 'In the meantime,' he thought, 'we should start to plan this wedding.'

Angela was glad that both Lucas and Kurt seemed eager to help her to plan the wedding. She had hoped that her mother would be the one to help her, woman-to-woman, but resignedly accepted that was not to be. She had called Pamela too, in a gesture of reconciliation. But her sister had come up with a host of very reasonable sounding excuses as to why she would be unable to traverse the seventy some miles between them and help out her sister with this very special moment in her life. Angela had not kept in touch with Christie and Becky. After leaving so suddenly, she felt bad about leaving them in the lurch at the office and her guilt had made her keep her distance. So she made do with the two men in her life helping her with such as they could and the rest she decided on for herself.

Lucas and Angela both decided that late May, just before summer travel season for the band started, would be a great time for a wedding. The flowers would be blooming and the weather should be good. Angela wanted to get married outdoors.

"In a clearing like our first time." she shyly told Lucas. He beamed at her, remembering too their first night together.

"That'll take a little looking for, unless you want to go back, and get married there." He asked.

"No." She stated emphatically. He raised an eyebrow at her but made no comment.

"There's lots of places we can look, my love." he assured her, "We'll go out driving on Sunday and I'm sure we'll find the perfect spot."

They did find the perfect spot all right, in a shoreline park right on the great bay that the city had been built up around they found a grassy clearing which had a grand old maple tree in the middle of it. The clearing was open on one side to the sandy beach and the bay beyond. They knew without a doubt that this was the place, they would look no further.

Lucas was losing patience with Belle Griffen. 'Doesn't she understand?' he wondered, 'Angie is her daughter and, like me or not, she should be here for her.' He was pacing round the house mid-afternoon alone as Angela was out on a temporary assignment. He took the Gibson up for a while and tried to play but his agitation did not diminish. Finally, he reached for the phone book and dragged the telephone closer to him.

He flipped through the listings for Angela's hometown, looking for the name he barely recalled of the small mortgage and loan where she had worked. Finally, it jumped off the page at him, Delta Valley Mortgage & Loan. His finger impatiently stabbed out the number. The phone was answered after three rings.

"Good afternoon Delta Valley Mortgage, Becky speaking." came the familiar voice and Lucas smiled.

"Hi Becky, this is Lucas Reeves." he said without any further explanation. On the other end of the phone Becky drew in a sudden breath then, as she recovered, she was waving to get Christie's attention.

"Hey Lucas," She greeted him, then her tone changed to concern, "Angie's okay, isn't she?"

"Yeah, Angie's fine Becky," Lucas replied, "We're both doing great. But I know she misses you and Christie a whole lot. That's kind of why I'm calling."

"We miss her too, Lucas." Becky told him and Christie nodded her agreement. "But when she never called after you two left, well...." she trailed off, unsure what to say.

"I know. She felt so bad about leaving you ladies with all the work and stuff." Lucas explained. "We've got big news though and we want you both to come and share it with us. We're getting married."

Lucas pulled the phone away from his ear then as Becky's shriek nearly deafened him. He heard her in the background telling Christie the news excitedly, and she came back on the phone not much calmer, but back with him. "Oh my God, getting married! Lucas, that's so wonderful!" she exclaimed, "Where? When? Have you told Angie's mom and sis yet?"

"Thanks Becky," Lucas responded, "Here, well in a beautiful spot we picked out in a park here, down by the water. Angie talked to her mom and sis, yeah, but they weren't very happy about it."

Becky had talked to Belle Griffen only a few days after Lucas and Angela had left together and knew that she did not like the handsome guitar player, but she was still surprised that Angie's mom had not softened when she had been told that Lucas was going to marry her little girl.

"Oh man, that's too bad." Becky said, by this time Christie was tugging on Becky's sleeve, frantic to get the whole story. "Maybe I can talk to her mom?"

"That would be great, Becky," Lucas told her, "I don't know if it'll help though, cause Mrs. Griffen just don't like me, ya know? But really I'd like you and Christie to come down for our wedding. It's kind of casual, just a few friends but I'd sure like her friends to be here too."

At this point, Christie simply wrestled the phone from Becky's grasp.

"Lucas, this is Christie." She stated shortly. "Not sure if you're just phoning to invite us but we're coming anyway." Lucas was laughing at the other end of the phone as Christie continued. "I'm coming down there this weekend anyway. So if Angie wants some help with a dress and stuff, tell her I'll be there for her. Now give us your number and the date of this big event."

Lucas supplied Christie with the details she wanted and told her that Angie would be overjoyed to see her at the weekend. When he hung up the phone, he had an almost triumphant look on his face. Now at least, his girl had a friend who could shop for her dress with her and do those other feminine things that were way beyond his or Kurt's abilities.

He sat back down with the guitar again, playing contentedly and planning for the coming weekend.

Angela was thrilled when Lucas told her that Christie was coming down for the weekend. She had been putting off shopping for a dress for the wedding because she kept hoping her mother may reconsider and come for a visit. Christie had always been Angela's best pal when it came to shopping for clothes so she knew that they would find the perfect dress together. She wondered, with a chuckle to herself, what Christie would think of some of the outfits that Lucas had helped her pick out; the slinky, sexy things that he liked her to wear when she accompanied him to gigs. 'Well,' she thought, 'I'll see on the weekend.'

Christie telephoned about three o'clock on Friday afternoon, letting Angela know she was in the city and would pick her up the following morning about eleven to go shopping. Angela chattered happily with her old friend for a few moments as Lucas watched her from across the room. When she hung up the phone, he casually commented,

"It's great Christie's going to shop with you Angie. I was getting worried my bride was going to show up in her blue jeans." he chuckled.

"Never, Lucas." she laughed merrily. "But I'm not sure I want the whole traditional fancy gown either. Maybe something sort of old fashioned? Something that looks right for our clearing by the sea?"

"Baby, you're gonna look awesome no matter what you wear." he told her emphatically.

Lucas was up early that Saturday, despite coming in at nearly two in the morning from his gig. Angela was surprised when she woke and he was already out of bed. She pulled on a pair of blue jeans and a t-shirt and went to look for him. In the kitchen, on the counter by the coffee maker, she found a hastily scrawled note.

"Angie, hope you have a great time shopping with Christie today. I'm running some errands of my own. Luv ya babe; Lucas"

Underneath the note was a wad of bills. Angela picked them up and was amazed to count over five hundred dollars. She smiled in wonder at how much he spoiled her.

Even as Angela was making a coffee and deciding what to wear for her shopping trip with Christie, Lucas's big Buick was speeding east along the highway in the direction of her home town. Lucas was smiling to himself as he thought of Angela shopping today. Christie had provided the perfect distraction.

He pulled up in front of the Griffen house at about quarter to twelve. He strode up to the front door and rang the doorbell. It was a minute or two before the door opened and Belle Griffen stared open mouthed at him. She looked past him, expecting her daughter to be there too. That gave Lucas enough time to put a hand out in an open palmed gesture of peace and also slide a foot in the door before he spoke.

"Mrs. Griffen, she's not with me." He answered her unasked question, "You and I need to talk."

Belle Griffen did not take the proffered hand; instead she started to close the door till it was brought up short by Lucas's booted foot.

"I have nothing to say to you, young man." she said haughtily, "Now please leave."

"I have something to say to you, ma'am." Lucas said, trying hard to remain calm. "And since we both love your daughter, you really need to hear me out. Then you can throw me out, if you still wish. Okay?" Lucas waited, hoping that she would at least decide since he'd driven all the way here that it wouldn't hurt to hear what he had to say. She looked at him for a long moment then, as if resigning herself to the inevitable, she swung the door open and stepped back to let him in. Lucas took off his boots just inside the door and then followed her lead through to the kitchen.

Once they were both seated at the table, she finally spoke.

"Well Mr. Reeves, what do you want?"

"I want Angela to be happy." Lucas said quietly. "That's my bottom line. It would mean everything to her to have her mother at our wedding."

"I love my daughter, Mr. Reeves." Belle Griffen told him. "And I will do anything in my power to ensure her happiness. However, I don't believe that marrying you will allow Angela to find happiness. I don't like you at all Mr. Reeves. You manipulated my daughter, took advantage of her lack of sophistication and her innocence to spellbind her and spirit her away. If she insists on marrying you, whether I'm there or not, so be it. But I'm not going to be there to silently condone something I believe in the end will only hurt my little girl."

Lucas looked at Belle Griffen as if for the first time. He hadn't quite expected that strength from her. He was silent for a long time before he spoke again.

"Mrs. Griffen, I don't really give a damn if you like me or not." he finally told her, "I'm not going to even try and prove myself to you, 'cause I know you ain't going to buy it. But I do care very deeply about your daughter. Please reconsider and let's just put aside our differences for one afternoon, for Angie's sake."

Belle chuckled a little then, much to Lucas's surprise. "Lucas," she said, addressing him by his Christian name for the first time, "You are either genuinely in love with my girl or the best damn liar I've ever met."

"What makes you say that, Mrs. Griffen?" He asked, completely baffled by her statement.

"Your eyes," she said quietly, "They are green, clear and honest. Eyes say a lot about a person, Lucas. And I've seen yours say volumes." She paused a long while, but Lucas offered nothing more. Finally Angela's mother spoke once more. "I will come to Angela's wedding, Mr. Reeves. But for her sake, not yours."

Belle rose from the table without another word and with a gesture only, ushered him towards the front door. Lucas followed in her wake, pulled on his boots and paused by the open door. He offered his hand to Mrs. Griffen and this time she took it in a brief hand shake.

"Thank you, Ma'am." he said with a respectful bow of his head. Then he turned and strode back out to his car.

Angela had decided several things while shopping with Christie. First, she decided that she would make her dress as nothing she looked at seemed to fit with their notion of a wedding beneath the maple in the clearing by the bay. Besides, she had bought a sewing machine with money earned from her temporary assignments and this was an opportunity to show Lucas it could do more than make curtains.

She and Christie had chosen an old-fashioned pattern for the dress. The dress would be a mid-calf length afternoon frock with a square neckline and an empire waist very much in the romantic styling of the 1920's. She bought the purest white Chantilly lace for the dress and a platinum coloured silk for the under slip which would accompany it. The effect of the flashy platinum silk shimmering through the fairy princess white Chantilly would be dazzling. Christie and Angela also found ribbon in the same platinum colour and white silk rosettes.

These Angela said she would weave into her long black hair instead of wearing a traditional veil and so keep her romantic theme intact.

The friends had stopped for lunch at a quiet little cafe, where they talked more about Angela's plans. Christie asked a question that hadn't occurred to Angela at all.

"What's Lucas going to wear?" she asked. "Cause, no matter what, he's gorgeous. But..."

"I don't know." Angela confessed. "I never even thought to ask. But Christie I've got another problem."

"What's that, hon?" her friend asked.

"Well, usually a bride has someone give her away, like her dad, you know?" Angela explained self-consciously. "But I don't have anyone like that."

"What about your sister's husband?" Christie suggested.

Angela chuckled wryly at her words. "I'm not even sure if Pamela's coming to the wedding and Brent and I have never been close. I thought about Lucas's brother Kurt, but Lucas has asked him to be best man."

"So what?" Christie told her. "There's no reason why he can't do both. It's unconventional anyway, having it in the park and all. Why can't he walk you there and then stand up for his brother too? I think that would be cool, kinda like their whole family is welcoming you."

"Do you really think so Christie?" Angela asked, but she was already feeling excited about the idea.

"Of course I do silly. It's perfect."

"Well, I'll ask Lucas first." Angela decided, "If he thinks it's okay, then we'll ask Kurt. And I'd better ask Lucas what he's planning on wearing too. Or he may turn up in a t-shirt and jeans." She finished with a chuckle. Christie laughed with her and then, as they turned serious once more, she asked a question that Angela had been anticipating but dreading a little none-the-less.

"So what about a bridesmaid?"

"Christie, I... umm..." Angela stammered.

"It's okay." Christie said with a grin. "I know you want to ask Becky not me, right?" When Angela merely nodded Christie continued. "I understand. You and I are pals. But you and Becky really know one another. I know you shared a lot more about Lucas and stuff with her. That's okay. I'm happy just to be your wedding consultant."

"Oh Christie, thank you so very much for understanding." Angela breathed with relief. "You are a good pal for sure."

That evening before they left together for Lucas's gig, Angela was sitting on the edge of the bed brushing her long dark hair. Lucas was just pulling on a fresh pair of denims.

"Lucas?" she ventured shyly.

"What baby?" He asked softly. He had been in a very relaxed mood ever since he got home from his own mysterious errand running trip.

"I'm going to need someone to 'give me away' like Daddy would have, you know?" She told him.

"Oh baby, don't worry 'bout that. I know your family's not being too cool." He intentionally made no mention of the conversation he'd had that day with Belle Griffen, knowing that Belle would not reveal it either. "Do you have any ideas who you would like to do that?"

"Well," she said hesitantly. He came and sat beside her on the bed, putting one strong arm round her shoulders and turning her face up to his.

"You do have someone in mind, don't you?" He chuckled. "Better tell me." He was being so light hearted that Angela couldn't help but smile too.

"Well, umm... Lucas, I thought maybe Kurt could walk me to the clearing and then stand up for you as best man? Do you think that might be okay?" She asked.

"I think that would be awesome." Lucas told her. "You can ask him tomorrow. I invited him for dinner." He took her in a firmer grasp and bent to her mouth for a long and passionate kiss. When he finally broke the contact, she was out of breath.

"Mm hmmm, you taste good today, baby." He chuckled. "We'd better get going. Or I may not be able to keep my hands off you."

She stood up and put her brush away, then turned back to him with her other question.

"Lucas what are you going to wear?" She asked.

He was taken aback by the question. It was true that he'd thought about not much else but marrying Angela ever since she'd accepted his proposal, but what he would wear for the occasion had not crossed his mind.

"Um, I don't know." He said. "Do I have to put on a suit for you?"

Angela almost laughed out loud when she heard that. "It might be nice." she told him. "But no, you don't absolutely have to wear a suit, because I know you wouldn't feel comfortable."

He was relieved to hear her say that. He thought a moment and then an idea came to him. 'But would she like it?' he wondered.

"Angie, I've got a pair of black leather pants that go with my black leather bomber jacket. You know the one?" She nodded and he continued. "That'd be kind of like a suit, wouldn't it?"

At first she was inclined to tell him, absolutely not. But the more she thought about it, the more she liked the idea. 'I'll have to go back and get some more of the platinum fabric,' she told herself, an idea formulating in her head. To Lucas, she said, "Yes darling, I love you in black leather."

Kurt had brought a case of beer and a bottle of wine with him when he came for dinner the next afternoon. He and Lucas each had two beers prior to eating while watching TV. Angela let Kurt open the wine for her, but she sipped very slowly on her first glass as she put the finishing touches on the meal.

All through dinner the three young people chatted quite merrily but although Angela tried to give Lucas several hints and openings to bring up her request to Kurt about 'giving her away', he didn't seem to notice. She sipped quietly on her second glass of wine, while pondering and worrying over how to ask Kurt herself. Just as they were finishing up dinner the phone rang.

Lucas went into the other room to answer it and Angela gathered from what she heard that it was one of the other members of Immortal Beat so the conversation may be long.

She started to clear off the table. Kurt got up and gave her a hand to take all the dishes to the counter. When she went to put her empty wine glass into the sink, he placed a hand over hers and stopped her short. She looked up at him, questioningly.

"Don't put the glass in the sink yet." He said smiling, "There's plenty more. Let me pour you another glass."

"Sorry Kurt," she murmured. "I was going to do the dishes." He gently wrested the glass from her grasp and filled it again. As he did so he spoke.

"Nothing to be sorry for Ange." He assured her. "Leave the dishes; I'll help with them later. Come sit down and relax."

She reluctantly left the mess on the counter and sat back onto her chair, taking the full wine glass from him without meeting his gaze. She knew there was no better time to ask Kurt than right now, but was still reluctant. She feared he would not understand and would just tell her no.

"How are your wedding plans coming along, Angie?" He asked. She took a small sip of her wine before answering.

"It's going fine, I guess." She told him. "I got fabric to make my dress yesterday and I'm going to make Lucas a little surprise too."

"That's great." Kurt said, grinning at her. "You're going to make a beautiful bride."

"Yeah, well everyone says that." Angie said, though Kurt could see her blushing a little at his words. "I kind of have a favour to ask you, though."

"Anything for you," he stated, "You've made my little brother happier than I've ever seen him. For that I would bring you the world on a platter if you asked for it." Angela blushed even more at those words.

"Well, you know it's kinda traditional for the bride's father to 'give her away'?" she asked, and Kurt nodded in reply. "And...Well... I don't have a dad to give me away." Her words started to come out in a rush and she felt like someone else was saying them. "I was wondering if you would.... could... well maybe... oh Kurt, you know what I mean." He smiled at her as warmly as he could.

"You know Angie, I really don't bite, hon." He said as lightly as possible. "It would be an honour to accompany you as you come to marry my little brother. Thank you for asking me."

Angela lay awake in the early morning of the day before her wedding. Lucas was sleeping peacefully beside her and she snuggled closer to his warmth. Her mind was busy ticking off a list of everything for the next day, worrying that she'd missed something. A lot of Lucas's musician friends had told him they were coming to the park for the ceremony, so she knew there would be a crowd there which made her a little nervous. She didn't know very many of his friends yet, except the few who'd been to the house to jam, were they coming just to check her out, she wondered.

Her mother and Pamela were coming. She had been completely taken aback when her mother had called earlier in the week to say that the two of them were driving down to be with her. Angela had thanked her mother warmly and, at Lucas's urging, suggested that both she and Pamela stay here at the house for Friday and Saturday evening.

Lucas would be going to Kurt's later on Friday, in keeping with the tradition of not seeing the bride on the night before the wedding and their wedding night surprise from Kurt had been an exclusive suite in one of the city's elegant hotels. Belle Griffen had, surprisingly, accepted her daughter's offer of hospitality for the two evenings. 'Perhaps she's just nosey about where Lucas and I live.' Angela thought unkindly.

The flowers had been picked out and she had made sure that a corsage was added for her mother. Angela would be carrying a dozen long stemmed white roses held together by platinum ribbon. Becky, who was wearing a sky blue lace dress in similar styling to Angela's Chantilly gown, would carry a lesser number of pale yellow roses. Kurt was wearing his navy suit so Angela had ordered him a white rose boutonniere, but Lucas, in his leather jacket, would not wear a flower.

Angela's surprise yesterday for Lucas had been the platinum shirt she had made for him to wear underneath the black leather. It was a simple round necked shirt, not unlike a t-shirt but made a handsome contrast to the black leather and, though she had not yet told him, would match perfectly the platinum silk in her dress. When he had tried it on, all she could say was, "Now you look like the image of a rock star." He had grinned mischievously at her and asked if she was only marrying him because he was such a big star. She blushed in that innocent way that he adored and he pulled her into a warm hug, where they had held each other for a long time.

Lucas stirred beside her and rolled over, sliding one arm round her shoulders.

"Morning, my love." he whispered. She turned towards him and he pulled her closer, at the same time starting to cover her forehead and face in tiny kisses. Her arms were caught up between them and her fingers traced soft trails all over his chest.

"Morning Lucas," she whispered back, "I love you."

"Love you too, Angel." He murmured between the kisses. "Baby, can I ask you something?"

He sounded so serious all of a sudden that Angela's fingers stopped in their tracks and her eyes, which were half closed in passion, reopened to peer at him.

"Anything, Lucas." She said softly.

"You are happy, aren't you?" He asked, "I mean, to be marrying me and well, happier now that your Mom's coming and all?" All of a sudden, he looked like a scared little boy. It was the first time that Angela remembered seeing him some-what unsure of himself, since the night he'd proposed and she had cried.

"Lucas, I love you," she told him again. "You've made me the happiest girl ever." He seemed to relax then and they spent another two hours of the morning playing and making love gently in bed. Finally, when it was almost lunch time, he made a move towards getting up and dressed.

"That, my love, will have to last the both of us till tomorrow night." he told her as he pulled on his jeans. "Let's go and make some brunch. Then I'd better get out of here before your Mom and Sis arrive."

Lucas left for Kurt's just after they finished lunch, taking his clothes for the next day and his Gibson with him. At the door, he took her in one strong arm and gave her a prolonged and passionate kiss.

"Till tomorrow my love." He said and without glancing back, he left.

Christie and her boyfriend dropped Becky off just a few minutes after Lucas had left. After giving Becky a quick tour of the house and showing her the spare room with the pull-out couch where she would be staying, the two young women settled at the kitchen table with cups of tea. Becky looked round the airy kitchen, and then grinned at Angela.

"Pretty nice little house, Angie." She complimented.

"Thanks Becky." Angela replied.

"You know," Becky said, "If someone had told me a year ago that you would be the first of us three to get married, I'd have told them that they were crazy! And wow, just look at you!" Angela grinned broadly.

"Becky, he's so wonderful. I love him so much." She breathed. "Just wish my Mom would try to understand that."

"Maybe she is trying, Angie." Becky suggested. "Just give her a bit more time."

At that moment, as though on cue, they heard a car door outside. Both Becky and Angela went to the door to greet Belle Griffin and her older daughter.

Belle said very little to her daughter about the house, but Angela thought that she seemed rather pleasantly surprised. The four women kept the afternoon light and enjoyable with mostly small talk and last minute plans. Angela had planned a simple supper with salad, rice and chicken breasts. All four pitched in to clean up afterwards.

The early evening found them all watching TV, but Angela was increasingly restless. She missed Lucas and the sound of his guitar in the house. She kept reminding herself it was just one night, but the distraction of the television and her guests was not sufficient to keep her mind off her handsome guitar player. She got up and slipped quietly out of the room.

She stood for a moment in the kitchen and then, as if drawn like a moth to a flame, she opened the basement door and went down the stairs to his music room. Angela was always very careful around Lucas's guitars, worried that her inexperience with the instruments may in some way cause an accident. But tonight, they seemed the only connection left for her to keep him somehow close till tomorrow. She carefully opened the case of the Fender Stratocaster, the first guitar she'd ever seen him play, and lifted the instrument out. She settled onto a low stool in the middle of the room holding the guitar much as though she was going to play it.

"I miss you, Lucas." she breathed, gently passing her fingertips over the strings. Belle Griffen was standing in the doorway watching her daughter.

"Are you learning to play, Angela?" Her mother's voice startled her and she let out a little shriek. She had been so engrossed in her own thoughts that she had not heard Belle come down the stairs.

"No Mom." she replied. Mrs. Griffen stepped into the room as Angela spoke. "It just makes me feel closer to him to hold it, that's all."

Belle Griffen drew up another of the low stools and sat facing her daughter. "I understand." She told Angela gravely. "I go into your old room at home sometimes and pick up one of your cushions and just hold it."

""Oh Mom." Angela softly groaned. "Don't be too mad at me about this. I love him. He's doing right by me, this house, our life...." She trailed off, unsure what else to say.

"I have no doubt that you love him, darling." Belle told her. "And I hope this all works out and he proves me very wrong. But, and I'd be a liar if I told you otherwise, I don't like Lucas very much. But, I'm not the one who's marrying him, you are. I love you Angela and wish you nothing but the best."

"Mom, I love you too. Thank you so much for coming." Angela felt her tears start to tumble down her cheeks. "It means so much to me that you are here."

"I'm tired, Angela." Her mother told her, "I'm going to turn in now. Tomorrow is your special day. We will speak of this no more." She rose from the stool and gave her daughter a kiss on the cheek. "Goodnight darling, I love you."

"Goodnight Mom." Angela said softly as the older woman left the room. She remained motionless on the stool, guitar clutched in her hands for several minutes before relinquishing her hold on it. She put the Strat carefully away and climbed the stairs to her own empty bed.

Angela was shaking like a leaf as they climbed out of her mother's car in the parking lot near the pathway to the beach and the clearing where Lucas was already waiting. Kurt, who was standing by Lucas's old Buick waiting to walk her to her wedding, drew in an awestruck breath when he first saw her. From head to toe, Angela was a vision of loveliness. The ribbons and rosettes contrasted perfectly with her shiny waterfall of black hair. The Chantilly lace with the platinum winking beneath gave one the impression she was shimmering.

Her mother and Pamela went on ahead to join the others. Becky, Angela and Kurt waited by the cars for a few minutes to give them sufficient time to get to the clearing. Then it was time, and Becky set off along the beach pathway about twenty five feet ahead of Angela.

Kurt held his arm out and Angela slid hers into the crook of his elbow. He leaned down towards her and whispered in her ear,

"Angela you are the most beautiful vision I have ever seen." He told her, "If you weren't marrying my brother, I'd be proposing to you myself." He chuckled softly and Angela blushed but managed to smile back too.

There were a lot of people in the clearing, under the steadfast boughs of the maple tree, but Angela had eyes only for Lucas. Looking every bit the dashing but somewhat dangerous rebel in his leathers, Lucas waited green eyes flashing with delight as he first saw her. Kurt walked her slowly down the aisle that people had naturally cleared through the throng when they saw her approaching.

The outdoor setting was close to perfect. There were spring and early summer blossoms showing through the grass here and there and birds could be heard singing in the woods around them. The sun was high and the water behind them a beautiful blue. Angela still barely noticed her surroundings at all. Her eyes had locked with Lucas's green ones and even if Kurt had not been beside her, she would have been propelled towards them without hesitation. Kurt stopped in front of his younger brother and gently lifted Angela's hand, placing it into Lucas's outstretched palm. He backed up a step and then came to stand beside his brother.

Lucas and Angela turned as one towards the Justice of the Peace who was to perform their ceremony.

It was a beautiful though short ceremony, mostly traditional, as that was one thing that Angela was quite sure about. But the young couple had also prepared short vows to be spoken to each other in addition to the service lead by the JP. Angela went first, her nervousness showing in her voice, but all the same the hush in the clearing allowed people to hear her quite plainly.

"Lucas Reeves, I love you. You are my strength, my life, my safe haven, my tall strong maple tree. You know my heart and my soul and you love me completely. I give you the only gift that is mine to give today. My love is yours as I become your wife."

She felt the tears of emotion which came unbidden as she finished speaking and looking at Lucas, realized that he was weeping too. Her heart pounded in her ears and, watching her, Kurt wondered for a moment if she might faint, but she remained quite still. Kurt reached to one of the musicians behind him, who had been holding Lucas's Gibson at the ready. The instrument was quickly passed to Lucas.

As his bride watched and listened, Lucas sang soft words of his love and passion for the angel he had been blessed with this day. The song was short but still the most beautiful thing that Angela had ever heard. Even Belle Griffen was moved by the pure emotion of the musical gift that Lucas shared with Angela and the throng. When the last chord faded, the guitar was passed back to Kurt and the JP took over once again.

"Ladies and Gentlemen, may I present, Mr. and Mrs. Lucas Reeves." He said solemnly, and then added. "You may kiss the bride."

Lucas and Angela each took one step towards one another and his strong arms wrapped her fragile figure, pulling her close to him. They kissed with an almost hesitant touch, as though it were a first kiss. Everyone in the party burst into spontaneous applause.

It was a merry group that strolled back towards the cars from the clearing by the sea. Lucas and Angela, arm in arm, led the way. They were followed closely by Kurt, now with Becky on his arm. Belle Griffen leaned close to her older daughter and cynically whispered, "Well, I'll give him this much, he is a good performer. This has been quite the show." Pamela looked at her mother in surprise but said nothing.

Lucas had made a reservation for Kurt, Becky, Christie and her boyfriend, Mrs. Griffen and Pamela, as well as Angela and himself to have dinner at a fine restaurant that evening. At the parking lot, they said good-byes and received the well wishes of many of Lucas's friends and colleagues, with a promise to see many of them later in the evening at their favourite blues bar. "We'll jam a little, hey Angel?" Lucas laughed.

Angela, much more relaxed now that the service was over, grinned up at her husband. Sure will, Lucas; For a little while anyway. That brought a lot of laughter and few rather risqué comments from the group. Angela blushed. Lucas helped her into the back seat of the Buick then slid in to join her. Kurt had already helped Becky into the front seat and he slid in himself and started the engine.

Angela melted into Lucas's arms in the car as he rained soft kisses on her forehead and cheeks. Kurt took a long circuit of the park's main drive before turning into city traffic, but the scenery was lost on the young couple in the back seat, who saw only each other.

At dinner, Kurt Reeves found himself seated between the vivacious Becky, who was chattering with excitement almost nonstop, and Belle Griffen, who was mostly silent. He was making every effort to be patient with Becky and eventually she did calm down some when the main course, prime rib, was served. Belle Griffen was quite impressed with how gracious the young man was in the face of Becky's over-enthusiasm. She looked from one brother to the other wondering a little at how different they seemed. 'Though,' she admitted to herself, 'My girls are very different people too.'

She pondered for some time before deciding to try and draw the older Reeves into conversation.

"Kurt, Angela told me you have your own business?" she ventured. Kurt turned towards her, looking almost grateful to her for taking his attention from Becky.

"Yes ma'am." Kurt told her, "Actually it's partly Lucas's business, but he's only a part time employee and silent partner, because he's got his music too."

Belle let that sink in a moment, before she responded. "Yes, his music." she said with a hint of contempt in her tone. "He may be more successful if he concentrated on real work like you." She was talking sufficiently in an undertone so that only Kurt could hear her words. He glanced surreptitiously at his brother and noticed that Lucas and Angela were both quite distracted by each other, and then he turned back to Mrs. Griffen.

"Depends on how you measure success, ma'am." He told her in a whisper. "Lucas is an amazing guitar player and, more importantly, he loves the music. You realize he wrote that piece he sang for Angie at the wedding?"

"Yes, Angela made that very clear." Belle conceded. "However Kurt, it's been my observation that even the most talented of musicians don't usually make a decent living at the game and he's got responsibilities now. I hope some of your work ethic, manners and self-control rub off on him."

Kurt was stunned by her rapid fire assessment of Lucas, partially because he knew the two of them had not seen a lot of each other but mainly because of the very frank and open way she delivered her judgment. He took some time to cut and eat a piece of the succulent prime rib on his plate before he replied.

"Lucas and I are very different people, Mrs. Griffen." Kurt told her, his tone still soft but with an underlying firmness that Belle couldn't misinterpret. Kurt Reeves had a fierce and admirable loyalty to his younger sibling. "He has the sensitivity of an artist and sometimes that shows in his quick temper or over enthusiasm. But, I can tell you that your daughter has had an amazing effect on him. I do not doubt for a moment that Lucas loves Angela very much. I believe they will be good for each other."

"I'm sorry, Kurt." Belle told him contritely, "I am a mother and my first instinct is to protect my girls. I most sincerely hope that you are correct." She took a short sip of her wine, and then held her glass up in front of her. She spoke in a stronger voice, addressing the whole table. "Angela, and Lucas, may you both find the happiness you so clearly share this evening is a lasting and strengthening part of your lives, always."

Everyone clinked glasses amidst merry cries of 'hear hear' and 'amen'. Lucas raised his own glass back towards Mrs. Griffen and, with a big grin, he toasted his new mother-in-law.

"Mrs. Griffen, thank you," he said, "First, for being here, because it means a lot to both Angie and I, and second, and most importantly, for raising this wonderful and special angel who is now miraculously my wife."

The rest of dinner passed in much the same pleasant way. Angela had had very little of the wine that they had ordered with dinner, not wanting a repeat performance of her birthday of giddy drunkenness. She was gratified that her mother and Lucas seemed to have at least made peace for today and wondered if perhaps it was something that Kurt and her mother had discussed. Their heads-down discussion had not escaped her observant eyes.

When dinner was over, Belle and Pamela excused themselves to go back to Lucas and Angela's house for the night. They intended to drive back home quite early in the morning. Belle gave her younger daughter a long hug that both women only reluctantly broke off.

"I love you, Angela." her mother said, "We won't see you tomorrow because we're leaving quite early. Be happy, sweetheart."

Angela had been down to Lucas's favourite blues bar, Louis' Blues, with him before and even watched him jam with various friends there. But that had been on a regular evening when the place was filled mainly with blues fans not musicians and, of course, she had not been resplendent in a white and platinum gown. When Lucas and she led their party of six into the bar, the whole room seemed to explode into spontaneous applause. Lucas was in his element but Angela almost felt like she wanted to hide behind him.

The guitar player in the small combo on stage waved the rest of the band quiet for a moment, and then he took the mike made a short announcement.

"Hey everyone, a good friend of ours, and it sounds like yours too, just walked in the door. This great looking couple down here in front of me is none other than Lucas Reeves and his new bride, Angela! Come on up here Lucas and let them all see ya!" He said. Lucas, with one arm round Angela's waist, stepped up onto the low stage, taking her with him. Everyone in the place was cheering and applauding. Angela clung to Lucas and felt herself flushing with a combination of embarrassment and excitement. Lucas took the mike and just had a couple of words for his colleagues.

"Hey, thanks all." He said, "Let's party, okay?" The room exploded in laughter, shouts and whistles. Over the din, Lucas had a hurried talk with the guitar player and released his grasp on Angela long enough to take the guitar from his friend's hands. He adjusted the strap and turned to the bass player, drummer and keyboard player, asking if they all knew Close to You. He strummed a couple of tentative chords till he was comfortable that he had a feel for the unfamiliar instrument, and then he counted the players into the number. When he turned back to the mike, he winked at Angela. She knew the song immediately and fell into place beside him as they moved together in the familiar rhythm, replaying their dance together which they had not done since the previous summer.

After the one number, Lucas turned the guitar back to his friend and led Angela to the table that the other four young people had settled in. Kurt had already bought a round of drinks for them all and they settled in, laughing and chattering merrily. Many well-wishers dropped by the table over the next couple of hours and Angela began to feel like she and Lucas were holding court. But the music was wonderful and it was nice for a change to enjoy it with him by her side instead of on stage.

Angela started to tire after a long and emotional day. Her sleepiness was making her feel cold and she shivered noticeably. She gently tugged on Lucas's sleeve and he inclined his head towards her, to better hear her tiny voice over the music and chatter of the bar.

"Lucas, I'm cold," she said apologetically, "And a little tired." He ran a palm along the length of her bare arm and she trembled with cold and excitement both. He chuckled lustfully and breathed softly in her ear as he spoke.

"Baby, you got goose bumps." he told her, "But you're blushing and all hot. Hmmm, cold or hot? Which is it you little vixen?" He teased.

His hot breath in her ear made her all the more aware of her longing to be alone with her husband. And as she thought it, the realization that he was her husband seemed to suddenly overwhelm her. She turned her face up towards his and his mouth covered hers almost instantly. He kissed her long and deeply and, for a moment, the bar and all the noise and people around them seemed to disappear. When he finally broke the contact, she shuddered again. He slid out of his leather jacket and placed it around her shoulders, then turned to Kurt.

"Hey man, would you mind giving us a ride over to the hotel?" He asked. Kurt grinned in response and held up the keys to his brother.

"You okay to drive, little bro?" he asked. "Cause my truck's out back too. So I'll take Becky back to the house in that."

"Yeah man, I haven't had much at all." Lucas said quite soberly. Kurt grinned and dropped the keys into Lucas's hand. Lucas helped Angela up and, to the accompaniment of more good wishes, they headed for the door.

Kurt had looked after everything at the hotel, remembering champagne and a tall vase filled with three dozen long stemmed white roses. Beautifully scented candles were lit by the bellman when he showed them to the suite and a silver platter with chocolate sauce, strawberries and whipped cream was placed on a low table. The suite had a large oval shaped Jacuzzi tub which was filled already with scented, steaming water bubbling invitingly.

As soon as the door had closed behind the bellman, Lucas turned to Angela pulling his bride to him. Both his hands started in her hair at the top of her head and traced their way down her cheeks, cupping her face briefly for a gentle but passionate kiss.

"I am the luckiest man alive." Lucas murmured.

"Lucas, I love you." Angela whispered, "I'm married!" she breathed in surprise. He stepped back, holding her at arm's length. He regarded her with his piercing green eyes. She blushed under his gaze.

"Yes my love, you're married." he said softly, "Not having second thoughts now, are you?" Angela squeezed his hands with hers and he squeezed her back in answer.

"No regrets," she murmured, "I just can't believe, with all the pretty girls in the world, you chose me."

He took her by one hand then, and led her across the room. He paused by the low table and gently fed her a strawberry dipped in the chocolate sauce. As she reached with her open mouth and tongue to take the last bite, he slid it into her mouth along with his index finger. She held on to his finger between her lips, sucking gently. His other hand was fumbling with the zipper at the back of her dress as he whispered in her ear.

"You are the most beautiful girl in the world, baby." He told her, as he slowly started to undress her. "I had no choice. I love you."

She trembled with relief and arousal. His lips followed his hands as he undressed her, gently kissing and tasting her as he uncovered her. When he slipped her bra off, he cupped her breasts in his hands and brought his mouth down on one nipple, sucking and licking gently. Angela felt her knees go weak and her arms went round his waist for support. She moaned softly.

Lucas brought his mouth back to hers and stretched one hand down across her belly to caress her through her panties. She was tugging at his shirt, trying to pull it from his leather pants. Finally, she daringly undid his belt buckle and the button of his pants. The shirt now came away in her grasp and Lucas smiled at how bold his shy angel had become this night. They undressed one another now and slowly made their way to the bed, for the moment forgetting champagne, strawberries or Jacuzzi. When her knees came in contact with the bed, he pushed her gently back onto it. She sprawled back across the satiny soft quilt and he gently crawled alongside her. He slid one hand down and caressed her lightly till her legs slid open for him. Then, bending to kiss her deeply again, he moved over her and she felt her husband enter her for the first time. She moved with him, their passion soaring and somehow, for Angela, it was different because she was his wife.

Immortal Beat started its summer season of small town gigs in the week following the wedding. Angela told her temporary office service company that she would not be available again until the fall. She and Lucas would travel together each week to the different spots where the band was playing and, as he put it, 'make it a summer long honeymoon.' Angela was thrilled. She hadn't been out to see him play as often while they'd been at home all winter and she was looking forward to watching Lucas working at what he loved so very much.

Their weeks fell into a routine of being away late in the week either Wednesday or Thursday until Sunday. Angela loved Sunday's because instead of driving straight to their home, Lucas got in the habit of stopping off at Kurt's for Sunday dinner, just like Sundays before he met Angela. They would visit with Kurt and Lucas would hear about what Kurt had in store for them in the way of work.

Monday was now laundry day, as Angela would look after that chore while Lucas was out with Kurt. It was her only major chore during their breaks from the gigs, so Angela became an avid reader and spent a lot of time at the library about a mile from the house. On the way there she passed a colourful but tiny park which was resplendent in a myriad of flowers in every possible hue. There were a couple of benches in the little park and one in particular, under the boughs of a beautiful maple, became Angela's favourite spot to spend some time in the fresh air with a book in her hands.

As she sat there one afternoon looking up through the dappled green towards the crystal blue of the sky, she thought about her home and her Mom. They had spoken only once on the phone since the wedding, when Angela had called to thank her mother for the cheque she had given them for a wedding gift. The phone call had been very stilted and uncomfortable which had quite surprised Angela. She had thought her mother's change of heart about attending the wedding had meant she was starting to warm a little towards Lucas. But now her mother seemed reluctant to talk and finally had simply said, "Look Angie, I'm really busy. You've made your choice; I think you'd best be making your own life."

Angela had been absolutely devastated. She kept the conversation from Lucas and tried to put it out of her mind. But sitting beneath the maple and letting her childhood memories flood back, she couldn't help but wonder about her mother's statement and the frightening finality of it. 'Perhaps,' she thought, 'it was not really Lucas at all, but herself that her mother was not very happy with.' She was pulled abruptly from her thoughts by the shattering squeal of an ambulance siren as it raced by on the road adjacent to the park. She gathered her bag of books and her purse and headed for home.

The middle of July found Lucas and Angela at a gig in a town only a matter of twenty miles from Angela's hometown. Lucas offered, their second morning there, to drive over to visit her mother. Angela shrugged as nonchalantly as possible and made the excuse that her mother would be at work so there was no point. Lucas didn't press the point, but instead drove them to a small lake nearby where they played in the sand and splashed in the water like a couple of children. The afternoon left them both relaxed for the evening's gig.

Though Immortal Beat hadn't changed their sets too much over the winter, they had changed keyboard players and the new man had brought a few new tunes to the mix. Lucas was still incorporating Angela and the song Close to You into the set at least once in every place they played. They all sometimes laughed that he only married her so she could continue to fulfill her role in the act.

The rest of each evening though, she had become unofficial den mother for all four men in the group. She was the one who sat at their table and made sure just before the end of a set that drinks for everyone were ordered. Once they discovered that she carried a small sewing kit with her, she was often called on to sew on buttons or mend a torn seam for one or the other of them. She enjoyed feeling useful in some way even though Lucas teased her about being 'seamstress for the band' like the Elton John song, Tiny Dancer. She never danced, except for rocking away in her seat and she rarely drank anything stronger than cola.

One evening, the club they were playing was very crowded. Their table was a little back from the stage, but she could still see well enough. There were enough drinks and cigarette packs littering the table top that it appeared quite obvious that Angela was not alone. However, despite all the signs, to Angela's surprise and discomfort, part way through the second set a man came and sat down beside her. He was somewhat older than either Angela or Lucas; in fact, she judged he was probably in his early thirties. He looked her up and down quite boldly and raised his glass to her. She shyly dropped her eyes. He shouted a greeting over the sound of the band but she never caught the name.

He didn't attempt any further conversation even in the lull between one number and the next, but every time Angela cast a glance his way, he was staring openly at her. Finally, just as Lucas had finished a pretty slow blues that was one of Angela's favourites, the man next to her spoke again.

"He plays pretty damn good." he said, sounding almost surprised. Angela smiled to herself proudly, 'That's my man he's saying that about.' she thought.

Out loud, she replied, "Yes, he's the greatest."

The stranger grinned at her, again openly staring and making her shift uncomfortably in her chair. Lucas, from the stage, could see the man who had joined his wife and was distractedly keeping his eyes in her direction. As a result, he missed a lead in that the keyboard player had given him. Angela started in her chair immediately, knowing the songs so well by now that she realized something was amiss. The stranger watched her as she watched Lucas and slowly sipped his drink.

The next song in the set was a popular rock number by Aerosmith, Walk This Way. The stranger leaned very close to Angela, putting an overly familiar hand on her forearm. She shrank a little away from him, but he just smiled broadly and half shouted, "Hey girl, I only wanted to dance with you."

"I'm sorry, but no thank you." Angela told him.

"What's the matter?" He asked, with a grin, "Don't you dance? Or are you his groupie or something?" He finished with a sneer, nodding in Lucas's direction.

She wanted to tell him she was Lucas's wife but hesitated, not wanting to either shout at him or cause a scene. She was conscious of his knee resting right against her thigh. 'Perhaps if I give him just one dance he'll be satisfied, then Lucas will be done this set and he'll know how to handle this' she thought. She managed a little smile at the stranger and then said, "Yes I dance, but only one dance though."

He took her hand and led her onto the floor. On stage, Lucas Reeves watched as Angela found herself suddenly wrapped in the arms of another man. Angela was overwhelmed, Lucas was angry. The stranger had wrapped her in his arms almost the minute they stepped onto the floor and she could not extricate herself at all. He pressed his body insistently against hers and she could feel his arousal. She wanted to scream for Lucas, but bit her lower lip instead and prayed for the song to end quickly. Because of her inexperience, she had no idea how to defend herself against this kind of predator. When Lucas played the final chords of the number, he was already removing the guitar strap and placing the instrument on its stand. He left the stage abruptly, leaving the bass player to cover for him and announce the set break.

By the time Lucas had reached the table, the stranger had melted into the crowd. He turned on Angela, eyes suddenly black as midnight. She didn't seem to notice his black look at first and smiled in happy relief that he was there to rescue her. He reached down, taking her wrist in an iron grasp and pulled her to her feet.

"We need to talk!" He fired at her.

"Ow! Lucas you're hurting me." she cried. He ignored her and half-walked half-dragged her across the room and out into the parking lot beyond. He said nothing at all until they were down at the end of the lot where the band's vehicles were parked.

He turned to face her as they stood between the Buick and the keyboard player's van. She had her back to the larger vehicle. He put both his hands on her shoulders and pushed her roughly up against the van. She cried out more in surprise than pain as she had only been a mere inch or so from the vehicle.

"What the hell was all that about?" Lucas growled at her. "That fucking jerk was practically doing you on the dance floor."

Angela stared in fear at her husband. "Oh god, Lucas, he scared me so much."

Lucas brought his right hand back and swung it at her then. Angela was totally unprepared for the smack and his palm caught her full across her left cheek. She was stunned by his blow and could only stand shaking and weeping uncontrollably. Lucas turned his back on her and stood with both hands at his sides, fists clenching and unclenching. If she could have seen his face, she may not have recognized it as it was so twisted with anger and fear. At last, he seemed to calm down and turned slowly back to her.

He took a step towards her and she shrank back against the van in fear. Lucas stopped and stared at her, his soft green eyes pleading. He held out his hands palm up towards her and spoke softly.

"Baby, I'm so sorry," he crooned, "I love you, Angel, please look at me."

She hesitantly looked up and her hand went, unconsciously, to her left cheek. It was still warm to the touch from the force of the blow and was red and angry with the promise of some bruising over her cheekbone. His hand reached out almost tentatively and he brushed her hair back from her face. Her eyes finally met his and she stepped slowly forward into his arms. She still had not spoken. He held her and rocked her gently there between the two vehicles, humming and singing a soft lullaby sound.

"My angel, I'm so sorry. I love you so much, couldn't stand to see you with that guy." He said finally.

Angela took one long shuddering breath that shook her tiny frame then she said softly, "I'm sorry Lucas. I couldn't stop him. Please don't be angry with me."

"Baby, it's okay. I love you." He told her. "We've got to get back inside. I've got one more set."

"Lucas, I couldn't face that place right now." She begged. "I'm a mess."

Lucas stroked her hair comfortingly with one hand and reached for his car keys with the other. He unlocked the door of the Buick and reached in and opened the rear door.

"Angie, why don't you just wait for me here in the car till I'm done?" He told her, "I won't be long and you'll be safe, locked in here."

She allowed him to help her into the back seat of the car and waited quietly while he quickly retrieved a blanket out of the trunk. He tucked the blanket round her, kissing her gently on both cheeks. When his lips brushed the bruised cheekbone, she winced just a little.

"Have a little nap, my love." He instructed. "I'll finish up the set in no time, I promise."

Then he was gone. Angela lay in the darkness cuddling the blanket to her, smelling Lucas on it and taking a certain comfort in his scent. She closed her eyes and was asleep almost instantly.

She stirred only very slightly when later on Lucas returned to the car. He slid into the front seat and deposited a paper bag next to him. He swiveled round and looked at his sleeping wife.

"Sleep Angel," he murmured, as he started the car. It was a short drive to the motel they were staying at. Once there, he left her in the car while he opened the door and took his package inside. Then he returned and opened the back door, taking hold of her still wrapped in her blanket. Angela stirred a little more as he slid her out of the car.

"Lucas." She mumbled sleepily.

"Yeah baby, it's okay." he told her. He carried her into the room and deposited her gingerly on the bed. She curled on to her side in an almost fetal position her hands tucked together under her chin. Lucas turned away and lifted a bottle of whisky out of the bag he had brought with him. He found a glass and filled it nearly full of the amber liquid. Dragging a chair up close by the bed, he sat and watched her in sleep as he sipped on the liquor.

He could clearly see the bruise forming on her cheek where he had struck her. 'Damn it.' he thought angrily, 'maybe I should just send her home? I can't protect her when I'm on stage and she don't know how to protect herself.' Lucas finished his first glass of whisky and poured another.

This time, he sat on the bed next to Angela. She stirred as he sat down and opened her eyes. Her first sight of him was with the glass raised to his lips head thrown back as he took a long swallow of the fiery liquor. She turned on to her back and stretched out her curled up legs. He looked down at her hungrily.

"Lucas, what are you drinking?" she asked him softly.

"Whisky." he said. Her eyes widened a little in surprise as he never usually drank anything other than beer, but she said nothing. His eyes drew her attention. They were a little glazed over from the effects of the alcohol and they had a carnal look in them. He took another long swallow of the liquor, his continuing silent stare enough to make her start to squirm a little uncomfortably. Finally, he smiled but it was a lascivious leer rather than his usually soft welcoming look.

"Your nap did you good," he chuckled, taking her squirming as an indication that she was aroused. "Take off your clothes, baby, now!" He ordered.

Angela was completely taken aback by his demeanor. She hesitated and reached a tentative hand to his knee.

"Lucas, maybe we should just get some sleep." she whispered. He emptied the glass in one quick swallow then took her hand and placed it on the crotch of his jeans. He held her hand there firmly and she felt his hardness pushing back against the fabric barrier.

"Sleep ain't what I got in mind, damn it!" He snapped, "Now take off your fucking clothes!"

Angela didn't argue further. She slid to the edge of the bed and started to undress. Lucas stood up, towering over her where she sat. She was already naked from the waist up and had just unzipped her jeans when his hands caught her wrists.

"Take my jeans off, baby." He told her. She carefully unzipped his jeans and leaned forward to slide them off his hips. As she slid forward, his cock came into contact with her bruised cheek. He stood over her watching her carefully.

"Kiss me, baby." He growled at her. She started to stand up, but he pushed her roughly back to the bed. "No, damn it, I want you to suck me, you stupid bitch."

Angela reeled at his words and started to shake. Lucas ignored her fear and, taking a handful of her long black hair at the back of her neck, he guided his cock into her mouth. She'd given him pleasure this way before but had never brought him to climax and he had never forced her to do it before. Lucas had always asked if she would touch and kiss him in this way. This time Lucas would have his satisfaction. He began to thrust into her throat, the force of it taking her breath away and bringing tears streaming down her cheeks. Angela detached her mind from what was happening, praying silently, as he continued to thrust into her mouth. When he climaxed, she thought she would choke but she held her breath and swallowed what he had deposited into her, feeling nauseous.

"Damn baby, you suck real nice." he told her. He pulled her to her feet then and went down on his knees in front of her to pull off her jeans and panties. She stood shivering and queasy beside the bed. But he was suddenly gentle again, putting his arms around her waist and gently kissing her stomach and the fronts of her thighs. Her nausea eased and she became aroused finally. Lucas laid her back onto the bed and pleasured her with his tongue and lips until she reached a small climax of her own. Then he pulled the blanket over them both gathering her slim form close to him and they slept. Angela slept in his arms, but fitfully, her sleep disturbed by images of the stranger at the bar and of Lucas and his angry lustful outburst.

When morning's light finally woke them both, Lucas was sweet, gentle and loving. Angela was tentative at first but relaxed as he went out of his way to please her with cuddling and soft whispered adoration. She never mentioned what had passed between them the previous night and Lucas behaved as though nothing had transpired. Her only reminder was the slight bruising on her left cheekbone.

During the last two weeks of July they were back in Angela's home town at Rock City. Lucas and Angela took long day time walks down the path by the river. On two separate days they took the hidden pathway to Angela's old backyard, knowing Mrs. Griffen would be out at work, and climbed to the tree house together. There they found a new peace with each other, making love in the soft green filtered sunshine.

She took him with her too, to visit her father's grave. Lucas crouched down behind her, as she knelt in the grass and talked softly to Paul Griffen. He was deeply touched by her naive surety that her father could still in some way hear her words. There was nothing in Lucas's background that compared to the open guileless faith his angel had in her father's love. A part of him felt a fierce jealousy of Paul Griffen and he wondered if Belle Griffen had felt shut out of this father-daughter relationship too.

The gigs went very smoothly at Rock City. Christie, now engaged to the young man who'd escorted her to Angela's wedding, was away both weekends. But Becky came down both Friday and Saturday nights and kept Angela company at the table. The two women reveled in each other's company and they even got up to dance together at least once in each set. Becky also gave Angela some girl-to-girl lessons in how to turn away the men who sometimes paid no attention to all the signs that a woman was already attached. Becky explained it pretty simply.

"You've gotta be firm, Angie," she laughed, "and sometimes even a little bit cruel. It's the only thing some jerks understand, you know?" Angela nodded at her friend, but wasn't sure how firm she could be. Becky saw the skeptical look in her friend's expression and continued.

"You'll learn to put them in their place, Angie." She laughed. "Cause your man's on stage and he can't help you from there. Think of him and just tell 'em to get lost."

Angela blushed at Becky's words, suddenly flashing back to that horrible night a few weeks before. Becky was right though, Lucas would have to expect her to look after herself when he couldn't protect her. She must get stronger for him as well as herself. 'No wonder he was so angry with me.' she thought.

Lucas and Angela had a room in the same motel where they had stayed their first full night together the previous summer. They went 'home' there every night and he would play the Gibson for her before they fell together into bed to make slow gentle love full of the memories of those first tentative days discovering each other.

For Angela, the only thing that was missing was a chance to see her mother. But Belle Griffen's words on the phone kept ringing in her ears, so she made excuses to Lucas why they shouldn't visit. Lucas was puzzled and finally, while strumming quietly one night, he asked her about it.

"Angie, baby, I kind of get the feeling you don't want to go see your Mom," he ventured. "Is that true?"

She considered her answer carefully, at first intending to just shrug it off, but finally deciding it was better he knew the whole thing. He was, after all, convinced that Belle had only rejected her girl because of him.

"Lucas, I talked to her, on the phone, after the wedding." She started. He raised one eyebrow questioningly, waiting for her to continue. Finally, after a deep breath, she spoke again. "She told me to go and make my own life. She was quite unkind about it."

"Oh baby, I'm so sorry." he told her, "It's all my fault. She can't stand me."

Angela shook her head and her tears started to flow. "No Lucas, it's not your fault." she replied, quite firmly. "My mother hasn't liked me much since I was a child. I know that now."

Lucas laid the Gibson aside and slid alongside her on the bed, taking her in his strong arms. He stroked her long dark hair and rocked her gently. "Baby, she told you that?" He asked in an amazed voice.

"No, not really, not in those words." she whispered, "But it was so obvious to me all of a sudden. She always resented how close Daddy and I were. Lucas, my mother hates me." She dissolved into tears then and he held her against his chest heedless of the salt tears soaking into his shirt.

"Go ahead and cry, baby." he crooned in her ear. "I'm here and I love you."
She heard those words through her grief and was comforted. She calmed and
relaxed in his arms and focused on listening to his heartbeat. When she closed
her eyes and drifted to sleep in his arms, Lucas shifted around to make himself as
comfortable as possible without disturbing her. For a long time he watched her
sleep, still marveling this angel was his.

Lucas and Angela had been back at home for a few weeks. Angela had started
taking assignments again from the Temporary Office Service, while Lucas and
Kurt worked a number of big contracts that Kurt had lined up. She was glad to be
back at home again because as much fun as it had been at first to be out to Lucas's
gigs all the time, by late August the excitement had worn off somewhat. When
they had driven into town on the last Sunday afternoon and she had first caught
sight of the city in the distance, she had felt an overwhelming pull to her home.

The third week back, she had taken a week long assignment at mortgage
office. They were very pleased to be able to get someone like Angela, who had
some mortgage knowledge from her job back in her home town and she was very
pleased to be settled in one place for a whole week. She had not been feeling too
well all week but it was a little easier not to have to search for a new office each
day on her way to work.

On Thursday at lunch time, one of the young women from the office had
joined her in the lunchroom to share some conversation with their sandwiches.
Something about this woman reminded Angela of her friend Becky, probably the
open and energetic approach both women seemed to have to life. Angela had
packed a ham and cheese sandwich that morning, her favourite kind, and she was
enjoying it immensely as she listened to her companion prattle on about the latest
popular TV show. A sudden wave of nausea caused a surprised Angela to drop her
sandwich to the table and rush across the hallway to the ladies room. She recalled
afterwards, her intense feeling of relief when she realized that the ladies room was
empty as she rushed into a toilet stall and vomited. It was bad enough, in her
mind, that her new companion must have guessed what had happened. She stared
at her pale face in the mirror as she used a paper towel soaked in cool water to try
and clean up. 'What on earth is the matter with me?' she wondered.

Feeling better, she returned to the lunchroom. Seeing the half-eaten sandwich
on the plate almost made her queasy again so, before sitting down, she wrapped it
back in its plastic paper and threw it into the garbage. Her companion watched
her with some concern.

"You okay, Angela?" she asked.

"Yeah, I think so, just a little queasy." Angela told her. "I feel kinda full, you know? I can't eat that sandwich now." The young woman studied her for a moment. They'd known each other a scant four days and she wasn't sure if Angela may think she was prying. Finally, just like her counterpart Becky would have done, she spoke her mind anyway.

"You're pregnant, right?" she asked, but it was more a statement than a question. Angela's eyes went wide and she stared uncomprehendingly at her for a few moments.

"I don't know." she murmured. She was trying desperately to calculate in her mind when her last period had been, but found she was blank. "I guess it's possible, but..."

"Well it's okay, isn't it?" her friend said, "I mean, you're married and all."

Angela's thoughts went straight to Lucas. 'Would it be okay?' She wasn't sure. They hadn't really talked much about children. "Lucas loves me," she told her companion. "Of course it's okay."

All afternoon she had thought of nothing else. Once she had time to think about it calmly, she was very sure that she was overdue. But before she could tell Lucas anything, she must know for sure. She resolved to stop in to a local drugstore on her way home from the office and pick up a home pregnancy test. The more Angela thought about having a baby, the more she became excited. A baby, their baby, could only strengthen Lucas's love for her.

She barely slept that night. On the way home she had purchased the home test kit and read the directions quickly before Kurt had dropped Lucas off at home. Finding that she was to take the test first thing in the morning, she carefully hid it in the back of the cupboard near the bathroom which held all their sheets and towels. Lucas did not seem to notice that she was distracted that evening as his mind was on the jam that he had been invited to the following night.

"There'll be a lot of really great players there." He explained. "Who knows, I might get a better gig with another band, ya know?" She smiled at his enthusiasm, which was making it easier for her to hide her possibly big news.

Angela had set the alarm a full fifteen minutes earlier than usual that Friday morning to allow herself time to go into the bathroom and take the home test before Lucas was up. The alarm never got a chance to ring. Angela woke from her restless sleep a few minutes before it was due to go off her anticipation was so great. She glanced briefly at her sleeping husband, then slipped out of bed and went quietly down the hall to the bathroom.

Twenty minutes later, she was sitting on the side of the tub still staring with a mixture of wonder and trepidation at the indicator which told her she was indeed pregnant. Her heart leapt went she tried to imagine the tiny life growing within her. Lucas could never be mad with her again, if she gave him this gift. Her thoughts were suddenly cut off by the sound of Lucas knocking on the door and calling through it to her.

"Angie, what are you doing girl?" He asked.

Angela looked around in a panic for a moment and finally pushed the evidence of the pregnancy test into the back of the cupboard beneath the sink. 'This isn't the time to tell him.' she thought.

"Sorry Lucas." She called back. "I'm done in here."

He gave her a long puzzled look as she came out of the bathroom. But she curled an arm round his waist and gave him a 'good morning' kiss on the cheek then padded past him and back to the bedroom.

When he joined her in the kitchen a few minutes later, she was already dressed for work and had a pot of coffee started in the coffee maker. He was only wearing his jeans and smelled fresh out the shower with an earthy aftershave that was one of her favourites. She turned from the counter as he walked in and he quickly took her into his arms, kissing her long and hard.

"There now," he chuckled, when he finally released her, "That was a good morning kiss." She grinned, pleased to see him in a good mood. Though he had never struck her again since that horrible night in the summer, his temper still sometimes seemed to boil just below the surface and she had become somewhat adept at 'walking on eggs' around him. The jam tonight must be his reason for being so upbeat. Angela decided her news must wait till after he was home from playing.

Lucas called Angela at work that afternoon which took her by surprise because she usually never heard from him. But she breathed a sigh of relief that it wasn't an emergency when all he told her was not to start anything for dinner as he and Kurt would be bringing home steaks for the three of them. He told her that they'd just finished up their current contract and netted some real big bucks so they wanted to celebrate a little.

She got home just a little before the men arrived and quickly changed out of her work clothes and pulled on a pair of jeans and a t-shirt. Glancing at herself in the full length mirror on the back of the bedroom door, Angela tried to imagine what she might look like in a few months. She heard Kurt's truck pull up out front and the men's boots on the driveway by the side of the house.

Lucas went straight around the back to light the barbecue while Kurt came into the kitchen carrying two large paper sacks. Angela came into the kitchen just as her brother-in-law was emptying the contents out of the bags.

"Hi Angie." He smiled warmly at her. "Are you hungry? Cause these steaks are great big slabs for sure!"

"Hi Kurt, I am a little hungry I guess." She told him, but wondered how her now sensitive digestion would deal with the huge pieces of beef he pulled from the bag. "Let me help, okay?" she added.

"Sure thing, it's your kitchen." he laughed. He pulled a six pack of beer from the other sack and put it into the fridge then he reached into the sack again and produced a bottle of white wine. "We brought a little something for you to drink too." He said, holding the bottle up for her. Angela spun around from where she was starting to clean vegetables in the sink for a salad.

She didn't want to hurt Kurt's feelings but she couldn't drink the wine, not now. She dropped her eyes shyly away from Kurt's gaze and murmured, "I don't think I really want to drink tonight, I'm sorry."

"That's okay, Angie." He assured her. "We just thought you'd like to celebrate with us. We made good money on this job. Lucas is gonna be able to afford that new guitar he's been looking at."

"That's awesome, Kurt." She told him. Just then Lucas came in, and crossed straight to his wife. He put his arms around her from behind, where she stood at the sink and she craned her neck backwards against his chest to look up at him. "Hi Lucas, I love you." she said to him. He brought his mouth down over hers and gave her a long deep kiss. His hands were caressing and rubbing her waist and tummy as he did so. When he broke the kiss, he squeezed her waistline between his forefingers and thumbs of both hands, pinching her just a little.

"Hey baby," he replied. "Hmm, you are putting on some weight girl?"

Angela wondered if he had somehow guessed, but from the casual way he spoke she felt sure her secret was still safe.

"Maybe a little, Lucas, I'm sorry." she confessed. "You men look after me too well is all, probably. Look at the size of these steaks."

Lucas chuckled at her, and Kurt joined in but shot Angela a quizzical look.

"So it's our fault, is it?" Lucas was laughing now. "I'm going to have to cut you off from rich food. And maybe chase you round the house more." Angela joined in his laughter with her own soft giggles.

Supper was wonderful and, as Kurt had predicted, Lucas announced that he was going to pick up the National Steel guitar that he'd had his eye on for some weeks now. He then turned to Angela and asked what she might like for either herself or her house from the money that they had realized this week. Her first thoughts were the many things which she'd started to dream of for her baby, but she held back. She wanted to tell Lucas when they were alone; this just wasn't the place or time.

"I don't know," she confessed. "Can I think about it?"

"Sure thing babe." Lucas told her. "I wish you'd have some wine though. Just so we could toast together."

Angela had just taken a bite from her steak and, like with her sandwich at the office, she got a sudden rush of nausea. Kurt watched her usually pale face turn a very sickly shade before she suddenly leapt up and raced towards the bathroom. Lucas stared after her in surprise.

"God," he said, "I didn't think that the thought of some wine would make her sick." Kurt chuckled at his brother but was still wondering what was really troubling his sister-in-law. When Angela returned to the table a few minutes later, she merely toyed with what was left on her plate while the men finished their dinner. She cleared off the empty plates along with her own half-eaten meal and put the kettle on to make some tea. Lucas had gone down to the music room to get what he needed for the jam he was going to; Kurt gave Angela a hand to clean up.

When Lucas came back up the stairs, he glanced at the clock on the wall over the table.

"I've gotta get going." He told Angela. "Babe, I'll be home late, probably two or three, okay?" She hid her disappointment at how late he was coming in. She was so tired now that she couldn't possibly wait up that late for him and her news somehow seemed unimportant in the face of his music.

"Okay Lucas," she told him in a near whisper. "You're going to be awesome, I know." While she was speaking he had pulled on his boots. He put on hand round the back of her neck and bent to give her a quick kiss.

"Yep, I'm gonna knock 'em on their asses, for sure!" he agreed, "Later Kurt. Angie, baby, be good."

She grinned weakly at him as he turned and headed out the door. When she turned back, Kurt was already making the tea. He looked at her over his shoulder.

"Sit down Angie." he suggested, gently. "You look tired."

"Thanks Kurt." she said and she did slump into one of the chairs gratefully. She folded her arms on the table and brought her forehead down against the cool surface. It seemed to help a little. Kurt watched her with great concern.

"Angie?" He ventured hesitantly.

She half raised her head at him in answer to his unspoken question. "I'm tired is all Kurt. I'm okay."

He looked at her skeptically, but finished pouring two cups of tea and carried them to the table before he spoke again. "Angie, you sure you're not sick? You don't look too well. How long you been feeling like this?"

"It's nothing, Kurt." she replied, steeling herself and sitting upright. "I'm just tired. It's been a long week." She put both hands round the mug of tea Kurt had deposited in front of her, as though drawing comfort from its warmth. Kurt hesitated an uncertain moment, then finally had to blurt out what was on his mind.

"Angie, you're pregnant, aren't you?" he asked. The silence between them seemed to stretch forever. Angela thought about lying to him, wondered how Kurt could know and Lucas not seem to notice and was suddenly very excited to share her news with someone. Finally her excitement won out.

"Yes Kurt, I'm having a baby." She confirmed.

He grinned from ear to ear. "Angie, that's great news. I really wondered, you know? You didn't want wine and then you got sick and everything." He explained. "But have you told Lucas yet?"

"No, Lucas doesn't know." She said softly. "I found out for sure this morning and I wanted to tell him tonight, after his jam."

Kurt nodded, understanding that his presence here at supper tonight had probably changed her plans. He suddenly felt like an intruder. He gulped his tea down. "Well Angie," He told her, "If it helps, I think that you are going to be a great mom. I really should get going." He rose, taking his mug to the sink.

"Thanks Kurt," she murmured. "I just hope Lucas is happy too."

He looked for a long moment at his sister-in-law, still marveling at how young and innocent she managed to look. He hoped Lucas would be pleased with the news too, but he wondered. "He'll be thrilled, Angie." he told her, "Why don't you go to bed for a while? That way, you'll be rested when he gets home and you can share your news with him."

"Great idea. Thank you Kurt." She stood up and walked him out to the front door, waiting while he pulled on his boots. He spontaneously gave her a hug and a brotherly peck on the forehead as they said their good nights.

Angela set her alarm clock and so was up about twenty minutes before Lucas walked in the side door. She still felt really tired but didn't want to delay any longer sharing the news with her husband, now that Kurt knew. When she heard his car in the driveway at the side of the house she plugged in the kettle to make them a cup of tea. When he walked in the door, he was surprised to see her, bathrobe clutched tightly around her solitary form, waiting for him to come in. The only light in the kitchen was the tiny one over the stove and in the semi-darkness she looked very fragile suddenly.

"Hey babe, you waited up?" He asked, surprised.

She shook her head and her arms seemed to wrap round herself more tightly. Lucas put his guitar in its case down right by the door and crossed to her. He took her face between his two strong hands and kissed her lightly on each cheek.

"What's up with you, baby?" He asked. He could feel her trembling beneath his hands. He dropped them to her shoulders and searched her face intently.

She dropped her eyes under his close examination and mumbled, "Lucas, the kettle. I'm making us tea."

He shrugged, leaving his question still hanging in the air between them. Taking up the electric guitar again, he crossed to the basement stairs as she turned to the counter to make their tea. When he came back upstairs, she already had two steaming mugs of tea on the coffee table in the living room. He took the Gibson out of its case and started playing soft melodies. Angela had curled herself into the big armchair and looked for all the world like a forlorn child as she watched him.

After pausing for a drink of the tea, Lucas went back to playing and watched his wife only out of the corner of his eyes. Angela sipped her tea, hugging the mug close to her between swallows. Finally, Lucas spoke softly, almost as though his voice was part of the quiet melody he was playing.

"Angela, my love," he said in calm undertone. "Something's up. You going to tell me what it is?"

She shifted uneasily in her seat, seemed to hold a silent debate with herself, then finally she looked up at him directly with a mixture of apprehension and excitement in her eyes. He looked up from the guitar and met her blue eyed gaze with his intense green ones.

"Lucas, I'm not feeling so good lately." She murmured.

"I knew that much, baby." Lucas agreed. "But what is it? You're not sick, are you?"

"Not exactly," she continued softly. "Lucas, I'm going to have a baby." Once the words were out of her mouth she started to tremble; fear for what he may feel, think, say and do. Several tense moments, which seemed an eternity to Angela, went by. His hands had stopped moving on the guitar the instant that he had heard her words. The room was eerily still. Finally, just when Angela was beginning to think he would never speak to her again, he broke the silence.

"My beautiful Angel love." he exclaimed. "A baby!" He laid the Gibson aside carefully and came to kneel in front of her chair. His arms stretched round her waist and he laid his head across her stomach. "Our baby, my god, Angela, when?"

She ran her fingers through his hair as her heart beat out a joyful rhythm which seemed to echo in her ears. She was elated at his reaction.

"I'm not sure, but probably while we were traveling still, around the beginning of August. The baby will probably come in early May." She told him.

Lucas came to his feet and his strong arms helped her up to her feet in front of him. After a prolonged embrace, he gathered her up into his arms and carried her through the house towards the bedroom. As he went, he was showering tiny kisses all over her neck and cheeks. Angela's relief at his reaction turned quickly to arousal and they made love gently before she drifted to sleep in the safe haven of his arms.

Kurt cursed under his breath as soon as he heard the telephone ring. He was on his hands and knees on the deck with a brush in one hand carefully spreading a fresh coat of wood stain across the re-sanded surface. He had just completed the area in front of the back door and was doubtful if he could successfully bridge the freshly coated area in time to grab the phone. He shrugged and decided to just let it go, 'If it's important, they'll call back.' he thought.

Twenty minutes later, he heard the unmistakable sound of Lucas Reeves' big Buick pulling up out front. He put his brush down carefully balanced on the rim of the stain can, picked up a rag to wipe his hands and strolled around the side of the house.

"Hey bro." he called just as Lucas was about to step up the stairs to the front door. The younger Reeves turned to Kurt with a grin all over his face. "Where's Angie?"

"She's taking a nap." Lucas told him. "I tried calling you. Didn't figger you'd be out, so...."

"No man, I'm out back, staining the deck." Kurt explained. "Let's go in through the front and grab a beer." He slid the keys out of his pocket and opened the front door. He retrieved a couple of cans of beer from the fridge and both men sprawled into chairs in the kitchen. "So what's up little brother?"

"Angie's pregnant, man." Lucas announced. Kurt did his best to look somewhat surprised but was unable to tell from Lucas's neutral tone whether his brother was pleased or not.

"Well, that explains her puking last night." he chuckled. "Hell and I thought she had the flu. I was scared I'd catch it, man."

Both men laughed at Kurt's attempt at humour. Lucas took a long swallow of his beer then, holding the can in both hands, studying the label intensely, not meeting Kurt's eyes.

"Don't know if I'm ready for this, man." he admitted.

"Is anyone ever ready?" Kurt countered. When Lucas didn't respond, his brother continued. "I take it this wasn't exactly in the plans?"

"Not exactly." Lucas confessed. "I mean, don't get me wrong, I'm happy 'bout it. But it's just I didn't expect it, you know?"

"Well man, Angie's going to be a great mom." Kurt said, "She's such a terrific gal. You just look after her, man, that's all."

"Yeah, I always look after her." Lucas said, a note of irritation creeping into his voice. "That's part of the trouble. I told her this morning I wanted her to quit the Temporary Job thing. She don't want to quit."

Kurt smiled a little at that. 'Poor Angie would go crazy spending months with nothing to occupy her.' he thought. Aloud, he said, "I don't know much about it man, but lots of women work when they're pregnant. Does Angie have a doctor? Maybe you could ask the doc?"

"Hell man, she ain't never had much more than the sniffles all the time we been together." Lucas admitted. "I dunno 'bout a doctor. I'd better see about that, huh?"

"Yeah Lucas, you and Angela had better see 'bout it, together." Kurt tried to gently correct his brother's usual tendency to take control. Kurt didn't think Angie would like it very much if her husband started picking a doctor out for her. "I can start next week's contract by myself man. Why don't you take Monday off so you and Angie can go a find a doc?"

"Not a bad idea, Kurt." Lucas agreed. He felt a certain calm having a least some direction. At least finding a doctor to look after his angel and their baby was something he could understand.

The two men finished their beer over a little business conversation about the contracts that Kurt had lined up. Then Kurt returned to his chore on the deck and Lucas headed back towards home.

As fall hurried along into a damp cold and universally grey winter, Angela became more and more aware of the life growing inside her. At first the changes in her had appeared slow and the whole notion of the baby seemed somehow unreal. But eventually, as clothes no longer fit properly, her belly started to swell and her feet were achy and swollen by the end of her work day, she really began to comprehend the reality that she was about to become a mother. That dawning revelation meant that Angela's thoughts turned to her own mother. She still hadn't called to let Belle know that she was going to be a grandmother; in fact, she hadn't talked to her mother at all for over six months. 'Perhaps she should discuss it with Lucas first.' she thought, looking for a justification to put off talking to her mother, fearing the previous rejection would be reinforced.

Lucas was out at a gig. Angela was curled in a big easy chair in the living room, with a sewing project for the baby on her lap. She glanced at her watch and decided they must be just starting the final set. Tonight she would probably still be awake when he got home. Perhaps then he'd be in a mood to discuss what to do about her mother.

The previous night, Angela had been sound asleep when he had arrived home and may not have heard him at all had he not slammed the door on his way into the house. The sudden banging of the door had brought her fully awake and she lay in the dark listening to him stomp down the stairs with his guitar. When he returned upstairs, she could hear him cursing but was unsure what he may be so angry about.

When he had come to bed twenty minutes later, the anger seemed to have passed. He undressed and slipped into bed with her, immediately wrapping an arm around her. His hand rubbed her swelling belly and he whispered in the dark, "Damn angel baby, I love you." She snuggled closer to him and mumbled, "Love you, too." And they had both slept.

But that had been last night. Angela suddenly stirred from sleep where she sat in the armchair, realizing that she must have drifted off for some time. Lucas was bending over her with a hand on either arm of the chair. His face was only inches from hers and she could smell whisky on his breath. She had not noticed the smell of whisky on him since that night in the summer when he had been so angry with her.

"Angie, wake up!" he nearly shouted at her. Her eyes met his only briefly, and then she had to look away. His normally animated green eyes were clouded with the liquor and something else, a dark fiery look that frightened her.

"I'm awake." she said, slurring a little with exhaustion.

"Barely!" he snapped. He put one hand round the nape of her neck and pulled her head to his, covering her mouth with a clumsy kiss which reeked of the odor of the whisky. She put her hands up gently on to his shoulders, applying no real pressure at all. He broke off the kiss but still held her by the neck keeping her face within a fraction of an inch of his.

"Lucas, I'm awake." She said softly. "Let me go, okay?"

"Let you go?" he was now shouting and her tiny frame seemed to shrink even more away from him. "I haven't hardly touched you yet, girl."

Angela tried desperately to control her shaking as his words brought a chill to her heart. He straightened up, not releasing his viselike grip on her neck, which forced her to her feet in front of him. His other hand came round her hips and grasped her by her once tiny waist. He pulled her in to him and forced another kiss on her, this time forcing her lips open with his tongue. She tried to remain unmoved and passive in his embrace but could not control the arousal that came mixed with fear. Angela felt his hardness, which would not be denied, as he pressed unrelentingly against her.

Despite her doctor's assurances that it would not hurt her baby to make love, Angela was terrified when Lucas was so intense and forceful that she would in some way hurt the fragile life within her.

Lucas had started to strip her clothes off her in a clumsy rush. His hands were pawing at her breasts and her crotch. She was shaking with fright, even though her body was responding to his drunken intensity and she felt the familiar dampness between her legs.

"Please don't Lucas," she begged. "The baby..."

Lucas had already removed her blouse and bra. She stood shivering, half-naked before him as his angry eyes bored into her. His hand which had been caressing her breasts tightened and he actually pulled hard on her nipple. She cried out in pained surprise. His other hand caught up her wrist and twisted until she was forced, by pain alone, to drop to her knees in front of him.

"This won't hurt the baby!" he growled at her, as he unzipped his fly and pushed his hard cock into her face. "I'm not going to go for months without any! 'Bout fucking time we got that straight! Now unless you want me to go look for it elsewhere, suck it baby!"

Angela, sobbing and on her knees before him, heard his words and hesitated only a moment before she took his cock first into her tiny soft hands and then guided it into her mouth. One of Lucas's hands was on her head, fingers loosely tangled in her hair. As she felt his cock swell and grow even harder, she heard him murmur, "Good baby, that's my angel." Then he started to thrust into her mouth, as she sobbed silently and thought only of her baby.

After Lucas had found his release, he pulled her gently to her feet. His showered tiny kisses onto her face and murmured softly, "Thank you, Angela.", before he gathered her up in his arms and carried her to bed. He tucked her in under the familiar quilt of her girlhood, gave her one last kiss on the forehead, and then left the room. A few minutes later, Angela drifted off to sleep listening to the sweet sounds that he was pulling from the new National Steel guitar.

Christmas came and went and still Angela made no move to tell her mother about her pregnancy. Belle had mailed a Christmas card with 'Merry Christmas, Mom' and nothing more written on it. Angela wrote one in return which seemed just as sadly impersonal. Angela very badly wanted her mother to be part of her life, especially now when the older woman's advice and understanding would have been a priceless gift, but she could do nothing to shake the feeling of rejection she had felt in their last conversation and would not risk such a thing happening again.

Lucas did not seem to notice his wife's growing anxiety as he was wrapped up in troubles of his own. Immortal Beat was undergoing the kind of upheaval that often occurred within bands of their ilk. The new keyboard player, as skillful as he was, was becoming very insistent on playing a major role in their choice of material and venues. Lucas, with his strong and intense character, was not so willing to bend on such issues which had been, for the most part, left to him by the others in the group. The tug of war which ensued caused the group to lose the cohesive and polished performance that they had been noted for in the past.

Lucas brought Jake, the bass player, home with him after a gig one night in early March and the two men sat at the kitchen table long into the wee hours talking of the possibility of simply forming a new band. Angela had been in bed when they had first arrived home but when the voices in the kitchen droned on for hours she got up to join them. Lucas was in the middle of saying something as she walked into the room but he held one hand out to her, beckoning her to him. She walked across the room, conscious of Jake's eyes on her and thinking she must look like an awkward duck with her now very obvious belly. Lucas slid an arm around her gently rubbing the small of her back. He finished what he had been saying, and then looked up at his wife.

"Hey babe, couldn't you sleep?" He asked.

"Well, just restless." she explained. "Hi Jake." Angela put one arm around Lucas's shoulders and leaned her body against his. He slid his chair back a bit more from the table and pulled her down onto his lap.

"Hullo Angela." Jake replied. "Did Lucas and I wake you?"

"No, it's okay." she said, almost apologetically. Lucas was still rubbing her back and she wondered just how he knew that she had needed his touch just there and then. She relaxed more and laid her head on his shoulder, content to listen to the men talk.

Jake addressed Lucas once more. "Well man, I dunno 'bout Phil, some of his ideas are good and all, but we made decent money and got regular gigs with you running the show. You and I could pick up a new drummer easy. But what about keys?"

Lucas was now idly caressing Angela's belly and she wondered if their baby could feel or sense daddy's touch.

"Yeah a good keys man is harder to come by." Lucas agreed. "But I already know a drummer. So maybe we should just bail on Immortal Beat, let Phil have it, ya know?"

"Well Lucas, this would be a damn good time to do it." Jake said, he tipped back his beer can and drained it, then continued, "We got no bookings till end of April. I say we dissolve it, get your drummer in and find a new keys man."

Lucas reached his free hand across the table and the two men shook hands. "Okay man, let's do it then. Angie, it looks like we'll be looking for a band name along with a baby name."

Angela laughed along with the two men, though she was almost a little surprised at how fleeting this business of her husband's seemed to be suddenly. Jake said polite goodnights to them both, opening the side door and walking out into a world already growing grey with dawn's coming.

Lucas gently pushed Angela off his lap then stood and put his arms around her, stroking his hand down the length of her hair. She laid her head on his chest and slid her arms round his waist. Content in each other's arms for the moment, they were both quite silent. Finally Lucas spoke, "We should get you back to bed." He said, "You both need lots of rest."

She pulled back a little to look up at him. "Lucas, the band..." she ventured, "You're just going to quit? It's gone just like that?"

He grinned at her and gently started to guide her towards the hallway as he replied. "Baby, you don't understand. It hasn't really been Immortal Beat for a while now. It's changed since Phil came. The chemistry just ain't there no more."

She nodded, trying to comprehend. In the bedroom, he gently helped her back under the covers before undressing and joining her. She lay on her side with her back to him. He snuggled up behind her and started again to rub her back.

She murmured softly in the dark, "Oh darling that feels so nice." He smiled in the darkness and continued the massage. Angela relaxed completely, no longer worried about the band, simply content in her husband's arms, but sleep would not come. Finally she turned towards him.

"Lucas, make love to me." she softly implored him. "I want to feel you."

Lucas was at first a little taken aback. But he lowered his caresses and she almost immediately started to moan under his touch. This time, he was the one who became cautious and concerned for their child as Angela practically demanded his attentions. He caressed her with hands and tongue alone until she found her release then he cuddled her in to him, as her ragged breathing slowly returned to normal. Her eyes focused briefly on him in the dim early morning light.

"I love you, Lucas." she murmured, before closing them and, almost instantly, falling asleep.

"You too, Angel." he told her. He lay awake for a long time marveling at her sleeping form. He rested one hand ever so lightly and very still on her belly feeling elated when the baby shifted and kicked. The wonder of a new life growing inside his shy angel touched Lucas deeply. But with the joy came a paralyzing fear of being unable to care for this miracle that she was about to bestow on them both. As the birds started singing outside, welcoming a new morning, Lucas lay next to his sleeping wife and wept.

Angela slept much of the next day and Lucas was happy to indulge her. He brought her breakfast in bed by mid-morning and perched on the edge of the bed as she toyed with the food. Her anxiety about the pregnancy along with her desire to somehow reconcile with her mother was more responsible for her malaise then anything physical. The closer to term she became the more she longed for Belle to be there and quietly reassure her as only another woman was able to do. Lucas watched, as she took a minuscule amount of scrambled egg on her fork, examining it rather than eating it.

"Angela, I thought your morning sickness was all over." he said. She looked up, but seemed to look past him rather that at him. The egg on her fork fell back to the plate.

"I'm tired." she said, and he was unsure if that was meant to be an answer or if she had even heard him. He gently took the fork out of her hand and lifted the tray away from her lap. Angela's eyes did follow him as he crossed to the dresser to put the tray down. When he turned back, she had her arms out to him.

Lucas came back to the bed and slid alongside her, placing one arm round her shoulders and putting his other hand onto her swelling belly. She leaned into him taking comfort in his nearness; his body warmth and scent enveloped her for a time in a sense of security. Lucas softly crooned a lullaby to her until he felt her go limp in his arms as sleep found her once more. He tucked her snugly back under the covers and, taking the tray, quietly left the room.

Kurt came over in the early afternoon and the two men got started on some renovations that they were making to the room that Angela had decided to convert to a nursery. Today's project was the soft turquoise paint that Angela had chosen for the walls.

"Where's Angie, man?" Kurt asked.

"She's sleeping." Lucas replied. "She was up kinda late with me and Jake last night."

"Well sleep will do her good for sure." Kurt acknowledged. He turned back to the brush work he was concentrating on round the window frame. Lucas continued to roll paint onto the wall in front of him, with his back to his brother.

"She isn't eating today, man." He said to the wall. Kurt's hand stopped in midair. "I'm worried 'bout what's up with her."

"Well Lucas, she's going through a lot of changes." Kurt said, and then added more tentatively. "And she's kind of all alone, you know? Maybe she's scared?"

"Damn Kurt." Lucas snapped defensively. "She ain't alone. She's got me."

Kurt shrugged and tried to remain as inoffensive as possible. "I just mean she maybe needs a woman, someone who knows what she's going through, ya know? I know I can't even begin to relate to being pregnant, like it's just foreign territory. Does her mother know she's expecting?"

"Don't think so, man." Lucas said. "Belle was such a bitch to her after the wedding; I don't think she's even talked to her since."

"Belle loves her." Kurt told him, remembering his conversation with Angela's mother the evening of the wedding. "Maybe she just needs to know that Angie needs her."

"Yeah man, maybe you're right." Lucas muttered in a thoughtful tone.

Becky was out for a stroll on her lunch break. She was the last of the original threesome who was still working at Delta Mortgage. Christie had moved permanently to the big city with her boyfriend turned fiancé just after Christmas. Although two new women had replaced Angela and then Christie in turn, Becky had never become close to either of them in quite the same way.

The spring sunshine felt great and seeing the tulips and daffodils in flower-beds along the way reminded her that Angela was getting very close to term. The women had exchanged phone calls once a month or so to bring each other up to date on their news.

Becky was about to turn in to the little park in the square that the girls had often lunched in, when she nearly ran into a woman coming the other way. Belle Griffen looked up in surprise at the bright face of her daughter's former co-worker.

"Umm, hi Mrs. Griffen." said Becky, a little apologetically.

"Becky," Belle smiled with recognition. "How nice to see you. I hope you're keeping well."

Becky grinned, "I'm doing well enough Mrs. Griffen. How about you?"

The older woman paused a moment before replying, as though wondering if she should say what was on her mind or not. "I'm alright Becky. Listen, do you think we might talk awhile?" she asked hesitantly.

"Sure thing," Becky agreed glad of the company. She indicated a nearby bench and the two women took seats at either end of it.

Belle wasted no more time on small talk. "Becky, have you heard from my daughter at all?" she asked.

"Umm well yeah," Becky answered. "Maybe three weeks ago. I think. Why, is anything wrong?"

"Not that I know of Becky." Belle stated. "How was she when you talked to her?"

"Well, you know." Becky started, unsure what it was that Angela's mother seemed to be fishing for with her question. "She's doing okay for almost seven months along."

Belle Griffen's eyes nearly bugged out of her head and her jaw slacked noticeably with shock. Becky realized instantly and with a lesser sense of shock; that Mrs. Griffen was hearing about her coming grandchild for the first time. She wondered why on earth that Angela had never told her mother. Belle was absolutely still for a timeless moment, then finally said very softly, "When is my grandchild due?"

"The beginning of May, ma'am." Becky replied then added. "I'm so surprised that you didn't know."

"Not as surprised as I am, Becky." Belle replied. "Do you have any ideas why my daughter would find it necessary to keep this a secret?"

"No idea at all," Becky confessed. "I just assumed that you knew. I'm sorry ma'am if you think I'm out of line, but Angela knows you don't like Lucas very much, perhaps that has something to do with it."

Belle Griffen heard Becky's words but was also giving thought to her last conversation with Angela. She sighed heavily then forced a smile for the young woman before her.

"Perhaps Becky," She said, "But perhaps I have had a hand in our estrangement too. Thank you very much for your honesty with me."

Becky acknowledged Belle's thanks with a nod, and then excused herself to return to the office. Belle remained on the bench, staring at a distant place in her memory when Angela was just a child. The young Angela had always been most sensitive and had hid in her room and later her tree house for many hours at the tiniest hint of rejection by anyone. Belle wondered if the silence from her daughter may not be the same habit of youth, intensified by age and the emotional stress every pregnant woman seems to endure. Whatever the reason, Belle resolved to at least attempt to mend the bridges between them.

Lucas and Jake managed to find a keyboard player. A younger man than either of them with an unassuming manner about him, Eric was eager to play with Lucas Reeves as he'd heard him several times before and knew of his good reputation around the city. Reed, the drummer, and Eric moved their equipment into Lucas's basement studio and the four men began to rehearse nightly working out the music and the personal bonds that make good players into better bands.

Angela had, at Lucas's urging, given up working to wait for her baby to arrive. She was still feeling lost and apprehensive about the coming birth of her child but was incapable of expressing her fears to Lucas and equally powerless to take the first step and call her mother to ask for her guidance. She settled into a routine which closely matched that of the band. She would stay up in the evening when they were downstairs rehearsing, keeping herself busy with crafts, reading or just the television as a diversion. Lucas would come upstairs once or twice during the course of each rehearsal and always took the time to check on his wife when he did. One such evening, he found Angela sitting at the kitchen table doodling with a pencil on a pad of paper.

"What're you doing, babe?" he asked, planting a kiss on her forehead.

Angela smiled up at him then slid her hands from the paper, where they had been covering her creation. The sheet she showed her husband had a pencil sketch on it of clouds of smoke and fire which resembled and explosion. Coming out of the smoky core of the sketch, in fancy scripted letters were the words 'Critical Mass'. Lucas studied the artwork carefully. Angela looked up at him waiting anxiously for his reaction. Finally, he handed it back to her, took her face in his hands and bent to give her and long passionate kiss. When he finally pulled his mouth away from hers, he asked, "Is this what I think it is?"

"I hope so." Angela told him. "It's kind of my idea for a name for the band. I know it's not the greatest but..."

He shook his head in a combination of amusement and amazement. "Not the best?" he asked with a chuckle in his tone. "Angie, it's awesome! It's perfect, just like you!" He grinned broadly at her.

"You really think so, Lucas?" She asked softly.

"Damn girl!" he exclaimed, "Of course I do. It's great. 'Critical Mass' is born, in an explosion of sorts!" he exclaimed.

The other three members of the group were as enthusiastic as Lucas so the name was adopted. Angela was elated to feel a part of this new group and even more gratified that Lucas seemed so content lately. He was playing every night with people who shared his love for music and she could almost see in his calm green eyes the peace that he was deriving from it.

Angela would go to bed after rehearsal was over and usually slept till mid-morning before arising to do it all again. Some mornings she would wake alone, because Lucas would have already slipped out of bed to join Kurt at a jobsite. Other mornings, they would wake together, cuddling and talking for a while before facing the day.

It was one of the mornings that Lucas had left early for work that Angela was jarred awake by the insistent ringing of the telephone. She awkwardly struggled from under the covers and reached for the receiver.

"Hello?" she said softly.

"Angela, its Mom," Belle's unmistakable voice brought a little jolt of emotion to her daughter.

"Mom? What a surprise!" Angela replied, her excitement at hearing her mother's voice tempered a little by her anxiety about why her mother was suddenly calling.

"Angela, darling," Belle said evenly; "I think we need to talk. I'd like to come down and visit for a long weekend as soon as I can arrange a Friday off. Would that be alright?"

Angela was taken completely by surprise and her hand unconsciously went to her swollen belly as she struggled for an answer. "I'd like to see you Mom. I've wanted to call, but....,"

Belle resisted the urge to vocalize the unkind thought that entered her head at that moment. "Angela, I love you. We've both kept out of touch and, in ways I suppose, we've had our reasons. But you are my daughter. Please say that you'll be willing to see me."

"Mom, I have to ask Lucas if it's okay that you stay." Angela told her mother. "And there's something I need to tell you, it's very important."

"Angie, I will stay in a hotel, if necessary. I'd rather not impose on you and your husband." Belle said politely. "Can your important news wait till say the first weekend of May?"

Angela gasped when she heard the date her mother proposed. Her baby was due in that same week. 'No' she thought, 'this news simply couldn't wait till then.' Aloud to her mother she said, with a nervous quaver in her voice. "No Mom, I need to tell you right now; should have called you a long time ago. Mom I'm so sorry. The truth is I may well be in the hospital that weekend. Lucas and I are expecting a baby."

There was a silence on the line which for Angela seemed an eternity. Belle Griffen, even though Angela's 'news' came as no surprise, was suddenly moved hearing the words from her own daughter's lips. She wiped at the tears which were creeping down her cheeks and finally composed herself enough to answer.

"Angela, I can't believe that you never called." she exclaimed, her voice thick with emotion. "I am happy for you, my darling girl. You will make a wonderful mother."

Angela was crying too now, but through her tears she managed a few words. "Mom, I've missed you, I need you. I'm so scared. Please Mom don't be angry with me anymore."

"Angela," her mother soothed, "Sshh now. I'm not angry with you but I do worry about you. I will take more time off, as much as you need. I'll be there soon."

After Angela had replaced the phone on its cradle, she wrapped her arms around herself in a hugging gesture and curled back under the covers in a fetal position. She wept with emotions which suddenly seemed out of control. Relief mixed with joy but still tempered with the panic and dismay she felt about the upcoming birth of her child reduced her to a certain emotional turmoil. Sleep seemed the only escape, so she closed her eyes. Lucas found her still in bed when he got in that evening at supper time.

Belle Griffen pulled up in front of Lucas and Angela's house just before suppertime on a Thursday evening. Angela was sitting at the kitchen table with a sketchbook working on a poster that Lucas had suggested she design for the new band. She was enjoying the diversion as, now less than one week to term, her anxiety was increasing daily. A pot of beef stew was simmering on the stove awaiting Lucas's arrival from working for the day with Kurt.

Belle sat in the car for a minute after turning off the engine, gathering her thoughts and composing herself. She still had not found much to like in her son-in-law but her daughter needed her so Belle was determined to put her feelings aside for Angela's sake. Angela had called her back the evening after their initial talk, insistent that it was both hers and Lucas's wish that she stay with them for her visit. The pleading note in Angela's voice had not been lost on her mother, nor had her repeated reassurances that Lucas definitely wanted his mother-in-law to stay with them. Belle doubted that Angela's husband had anything but his own motives in mind for wanting her in his house. She got out of the car and, carrying her one small suitcase, walked up to the front door.

Angela was very surprised when the doorbell rang, wondering who it could be. She had assumed that her mother would wait till a weekend to make the trip.

She got up from the table and made her somewhat awkward way to the door. When the door swung open and she saw her mother standing there, she gasped with joy.

"Mom, you're here!" she exclaimed, wrapping her arms around the older woman. Belle put her case down and returned the embrace. Even though she had known that Angela was pregnant, she was still surprised somehow seeing her little girl so heavy with child.

"Angela, darling." She said, "Yes I'm here."

Angela stepped aside to allow her mother to come through the doorway into the living room. Belle came in, studying her daughter's face as she did so, she saw the tears which had filled Angela's eyes and were starting to spill down her cheeks.

"Angela, are you alright?" she asked with concern, "You're crying."

Angela wiped a hand across her face as though trying to hide the tears away from sight. "I'm okay, Mom." she said softly, "Just happy to see you is all."

Belle smiled warmly and patted Angela's arm. "Just look at you," she told her daughter, "That baby's going to be here very soon."

"Yeah Mom, I guess." Angela murmured in subdued tones. "Let me show you your room, okay?" She added, obviously changing the subject. She led her mother through the kitchen and down the hall to the spare room. Belle couldn't help but notice the wonderful smell of the stew simmering on the stove.

"Beef stew?" she asked, "It sure smells good." "Yes, Lucas loves it. And there's plenty." Angela explained, "You didn't eat yet did you?"

"No, I had lunch at home, and then dropped by Pamela's before I drove in to the city." Belle told her.

"Well, I'll leave you to wash up and get settled," Angela said. "Lucas will be home any minute from work and we'll eat." Just as she was speaking, she heard the side door in the kitchen open. "There he is now." She laughed. She left Belle alone in the simply decorated bedroom and turned towards the kitchen as Lucas yelled.

"Angie, baby I'm home!"

Angela walked into the kitchen where Lucas was already reaching in the fridge for a beer. He spun round when she walked in and looked past her. He had seen Belle's car out front and knew his mother-in-law had arrived.

"Where is she?" he asked.

"Just got here, Lucas." Angela told him. "She's freshening up before dinner."

"So baby?" he said, putting his arms around her shoulders and moving close to whisper in her ear. "Are you happier now?" He was kissing and licking round her tiny ear and Angela could feel his arousal as he pressed his body against her. She turned her face towards his and kissed his cheek.

"Yes Lucas, I'm glad she's here." She whispered. "I just want the baby to come soon. I'm so tired all the time."

Lucas pulled away from her abruptly and popped the top on his beer can. "Yeah I know. You're too damn tired for anything." He snapped at her. Angela blinked back her tears and turned to the pot on the stove.

"I'm sorry Lucas, I'm so sorry." she murmured.

"Well I hope you drop the kid soon too. So we can get back to normal round here." He said unkindly. He had crossed to the table and was studying her handiwork on the poster. In a happier tone, he told her, "This looks not bad, kind of cool."

Angela smiled, relieved that Lucas had changed the subject. She was just putting the stew into bowls and pulling some dinner rolls out of the oven where they'd been warming, when Belle walked into the kitchen. Lucas greeted his mother-in-law in polite but distant tones and the three of them sat down for dinner.

Their conversation was minimal as they ate. Belle and Angela carried most of the talk about doings back home and Belle told Angela that it had been Becky who had unwittingly let the news of her pregnancy slip. Lucas merely ate in silence, keeping his thoughts to himself and watching his wife closely. Angela noticed his long and lustful look at one point and dropped her eyes to her plate, flushing with some embarrassment as she realized what he was thinking about. He smiled to himself, knowing he could still touch her like that with just a look.

As Lucas popped the top on another beer and Angela put the kettle on for tea after the meal, he finally entered into some conversation by making an announcement of sorts.

"Well this is our last rehearsal tonight." He said. "We've got a gig on Saturday."

"Lucas, really?" Angela exclaimed. "That's awesome!" She turned to her mother. "Mom, Lucas has a new band; they've been rehearsing for nearly two months. They sound so great!"

"Yeah, we're playing Louis's Blues Club." Lucas told them both.

"That's nice, Lucas." Belle told him evenly.

"It's awesome, darling." Angela said again. "Only wish I could be there for you."

"Angie, baby," Lucas crooned at her, putting an arm round her and patting her swollen belly with his free hand. "You are here for me. You are giving me the most amazing gift, our baby."

The kettle started to whistle and Lucas released her, but not before he kissed her gently on the cheek. Belle wondered fleetingly if perhaps her judgment was a little hasty. He certainly seemed to be gentle with her now.

Tea made the three of them moved to more comfortable seating in the living room. Lucas got out the Gibson acoustic and played as he sipped his beer, warming his fingers up a bit for the evening rehearsal. Angela loved this quiet time for them as it reminded her of the days when she would stay with him in motels and he'd play the Gibson just for her, late at night. She sipped her tea, content that she had both her mom and Lucas so close, at least for a little while.

The rest of the band arrived one by one so eventually Angela and her mother were left by themselves in the living room. Angela picked up a needlework project and got as comfortable as her awkward, swollen body would allow on the big easy chair. Both women sat in silence for a time. Angela's ears were tuned to the sounds coming from below. Though Kurt and Lucas had soundproofed the ceiling, the barrier was not perfect and here in the living room directly above the music room one could hear the music from below. Finally Belle broke the silence.

"Does this go on every night, Angie?" she inquired.

Angela glanced up at her mother briefly, and then explained. "Yes mostly every night for the past couple of months. Jake and Lucas have played together before, but the other two are new. They're rehearsing, picking the stuff that works, learning to play together. The band needs to be tight if they want to work."

"And you've been staying up half the night with him, then?" She asked, pointedly.

"Mom, please don't go looking for trouble, okay?" Angela told her mother in an almost pleading tone. "Yes, I do stay up with him, I'm his wife. But I sleep from whenever they quit till noon or later."

"That can't be good for you." her mother stated flatly. "Doesn't he understand you need so much rest right now? Angela you look exhausted."

"Mom, let's not fight about Lucas." Angela said sadly. "I need you here now. Mom, I'm scared. I've read all the books about being pregnant and they're great, you know? But what's it really gonna be like, having the baby? I'm so scared; it's going to hurt so bad!"

Even as Angela was speaking, Belle had moved from her place on the couch and settled on the arm of Angela's chair. She wrapped her arms around her daughter's shoulders and pulled her head onto her breasts. Gently stroking Angela's long black hair as her daughter wept, Belle tried to comfort and to reassure her.

"Angela, it will be alright." she told her. "You're much stronger than you can ever imagine. You will handle it. You need to find something to focus on, a picture or something that makes you feel safe and loved. Focus through the pain and always remember what is waiting at the end for you, your beautiful baby. Everything will be alright darling, I promise."

"Mom, stay with me, when I go into labour, please?" Angela begged.

"Oh darling, I would think you'll want your husband there." Belle reminded her. "But I will be very close by, that I can promise. Now I think you should go to bed."

Angela allowed her mother to take the needlework from her and then uncomplainingly let Belle lead her down the hall to her bedroom. She glanced hesitantly at the door to the basement staircase as they passed through the kitchen. Her mother gave her a few minutes alone to get out of her clothes and slip on a nightie but then came back in and gently snugged the covers around her daughter. She kissed her on the forehead, said a soft goodnight and closed the door softly behind her. Before Belle was back in the living room, Angela was asleep.

An hour or so later, Lucas came upstairs for more beer and was surprised to find his mother-in-law alone in the living room.

"Where's Angie?" he asked.

"I sent her to bed." Belle said shortly. "In case you hadn't noticed, she's exhausted."

"Thanks Belle," Lucas told her, sounding quite relieved. "I was hoping having you here would help and it already has. She won't listen to me about getting her rest, ya know?"

Belle was taken aback by his gratitude and manner. She merely nodded in response. Lucas grinned to himself, seeing her discomfort.

"You know Belle, I ain't no monster." he said, winking at her, "Just a guitar player." He spun round, not giving her a chance to reply, and left the room. Belle sat up for another hour trying to come to terms with the many faces she'd seen of Lucas Reeves. She could well appreciate how her daughter had come to fall so fast and so completely in love with him; his charm was quite overwhelming. But she still couldn't shake her visions of him in her own home, his green eyes turning black with anger as he clearly challenged her for control of Angela's affections. 'No' she decided, 'Lucas Reeves still frightens me and I will worry for Angela as long as she is with him.'

Lucas finally wrapped up the rehearsal about three a.m. and came up the stairs. The three other men left quickly, eager for their beds, and, although they had tried to be quiet, Angela was awake when Lucas came to bed.

The light spilling from the hall was enough for him to see her there under the blankets looking innocent, almost childlike, despite her pregnant form. He kicked the bedroom door shut behind him, slipped out of his jeans and shirt and kneeled on the edge of the bed beside her. Angela rolled to her back and looked up at him. He grinned lasciviously down at her, placing on hand on either side of her head on the pillow and bending to kiss her deeply. Angela responded to him eagerly.

When their lips finally parted, Lucas spoke in a husky whisper.

"I want you, baby." He told her. "Damn girl you make me so hot."

Angela's eyes flew briefly to the door, knowing her mother lay asleep just down the hall. She gently caressed Lucas's powerful forearms and softly murmured, "But Lucas, mom's right there."

Lucas chuckled and kissed her very deeply again, forcing his tongue into her mouth this time and bruising her lips with his intensity. When Angela did not respond to him and shifted uncomfortably in bed, he reached for her breasts through her nightie and squeezed them hard enough to make her moan. They were becoming full and heavy with milk for the baby and his attentions brought tears to her eyes.

"Yes," he growled at her, "Your mother is here. You still need to thank me for that. I didn't need to let her stay here, you know." As he was speaking he had shifted position so he was kneeling right next to her head. He roughly pulled her head to the side and guided his hard cock into her mouth. Angela was more frightened that her mother would hear if she struggled; she meekly accepted his invasion and sucked him. Lucas fondled her tender breasts and reached under her nightie to find her clitoris, trying to arouse her. Despite her fear, Angela responded to her husband's caresses and moaned even as he climaxed all over her face. He allowed her to awkwardly roll out of bed and go to the bathroom to clean herself. When she came back to bed, he was already soundly asleep.

Angela was excited even early on Saturday morning. Critical Mass would play its first gig tonight and, better still, at a blues club. She was so happy for Lucas; this was like a dream come true for him, his own band in a blues venue. She was up before either her husband or her mother, but the smell of coffee brewing soon penetrated their senses so she wasn't alone long. Lucas came into the kitchen first, wearing only his jeans.

Angela was at the counter when he came in, pouring milk onto a bowl of shredded wheat. He came behind her, arms encircling her form and one hand rubbing her belly gently. She carefully put the milk carton down and twisted round in his loose grasp to face him. She snuggled against his bare chest, enjoying the feel of his skin against her cheek.

"Morning baby," he crooned at her as his hands slipped down to cup her buttocks. Angela nuzzled his chest with tiny kisses, loving the taste of him.

"Lucas I love you." She murmured to his skin. Her mouth found one of his nipples and she was gently sucking on him when her mother walked into the kitchen. She broke the contact between them immediately, flushing scarlet with her embarrassment. Lucas squeezed her bottom one more time, grinning mischievously, and then he turned to his mother-in-law.

"Morning Belle." he said brightly, "Would you like a coffee?"

"Umm, yes please." Belle said, surprised by Lucas's casual familiarity with her but a little more astonished at her daughter's behaviour. 'Had she not remembered they had a houseguest?' she wondered.

"Good morning Mom," Angela mumbled, still trying to regain her composure. She had almost forgotten her mother was in the house in her excitement about Lucas's gig.

"Angela, you're in a bright mood today." her mother said, somewhat sarcastically.

"I'm just excited about the gig tonight." Angela explained, "Only wish I could be there." She picked up her cereal bowl and moved towards the table. Halfway there, the bowl slipped suddenly from her hands smashing on the floor. Angela bent over in some discomfort, her hands going to her belly. "Oh my god." she breathed.

"Angie?" Lucas came to her side instantly. "You okay babe?"

Angela slowly straightened up and looked from her mother to Lucas in surprise. Belle had already reached for paper towels to mop up the milk puddle on the floor.

"I'll clean this up Angela." She said practically. "Perhaps you should sit down darling."

Lucas helped her to a seat at the table and then turned to help Belle. Angela remained silent, watching them impassively. The pain had not been a kick, she was used to those now, but rather a twinge that she'd never felt before. It hadn't been too painful, just took her by surprise. She had a funny feeling suddenly, about that twinge, sure of what it was but unwilling to let Belle or Lucas know. 'Especially Lucas,' she thought, 'nothing must spoil his first gig with the new band, this was his night.'

Both Belle and Lucas quickly joined Angela at the table and Lucas put a fresh bowl of shredded wheat in front of her. She smiled her thanks at them both.

"Thanks," she said, almost apologetically. "I don't know how I could be so clumsy. I'm okay now, I promise."

"Damn it girl!" Lucas exclaimed, with a chuckle in his voice, "You had me scared."

Belle studied her daughter's face closely. She was fairly sure that was no accident; the girl may be in labour and, with her inexperience, may not realize it. But Angela's face remained outwardly calm and Belle relaxed. Twenty minutes or so later when Angela felt another twinge, she breathed through it and gave no outward indication of the sensation. The twinges remained twenty minutes or so apart all afternoon and Angela had no trouble disguising them from either her husband or her mother.

At suppertime, she merely played with her food and then, saying she was feeling tired, went to lie down. Belle had taken over in the kitchen and Lucas, not wanting to be alone with his mother-in-law, went down to the music room. Angela couldn't sleep but was glad of the time alone. It wasn't long however, before she heard the sounds of the other men from Critical Mass arriving to load their equipment. She struggled up from bed and went to see them off.

As she walked into the kitchen, another of the twinges hit her, this one unexpectedly. She bent over with the pain again, clutching at her belly. Belle, who had been drying the last of the dishes, put down her cloth and was quickly at her daughter's side. She put an arm around Angela's shoulders and assisted her to a chair.

"Angela," she asked, "How many of these pains have you had today?" Angela looked up at her mother, shaking her head in negation of what Belle was thinking.

"It's okay Mom," she said, "I'm fine. Don't say anything to Lucas."

Belle was taken aback, but she just shrugged as Lucas and Eric came through the room behind them with the electric piano hefted between them. Lucas grinned when he saw Angela.

"Feeling better babe?" He asked without stopping.

"Yeah darling, I'm fine now." Angela lied.

Once they had finished loading, Lucas came back in. Angela stood up and wrapped her arms around him. They kissed deeply. His arms were still around her when she felt another twinge start to assault her. Lucas felt her tense under his touch and looked down at her quizzically.

"You getting pain again?" he asked.

She breathed deeply, waiting for the pain to pass, before replying. She smiled weakly at him. "It's nothing. I'm fine. Go now; play These Arms of Mine, just for me, okay?"

He grinned at her, kissed her once more quickly and abruptly headed for the door. When the door closed Angela turned back towards her mother.

"Why didn't you tell him?" Belle asked simply.

"The gig Mom." she said, not expecting her mother to understand anyway but trying to explain. "This band, this first gig, he's lived for it for months. He plays Mom, it's what he does."

Belle shook her head, uncomprehendingly. "You'd think he'd want to be here with you. How often are the pains coming Angela?"

"Every ten minutes or so now." Angela told her, amazed herself at how calm she was now that she knew her baby was coming. "I'm going to call Kurt, so he can let Lucas know after the gig and bring him to the hospital instead of home."

Belle shook her head in a combination of confusion and anger. "Angela, he should be with his wife! What kind of a man is he? You're willing to have his baby alone while he's out playing guitar?"

"Mom," Angela said, her usually soft voice raised with emotion. "I'm not alone, you're here. And Lucas can't really help me with this part. He's playing guitar because it's what he does, not an idle hobby, but his work! Wasn't Daddy away on business when I was born?"

Belle was surprised by the force of Angela's words. She was silent for a long moment and then turned to the practical for comfort.

"Do you have a bag packed for the hospital?" She asked. "I'll get it and start the car."

Angela smiled, then immediately winced as another of the now more frequent pains started. She held onto the counter by the phone waiting for it to pass before she spoke.

"My bag's just inside the bedroom door. Thanks Mom." She said. "Don't start the car. I'll get Kurt to drive us, he knows the way better than me, and then he can go for Lucas."

Belle went in search of her daughter's overnight bag and her own purse while Angela turned to the phone.

Melissa Belle Reeves came into the world at twelve twenty a.m. on May the eight as, across town, her father was playing Stevie Ray Vaughan's Pride and Joy for his encore song. Kurt led a standing ovation at the packed little blues bar then pushed his way none too gently up the tiny stage.

"Hey Lucas, way to go man!!" he exclaimed.

Lucas grinned at his big brother with elation. "Damn Kurt; that felt so good!" He said enthusiastically. "Thanks for coming, man."

"Lucas, I came 'cause Angie asked me to, man." Kurt explained. "I drove her and her mom to the hospital nearly four hours ago. You're probably a daddy by now."

Lucas had been packing the Stratocaster into its case and he stopped dead as Kurt spoke. "Damn Kurt! She's had the baby? Help me get this gear packed, will ya? We gotta get over there."

Kurt grinned at his little brother, but pitched in willingly. There were a lot of people in the club, especially other musicians, who wanted to talk to Lucas as well as the other members of Critical Mass to pass on congratulations for a fine debut gig. Lucas was polite but short with most of them. Finally, Jake grabbed a mike which was still live and made a quick announcement.

"Hey people, thanks to all of you for your support and all. But Lucas has to get outta here. His wife is having their first baby, right now! So if you all can just give him a little space. Critical Mass will be back again next weekend; we'll see y'all then, have a nice night."

Lucas looked gratefully at his friend as he snapped the last case shut. Kurt and he carried everything out to Lucas's car in one trip then Lucas jumped in and started the big Buick with a roar. His brother leaned down to the open driver's side window.

"I'll follow you over in the truck, man."

Lucas nodded and impatiently gunned the engine as his brother unlocked and started his truck. Then they were on their way. As Lucas drove, he realized that he had been shaking almost uncontrollably and had to grip the steering wheel tightly to be sure of keeping the car straight. His band had been a smashing success and now this, his baby, all on the same night.

Kurt and Lucas both walked into the hospital together and Kurt asked at the desk where they would find the maternity wing. The woman on duty gave them directions and Lucas moved immediately in that direction, already nearly three steps ahead of his brother by the time they reached the elevator. They rode to the fourth floor, Lucas tapping his foot impatiently as the elevator seemed to run far slower than he had hoped.

"Should a taken the stairs, man." he complained.

"Relax Lucas, we're here." Kurt said, chuckling, as the doors slid open.

The men encountered another desk at the nurses' station where they were told they would find Mrs. Reeves in room 406. The nurse smiled broadly at both of them and asked. "Which one of you gentlemen is the father?"

"I am." Lucas said impatiently, already starting down the hall.

The nurse called after him, "Congratulations Sir, you have a beautiful baby daughter." She looked at the retreating figure, black leather clad and dangerous looking with some amazement. Kurt grinned at her and nodded his head after his brother.

"He's a guitar player, ma'am. Just finished a gig." He explained. The nurse merely nodded in response, still watching Lucas as he strode down the hall. She wasn't about to tell his companion that she was openly admiring the handsome young man. Kurt hung back wanting Lucas to have time with Angela alone.

Lucas turned in to the doorway marked 406, stepping tentatively through the threshold. Angela was in bed, with a small bundle held comfortably in her arms. Belle had been sitting in a chair beside the bed but rose when Lucas came in. She inclined her head respectfully to her son-in-law and without a word, left the room.

Angela looked exhausted but elated. She beamed at Lucas, her bright blue eyes sparkling.

"Hi darling," she said, "How'd the gig go?"

Lucas came up beside the bed and reached one cautious hand towards the bundle his wife was cuddling. The blanket fell away to reveal his tiny daughter's sleeping form for the first time. He gasped. He sat down carefully on the edge of the bed, not taking his eyes off the infant. Finally, after a lengthy silence between them, he leaned across the child to his wife and kissed her slowly, passionately and gently. He felt his daughter as she shifted around between them and marveled at the tiny life that so recently had still been a part of his wife's body.

"Angela, my angel," he whispered, his voice heavy with emotion. "She's perfect. You've brought us a miracle. Baby, I love you so very much."

They kissed and whispered to each other; talking excitedly about the gig as well as the baby. When Angela told Lucas the time his daughter had come into the world, he had laughed and told her the song he had been playing. Pride and Joy would be forever, in his mind, Baby Melissa's song. Angela had already chosen Melissa and it was Lucas who asked her if she would add Belle as a middle name. Angela's joy was complete now that Lucas was here. Finally, after ten minutes together, she offered his daughter to him. Lucas was hesitant at first and Angela saw in his green eyes a sudden flash of fear.

"It's okay Lucas." she said gently. "She's tiny but tough. You won't break her."

He smiled weakly at his wife, and then almost reverently held his little girl for the first time, staring down at the tiny face in amazement. Angela reached for the call button on her pillow and buzzed for the nurse.

"Yes Mrs. Reeves?" Asked the voice over the small intercom.

"Would you send the rest of my family in now, please?" she requested politely.

A moment or two later, Belle and Kurt both came into the room. Kurt looked over his brother's shoulder and had much the same amazed reaction at the tiny fragile looking form Lucas now held. Belle went round to the far side of the bed and took one of her daughter's hands in hers.

"Angela, she's beautiful." Belle told her and Angela grinned at words her mother seemed to have said many times over since Melissa's birth. Then Belle turned practical. "But darling, both you and this little one need some rest. I think perhaps it's time we let you sleep."

Lucas glanced up at Belle and nodded. "Yes darling you need to rest." He gently passed his daughter back to Angela and then turned to Kurt and Belle. "Kurt, can you drive Mrs. Griffen back to the house? I'm staying with Angie for a while."

Belle looked as though she may protest, but Lucas merely handed her a set of spare keys for the house and turned back to his wife. Angela said soft goodnights to her mother and Kurt as they left the room.

After Kurt and Belle had left, the nurse came in and took little Melissa from Angela. Angela looked longingly after her baby as they placed her into a bassinet to wheel her back to the nursery. Over her shoulder, the nurse said, "Get some sleep young lady. I'll be bringing her back for a feeding in four hours."

Lucas slid a little closer to Angela and took one of her tiny hands in both his large ones. Angela's eyes were already heavy with sleep but she still managed a delighted smile at her husband. He bent and kissed her forehead.

"Close your eyes, my love." he murmured. When her eyes were shut, he gently kissed each eyelid very delicately, then he straightened up but did not let go of her hand. He started to sing very quietly to her, a cappella, some of their favourite slow blues. Angela slept. Later, when a nurse looked in, she saw Lucas dosing in the chair by his wife's bed but he was slumped forward with his head on the edge of the bed and even in sleep he still held her tiny hand.

At three weeks old, Melissa was her mother's pride and joy. Never had Angela felt so much in awe of anything as she did of the tiny babe in her arms. But at the same time, she had a new resolve about her that was born of her inborn ability to nurture. Angela was so comfortable with motherhood that when she was with Melissa it was hard to recognize the shy innocent girl that had stood beside the dashing and dangerous Lucas Reeves just one short year before and promised to give him her love.

This day was Lucas and Angela's first anniversary. It was also a first check up for both baby and mom. Lucas drove them both down to the doctor's office and saw them safely inside. He told Angela he had an appointment with a club owner across town, but he'd made arrangements for Kurt to drop by and pick her and the baby up in an hour. Angela gave him a brief hug and a soft peck on the cheek then took her place in the doctor's waiting room with tiny Melissa sleeping peacefully in her arms.

Angela had been comfortable with her doctor from their first meeting early in her pregnancy. Dr. Kendall was an older gentleman with an open and kind face. His hair once light brown was now salt and pepper with the grey shading giving him a distinguished and knowing look.

His easygoing, almost small town, manners had put Angela instantly at ease with him. When it was Angela's turn to see the doctor, she followed the nurse to an examining room, carrying Melissa comfortably in the crook of one arm with her purse and child car seat balanced in the other. The nurse took the car seat from her and Angela smiled gratefully for her assistance.

"Your husband didn't come with you today, Mrs. Reeves?" She asked.

"No, he had another appointment, though he would have liked to have been here." she said hastily. She suddenly worried that Lucas not being there for the first checkup somehow reflected poorly on her little family.

"The nurse smiled reassuringly. "It's okay," she told Angela, "My man was never around for Doctor's appointments, home and school meetings, little league, you name it. Some men are like that."

Angela relaxed. The nurse left the small room, pulling the door shut quietly as she went out. Melissa was stirring just a little but as soon as Angela's soft voice started to croon a quiet lullaby the child immediately calmed again. When Dr. Kendall came in to the examining room ten minutes later, Melissa was just as quiet as a porcelain doll in Angela's arms. He genuinely liked the shy soft-spoken girl, who he'd only known as a patient for a matter of just over seven months. Her calm manner and quiet good sense made her a wonderful mother. He could only hope that some of her calm would rub off on her firebrand of a husband. He'd seen Lucas at a few of their frequent visits during the pregnancy and had the impression that the intense guitar player was a hot head who was a little overbearing with his young wife. But Lucas did seem to be very concerned with her health and well-being and all-in-all the pair appeared to make a good couple.

"Good afternoon Mrs. Reeves." he said warmly. "And how is our little Melissa doing?"

Angela smiled back Dr. Kendall. "She's the greatest, Doctor." she told him. "She's such a good baby. Hardly ever cries at all."

"I can see that," He said, nodding towards the examining table. "Let's have a closer look at her then; though I must say she looks the picture of health."

Angela gently laid Melissa on the examining table and carefully uncovered her from the blankets she'd been snuggled inside. Dr. Kendall gave the infant a brief once over, checking heart rate, skin tone, temperature and other standard measurements. Content, he stepped back and beamed at the young woman beside him.

"My dear," he told her, "You are doing a wonderful job. Melissa is just fine."

Angela beamed at him with gratitude. "Thank you, Doctor."

Dr. Kendall continued. "Now, make her comfortable for a moment because it's your turn, young lady. How are you feeling?"

Angela busied herself with redressing little Melissa and didn't meet Dr. Kendall's eyes as she replied. "A little sore still, Doctor. But I'm okay." She told him, blushing as she spoke.

"That's natural, Angela." he assured her. "Now I'm going to give you a few moments to get undressed for me and I'll come back and we'll be sure you are well."

Dr. Kendall returned with his nurse in a few minutes as promised and Angela, somewhat self-consciously, submitted to an examination herself. The doctor was well aware of his young patient's modesty and did his best to remain aloof, businesslike and quick in his assessment to give her the least emotional discomfort possible. He did, however, notice a rather nasty bruise on Angela's shoulder and asked her gently about it.

"Oh that," Angela said with a delicate smile. "I banged it on the car door the other day."

"Ouch." Dr. Kendall replied with a little wink. "You should watch out for those old car doors. You're fine, Mrs. Reeves, you'll be back to normal in no time. You're a very healthy young woman."

"Dr. Kendall," Angela asked tentatively.

He looked at her searchingly a moment. "Yes." he said. "Is there something else?"

"Umm, well... Yes, Doctor, there is." She hesitantly told him. "I need to ask you something."

He studied the young woman's face for a moment more, and then glanced at his nurse. When he turned back to Angela, he said matter-of-factly, "Then get dressed, my dear. I'll wait for you in my office directly across the hall here."

Angela stepped into the Doctor's office, carrying Melissa, now in the car seat, in front of her. Dr. Kendall came round the desk and closed the door behind her. Turning back to her, he smiled and said, "Take a seat, Mrs. Reeves."

Angela placed the car seat carefully on one of the two chairs in front of the desk and perched herself on the very edge of the other one. Dr. Kendall returned to his chair across from her and waited attentively.

"Dr. Kendall," she began. "I was wondering if it was possible for me to start on birth control pills. I mean after my period's all back to normal and everything."

He raised one eyebrow at her, but other than that did not seem ruffled by her request. Angela felt somewhat comforted by that.

"Mrs. Reeves, have you ever taken birth control pills before?" he asked.

"No doctor." she replied. "Lucas was, well he...." she stammered, not sure how to explain without further embarrassment.

"Mrs. Reeves, I only wanted to know if you'd used the pill before and whether you'd had any side effects." Dr. Kendall explained, somewhat bemused by Angela's discomfort. "I can certainly give you a renewable prescription for birth control pills. It is a rather mild dosage, which should be more than adequate for you. I have to caution you that you must wait till you have a normal period prior to starting the first month's pills. Also, if you haven't done so, I would urge you to discuss your decision with your husband first."

"Yes Doctor," Angela responded meekly. "Thank you very much."

After writing her the prescription, which Angela tucked safely into her purse, Dr. Kendall saw her out to the waiting room where Kurt was standing near the door looking most uncomfortable.

"Hi Angie." He said with relief when he saw her.

"Thanks again Doctor." Angie said, as she allowed Kurt to take the car seat out of her hands. "There now, Melissa," she cooed to the infant. "Uncle Kurt's got you."

In the truck on the way home, Angela clutched her purse tightly to her, as though someone may discern her secret hidden in its interior if she didn't keep it closed. She kept glancing over the seat to the back cab of the truck where Melissa's car seat was secured. 'I love you my darling baby girl.' she thought to herself. 'Maybe someday, I'll give you a brother or sister. But right now, I couldn't face that again.'

Instead of driving Angela straight home, Kurt took a turn which brought them into the park where one year before she and Lucas had pledged their love and truly started a life together. Angela's eyes widened a little when she saw Lucas's big Buick parked in the lot. Then she grinned happily at Kurt.

"What are you boys up to this time?" she asked, laughing.

"Not me, Angie." Kurt told her innocently. "This is all Lucas's idea." He pulled the truck in next to the Buick, then came around and helped Angela out. He took Melissa, in her car seat, out of the back. Then, like one year previously, offered Angela his arm. She smiled, just as shyly at him as then and allowed him to lead her along the path down the beach.

When they turned into the clearing, Angela gasped with surprise. Lucas had a blanket spread beneath the maple tree, with a picnic basket, champagne and the ever-present Gibson acoustic. As Kurt led her a little closer, she noticed that the blanket that Lucas had spread for the picnic was the very one he'd taken with them to their very first tryst in a clearing. She blushed a little remembering that magical night which now seemed so long ago.

"Happy Anniversary, my love." Lucas said, standing to greet her. Just like the year before, Kurt passed Angela's hand ceremoniously to his brother, but this time he also passed Lucas his daughter comfy in the car seat.

"Later, kids," he told them with a wink. "Congratulations." Kurt went back the way he had come. Lucas bent to Angela and kissed her long and deep. She responded to him immediately, her arms linking round his neck, stretching nearly on her tiptoes in the soft turf. When they finally broke the kiss, she felt nearly out of breath.

"Lucas, this is wonderful." she breathed. Melissa started to fuss then and both her mom and dad smiled down at her. Angela lifted her from the car seat and cuddled her in between herself and her husband. Melissa continued to cry softly. "She's hungry darling." Angela told him.

Lucas put the car seat aside and took the baby carefully from his wife's arm. "Get comfortable on the blanket, Angel. Then you can feed her." He told her.

Angela looked around the clearing and out towards the beach where people were strolling by on the pathway. She turned back to Lucas, who was allowing Melissa to suck the end of one of his callused fingertips. "But Lucas, we're out here." she said self-consciously.

"It's okay Angela," he assured her. "I'm here with you. Feeding your baby is natural. Feed her first, and then we'll eat."

Angela sat down and Lucas passed the baby back to her. He dropped to the blanket himself, sitting very close in front of her, so Angela felt less exposed as she lifted her blouse and freed first one breast and then the other for Melissa to suckle. Lucas loved watching her breast feed their baby, the gentle bonding of his angel and their tiny miracle wakened gentleness in him that he had not known existed. He reached into the picnic basket and brought out some fresh strawberries, which he fed to Angela one by one as she fed Melissa.

After Melissa had her fill, Angela looked after her daughter's other needs and made her comfortable in the car seat again. The baby slept peacefully. Lucas got out the rest of the goodies he'd packed and spread them out. There was Angela's favourite jumbo shrimp, slices of cheese and sausage meat and freshly baked croissants. He leaned his back against the maple tree and Angela half-sat, half-reclined against him with her head on his chest as he fed bite size morsels of everything to her. When he reached for the champagne, Angela gently reminded him that she was breastfeeding the baby and shouldn't drink. He grinned broadly.

"I thought of that, silly girl." He chuckled, showing her that label on the bottle. It was one of those non-alcoholic sparkling wines. She laughed softly and held her glass for him to fill it, marveling at how gentle and thoughtful he seemed to have become since the baby was born.

Lucas raised his glass and offered a toast. "Angela, my love, my wife," he said, "Here's to you and sweet Melissa. I am the luckiest man alive." They drank together then Angela put her glass down and laid back against his chest in the comfort of his arms.

"Lucas," she ventured softly.

"What darling?" he asked, as his fingertips gently caressed the back of her hand and wrist.

"Maybe we could come back here every year? Like a family tradition?" She had turned her palm up towards his and laced her fingers with his longer ones. His other hand came round to her chin and gently pulled her face up towards his. Smiling down at her, he whispered.

"Of course we will. Here beneath the maple tree in our place." He bent and kissed her very softly. "I love you, Happy Anniversary."

Angela was very comfortable with a combination of the afternoon sun and the warmth of Lucas's arms around her. She looked up at his green eyes, sparkling in the sunshine, through her own eyes heavy with sleepiness.

"I love you, Lucas Reeves," she murmured before allowing herself to drift into a cat nap. Lucas shifted just enough to make her slightly more comfortable resting his knee against the corner of Melissa's car seat. He marveled at both sleeping forms and found himself wondering if such tenderness as he felt at that moment could be real. Nothing in his experience of family had prepared him for Angela's innocent, kind ways and the miracle that was baby Melissa was wholly incomprehensible to him.

When Angela stirred a few minutes later, as two children raced by on the beach calling loudly to one another, she looked first to the baby, then to Lucas, who was sitting immobile with tears streaming down his cheeks. Angela was dumbstruck at first. She came to her knees beside him, taking both his hands in her tiny ones. She gazed at him with some worry.

"Lucas, what's wrong?" she asked. He focused on her through his tears, seeming to see her for the first time.

"I'm okay." he lied, pulling one of his hands from hers and wiping it across his face. She put both her hands onto his shoulders and leaned forward gently licking and kissing the tears from his cheeks. His arms went round her and she felt the tension in them immediately.

"Please Lucas, talk to me." She murmured, continuing to kiss him softly.

"I just love you so much." He told her then added an unfathomable statement. "Angie, I don't understand what makes life beautiful. I mean except for you and the music, life sucks baby. I hate it sometimes."

She pulled him to her, this time cradling his head against her breasts as though he were also a child. "Life is quite miraculous, darling. Miraculous that a shy girl like me was even noticed by a handsome and talented man like you, miraculous that you love me and miraculous that Melissa has come to bless us. My daddy used to say, 'Never question miracles.' So I don't."

He heard her words and marveled at her quiet faith. "Angela, I don't know how to love as deeply and wholly as you do. I love you, of that I am most sure. But even being sure, makes me afraid."

She could feel him shaking as he spoke and her heart leapt. They had talked before about how little real love or caring was ever shown in the Reeves household when Kurt and he were growing up and how different that made his experience from hers. But she was unsure how to help him except by always loving him, no matter what. Her arms tightened round him, giving him as strong a hug as she could manage.

"Play for us, Lucas." She asked. "You do know how to love wholly; I hear it every time you play for me."

Lucas had managed to line up gigs for Critical Mass with several of the club managers on the small town circuit that Immortal Beat had traveled every summer. That meant at least every two weeks or so throughout the summer he would be gone for three days at a time. Angela missed his presence in the house at times but was glad of the bonding time with Melissa. She wasn't too nervous of being home all alone with the baby because Kurt was always just a phone call away.

Every day that the weather was warm and dry, she would take Melissa for long walks in her stroller. No matter how far they went, she always wound up at the children's play park not quite a block from home. Angela would take Melissa on her lap so the child could enjoy the sights and sounds of the older children. Angela herself loved the park for its five beautiful maple trees which so reminded her of home.

When Lucas came home on Sundays, he would always bring something for Melissa. Angela laughed because the baby was still so tiny that she couldn't yet appreciate the surprises. But it always brought a joyful tear to her eyes to watch Lucas take her in his arms and tell her how much he had missed her.

Angela got her share of surprises too. Lucas usually brought her ribbons for her hair, pretty scented candles or once he brought a small painting of a young couple picnicking beneath a maple tree. He had found it in a small shop in one of the towns they had played in and knew she would cherish it. Angela found it a place of honour on their bedroom wall where, even when he was away, it would remind her of their special bond.

Angela came to love Sunday night's because Lucas was so gentle and relaxed coming home after missing her for a few days. Once Melissa was tucked in, for a few hours at least, Angela would make them tea. Then Lucas would play the Gibson for her, or sometimes the National Steel. Then he would lead her down the hall to bed and, almost like their first times together, gently make love to her, without any rush or intensity. Angela was radiant and contented for most of that summer.

Lucas finished the first set with a hard driving version of When the House is A 'Rocking and he and Eric, on keyboards, traded some great licks. He put the Stratocaster on to its stand and wheeled around headed towards the bar. He was hot and sweaty but elated that yet another club date seemed to be receiving Critical Mass so very well. As he stepped off the stage, two women and a man approached him. He nodded politely to them all. The brunette girl and the young man were obviously together and were full of enthusiasm for the music. The tall and buxom blonde woman made it rather obvious her enthusiasm was more for Lucas than his music. She was dressed in a rather revealing white summer tube top which covered only the bare essentials and a red leather mini skirt that made her long legs look even longer. When she spoke to Lucas, she leaned very close, almost whispering in his ear and he could easily smell the musky odor of her perfume mixed with the whisky on her breath.

"You're just awesome, man." she breathed, huskily.

"Yeah, thanks." Lucas told her. He felt himself grow aroused by her nearness. Pushing the feeling out of his mind, he pushed past her, speaking back over his shoulder, "Excuse me, I got to get a drink. Enjoy the rest of the show, okay?"

He strode over to the bar where the bartender handed him an ice cold can of beer. Popping the top on the can, he immediately downed nearly half of it in one long swallow. Eric joined him at the bar, grinning with excitement.

"Great set man." the younger man said.

"Yeah, it was awesome." Lucas agreed. "This should be a great gig."

"Hey man, that blonde you were talking to, you know her?" Eric asked.

"No. Why?" Lucas snapped shortly.

"No reason, man." Eric said. "Just she's really hot, huh? Kind of too bad you're married, way she was talking to you, I thought she was gonna fuck you right here!"

Both men laughed cruelly. But Lucas turned uncomfortably away from the room; hiding the evident arousal he felt when he had again pictured the obviously willing blonde in her scanty clothing. He took another long swallow of the beer and changed the subject. For the rest of the break, he and Eric discussed possible new material that they may want to add into the current playlist.

The second set really rocked. The band had incorporated a lot of rock and roll along with rocking blues into the middle set to ensure that the dance floor was filled to capacity. Lucas thrived off the hard driving tunes and had included several blistering guitar solos in their arrangements. The one beer that he had gulped on the break had relaxed him sufficiently so he was having a great time.

Between two numbers, as he was switching from the Stratocaster to the Telecaster, one of the waitresses came up to the edge of the stage with a beer and a shot of whisky on her tray. She motioned to Lucas and he came to where she was standing, bending over a little to catch her words.

"Lucas, this was sent over for you." she explained, indicated the beer and shot.

He looked quizzically at her, "Who?" was all he asked.

She looked around for a moment then motioned discreetly with her arm at the blonde sitting at a table near the corner of the stage. "That lady told me she wanted to buy you a beer and a shot."

"Okay, thanks," he said to her. He took both glasses off the tray and set them behind him on the amplifier without taking a drink from either. As he straightened up and counted down the band into the next number, Eric caught his eye and winked at him. Lucas ignored the young keyboard player.

At the end of that song, Lucas strolled back to the amplifier, picked up the shot glass and downed the shot with a flourish. He then raised the glass of beer in a silent salute towards the blonde's table. As he took a sip of the beer, the woman smiled lewdly at him and ran her tongue around her lips in a gesture that could not be mistaken. Lucas spun away from her quickly, replaced the beer on the amp and got back down to business. The second last number in the set was the slow blues tune that Angela liked so much, These Arms of Mine. Lucas found himself close to tears as he felt every note and wished that his angel was here with him, instead of so many miles away.

Lucas stayed on stage during the next set break, sitting on the corner of the amplifier changing one string on the strat and sipping the rest of the beer. He had his back to the room and head down, so he didn't see the blonde till she stood right beside him. Then his first vision of her was her incredibly long legs. He drew in a sharp breath and looked up at her questioningly.

"If I didn't know better, Lucas Reeves," she said coyly, "I'd swear you were avoiding me."

"Yeah," he half agreed, "Well, thanks for the drink, that was nice."

She laughed then, a deep throaty sound that was loaded with sexual overtones that were unmistakable. "Don't tell me you're shy?" she asked, "A handsome, take-charge kind of guy like you."

Lucas grinned at her then shrugged. "No, I'm restringing a guitar. So I can do my job, you know?" he explained.

That elicited yet another carnal chuckle from the blonde. Again she licked her lips hungrily as she leaned down close to his ear and told him, "We'll just have to see if you can do your job, you know?" That said, she turned and left the stage without a backward glance.

Lucas watched her go, with his hands clenching into tight fists and a feeling of arousal that bordered on pure animal passion. It took him a few moments to compose himself and complete the restringing.

The third set went very well and Lucas spent some time chatting with several of the young patrons of the club before he packed up to head for the car. He had not seen the blonde woman after the show at all and had hopefully assumed that she had given up and left for home.

He had put both the Stratocaster and Telecaster into the backseat of the car and was about to slide into the driver's seat, when he froze, suddenly conscious of a movement behind him in the dark parking lot. He wheeled round, ready for anything, and looked into the smiling eyes of the blonde. She stepped closer as soon as he turned towards her and was now pressing her leggy body against him. She looked coyly into his flashing green eyes and once their eyes had locked, she boldly slid her hand down and rubbed his cock through his jeans. Lucas was aroused instantly, but glanced quickly around the lot. Satisfying himself that no one was observing them, he put an arm around the woman's waist and drew her tightly against him. His other hand went to the hem of her very short skirt and then brazenly reached beneath it as he rubbed her through her panties. He broke the contact very quickly and pulled her past him towards the open driver's door.

"Get in, now!" he growled at her. She giggled softly but quickly slid into the car moving across the seat just enough to let him slide behind the wheel. He started the car and pulled out of the lot. In minutes he pulled up in front of the motel he was staying in. All the way there in the car she had continued to caress his hardness through his pants.

He turned off the engine, opened the door and practically dragged her out of the car with him. He held her tightly by one wrist as he unlocked the door to his room then pushed her through the door into the darkened room beyond. She had stumbled a little but managed to regain her feet and turned to face him as he kicked the door shut behind him.

Lucas advanced on her now, one hand pushed roughly against one of her shoulders, causing her to step backwards against the bed and fall backwards on to it. She laughed sexily again and held her arms up to him. He stared down at her for a moment then very deliberately started unbuckling his belt and unzipping his jeans. He pushed her arms out of his way and roughly pulled her head to the edge of the bed.

"Suck me!" he demanded. She willingly took his now hard cock into her mouth. As her mouth worked up and down the length of his arousal, he reached for her skirt and pushed it up around her waist. He then literally tore her panties off her and, for the first time, she became a little frightened of her handsome conquest. She let his cock slip out of her mouth and gasped in surprise and a little fear.

It was Lucas's turn to chuckle as he grabbed her legs and drew her to the edge of the bed, driving his still hard cock into her. He plunged into her forcefully bringing tears to her eyes. Lucas didn't even see them; his eyes were closed, head thrown back. When he climaxed, he cried out Angela's name. He stretched onto the bed beside the blonde woman, face down on the bedspread.

She rolled to her side and put a hand tentatively on his shoulder. "Lucas," she murmured softly.

At first he didn't move or react in anyway. But after a moment, he stood up and pulled on his jeans, digging his wallet out of his back pocket.

"Lucas, what's wrong?" she asked.

"Nothing." he snapped at her. He tossed a bill on the bed beside her. "Cab fare," he explained. "Get out of here."

"Who's Angela?" she asked, as she picked up the bill and tried to straighten her clothes.

He glared at her and the black look in his eyes terrified her completely. "Just get the fuck out!" he told her forcefully.

She left hastily, making her way down to the office of the motel to call for her cab.

Lucas sat silent in the dark for long minutes after the door had closed then crossed to the bathroom and vomited into the toilet. He stripped and took a shower, drank some water and, at last, collapsed on to the bed to sleep fitfully for what was left of the night.

The following day, Lucas went shopping for the gifts he would take home to his family and it was in a small gift shop that afternoon he found the small painting of the young couple picnicking beneath the maple that Angela cherished and that brought tears to his eyes.

Just after supper on a Sunday evening, Lucas was stretched out on the couch with baby Melissa on his chest. Angela came in from the kitchen and smiled at the two of them. Melissa was three months old now and would sometimes even sleep right through the night.

"My two favourite couch potatoes." She laughed.

Lucas grinned at her. "Yep that's us, babe." He said, "You know I love Sunday's, coming home and being with you and Melissa. I miss you so bad when I'm gone."

Angela lifted the baby gently out of Lucas's arms. "I miss you too, darling." She told him. "I'm gonna feed her now and see if she will settle for us." Angela curled into the easy chair and unbuttoned her blouse to offer her nipple to her tiny daughter.

Lucas sat up, swung his legs down to the floor and reached for the Gibson which had been leaning against the arm of the couch. He never got tired of watching Angela nurse the baby, there was such a closeness and sense of love in the act that he found entrancing. He played soft melodies, like lullabies, as Melissa suckled at her mother's breasts.

"Dinner music." he chuckled softly.

Angela smiled back at him, thinking how wonderful it was to have this time of quiet togetherness. The baby was content and so, it seemed, was Lucas. When Melissa had taken her fill, Angela changed her and cuddled her comfortably in her arms till the baby slept. Lucas stood and followed her through to the nursery, standing behind her, as Angela gently laid the baby in her crib.

Lucas linked an arm around Angela's waist and for a long time they just stood together and watched their daughter sleep. Finally, it was Angela who turned towards Lucas, reaching up to slide her arms around his neck then pulling his head down to her lips and kissing him hungrily. He responded to her with surprised pleasure. It wasn't often that Angela initiated intimacy between them.

"I want you." she murmured against the skin of his neck and even the caress of her warm breath moved him deeply. She stepped back and put one small hand in his, leading him from the baby's room.

Once they were into the bedroom, she pulled his head down to hers again kissing him deeply. As their mouths and tongues explored one another, she reached for his shirt, tugging it gently out of his jeans. She broke off the kiss long enough to pull the shirt over his head, then her lips were back on him, licking and kissing across his now bared chest. Lucas caressed her hair, neck and shoulders as she continued to explore his skin with her mouth.

"God Angie, that feels so nice." He murmured.

She continued down across his stomach till she reached the edge of his jeans. Her hands unbuckled his belt, opened the fly and slid inside round his hips pushing the jeans down and round his ankles. Lucas was already very hard, aroused by her boldness. As he stepped out of the jeans, Angela slipped to her knees in front of him and gently took his cock into her hands. Lucas reached for her head and she whispered firmly, "No Lucas, let me do this, don't make me do this."

Surprised, he dropped his hands away from her even as she took his hardness into her mouth. She sucked on him gently, exploring with her tongue, feeling him grow even harder and marveling that she could enjoy the sensation without feeling shamed. Lucas was trembling with an inner turmoil he did not comprehend. His arousal as she kneeled before him brought him a strangely disquieting feeling of humiliation. Her words had bitten him viciously though they were softly whispered. He wept.

"Angela," he murmured tentatively, "I want to be inside you, my love." He placed one hand softly on her shoulder and reached under her chin with the other. She allowed his cock to slide from her mouth and stood up. Lucas, gentled now by her example, slowly and lovingly undressed her and together they moved onto the bed. Angela was at once trembling with arousal and elation that their love was so very gentle, at least this night. Lucas moved over her and, kissing her deeply, guided his hardness into her. He continued to kiss and lick her gently as they moved together, until he neared climax, then he threw his head back and a sound that was a combination of moan and scream rose in his throat. Angela felt her own climax rise with his and was overwhelmed by sensation.

As they lay entwined afterwards, she murmured softly, "Lucas, I love you."

Lucas, silent tears covering his face, nearly choked on his words of reply, "My love, I don't deserve you."

Angela was stunned by his words and even more unsettled when she tasted his tears. She lay safe in his arms in the darkness and could find no words to comfort him. He drew the quilt up over them and the warmth lulled them both into the peace of sleep.

Melissa was growing like the proverbial weed. Now over six months old, Angela had started weaning her from breast milk and varying her diet with pabulum and other very mild baby foods. Bedtime was now the only time that she still let the baby suckle as she seemed to settle for the night so much better that way.

But Angela herself was growing restless. The weather in mid-November was chilly and brisk at best, damp and freezing at worst so she felt trapped in the house more and more. She still had not seen Lucas's band play live, though they had gigs fairly regularly all over the city. He seemed reluctant for her to leave the baby even for an evening. Though she had broached the subject a couple of times, his swift censure of the idea caused her to shyly keep her feelings to herself.

Kurt joined them for Sunday dinner more often than not and it was gratifying to watch him with baby Melissa. It seemed he took the duties of being an uncle very seriously. Often he would take the baby on his lap and patiently feed her whatever cereal that Angela had prepared. Watching them together one evening put an idea into Angela's mind.

Lucas was down in the music room with Jake and Eric working on a new number, so she slid into a chair next to him and softly ventured, "Kurt, can I ask you a question?"

"Sure Angie," he told her, as he gently wiped Melissa's chin where she had dribbled some of the pabulum.

"Do you think that you would like to maybe baby-sit her one night?" She asked nervously then tried to explain. "I'd like to go see Lucas play and well......"

"Sure Angie." He confirmed without hesitation "Just say the word. But maybe you and Lucas should pick a night when he's not playing and go out for a romantic dinner or something, too?"

"Oh, no." She said quickly, "I really want to see him play with the band, like we used to, you know? But don't say anything to him, okay? I want it to be a surprise."

Kurt studied her face, trying to fathom her sudden secretive hesitation and was a little surprised that her eyes seemed clouded by a look that could only be described as fearful. He shrugged away an urge to reach out to her and instead merely nodded his understanding of her words.

"Just tell me when you'd like to go then, Angie." He assured her, "I'll be here."

"Thank you, Kurt." She replied. She stood and lifted Melissa from his lap. "I'd better change her and make sure she's comfortable before dinner," and went down the hall to the nursery. Kurt took the small dish and spoon he'd been feeding the child with across to the sink, even as he heard his brother and the other two men coming up from the basement.

Angela waited two weeks before calling on Kurt to stay with Melissa. Lucas and Critical Mass were playing at Louis' Blues that night and she felt familiar enough with the club to be able to go there alone. Kurt arrived about nine thirty in the evening and Angela called a cab as soon as he got there. She would probably miss the first set but hoped to arrive to see most of the second and all of the third sets. She was radiant, made more so by the excitement of going out for a change. The long walks she took so regularly with Melissa had allowed her to regain her girlish figure very soon after the baby's birth so her tight jeans and a pretty white shirt with gold thread sparkling throughout looked fabulous on her. Kurt nodded his approval as she waited by the front door for the cab.

"You look great, Angie." He told her.

"Thanks," she said, blushing. "Not too flashy for a blues bar?"

"Naw, you're perfect." He assured her. "Besides, you're the star's wife. You gotta look the part."

She grinned at him then, spotting the cab pulling up out front, she waved goodbye. "See you later, Kurt. Thanks so very much for this."

The cab whisked her downtown through the hypnotic rush of traffic and city lights. As they sped through traffic she thought about the last time she had been at Louis' Blues, on her wedding night. She smiled wryly to herself, thinking that tonight's welcome may not be quite as jubilant as that night had been, but hopeful that Lucas would be pleased that she wanted to be close to him and watch him play.

The young man at the door of Louis' Blues was quite surprised when Angela got out of her cab alone. Not many women ventured out to bars unescorted even in these enlightened times unless in groups of two or three women. He was about to key in her cover charge on the small cash register in front of him when a voice came from behind him.

"Hey Tom, don't be charging this fine young lady." The speaker said in a deep jolly sounding voice. "She's Lucas's wife." The voice materialized into the tall, very stocky figure of Louis himself, who came past the counter and took both Angela's hands in his. Tom whistled under his breath. He'd heard that Lucas Reeves' lady was a real beauty but now the evidence was standing in front of him, he had a new reason to envy the guitarist.

"Angela, my dear girl," Louis was saying, "What a pleasure to see you! It's been too long since you graced my humble establishment."

Angela squeezed Louis' hands warmly and smiled shyly up at the big man. "Thank you, Louis. You're very kind."

"Lucas never said you were coming," Louis continued, as he protectively walked her through the doorway. "I'd have rolled out the red carpet for sure, if I'd known."

Angela could hear Critical Mass, though couldn't yet see the stage. 'They must be in the second set.' she thought. To Louis, she said, "Lucas didn't know I was coming. This is kind of a surprise."

"Well then, you must come and sit at the bar next to me." He told her firmly. "Great view from there and you'll be safe from all these yahoos." He gestured at the rather large crowd of mainly men. A few heads turned as she made her way through the crowd, following in Louis' wake, but she focused on the music and the few glimpses she caught of Lucas as they traversed the back side of the room.

The bar was to one side of the room close to the front of the space and the bandstand. From the bar stools one had a clear view of the stage over the heads of any seated patrons. Angela slipped up onto the stool beside Louis' and, when he asked, requested only a ginger ale. Then her full attention was focused on the stage, her eyes sparkling with excitement.

Lucas had not noticed her arrival at first being fully absorbed in what he was playing. But as the band slipped from one number to the next he had glanced over to Louis' usual spot by the bar. He took a sharp inward breath when he saw Angela sitting next to Louis. She smiled happily when their eyes briefly locked and Lucas nodded in return. Though outwardly he showed little emotion, inwardly his mind was racing. 'What on earth was she doing here and all alone?' he thought.

The last number in the set was usually Walking Blues but before the band played the opening notes, Lucas had a hurried conference. Tonight, he told them, they would add one more number before the break; Close to You, a Stevie Ray

Vaughan tune. They nodded their agreement and Jason grinned at Lucas, "Like old times, huh, my friend?"

"Yeah man," Lucas replied, "Something like that."

When Lucas stepped up to the mike to introduce the last number, Angela smiled to herself. She knew right away which song he was leading up to and was already slipping off her barstool when he called her to the stage. She slipped into his arms with the guitar in front of them both and good-naturedly played her part in the little dance performance.

As the tune ended, Lucas released the guitar and took his wife firmly in his one free arm. He brought his mouth down over hers and kissed her deeply, forcing his tongue between her parted lips. Angela squirmed a little in his grasp, conscious of the numbers of people witnessing the very passionate grip he held her in. But Lucas did not release his hold; in fact, he did not let her go even as he broke off the kiss and replaced the guitar on the stand behind them.

He turned back to her, his now free right hand cupping her chin and she looked into his eyes, immediately frozen by the anger she saw there. The rest of the band had left the stage and someone had turned the lights off for the break. Angela stood transfixed by her husband's look alone and a tense silence only moments long, seemed to her like an eternity. Lucas leaned down as though to kiss her again but instead his lips brushed her ear. He spoke harshly but softly, so no one but Angela heard him, "What the hell do you think you're doing here?" He asked, then stung her brutally with words alone, "You belong at home minding our daughter, you stupid little bitch." Angela tried desperately to hold back her tears, praying that he would at least decide his anger could wait till they got home.

Lucas took her firmly by one hand and led her from the stage. Not wanting to cause a scene in front of everyone, Angela meekly allowed him to lead her past the bar and through a short hallway adjacent to the kitchen which led out the back of the club to the alley.

Once they were out in the night air, he wheeled on her, eyes flashing angrily. "I thought I'd told you that I wanted you home with Melissa!" he snapped at her, "Who the hell is with her anyway?"

"Kurt's with her Lucas," Angela said, shaking with fear, "It's okay."

"Okay?" he growled. "No it is not okay! Damn you!" He brought his free hand round in an open handed slap which connected with her skull right over her ear. She reeled and almost stumbled, crying out in pained surprise. Lucas put both hands on her shoulders and shook her violently; her tiny form was like a rag doll in his grasp. The shaking only lasted a few seconds then with one last violent push he shoved her away from him. She fell backwards against the unyielding surface of the brick building wall behind her, barely noticing the stabbing pain which shot through her shoulder. Both her hands had come up to her face as she stood there sobbing and trembling. Lucas shot her a last disdainful look and said, "Clean yourself up and get inside. Sit beside Louis and don't move a damned muscle till I'm done. We'll discuss this at home." He left her there and went back inside.

The alley was a frightening place, made more so by being left alone there by Lucas. She took several deep breaths, trying to clear her head then quickly went through the door into the dimly lit back hallway. There were doors to her right which lead into restrooms and she quickly went into the ladies room which she found thankfully empty. She hardly recognized the frightened figure in the mirror. Her head was pounding and makeup smeared. She did a little repair work on the makeup and was relieved that Lucas's blow had hit her where her long black hair would easily hide any bruising. After a small drink of water and a few more deep breaths to clear her head, she made her way back to the bar. Louis gave her a curious look but did not venture any comments about her long absence.

When the last set was over, Lucas took his time packing up. Louis had made several attempts to start conversation with Angela but her one word mumbled responses soon made him realize that she would not be drawn out. He made sure she had a fresh ginger ale while she waited for her husband then, as the club was slowly emptying, he sat down at the Hammond organ and idly played snippets of tunes and scales.

When Lucas had the car loaded, he came back in for Angela. He was utterly silent, which frightened her more somehow than if he had said anything. She slipped down off the barstool and put her hand into his, following him into the night. Louis called out a goodnight to them both, which Angela was content to let Lucas answer.

Lucas remained silent all the way home and the longer his silence dragged on the worse Angela's tense trembling fear became. They pulled into the driveway and he finally turned towards her.

"Go and tell Kurt we're home." he said. "I've gotta move this gear inside."

"Yes Lucas." she said, sliding out of the car and fishing her keys from her bag.

Kurt was all smiles as Angela walked through the kitchen door. She managed to grin at him not wanting him to know her 'surprise' had turned into such a disaster.

"Your little one has been a perfect angel," he told her, "Just like her Mom."

Angela winced a little at his words. "Thank you so much, Kurt." she told him, trying to keep the apprehension out of her voice. "I really appreciate this."

Kurt was already pulling on his boots. He straightened and politely nodded at his sister-in-law. "Take care, Angie. Good night." He went out the door she had come through and she heard him call to Lucas. She turned and went to check on the baby but not before she heard Lucas's voice raised in anger outside.

"Kurt damn you!" Lucas exploded, at his brother as soon as the door behind the older man had closed.

"What the hell?" Kurt replied, baffled but wary.

"If we need someone to look after Melissa, I'll call you myself." Lucas told him. "What the fuck were you thinking letting her go out to a bar alone?"

"Now hold on, Lucas." Kurt tried to explain, "She wasn't going to just any bar she was coming to see you."

Lucas blindsided Kurt with an unexpected closed fisted smash that caught him right below his left eye. Kurt staggered one step then held both hands up, palm out, in a gesture of placation or possibly supplication. Lucas stared disdainfully at him.

"Don't ever let her pull this shit with you again!" He growled. "She's my wife, stay the fuck away from her."

Kurt backed off a pace down the driveway and replied in as even a tone as he could. "Lucas, I thought I was doing you both a favour. I'm outta here man. We'll talk to you Monday, okay?"

Lucas seemed to calm a little and bent to pick up the amplifier that he'd left in the middle of the driveway. As he straightened up, he glared at Kurt and said quietly, "I ain't coming on Monday. We need a break from you man."

Kurt only nodded and turned towards his car. Lucas moved towards the house with his burden without giving his brother another thought.

Lucas moved his gear into the house then locked the kitchen door, turned off the lights and went down the hall in search of Angela. He found her sitting in the rocking chair in the nursery next to Melissa's crib, watching the baby sleep. His still booted foot stopped the slow sway of the chair abruptly and she looked up at him in fear.

"She's asleep, Angela." he said softly. "Come now, we don't want to wake her." He reached down and took an iron grip on one of her wrists and literally dragged her from the chair. She cried out in pain and he glared at her.

"Sssh, damn you."

She did not fight him, but allowed him to lead her out of the room. He was completely silent as he dragged her through the hall and into their bedroom, slamming the door shut behind him. He turned to face her, cruelly twisting her arm by the wrist, till she cried out in fear and hurt.

"Lucas please don't." She whimpered. He ignored her plea and slapped her with his open hand across first one cheek and then the other. Her head was ablaze with the pain of his blows, her tears flowing like rivers carrying blackened trails of eye makeup across her reddened cheeks.

"Don't you ever cross me again, Angie!" He bellowed, and she cowered more from his angry voice and eyes than from his hands. "Now get your god damned clothes off before I rip them off!"

Hands shaking, she quickly did as he asked. Soon she stood naked and shivering, more from fear than cold, before him. He advanced on her again, taking the same wrist which was already bruised by his hand and twisting her arm up behind her. Again she cried out and he smacked her swiftly across the back of the head.

He pushed her onto the bed face first in front him still holding her one hand behind her back. She felt like she was going to suffocate with her face in the pillows and turned her head just a little so she could still breathe. Lucas fumbled one handed with his belt and fly and Angela lay face down and frightened for what seemed to her to be an eternity. Finally she heard his jeans fall to the floor and his other hand roughly grabbed her backside. He let go of her arm and she felt an instant of relief as the pain subsided. Then she was horrified as she heard him first spit onto his hand and then felt that hand rub his spittle into the crack of her ass. She suddenly realized what he intended but didn't dare to protest. She turned her face back into the pillow even as he plunged his cock into her anus. Her agonized screams were muffled by the corner of a lacy pillow which she took into her mouth as a self-imposed gag. Angela prayed as Lucas punished her brutally.

Angela woke to the sound of Melissa's cries from the nursery at about five in the morning. She winced in pain as she rolled out of bed and dare not even look at Lucas. He did not stir as she pulled on a robe over her naked form and shuffled from the room. She gathered Melissa into her arms, trying to put as little of the child's weight onto her bruised and swollen wrist as possible. She made the baby comfortable with a clean dry diaper and sleeper then carried her through to the kitchen.

She clumsily warmed a bottle of formula for her baby using only her sore arm. Not willing to put Melissa down for even a moment, she was cradling her daughter on her hip safe in the grip of her uninjured left arm. Melissa's crying had been replaced by happy gurgles as she clutched with her tiny fists at handfuls of the soft flannel fabric of Angela's robe. Once the bottle was warm, she carried the baby through into the living room and curled into a corner of the couch to feed her.

Outside it was raining heavily. Angela listened to the deluge and tried in vain not to think about the previous night. Her tears surprised her, as she had thought she had no more to cry. She wept silently as Melissa hungrily devoured the bottle of formula. When the baby had finished her morning bottle she was content to gurgle in Angela's arms as her mother watched her through tear filled eyes, one blackened and swollen. The young woman suddenly felt she had not the strength to move from where she was. She pulled a blanket over her legs from the arm of the couch, tucked the baby safely between her own body and the back of the couch then stretched full length with her back to the room. It was there, both contentedly asleep, that Lucas found his wife and daughter three hours later.

Lucas stood over them for long minutes then, as the baby had started to stir, he bent down to lift her from behind her sleeping mother. Angela's eyes flew instantly open and, despite her pain, she arose quickly. Her fear was evident in her downcast demeanor but she put her arms out towards the baby.

"It's okay, Lucas," she almost begged, "I'm awake, I'll look after her."

Lucas was noticeably shaken now that he could see all of Angela's face and readily see the terrible bruising on her left cheek and eye. The baby, oblivious of the tension between her parents, was clutching at gold chain which hung round his neck. He unconsciously untangled her tiny hand from the chain as he spoke to Angela.

"Oh baby," he told her, "I am so very sorry. I was just so angry, you know, so worried about you, going out all alone."

Angela hardly heard his words as her focus remained on Melissa. She stood up slowly and cautiously, her hands still reaching towards the child.

"Please Lucas;" she murmured plaintively, "I'll look after her. I promise."

He gently handed the baby back to her and silently watched as she moved somewhat painfully to the kitchen holding her daughter thankfully in her arms. She put the baby safely into the high chair drawn up near the counter where she could keep an eye on her and reached for the baby cereal box to prepare some breakfast. Melissa babbled happily playing with a plastic baby toy on the tray of her chair and Angela prattled on at her reciting nursery rhymes more to keep her own emotions in check than to entertain the baby.

Lucas had sat down in the easy chair in the living room and picked up his Gibson six string. The sound of his playing was like a double edged sword to Angela's tattered emotions, at once calming her and bringing dark images of his rage to assail her.

Before she started to feed Melissa, Angela started the coffee maker. Then, moving Melissa's chair back to the kitchen table she sat in front of her daughter and fed her breakfast. In the living room, Lucas played on, seemingly oblivious of either mother or child.

After she'd fed the baby, Angela poured him a coffee and placed it on the coffee table, not daring yet to meet his eyes. He put the Gibson aside and reached for the steaming mug.

"Thanks baby," he said softly, when she didn't look at him or acknowledge his words, he spoke again, "Angie?"

"You're welcome, Lucas." she whispered. Then, head bowed and eyes averted from him, she turned back to the kitchen.

Angela gave Melissa a bath, changed her into fresh clothes and carried her into the main bedroom while she got dressed herself. She was horrified when she caught a glimpse of her bruised face in the mirror and tried somewhat unsuccessfully to mask the marks with some makeup. She pulled on fresh underwear, comfortable jeans and a pullover, drew a brush through her long hair then gathered Melissa up and took her to the nursery. She was playing on the floor with the baby when she heard the outer kitchen door open and then close again followed by the sound of the Buick's engine as Lucas started it and she realized with relief that he was gone.

The baby settled down for a midmorning nap and Angela went and washed up the porridge bowl and Lucas's coffee mug. She still hadn't eaten herself but couldn't seem to find any appetite for food. She went back to the nursery and dozed in the big rocking chair as Melissa slept.

Lucas came back in just about lunch time and came through to the nursery looking for her. In one hand he carried two dozen long stemmed roses, half red and half white. Angela had heard him come in and was fully awake when he found her.

"Angela," he began, tentatively.

"Yes Lucas," she replied meekly with a noticeable edge of fear in her tiny voice.

"Baby, please tell me you forgive me." he begged. He stepped slowly in front of her and dropped to his knees at her feet. He offered the flowers to her on both outspread palms. Angela stared for a long moment at the hands, not the flowers, vividly remembering how he had hurt her the previous night. Finally, shaking violently, she reached out and took the roses on to her lap.

"I love you, Lucas." she said through her tears. "I'm so sorry."

He reached out his hands and took one of hers in both his, gently kissing the back, the palm and the inside of her wrist as she cried bitter tears. Finally he helped her up and together they went to the kitchen. He kept one arm around her, but reached a vase, filled it with water and helped her put the roses into it. Then he led her down the hall to their bedroom where he took her in his arms on the bed and held her till her weeping finally subsided and she slept.

Angela's bruises healed. Her focus turned almost entirely to Melissa over the weeks that followed as the Christmas season took Lucas away from home most nights for gigs. He would usually get home at two or later in the morning and sleep most of the day. When he did come in, Angela would slide out of bed and put the kettle on for tea. They would talk as they sipped their tea and he usually would play for her, but she carefully avoided speaking of the things she thought may anger or upset him. Lucas was gentler in their lovemaking but Angela would always feel some small sense of resignation to his needs and will as she sought to gratify him rather than risk his wrath.

They were just finishing supper one evening, with Melissa making a happy mess of a teething biscuit on her high chair tray, when someone knocked on the kitchen door. Angela glanced quickly at Lucas, wondering if he'd forgotten yet again to tell her the band was rehearsing at the house. But he too looked surprised as he put his coffee mug down and rose to see who was there. He swung open the door and found Kurt standing hunched against the damp windy air.

"Hey man, am I interrupting dinner?" Kurt asked somewhat sheepishly. Angela looked from one to the other of the brothers, knowing that they hadn't spoken since the night that Kurt had baby-sat for her and she had made Lucas so terribly angry. She felt responsible somehow for the brothers' distance.

Lucas was utterly silent for a moment or two, staring with a mixture of anger and amazement at his older brother. "What you doing here, Kurt?" he challenged, making no move to step aside and let his brother into the house.

"We need to talk, Lucas." Kurt replied, looking the younger man in the eye and resisting the urge to glance past him at either Angela or the baby.

Lucas paused again for a very long time before he responded at all, almost as though debating with himself. Angela watched his hand, closest to her, clench and unclench several times and she worried a little that he may take a swing at Kurt. Finally, he spoke evenly, "Okay man, let's talk. Come on in."

Angela smiled with a sense of relief as Kurt walked through the door. He turned his attention immediately to his niece, though he nodded a polite hello to Angela too. The baby was a sight with cookie all over her mouth, face, hair and clothes but she grinned with delight when Kurt smiled at her.

"My God, she's grown so much!" he exclaimed and Angela beamed with pride.

"Nice to see you, Kurt," she said shyly, "Would you like a cup of coffee?"

"Thanks Angie, that'd be nice." He replied. She crossed to the counter to pour another mug as the men took seats at the table. Once she had put the coffee down in front of Kurt, she turned to Melissa and lifted her from the high chair.

"Time for a bath for this young lady." She announced and carried her from the room.

Lucas watched her go before he spoke again.

"So talk, Kurt." He said tersely. "What you want?"

"I would like you to come back and give me a hand, man." Kurt said evenly. "I got a couple of big contracts between now and mid-January and I could use your help if you're willing. Money's good."

"Well, we're gigging a lot right now, with Christmas and all." Lucas told him then took a long thoughtful sip of his coffee before continuing. "Money's always good with you, man. I'm thinking maybe just early in the week, ya know? Like Monday, Tuesday, maybe even Wednesday when we're not playing so much?"

Kurt's eyes betrayed his delight though he still kept his voice and manner as neutral as possible. "Yeah Lucas, three days a week would be great. It'll probably guarantee that these jobs are done on schedule. I'll pick you up 'bout eight in the morning, like we used to?"

Lucas put his coffee mug down and stretched a hand across the table. Kurt met him half way and the two men shook hands somberly. Then Lucas softened and grinned. "Sure Kurt, same time same place." he chuckled. "Baby needs new shoes!"

Both men laughed and, by the time Angela returned with the freshly bathed and dressed Melissa on her hip, they had switched from coffee to beer and Kurt was drawing floor plans on a scratch pad to show Lucas the current project. Angela smiled with relief and joy that the men seemed to have come to terms.

During the last week before Christmas, Angela barely saw Lucas. He was either on jobsites with Kurt or out playing gigs and seemed to come home only long enough to have a quick meal or shower and change clothes. Melissa was crawling everywhere now and the lights and shiny baubles on the tiny tree that Angela had decorated in the living room were an irresistible magnet to the baby's eyes and hands. Just as Angela rescued the tree from yet another onslaught, the phone rang. She took the child on her hip, dangling a brightly coloured plastic rattle in front of her to distract her. The child took the toy in one tiny fist and Angela picked up the receiver.

"Hello?" she said softly.

It was her mother's voice that greeted her. Angela was ecstatic. They had rarely talked since Melissa's birth. Angela had been especially reticent about contacting her mother, knowing how she felt about Lucas and worrying that she may sense that something had not been right between her and her husband.

"Hello Angela." Belle said quietly. "How's my granddaughter?"

"She's fine, Mom." Angela told her. "Growing like a weed. I'm so happy you called."

"I'm happy for you darling." Belle replied. "And things are okay with you and Lucas?"

Angela drew in a sharp breath when she heard that and wondered if somehow Belle knew. "Fine Mom, he's out right now at a gig. Melissa and I are just playing."

"I see," her mother said rather flatly. "Angela darling, remember I told you I was going to try and come down to see you and the baby at Christmas?"

Angela's original excitement was dampened by her mother's somber tone. "Yes Mom, I've been really excited about it too. I can't wait for you to see my girl." She said hopefully.

"Well, I'm sorry," Belle told her, almost coldly. "Your sister and her husband have paid for me to join them on a trip to Disneyworld for Christmas. I won't be joining you, this year."

"Oh," Angela murmured, completely devastated and unable to utter more than the one syllable.

"Take care Angela, and Merry Christmas." Her mother finished with an air of finality.

Angela mumbled a "Merry Christmas" back but it seemed the line had already gone dead before the words were out of her mouth. She replaced the receiver and sat back on the couch cuddling Melissa. It was almost the baby's bedtime and she was content to snuggle into the warmth of her mother's arms, while Angela fretted about her mother; she took comfort from her daughter's nearness.

When Lucas came in from his gig that evening, he found Angela dozing in the rocking chair in the baby's room with the comforter from her childhood bed wrapped round her. He could see, even in the dim glow of the night light, that his wife had been crying. He gently shook her awake.

"Hey baby," he chuckled, "You shouldn't be sleeping here. Gonna get up and have some tea with me?"

She pulled the comforter aside, got up from the chair and moved resignedly towards the hall and the kitchen. Lucas followed after her, only after standing for a moment next to his daughter's crib and gently caressing her brow with his callused fingertips. He folded Angela's comforter over his arm and carried it from the room with him.

In the kitchen, she had put the kettle on, lifted out mugs and was sitting at the table waiting for the water to boil. Lucas put the comforter down on one chair and drew another round to face his wife. He sat opposite her and put one hand under her chin, bringing her downcast face up to meet his gaze.

"What's up with you, baby?" He asked her softly. He could see that her eyes were brimming with tears not yet shed.

She met his piercing gaze for mere seconds before she dropped her head once again and started to cry softly. At that moment the kettle started to whistle and she broke away from him to make the tea. He did not press her any further but took the comforter through to the living room and sat down with his Gibson acoustic while she was still filling the mugs. When she brought them through to the living room, he patted the couch right next to him and, taking his cue, she sat down.

He had a drink of the tea, put the mug on the coffee table then started to play a soft melody. As the music filled the room, he spoke again.

"Baby, when something is bothering you, I need to know." He told her. "Now out with it. What's wrong?"

Somehow, Angela found it a little bit easier to talk to him when she didn't have to look him in the eye and with the calming effect of his music; she related her phone conversation with her mother.

Lucas listened, strummed and drank his tea, as Angela tearfully told him that she felt betrayed or even abandoned by her mother. He said nothing for a long while after she had finished, except to urge her to finish her tea. Then he put the guitar aside and wrapped the comforter round them both, taking her into his strong armed embrace.

"Angie," he said, a hesitant note creeping into his voice. "Sometimes I get so mad at your Mom. I don't think you're imagining things at all, she really does favour Pamela. It just ain't fair for a Mom to be like that."

"Do you really think so, Lucas?" Angela asked, craning her head a little to try and see his expression more clearly.

Lucas squeezed her reassuringly but at the same time there was still certain trepidation in his manner. He stroked her long black hair, kissed her brow several times then finally drew a deep breath and spoke again.

"Angela, I was never going to tell you this, but now that your mother's done this to you, I think I'd better."

Angela tensed up under his arms and started to sit up straighter, a frightened look in her blue eyes. He continued to caress her with his hands and spoke again.

"Baby, remember when you and Christie went dress shopping for the wedding and I took off to do some errands?" He asked her.

"Yes Lucas." she whispered.

"Well my errand was a drive in the country." he told her. "I drove out to see your Mom, because I wasn't going to let you have a wedding without her here. I made sure she came to her daughter's wedding."

"Oh my God, Lucas." Angela breathed. "You mean she wasn't going to even come?"

"Baby, I'm so sorry." he crooned, then continued. "Damn that woman makes me angry. You're her daughter just as much as Pamela and she shoulda just come. But I had to practically threaten her to get her here."

"She doesn't love me, Lucas." Angela said very softly, her voice cracking with emotion. "I'm a disappointment to her."

He didn't say anything more, merely held her as she wept. Slowly her tears subsided. Lucas kissed her cheeks tasting the still damp and salty trail of her tears then brought his mouth over hers. She responded immediately, feeling an overwhelming urge to reconfirm their love. When Lucas felt her move hard and rhythmically against him under the comforter, he smiled to himself. 'Oh yeah,' he thought, 'You're mine baby.' Aloud, he told her, "I'm your family, babe. Melissa and I, we love you."

Spring's warmth brought tulips, daffodils and crocuses to brighten Angela's afternoon walks with Melissa. They had been housebound so often by heavy rains all through the winter months that it was sweet relief to be able to get out in the fresh air again. Melissa, just turned one now, was just starting to walk and eagerly clung to Angela's hands as they explored the universe of the small park close to the house together. The great maple trees in the park were just getting their leaves and the sunshine gleaming through the pale green of new growth cast pretty shadowed patterns on everything beneath them, including the blanket that Angela always brought for Melissa to play on.

Angela looked up through the trees at the brilliant blue of the sky beyond and it reminded her of that wonderful afternoon almost two years before, when she had married Lucas beneath just such a stately old maple tree. Their anniversary was in just two days and she hoped that perhaps he would remember, but knew that the band was playing that evening and so resolved not to be too disappointed if he forgot. Melissa distracted her thoughts as she chose that moment to half-crawl half-walk towards the swings where some older children were laughing and calling to one another as they played. Angela caught Melissa up in her arms well out of harm's way. Then she went herself to the remaining free swing and, with the baby on her lap, she gently pushed the swing just enough to make her daughter laugh with joy.

Two days later, Lucas was up early in the morning with Angela and the baby, drinking a mug of coffee and waiting for Kurt to pick him up. Angela was trying unsuccessfully to assist Melissa with her breakfast. The little girl was quite insistent on trying to use the spoon by herself and the result was porridge nearly everywhere but her mouth.

Lucas was laughing at the sight.

"You're both going to need a bath by the time she's done." he observed.

Angela laughed too. "I expect so. But it's so cool she wants to do things all by herself."

"Hmm," Lucas said thoughtfully. "Would love to stay home and watch my girls in the tub."

Angela blushed at his words, causing Lucas to grin and wink at her lustfully. She self-consciously lifted a cloth from the table to wipe at some of the porridge Melissa had managed to deposit on the front of her mom's blouse. As she was doing so, the kitchen door rattled, knob turned and in walked Kurt Reeves. Angela smiled up at her brother-in-law shyly and slipped out of her chair as he stepped into the room.

"Morning Kurt." she said. "Got time for a coffee?"

Lucas nodded a greeting at his brother and rose from the table too, finishing the last of his mug of coffee in one long swallow.

"Doesn't look like it, Angie. Thanks anyway." Kurt told her, laughing. He turned to Melissa in her high chair. "How's our sweet little girl today?" He said, bending towards her. Melissa grinned up at her uncle and waved the porridge spoon in her tiny fist. Lucas laughed deep and heartily as porridge sprayed across Kurt's face and hair.

"She's learning to feed herself Kurt." Lucas told him. "Ain't that great?"

Angela gasped when she saw what the baby had done and quickly took the spoon from her grasp before she could do further damage. Melissa started to protest rather vocally the removal of her spoon, while Kurt went to the sink and cleaned off most of the porridge. The two men, both still laughing, headed out the door to work. Angela turned to the baby with a rueful smile.

"You'd better not treat your boyfriends like that when you grow older." she told her. "You're lucky Uncle Kurt is pretty patient."

In the truck, Lucas turned to Kurt as they pulled away from the house.

"What time do you think we'll be done today?" he asked.

"Probably early man." Kurt told him. "We just got some finish up stuff to do. You got plans?"

"Well yeah." Lucas answered a little uncertainly. "At least I have if you would be willing to look after Melissa tonight? It's our anniversary. Thought I'd take Angie out to dinner then let her tag along to the gig."

"I'm sure she'd love that. Been a while since she's seen you play, huh?" Kurt replied evenly. "Sure man, I got no plans. I'll watch the tyke for you."

"Thanks man." Lucas told him. The two men lapsed into silence. Kurt thinking about the last time he had stayed with the baby. 'At least this time,' he thought. 'Lucas won't have cause to take a swing at me.'

About three thirty that afternoon, Kurt and Lucas pulled up in front of the house. Angela was on the floor in the living room with Melissa in her lap. Together they were looking through a picture book. She heard Lucas's key turn in the lock and looked up startled.

"Hi," she said, as they came through the door. "You're home early." Melissa put her arms out towards Lucas smiling with delight. He bent down and swept the baby into his arms, planting a kiss on Angela's forehead at the same time.

"Hey there babe." he said softly. "Yeah we finished early. And that's a good thing."

"Hi Angie." Kurt said from behind Lucas.

Lucas put one hand down and helped Angela to her feet, then turned most of his attention back to his daughter. Very casually, he glanced across at her as she started to turn to the kitchen to make dinner.

"You'd better go straight down the hall and get dressed and pretty, babe." He told her. She turned back to him with a surprised and questioning look. He grinned in return and continued. "I thought I'd take you out for dinner, Mrs. Reeves. It is our anniversary after all. Then you can come along and catch Critical Mass."

Angela froze for a moment in the doorway between living room and kitchen then flew at Lucas. He put one arm around her and held Melissa comfortably between them in the other. Angela linked both her arms around her husband and kissed him gratefully on the cheek.

"You remembered." she murmured softly.

The brothers played with the baby while Angela took some time bathing and dressing. Lying in a luxurious tub full of softly scented bubbles, she shook her head in amazement. Lucas had remembered and had chosen to surprise her with a night out. She felt a little sheepish that she had ever doubted him.

When she finally came back into the living room, both brothers looked up in some surprise. She had chosen a soft butter yellow blouse with a feminine but quite short denim mini skirt. Lucas whistled softly. Kurt diffidently nodded his approval.

"God babe, you are gorgeous!" her husband exclaimed. He passed his daughter to Kurt and stood up as Angela walked the rest of the way into the room.

"You sure I'm okay?" Angela asked uncertainly. "I don't know where we're eating, but I didn't want to be overdressed for the club."

Lucas pulled her into his strong armed embrace and bent as though to kiss her. Instead, he gently whispered in her ear, "You look good enough to eat, baby." Angela flushed with embarrassment.

Lucas's hands roved across her back and down to cup her buttocks. He grinned down at her, "You look just perfect to me, my love." He said aloud. He allowed her to gently push him away for the moment and went to get his guitars for the gig while she gave Kurt some brief instructions for Melissa.

When they left a few minutes later, each of them carried one of the guitars and Angela had a wondrous sense of camaraderie with her husband suddenly, much like she remembered from early in their relationship. She wanted to tell him that her hope was their lives could always be like this, but hesitated to even allude to the times when he was not so gentle lest she arouse his anger once again.

Dinner was wonderful. Lucas took her to a restaurant which was built right on the water's edge overlooking a marina full of sleek looking yachts. Their table was right next to the windows and Angela delighted in the view.

Lucas looked mainly at her, marveling to himself how very innocent she still managed to look and proud that she still turned heads whenever they walked into a room. He talked animatedly about the band, excited about some new numbers they had added to the mix. She listened sharing, with smiles and soft words, his enthusiasm.

A few heads turned later that evening when Lucas and Angela walked into Louis' Blues together. They had nearly an hour before the first set so Lucas led the way to a pair of stools at the bar. The few times Angela had been in Louis' Blues with Lucas, she had always felt like she was on the arm of a celebrity, as so many of the other musicians and blues devotees seemed to know and respect him. She was proud and a little overwhelmed by their attention.

Lucas ordered a beer for himself and a glass of white wine for Angela. When the drinks were placed in front of them, he tapped the rim of her glass with his fingertip and grinned at her.

"One glass per set, okay?" he cautioned. "You've already had champagne; I don't want to be carrying you home."

She smiled shyly up at him, placing one small hand on his knee and taking the glass in the other. "I will be careful. I love you, Lucas. Thank you for bringing me to a gig; this is a wonderful anniversary present."

His larger hand covered hers where it lay on his knee and he gave a reassuring squeeze. Even as he did so, his attention was drawn away from her by a friend wanting to talk guitar gear. Angela paid very little attention to the men as they spoke for the conversation was rapidly over her head. Instead she gazed around the room, content to watch the people, characters all, who were the denizens of the little club.

One man, a slim built blonde with hazel eyes, was studying Angela from his seat at a table near the corner of the stage. Their eyes met briefly and the blonde man smiled warmly at her. She was not sure why but something in his open stare had made her feel suddenly uncomfortable. Her eyes immediately flew back to Lucas and she shifted restlessly in her seat. Lucas did not pause in his conversation but acknowledged her with a squeeze of his hand. She relaxed, smiling up at her husband and had another dainty sip of her wine.

Lucas drained his beer and slipped down off his barstool. He wrapped his arms around her, kissing her affectionately on both cheeks.

"Be good," he chuckled then glanced at the bartender. "Keep an eye on my angel, will ya Tom? I gotta go to work."

Tom, Lucas and Angela, along with a few others nearby all laughed merrily. Lucas gave her hands one last squeeze and headed up to the little stage. Angela felt really excited all of a sudden. Watching him play, experiencing his energy and passion for the music was something she had missed very much now that she was mostly at home with the baby and this was her chance to enjoy that feeling once again.

Critical Mass sounded great; with a full year of playing together they had become a very tight unit. Each played off the other's strengths very well and all of them clearly played for the love of the music. Angela was drawn fully into the emotional journeys that Lucas's guitar led her on and the room seemed to fade away. She saw and heard only him. Even if he had not warned her in jest about moderation, her wine was untouched for most of the set. She did not notice when the blonde man, she'd seen earlier, arose from his seat and came to stand next to her at the bar.

Between songs, as Lucas was changing from his Stratocaster to the Telecaster, the blonde man spoke to her causing her to jump in surprise.

"Hi there, beautiful." he said grinning, "Great band, huh?"

Angela took a deep breath to calm herself, looking cautiously at the stranger. "Yes, they're awesome." she agreed.

"Never seen you in here before." he commented, staring quite openly at her, which caused her to shift nervously in her seat. "You a big blues fan?"

"I'm here with Lucas." she said softly, though her words were lost as the band kicked into another number. The blonde man turned towards the bartender and spoke to him over the sound of the music. Angela saw Tom shake his head negatively, but didn't hear the words exchanged. Finally Tom nodded and moved to the other end of the bar. A moment later, he returned with a beer for the stranger and a fresh glass of wine for Angela. He indicated to Angela that the blonde man had purchased the drink.

Angela's eyes flew first to Tom in surprise then she whirled round to Lucas on the stage and, she hoped, oblivious of the scene at the bar. He was playing a solo with his eyes half closed and she breathed a soft sigh of relief. She nervously played with the wedding ring on her finger and concentrated on the stage, never taking her eyes from Lucas to even glance at the man beside her.

As the number ended, she spoke, in what she hoped was a firm voice, "Thank you for the drink," she told him, "But you really shouldn't have. I am Lucas Reeves' wife."

The blonde man shrugged nonchalantly, still smiling boldly at her. "Never wrong to buy a pretty girl a drink." he said with a chuckle. "And Lucas Reeves, whoever he is, is a lucky bastard." He gave her a rather formal hand shake then turned abruptly and returned to his table. On stage, Lucas had watched the tableau unfold in silent rage.

When the set ended, he came straight to Angela, hugging her warmly. Tom slid a full icy beer mug onto the counter. Lucas kissed her possessively on the forehead and both cheeks, then whispered a question in her ear.

"Who was that?" he demanded.

"Lucas, I don't know." She confessed, shaking a little in fear. "He just came over. Lucas, he bought me a glass of wine. Tom tried to tell him no, I saw him."

Lucas was still holding her gently in his arms. He kissed her deeply on the mouth forcing his tongue between her lips as if, by his open demonstration of intimacy, he was letting the whole room know she was his woman. He broke off the kiss and stepped back a pace, studying her face closely.

"Did he upset you, babe?" He asked.

"Only a little, Lucas." she told him. "I just didn't know what to say. He didn't seem to notice that I was married, you know?"

"Son of a bitch!" Lucas cursed, under his breath. He looked round, searching the room for the face of the stranger. When he spotted him making his way down the hall to the men's room, he smiled with a dark glint coming into his emerald eyes. He patted Angela on the knee.

"I'll be right back, babe." He told her, "Gotta make a call, you know?"

He strode across the room and intercepted the blonde man just as he was coming back out of the men's room. He blocked the man's way in the tiny hall which led past the kitchen to the alley.

"Excuse me." the blonde man said, as he tried to pass Lucas.

Lucas stood his ground and put a finger disdainfully against the somewhat shorter man's chest. "There ain't no excuse for some people, asshole." He growled. "What the hell are you doing messing with my wife?"

The blonde man stared for a moment at the leather clad guitar player in front of him then tried to ease the situation as diplomatically as he could.

"Hey man, I'm sorry." he said, holding both hands palm out in a gesture of peace. "I only bought her a glass of wine. No biggie. I didn't know she was married."

As he had spoken, Lucas had stepped towards him, causing the stranger to back away a half pace at a time. Lucas kept up the pressure, actually pushing him now with both hands as he spoke again.

"No big deal!" he said, still quietly but with an anger that was unmistakable. "She is my wife. Nobody messes with her, ever!"

The blonde man was backed right against the door leading out to the alley. Lucas pulled back one arm and punched him, catching him squarely in the face. The force of the blow caused the latch to open on the door and the stranger fell backwards into the alleyway. Lucas followed him through the door, bending down and grabbing him by the fabric of his shirt. He pulled him up till they were face to face.

"Keep the fuck away from mine, asshole!" he bellowed at him. He pushed the man back down onto the asphalt of the alleyway into a black puddle and leveled a kick at him before turning back into the club.

In the hallway, Lucas met Jake who looked curiously at his friend.

"What's up man?" he asked.

"Nothing much, Jake." Lucas said, rubbing his hands together as though trying to rid them of something distasteful. "Just taking out the garbage."

Lucas returned to Angela, standing beside her barstool with a protective arm around her shoulders as he calmly sipped his beer. She had seen him intercept the blonde stranger and felt some fear when they had disappeared down the back hall. She laid her head against his chest and took comfort in his strength. He stroked her long black hair, gently whispering in her ear.

"It's okay, my love." he crooned, "He won't bother you again." His words brought her mixed feelings of fear and security. 'What had he done?' she wondered, afraid to find out.

A minute or two later, she watched the blonde man come back through the bar. His clothes were dirty from falling into the greasy puddle in the alley and there was a little blood on the corner of his mouth from a split lip. He paused at his table long enough to retrieve his jacket and cigarettes, then left without glancing in their direction at all. If Lucas had seen him, he made no indication. Angela hugged him tighter and he bent and kissed her lightly on the mouth. The rest of the evening passed without incident.

After they arrived home and Kurt had left them alone, Lucas took her in his arms, speaking softly.

"I love you, babe." He whispered. "I want you to tell me if anyone ever bothers you like that. Promise?"

She nodded mutely. He was slowly unbuttoning her blouse as he spoke, kissing her face and neck in between the words. "You're mine, baby, I protect what is mine."

Angela hardly heard any more of his words then, caught up in the sensations of his attentions. She trembled at his touch and reached for him like a drowning man clings to anything solid. He kissed her deeply and gathered her up into his arms. As he carried her towards the bedroom, he murmured, "Happy anniversary baby."

Her breathing was already ragged and uneven; she kissed his neck and shoulder as he carried her through the house. She wanted to tell him it had frightened her when he had gone after the stranger but she couldn't find her voice. "Love you, Lucas." were her only three words, before becoming lost in his passion.

The summer passed very quickly with Lucas away three or four nights nearly every week for gigs on the small town circuit. Angela and Melissa traveled further afield by themselves now than when the baby was younger. Angela had become very familiar with the public bus system and was determined to take her little girl everywhere she could. One of their favourite haunts was the park where Lucas and Angela had been married.

Melissa would play in the sand on the beach while her Mom kept a watchful eye on her. They waded ankle-deep into the water until Melissa would start to stamp her little feet, throwing spray up over them both. Before they left the park, Angela would always spend a little quiet time with her daughter under the protective bows of the maple tree in the clearing where her wedding took place.

She always talked to the little girl about the maple and its beautiful twin in Angela's childhood home. Melissa would listen too, as her mother told her about her grandfather and the wonder of growing up with such a man. Though she was too young yet to really understand Angela's words, the telling gave her mother some comfort.

Lucas still worked with Kurt whenever he was back in the city, so mother and daughter saw little of him. But Angela always kept to their routine of having tea late in the evening before bed and Lucas would take out one of his acoustic guitars and play for her. Sunday nights were the best; he would be just home from the weekend's gig and eager to spend time with both of his girls. While Angela made dinner, Lucas delighted in spending time with his daughter, sometimes even taking her over to Kurt's to visit or just exploring the backyard together. On rare occasions, he would read to her, but he would always get out a guitar when she pointed to the case and entertain her with silly verses made up on the spur of the moment. Angela delighted in hearing her daughter's laughter as Lucas sought to keep her amused.

Summer again turned to fall and before Angela knew it she was facing another winter. Melissa followed her round the house, already starting to imitate her mother's actions of dusting and tidying. On days when Lucas wasn't working with Kurt, he would sleep later than Melissa and his wife, but once up, he was happy to take them out in the car spending some early afternoon time in the fresh air. Melissa, in a cosy jacket and hand knit mittens and hats, toddled happily along beaches near the perimeter of the city that Angela was not able to take her to on the bus. Those afternoons, the child returned home braced by fresh air and exercise and had a two or three hour nap before dinner.

Lucas and Angela sometimes talked during those times when their daughter slept, but Angela's gentle attempts to draw her husband into sharing his childhood and his dreams or fears with her were usually met with his moody silence. She adored him and only sought to know him better, but rapidly realized that there were some parts of Lucas that would remain closed to her. They would often make love as Melissa slept. Though he was usually gentle, Lucas was quietly forceful with her whenever amorous but Angela's adoration tinged somewhat with fear would no longer allow her to protest. Her little family was at peace.

In the January following her second Christmas, Melissa was over a year and a half old and full of the curiosity of most children her age. She also was devoid of any fears and Angela seemed to be constantly behind her as she played waiting anxiously to avert disaster. Mostly though her daughter was like a little shadow, never far behind her mother as they moved through their days.

Angela slid out of bed one morning, knowing that Lucas was home for the day so careful not to disturb him. She had not yet heard Melissa, so she went first into the bathroom. Teeth brushed, face washed and hair combed she stood for a moment contemplating her reflection in the mirror. She had a tiny bruise on one cheekbone that was almost healed and she winced ever so slightly as she recalled Lucas's annoyance with her for suggesting she may go back to temporary work. He had been enraged at the notion that the mother of his child would want to abandon her baby. "You should be pregnant with another by now." he had shouted and punctuated his statement with an open handed smack which brought tears to her eyes. Now she swallowed hard and tried to dismiss the memory, pulling the packet of birth control pills from their hiding place beneath the bathroom sink. Just as she popped the tiny pill into her mouth, there was a sudden frightening clatter and smashing sound which came from the kitchen.

Angela left the packet of pills where they lay and ran panic stricken towards the sound. Even as she ran, Melissa's squeal of fear and hurt cut through her heart.

She stopped short just inside the doorway to the kitchen and gazed in stunned silence at the scene in front of her. Melissa was seated on one of the kitchen chairs, sobbing piteously. Around her, on the floor were the dangerously sharp shards of glass from what had been a huge vase in the middle of the table. Spilled water and flowers were everywhere. Angela spoke softly to Melissa as she moved cautiously into the room.

"It's okay sweetie," she told the child. "Just sit real still for Mommy. Stay where you are Melissa, Mommy will get you." It appeared that the vase had not broken until it hit the floor and Melissa, being up on the chair, had been away from most of the danger. Though she did have both flowers and water spilled on her; the latter being most responsible for her fright.

"Fall down." she stated with childlike certainty. Angela almost burst out giggling, relieved as she drew closer to realize that her daughter was unharmed. She picked the girl up from the chair and, hugging her gratefully, admonished her gently for playing with the pretty flowers. As she was talking to Melissa and calming her fears, she heard Lucas move down the hall to the bathroom.

Melissa was quickly changed into something clean and dry while Lucas was showering. By the time he joined his wife and daughter in the kitchen, the mess on the floor was cleaned up and the coffee pot was full and ready.

"Morning Angie." He said, as he walked in already dressed and ready for the day. "What was that crash? You throwing the pots and pans again?"

"Hi Lucas. Coffee's made." She answered. "Melissa decided she wanted the flowers in the big vase. We're now short one big vase."

"Damn Angie." he cursed softly. "She's okay isn't she?"

"Yes Lucas, she's fine." Angela answered, feeling guilty about not hearing Melissa get out of bed. "She just scared herself and me, is all."

He shrugged thoughtfully, poured himself a coffee, gave his daughter and quick hug and kiss, then went downstairs to his music room. Minutes later, Angela heard the wail of the Stratocaster. She smiled to herself. 'At least he always seemed more content after he'd played for a few hours.' She and Melissa went on with their morning routine of half-chores and half play to the accompaniment of Lucas's Blues.

Lucas came upstairs again and joined them for some lunch. Angela had made them soup and sandwiches. The soup seemed like a great idea as the weather outside was bitterly cold and damp with rain falling heavily and occasionally becoming sleet driving icy blasts against the outside walls of the little house. There would be no drives to the park today.

Lucas was very quiet as he ate his lunch, though he took some time for a playful game of peekaboo with his daughter. After they had eaten, Angela cleaned up the kitchen and washed the dishes while Lucas entertained Melissa. They went through to the living room and he tickled and rough-housed with her until she was in paroxysms of laughter. Then he lay on the floor and allowed her to crawl all over him pulling on his ears, his nose, and his fingers as he laughed too. Melissa feeling she was taking her turns to tickle Daddy, delighted in the game. Angela eventually separated the two of them, whisking Melissa off for a nap before her excitement made her over-wrought and fretful.

When she came back into the living room, Lucas was standing with his back to her staring out the window at the grim weather. She picked up some mending she needed to finish and settled comfortably into the big easy chair. Neither of them moved nor spoke for a long interval then Lucas spun round towards her.

"Angie," he began, waiting till she looked up at him before continuing. "Melissa ought to have a brother or sister, before she gets much bigger."

Angela looked up at him cautiously. He'd mentioned this when they'd fought about her going back to work and apparently it was still on his mind. "Lucas, I can't decide when I'm going to get pregnant again. It'll just happen when it happens."

Something in the disdainful and angry glance he cast her then rang awful alarm bells in her mind. He crossed the living room in three quick paces and stopped abruptly in front of her knees. He shoved one hand into his jeans pocket and pulled out the packet of birth control pills he had discovered on the bathroom counter that morning. Glaring at her now with undisguised anger, he threw the packet into her lap.

"You can't decide!" he bellowed at her and she physically cringed from his voice alone. "What the fuck are these then? It seems you did decide not to have any babies without even asking me!"

Angela was shaking terribly but took a deep breath and tried to remain calm and explain. "Lucas, I was going to tell you. But after I had Melissa, I just didn't want to face being pregnant again quickly is all." She would have said more but he cut her off, pulling her up by an iron grip on both her shoulders to stand in front of him.

"Was going to tell me ain't good enough, damn it!" He yelled again. "I'm your fucking husband, I got some rights round here and don't you forget it! You should have told me, we should have agreed before you did that!" He said this last while shaking her violently by the shoulders.

"Lucas, I'm so sorry." She sobbed. "I was so scared. I didn't want to go through all that again. I was so scared."

He stared at her, uncomprehendingly. "Hey it's supposed to hurt giving birth, you know? Didn't your mother ever tell you that?" Even as he spoke, the images that went through Angela's mind were not of the giving birth but black images of Lucas forcing her to her knees to pleasure him even as she felt sick and exhausted by the baby she had been carrying. She could never explain her fear. Tentatively, she reached out to him now, winding her arms around his waist and sliding down to kneel before him. He reached down and stroked his fingers through her long black hair, as she spoke again.

"Please forgive me, Lucas." She begged. "I will not take any more of the pills. I'm so sorry for not telling you. Please, oh God, please forgive me."

He looked down at her and, even though his eyes remained unwaveringly angry, he chuckled softly. "Damn right you won't take any more of these pills." He stated flatly. "I'll forgive you alright. If you want to show me how sorry you are." He pulled her to her feet, taking her by one wrist and she followed him in silence down the hall to the bedroom. He pulled the bedroom door shut behind them, turned back to her and, grabbing a handful of her hair, pulled her to him in a violently passionate embrace.

Four months later, Melissa turned two years old. She toddled round the house with an air of self-assurance that her mother couldn't ever remember possessing.

Angela encouraged Melissa in all things and together they made games out of chores like putting the toys away or folding laundry. Lucas watched them with pride but some bafflement as the mother of his experience had been almost totally silent and very nearly invisible in his life.

Lucas had bookings for almost every weekend of the summer once again. On the second weekend of July, Critical Mass would be playing once again in Angela's home town at Rock City. When Angela saw that date on the calendar that they had placed on the door to the basement stairs, her thoughts went to her mother. The two women had talked on the phone sporadically but their old closeness seemed lost to them. Angela wondered if Lucas would consider letting her and Melissa tag along that weekend to visit Grandma. Somewhat to her surprise, he was in favour of the idea. Even more surprising to her was Belle's reaction when she called to tell her they were coming. Her mother invited them to stay at the house rather than in a motel, saying that she wanted some time with her granddaughter.

Grandmother and granddaughter seemed to instantly take to one another and Angela felt some sense of relief on seeing how well they got along. Belle was a gracious hostess and seemed to go out of her way to make her daughter's family welcome in her home, but there was a distance between mother and daughter that seemed almost insurmountable. The band had a three night date and Angela stayed home with Melissa and her mother both Thursday and Friday nights.

After she had bathed Melissa and settled her to sleep in Mrs. Griffen's guest bedroom, Angela joined her mother in the living room to watch TV. The first evening, the two women had sat mostly in silence except for occasional exchanges about inconsequential things like the weather or a little hometown gossip. Friday evening, however, Belle seemed more anxious to talk to her daughter.

"Angela, you're doing a wonderful job with Melissa." She told her, "She's an absolute treasure."

"Thanks Mom." Angela replied. "Melissa is a blessing. I'm thankful for her every day."

Her mother gave her a long searching look, before she spoke again. "And you and Lucas?" she asked. "Are you happy, Angela?"

"Mom, I'm fine." She answered evasively. "I know it's hard to understand, when he goes out at night all the time, but this is what he does, what he loves. I married a musician. I have to accept his lifestyle, his hours and his moods. It's all part of living with an artist. We compromise."

"Compromise." Belle repeated, thoughtfully. "It seems to me like you're the one doing all the compromising. Angela, I think my question is, does he treat you right?"

"Of course he does." Angela answered, a little too quickly and adamantly. Belle raised one eyebrow but said nothing. Angela continued. "He looks after

Melissa and me." She was suddenly very defensive about the turn the conversation seemed to be taking.

"That's good, Angela." Belle agreed. "I know we've been distant the past couple of years. But I want you to know I'm always here, if you really need me. Okay?"

Angela was baffled by her mother's sudden assurances, but also very gratified. "Thanks Mom. I love you too."

The following evening, Belle was pleased to look after Melissa so that Angela could join Lucas and catch the gig. The band was great and in some ways the evening reminded Angela so much of the summer they had first met at Rock City and Lucas had so charmingly won her heart. That same memory must have touched Lucas too, because when they left Rock City and drove back to the house, he pulled up out front and drew her into his arms for what almost felt like a goodnight kiss. He chuckled softly as the long deep kiss ended.

"Should I just walk you to the door now?" he asked her.

"Lucas, I love you." she told him, also giggling. "This reminds me so much of when we met. But now you can come inside."

He chuckled again, then bent to kiss her once more and she was caught up in his passion almost instantly. This time when he broke off the kiss, he opened the driver's door and slipped quickly from behind the wheel. Angela, as she watched him walk round to her side of the car, was suddenly nervous about being so openly physical with him here in front of her mother's home. Even all grown up and married, she felt very self-conscious of her mother's presence and the feeling was overwhelming and quelling her earlier passion.

Lucas helped her from the car then and with one strong arm wrapped tightly round her, walked her up to the house, still kissing and nuzzling at her as he went. The house was dark and quiet when they went inside, except for the soft glow of a night light from Melissa's room and a line of light shining under Belle's closed bedroom door. Angela moved to free herself from Lucas's grip to go towards her daughter's room and check on the sleeping child. Lucas tightened his hold on her, impatiently denying any interruption to his passion.

"She's sleeping, Angie," he whispered, with some exasperation. "Come on baby! Now!" He opened the door to their bedroom, her old room, and pulled her forcefully in behind him. Angela shook with fear and disappointment, which he mistook for ardor, as he started to clumsily remove all her clothing. She reached tentatively to his hands looking up at him with pleading eyes, stopping him momentarily.

"Lucas, my Mom, she's still awake." She murmured, nervously.

"Damn it," he hissed at her, pushing her hand away, "So what? We're married. I'm sure she knows that we fuck! Where does she think Melissa came from?" He glared at her, almost daring her to protest further. Angela's eyes dropped away from his and she submissively allowed him to finished stripping her. He pushed her back on to the bed and stood staring down at her as he took off his own jeans and leather vest. Then he crawled onto the bed beside her and started kissing her on the face and neck, making his way rapidly to one of her breasts which he sucked hungrily into his mouth. When his teeth took in her nipple and bit it rather sharply, she cried out in pained surprise.

Laughing cruelly, he told her, "Hush now, your Mommy will hear you."

She was utterly silent after that, as Lucas brutally released his frustration and pent up energies on her body. When he finally found satisfaction, he lay back pulling her against him. Before he drifted to sleep, he kissed her salty tears from her temples and quietly whispered.

"See, you can be such a good girl. Mommy never heard a thing." He chuckled and squeezed her tender breasts in his hands. She winced a little with pain, but made no sound. Simply seeking some small comfort in the warmth of his body against hers, she slept.

Summer passed again into fall. Angela and Melissa continued to spend as many afternoons as possible outdoors and, like her father before her, Angela would help Melissa to explore her world. They played in the brightly coloured fallen leaves of the maple trees in the small park near home. When they went to the beach, bundled against the chilly winds of fall, they collected shells and pretty pebbles. Angela watched her girl grow with pride, as Melissa sprouted from baby to child with the passing weeks.

After their visit in the summer, Belle Griffen had continued to keep in more regular contact with her daughter. She would call at least every two weeks or so to hear how Melissa was doing. Angela looked forward to her calls as her only other adult company, besides Lucas, was Kurt when her brother-in-law happened to stop in for dinner.

Melissa's third Christmas approached rapidly. Angela slipped tiredly out of bed one December morning, shivering against the damp cold air. She was about to step into her daughter's bedroom when a sudden wave of nausea overcame her. She moved in a panic stricken fog to the bathroom, just reaching the toilet in time. She slowly straightened up and caught a glimpse of her face in the mirror, hair tangled and beads of perspiration shining on her forehead suddenly. 'Oh god,' she thought, 'I can't be sick.' Behind her, both her daughter and husband suddenly appeared in the bathroom doorway.

"Mommy sick?" Melissa asked with a child's innocence. Angela smiled weakly at her and was about to speak when a wave of dizziness hit without warning. Lucas's voice cut into her suddenly foggy senses as though from a great distance.

"Baby, you okay?" he was asking her. Angela's next moment of awareness was of being in Lucas's arms as he lifted her limp form from the bathroom floor. She had lost any clarity of the moments or perhaps hours in between. He carried her back into their bedroom with a frightened and sobbing Melissa following behind. As he deposited her gently on to the bed, she finally managed to sort out what had happened and reacted first to Melissa's dismay.

"It's okay Melissa." she told the girl, reaching one hand towards her. "Mommy just fainted."

Lucas had sat on the edge of the bed and was caressing her forehead with one hand. He scooped Melissa onto his lap and gave her a reassuring one-armed hug.

"Angie, are you sick?" he asked her softly.

She looked up at him in silence a moment, baffled herself that she suddenly felt perfectly normal again. Then realization seemed to come to her and a rush of mixed and overwhelming emotions made her head swim again. Lucas saw the disconcerted look that passed over her face and was about to speak again, when Angela finally answered.

"I don't think I'm sick, Lucas." She said, "At least not exactly."

A light of recognition appeared in his eyes too. He put Melissa back on to the floor and looked at her gravely.

"Your mother and I need to talk for a moment, sweetie." He told the child. "Run to your room and find the clothes you want to wear today."

Melissa smiled happily up at him and quickly went off down the hall content now, having heard her mother's calming voice; everything was now all right. Lucas turned back to Angela as soon as the girl had left the room.

"You're pregnant?" he asked.

"Yes Lucas, I think so anyway." she replied timidly, unsure of his reaction.

He bent and kissed her on both cheeks then took both her hands in his large ones before speaking again.

"It's about time!" he stated, but with a chuckle in his voice that softened his words some. "Right after breakfast you'd better be getting on the phone and making a doctor's appointment, okay?"

"I will, I promise." She answered. She started to rise, feeling very much better and ready to get back to the normal routine for Melissa's sake. But Lucas gently pushed her back on the bed.

"Why don't you stay in bed for a little while longer?" he suggested, "I'll give Melissa her breakfast."

"Thanks Lucas." She murmured.

He gave her another quick kiss on the cheek then left in search of his daughter. Angela snuggled down under the quilt which Lucas had hastily tossed to one side when he'd rushed to her in the bathroom. The warmth of the quilt was very soothing to her still muddled emotions and senses. 'Another baby,' she thought. 'Please Lucas; be gentle with me, just like today.'

A week and a half later, when Belle called as usual, Angela told her that she was going to be a grandmother again. Belle certainly sounded pleased for her, but then dropped a small bombshell of her own. For several months now she had been seeing a gentleman who had been working in town on a contract assignment for a security firm. He was, she told her daughter, a very decent man, a former police officer who had retired early and did private consulting work. Michael's home was in the big city, not too very far from Angela's home with Lucas. Belle told her daughter that she had decided to pick up and move into the city with Michael, now that his contract was over.

Angela couldn't believe what she was hearing and perhaps, she thought, was slowly beginning to understand how her mother had felt when she suddenly up and moved in with Lucas. Though she was partially pleased that her mother would now be close at hand, she was filled with concern at her mother's seemingly rash behavior. Looking back, Angela couldn't remember her mother ever seeing a man since her father's death. This somehow seemed disloyal to his memory. She admonished herself as soon as the thought crossed her mind because, of course, she must admit that her mother deserved some companionship and happiness too.

Lucas seemed greatly amused by the notion of Belle Griffen with a gentleman friend, as Angela had phrased it when she told him at supper time. His response came amidst mocking chuckles.

"So Mommy found a man." he exclaimed. "Well maybe it'll mellow her out some."

Angela let the remarks pass and secretly hoped that Michael was as gentle and decent as her mother seemed to believe. Lucas took his after dinner coffee and went down to the music room. Angela entertained Melissa until bedtime, all the while thinking about how nice it was going to be to have her mother close at hand when she moved to the city in six weeks.

As morning was greying the sky, Angela opened her eyes to pain. When Lucas and Kurt had returned from their 'boy's night out', she had been roused from sleep by the clatter they made coming in the door. She had snuggled deeper into the covers but that was before Lucas had stumbled drunkenly into the bedroom smelling of whisky and cigarette smoke. Enraged that she had not waited up for him, he had dragged her from the bed. Even as he had battered and abused her rather pregnant body, her mind became detached from the nightmare and she had wondered, with shame, if Kurt could hear them.

Dawn's light was quickly softening all the deeper blackness of the shadows in the room. Lucas's deep even breathing told her, without looking, that he was still sound asleep. She eased awkwardly out of the bed and, after first gathering clean clothing for the day ahead, shuffled painfully to the bathroom.

She washed up quickly then pulled on slacks and a maternity top. Despite the very warm June weather, the top was long sleeved, chosen purposely to cover the hand-print shaped bruising on her upper arms. But nothing could easily hide or disguise the nasty purple bruise on her right cheekbone. She bit hard on her lower lip, taking a couple of deep breaths to dispel the tears threatening to well up again. Then she went through to the kitchen.

She could hear Kurt snoring in the living room and again felt acute embarrassment that he had been in the house and may have heard Lucas and her the previous night. With determination, she turned to morning chores, hoping the routine would help ease her pain and fear once again.

Melissa was out of bed very soon after her mother. Angela made porridge for both of them and sat down with the girl. Melissa was very excited that Uncle Kurt had spent the night and was eager to wake him immediately. Her mother was careful to gently tell her that Uncle Kurt was very tired and needed to rest a while longer. After breakfast, she sent Melissa to collect a colouring book and crayons from her toy box then sat her back at the kitchen table. Angela then went into the living room to get a partially completed crocheted baby sweater that she had been working on the day before. As she was going back to the kitchen, she glanced down at her sleeping brother-in-law.

Kurt looked ruggedly handsome, if somewhat younger in sleep. Some small part of Angela hoped briefly that he had indeed heard his brother's anger the previous evening. It was a faint hope, that somehow Lucas's older brother may be able to help him see that he was hurting her. As soon as the thought was in her mind, she rebelled at it, angrily pushing it from her head. Such disloyalty would surely mean that Lucas would leave her and she was more frightened of being without him than of anything.

Kurt Reeves must have sensed her eyes on him, because he woke quite suddenly as she stood there. He took a moment to focus on her then the sight of the nasty bruise on her face brought last night's events back to him with a nauseating suddenness. With the very immediate memory came other vaguer recollections of times past when he'd noticed odd bruises on his sister-in-law. She smiled very shyly down at him.

"Morning Kurt, can I get you a coffee?" She murmured.

He managed a weak smile in return, amazed and confused by her calm everyday manner. Then slowly, holding his head in his hands, he sat upright.

"Yeah, please Angie." He replied, regretting already how much he'd drank the night before. "Are you okay? You've got a nasty bump there."

Angela shrugged. "It's okay." she lied. "Don't hurt much." She heard the telltale sounds of someone moving through the hall to the bathroom and realized that Lucas was up also. Without waiting for a further comment from Kurt, she went back to the kitchen to start the coffee. Kurt watched her go and fought the urge to go after her and offer comfort. He sat for a very long time on the couch head in hands, despair, fear and self-loathing all combining to render him impotent, frozen by the nightmare that he knew would haunt him each time he looked at her.

Lucas was solicitous and gentle when he joined her in the kitchen. He gave his daughter a good morning kiss and hug and she ran off to the living room to see Uncle Kurt. He then turned to Angela and took her gently in his arms, kissing her cheeks and forehead.

"Sorry baby, I shouldn't have woken you last night." He told her. "Maybe you should just go back to bed now. I'll watch Melissa for a while."

She laid her head against his chest and started to cry very quietly. He smoothed her hair beneath his hand while the other arm wrapped round her shoulders.

"Hush, now." he crooned. "Off to bed. I'll wake you later."

Even as he spoke, Kurt and Melissa came back into the kitchen. Kurt felt some relief when he saw Angela in his brother's arms. 'She's obviously forgiven him' he thought. 'Maybe I'd best stay out of it.'

Lucas released his hold on Angela and gently pushed her in the direction of the hall. Docilely, she went down the hall to the bedroom without a backward glance. Kurt suddenly had no stomach for the coffee that Lucas was offering him. He glanced down the hallway briefly, then crossed to the door and started pulling on his boots.

"I'll pass on the coffee, man." He told Lucas, "I got a lot of stuff to do today. I got to go."

Lucas looked at him in surprise, but merely nodded wordlessly. Kurt went out the door, climbed into his truck and pulled out of the driveway. He drove miles without even consciously thinking about where he was going, but he ended up pulling into a small side road that ran down to the beach, very close to the house that he and Lucas had grown up in. He parked the truck and walked down through the trees till he reached a small clearing which looked out on the water beyond. This was where he knew, when they were boys, he could always find Lucas sitting and playing his guitar endless hour after endless hour. Kurt sat on an old driftwood log staring unseeing out across the water and cried till he had no more tears.

Tyson Kurt Reeves made his appearance in the world on July fifteenth, a Saturday night. His father was one hundred miles away playing yet another gig. Angela had called her mother this time, once her contractions had reached the point where she knew that she must get to the hospital. She already had a bag packed for herself and a bag for Melissa who would have to visit with Grandma and Michael for at least one night until Lucas returned from his gig. Just before Michael and Belle arrived to pick her up, Angela had also called the motel that Lucas was staying at and the cabaret that the band was booked in. She was not able to reach Lucas directly but the man she spoke with at the cabaret assured her he would give her husband the message. Her hand hesitated after hanging up the phone, as she wondered if she should call Kurt too. They had not spoken for six weeks ever since Kurt had spent the night that black evening in June. Before she picked the phone up again, Belle and Michael arrived and, with much fuss and excitement, they left for the hospital.

As Michael had driven carefully through Saturday evening traffic to the hospital, he had expressed his annoyance that Angela's husband was not even in the city for the birth of his child. Belle shook her head sadly, remembering the night Melissa had been born as her father was in some smoky bar downtown. Angela, sitting in the front seat next to Michael, breathed silently through another contraction then, as the pain faded, she stunned her mother and Michael alike by her angry outburst.

"He's a guitar player!" she almost shouted. "He's working! It's what he does! He'll be here tomorrow as soon as he can!"

Michael glanced briefly over at the young woman beside him. He'd met Angela several times since Belle and he had moved in together and had never once known the shy beauty to raise her voice. 'Must be the labor pains.' he thought. Belle hurriedly changed the subject.

"Angela, can Melissa stay up and wait with us at the hospital for the baby to come?"

"Yes Mom," Angela said, her soft tones returning. "It won't be long now, I'm sure." Just as she finished speaking another contraction hit her and she breathed stoically through the pain. Melissa, sitting in the back next to her grandma, was excited and chattering on at Belle about her new brother or sister coming soon. Somehow, the sound of her daughter's voice calmed Angela and helped her focus each time a contraction gripped her body.

Lucas was given the message from Angela right after he'd finished the first set and immediately asked to use a phone. The bartender grinned at him and directed him to the phone on one corner of the bar. Lucas called Kurt, knowing that his brother should be home. Angela and he had already agreed that she would call Belle and Michael if she needed them while he was out of town. After three rings, Kurt picked up the phone.

"Hello?" he said.

"Kurt, did Angie call you?" Lucas asked.

Kurt was a little taken back by the abrupt start to Lucas's conversation. The brother's had argued two days after their 'boy's night out' and Lucas, feeling the luxury of plenty of money from regular gigs, had told Kurt he was through being a carpenter's helper. They had not spoken since. Though Kurt's business would always be open to Lucas, since the older brother had given his guitar playing sibling a forty percent share years before, he thought it was probably better for now if they lived their separate lives.

"No, she didn't." Kurt answered. "Is something wrong?"

"No man, not wrong." Lucas told him. "She's in labour. Belle and Michael were driving her to the hospital. Just thought you might like to know and maybe go down there?"

Kurt realized that Lucas was calling from a gig somewhere. He could hear the bar noise in the background and also reasoned that if Belle and Michael had driven Angie to the hospital, Lucas was out of town. He was also amazed that his little brother would leave when Angela was so close to term, but he refrained from commenting.

"Yeah man, I guess I could go down there." he answered. "You got some message for me to pass on?"

Lucas thought for a moment, then answered quickly, "Yeah, tell her I'm going to play Close to You just for her and the baby and that I'm driving home right after the gig. And that I love her."

Kurt hesitated as he heard the words Lucas spoke, then after an uncomfortable pause, he finally replied. "Okay Lucas, I'll tell her. You just get your ass home, you ought to be here." Kurt spoke in a lighthearted tone to avoid arousing his brother, but he felt at least minimally better for having spoken at all.

Lucas ended the conversation abruptly with, "I got a damn gig to finish. Then I'll be there."

Lucas immediately started packing up his gear at the end of the gig. Several young people were hovering around at the edge of the small stage waiting for an opportunity to speak to the guitar player, but with his mind elsewhere, he simply ignored them. Though he hadn't said anything, Jake guessed the reason for Lucas's distraction. He covered for his friend by intervening to politely tell the waiting fans that the band was on a particularly tight schedule and would not have time to stay and chat. Then he grabbed Lucas's amp and together they carried his gear out to the big Buick.

After a brief stop at his motel to throw his personal belongings in the car and checkout, Lucas was speeding west through the night towards home. There was little traffic on the road in the post-midnight darkness, he cranked up the stereo and leaned heavily on the accelerator. As the big Buick ate up the highway miles, Lucas Reeves found his mind wandering to another dark road in a different speeding car.

He must have been about nine years old. Kurt and he were in the back seat of their father's big Pontiac Parisienne. His mother was sitting, silent as usual, in the front seat cringing against the car door seemingly as far away as possible from her husband. Karl Reeves was angry. Even his boys knew better than to say much when his mood was black.

They were returning from a few days spent camping at the lake. Kurt and Lucas had enjoyed the trip, but for different reasons. Kurt had been up with his father every day at the crack of dawn to go fishing. Lucas had brought his guitar and spent hour after hour practicing. Now listening to his father harangue his mother, the boy wished the holiday mood could be recaptured.

"Damn it woman!" Karl Reeves shouted. "I work hard all the time god damn it, I'll spend my money the way I want! Maybe I should be spending it on a fucking whore 'cause I ain't getting much from you!"

His mother's soft voice was barely audible above the sound of the car's engine, but Lucas, directly behind her, heard her plainly enough.

"I'm sorry Karl." She told him apologetically, "I only thought that maybe we spent too much this week."

"That's the trouble with you." Karl snapped, "You think too much. Just take care of the boys and leave the thinking to me."

"Yes Karl." she answered quietly. "I'm sorry."

Karl pulled the car to the side of the road at a dangerously high speed but kept it under control until he had stopped. He got out and strode around to the passenger side door, pulling it open and dragging his wife from it. She cried out in protest.

"No Karl, please." But the words fell on deaf ears. Karl Reeves took her by the wrist, pulling her into the deeper darkness of a stand of trees on the perimeter of the road.

Lucas and Kurt could still hear their father's voice though they could not see their parents.

"You're always sorry, damn you!" he growled at her. "You know bitch, you're only good for one thing!"

The boys heard Karl's hand connect with a smack against her face but only Lucas's sharp ears heard her pained whimpering cry. Kurt picked up the blanket which was folded on the seat next to him and beckoned to his little brother. The two boys huddled under the blanket more for the comfort their closeness brought than from cold, for it was a mild evening. It wasn't very long before their parents returned to the car. Lucas heard them get back in and heard also his mother's soft weeping, but he kept his eyes closed and snuggled deeper beneath the blanket blocking out the world.

The adult Lucas Reeves swore softly under his breath wondering why the memory had dared to assail him. 'I am nothing at all like Karl Reeves,' he thought. Then he came abruptly back to the present as the lights of the city were starting to dispel the deeper darkness of night, he wondered why Angela had to have the baby at such an awkward time, when he was away on the road.

It was three thirty in the morning when Lucas walked into the maternity wing of the hospital still wearing his leather vest and jeans from on stage, still smelling of sweat, smoke and beer. His son was just four hours old. Kurt and Michael were still in the waiting room, both men deciding to stay and wait for Lucas when Belle had taken Melissa home to bed just after midnight. Lucas barely glanced at Michael but turned directly to Kurt.

"Where is she?" he asked, without preamble. "And did she have it yet?"

Kurt started to speak but was cut off by Michael who angrily stepped between the two brothers to confront Lucas.

"Yes, your wife gave birth to your son, you damn son of a bitch. Where the hell were you?" he said vehemently.

Lucas stared at the older man in front of him as Kurt watched his eyes go from tired but placid to angry and black. Finally Lucas spoke, barely above a whisper but biting off each word in his rage.

"I was on a fucking stage for four hours working for a living!" he said, "and then I drove two fucking hours straight to get here!"

Michael didn't flinch as Lucas delivered his angry outburst, which surprised both Lucas and Kurt. Lucas, however, turned back to Kurt.

"I've got a son?" He asked in an awed tone. "That's just amazing!"

Michael was unwilling to allow Lucas to merely dismiss him so easily. He had talked many times with Belle about her son-in-law, also observed him at close range several times since Belle had moved in and what he saw he did not like much. He took one pace which put him once again in front of Lucas Reeves, blocking his path.

"Maybe son, you shouldn't have booked a gig at all this weekend, in respect for your wife's condition." He stated, voice quiet but still very firm. "Then you could have been here for your son's birth."

Lucas made an almost animal sound deep in his throat and, without any real warning, swung viciously at the older man's head with an iron hard fist. Michael, years of police training on his side, reacted with lightning speed to the younger man's attack and grabbed his forearm, stopping Lucas before he connected. Kurt stood rooted to the spot; watching the frightening tableau before him. Michael released Lucas's arm almost immediately then pointed one disdainful finger at his face.

"Don't ever take a swing at me again, Lucas." He stated simply. "Cause I swear I'll hurt you if you do. Now go and see your wife. And be a man, apologize to her for not being here and pray she forgives you."

Kurt was utterly speechless as Lucas nodded almost politely to Michael, backed off a pace and then turned to his brother. His eyes were absolutely calm, the anger defused.

"Which room, man.?" Lucas whispered, "I gotta see her."

Kurt led him down the hall. Behind them, Michael took one long deep breath, searched for his wallet and went to call a cab to go home. Kurt showed Lucas to the door of Angela's room then bid him goodnight also.

Lucas walked tentatively into the room. Angela was asleep, her long dark hair spilling all across the pillow and making her face look even paler and younger in the glow of the light from the hallway. Lucas crossed to the side of the bed and stared down at her, Michael's words still ringing in his ears. He wanted to reach out and touch her but was actually afraid he would waken her. As quietly as he could, he moved a chair alongside her bed then slumped into it stretching out his legs.

"Angela, I love you." he whispered. "I'm so sorry. I got here as soon as I could. A son! I have a son!" Angela didn't stir or make any sign that she had heard his words.

He said no more. Soon his head lolled to one side and he slept where he sat.

Just a couple of hours later a nurse woke Angela bringing her tiny son to be fed. The sudden activity in the room brought Lucas awake with a start. The first sight that met his eyes was Angela with their son cuddled to her breast as he fed. She smiled shyly at her husband.

"He's a boy, Lucas." She told him. "Tyson Kurt, just like we wanted."

Lucas straightened up in his seat and leaned forward onto the bed. He reached one hand out gently to the baby and touched his tiny fist. The baby's fingers instinctively clung to his father's pinky finger. Angela watched fascinated as Lucas softened before her eyes. He gazed up at her.

"Angela, he's perfect." He told her in a husky whisper.

Her hand touched his and the baby's tiny fist at the same time then she smiled at him. "He looks like you already. Now I have two very handsome men in my life."

When the baby had finished feeding, Angela passed him to Lucas and padded to the bathroom. Lucas sat holding Tyson with an awed look on his face. Images flooded his mind, but the wonder of the fragile life in his hands was foremost in his thoughts. When Angela came back and stood leaning against Lucas's shoulder one hand touching her new son's face, she heard the soft sounds of Lucas's voice singing words and a tune she did not know. It was a soft bluesy sound that touched her deeply and lulled the infant to peaceful slumber. Angela was content.

The rest of the summer and into September, Critical Mass had gigs three nights a week regularly. Most were in surrounding towns so Lucas would be gone from late afternoon on Thursday till Sunday around lunch time. The rest of the week he chose not to work with Kurt as they had kept a certain distance between them ever since their fateful 'boy's night out'. So Angela had his help with the kids for most of the week. Lucas was a help too as he would often take Melissa out for a few hours during the day giving Angela time alone with Tyson. Or he would watch both children while Angela took a long bath or had a much needed nap. She was beginning to believe that giving Lucas a son was the magic that it had taken to soften his temper.

Belle visited once a week, but prudently came down on weekends when she knew Lucas would not be there. Angela seemed very happy in her mother's eyes and both her grandchildren were a delight. She still did not trust her daughter's husband and that mistrust was reinforced by Michael's opinion that Lucas was manipulative at best and abusive at worst. But Belle kept her own counsel on the matter not wanting to alienate Angela now that they were becoming closer once again.

Near the end of September, Lucas looked at his big calendar and announced that the band had only four gigs lined up during the next month, all in town.

"Time I went back to some day-work," he told Angie late one evening as they sipped tea.

She nodded at him, trying to hide her surprise that he was sharing his plans with her at all. "So back to working with Kurt again?" She asked quietly.

"No, not Kurt." he said, a little too abruptly. "I heard that Bill Ross Music wanted a guy full time. I'm going to talk to Bill; we've met a few times down at Louis' Blues."

Angela felt almost relieved when he had said 'Not Kurt'. She had felt very uncomfortable when her brother-in-law was around because she knew in her heart that he was aware how Lucas had treated her and she was confused and unsure of herself around him as a result. And her hesitation included what her brother-in-law's silence in the face of his knowledge meant.

Lucas got the job at the music store and life seemed to settle into a regular routine. For the first time since they were married, they all got up in the morning like a regular family and Lucas went off to work like other dads. Mostly, he was content with his job at the store. In lulls, he was always able to pick up a guitar and play. In fact Bill encouraged him to do so as it was a great incentive to customers to see and hear the wonderful sounds that Lucas could pull from the merchandise.

Angela would have dinner ready when he came home and the little family found some degree of peace. She still cringed on days when he was not in such a good mood. But mostly the storms passed with nothing more than a few harsh words spoken or a broken dish that he had thrown in anger. Critical Mass was still playing gigs though not as frequently as they booked strictly in town now to work around Lucas's work schedule.

The weeks rapidly stretched into months, Melissa was just as excited by her baby brother as when she had first glimpsed him at the hospital. The little girl seemed to take her big sister role very seriously and Angela was delighted with both her children.

By the time Tyson was six months old, he was sleeping through the night. On nights when Lucas was playing, Angela would wait up for him and make them both tea before bed. Some nights though, he would bring Jake or even some other players he knew home and Angela would find her house full of men either jamming or talking music and the gear and gadgetry which they all loved. Other nights he wouldn't arrive home till the early morning hours, having gone out after the gig to jam or drink at someone else's house.

Angela was always very restless when he didn't come home. She slept only fitfully and found herself pacing the house and checking on the children, tucking their blankets around them and watching them sleep as her ears strained to hear the sound of his car.

One night, just before four in the morning, she had managed to resettle an equally restless Tyson when she heard the Buick pull into the driveway. Something about the way Lucas slammed open the kitchen door, caused Angela some alarm but she padded down the hall to offer him a cup of tea anyway. When she walked into the kitchen, he was standing with his back to her looking into the fridge.

"Hi Lucas." she said softly.

He wheeled towards her and she drew in a sudden breath of apprehension when she saw the angry expression on his face.

"We got any beer?" he demanded.

"Downstairs in the spare fridge." she told him, wondering if he needed any more beer. He was obviously a little drunk already and had an intense look on his face.

"Well damn it girl. Bring some upstairs!" he snapped at her.

Without a word, she nodded and went to the basement stairs; he followed her after picking up the strat from where he'd left it by the door. He went into the music room and immediately took the strat from its case. By the time she had taken a half a dozen beer to the upstairs fridge and returned to him with one open can, he had cranked the amplifier up and was playing the same heart breaking slow blues she had heard him play so many times before. He motioned for her to sit and she put the beer on the corner of the amplifier then curled on to an old easy chair in the corner of the room.

She could see the tension in him as a tangible and visible force as he played. The intensity of it brought tears to her eyes though she couldn't have said why. He did not look at her as he played but had thrown his head back, eyes closed lost in the music. When he finally paused and opened his eyes, he stared directly at her with an appraising look that made her shift uncomfortably in her seat.

"You're crying." His comment was calm and without inflection.

She swiped at her tears as though realizing it herself for the first time. "Yes I guess I am." She agreed.

"What's wrong?"

"The music, Lucas." she tried to explain, "It hurts so much. I can feel it hurting."

His fingers returned to the strings and he now played gentle sounds as a quiet counterpoint to their conversation. "Why, my love. Why does it hurt?" He asked again and she felt a little like he was interrogating her.

"I don't know," she confessed. "It simply touched me somehow. I hardly even knew I was crying till you spoke."

He smiled a little then and softened a bit. He stopped playing long enough to take a drink from the beer she'd brought him then returned to the guitar. He played only a little while longer then laid the instrument aside. Without looking up at her, he spoke again.

"Jake is leaving Critical Mass." he said matter-of-factly.

"Oh no, Lucas." she responded. "But you can get a new bass player, can't you?"

"I can try, I guess." He conceded, but she sensed the anger rising in him again. Angela wondered what she had said wrong. "It don't fucking matter. He's moving back to his old lady's home town. Geez! We were gonna make this band work!"

"Well it did Lucas." she tried to placate. "Critical Mass was great!"

He wheeled round from where he now stood with his back to her. His angry eyes bore into her.

"Was great?" he shouted. "Damn it, you've already written it off. I want your support not your criticism!"

She started to shake, still unsure as to what she had done wrong and frightened to speak further and risk his wrath. She tentatively started to rise from her chair. He quickly crossed to her and pulled her the rest of the way to her feet.

"Where the hell are you going?" he demanded, holding her firmly by the shoulders and glaring down into her frightened face.

"It's late. I was going to get a little sleep before the kids are up." she managed to tell him.

"Go then!" he growled, shoving her roughly away from him. She stumbled a little but recovered and stood, shivering violently. He glared at her.

"You still here?" he asked. "Come here then, I want you." He beckoned with one hand.

She took a tentative step closer and he took the front of her nightgown in his hand and forcibly pulled her hard against him. She stifled a tiny scream. Lucas wrapped both arms around her and bent his mouth to hers, kissing her deeply and forcefully. She tasted the blood in her mouth as his lips and teeth roughly assailed hers. When he broke the contact, she relaxed a little in his arms.

"Lucas," she murmured against his chest.

"What baby?" he said, his voice softening a little.

"I love you, but..." she stammered to a stop unable to say more. She felt his whole body tense and one of his hands grasped a handful of her hair at the nape of her neck.

"But what?" he demanded, his eyes flashing angrily down at her.

She was unable to meet his gaze; her eyes fell to the floor even as her heart was in her mouth. "I'm scared sometimes." She managed to say in a whisper.

He released his hold on her and turned back to the guitar. From upstairs, they both heard Tyson as he cried to announce his need for attention. He didn't turn around at all.

"Go and look after my son!" he snapped angrily. Before she had reached the top of the stairs the guitar was crying in anguish yet again. She brushed away her own tears and went to see to the baby.

Two nights later, Lucas slammed out of the house in a touchy mood to play Critical Mass's last ever gig. He had already been annoyed that Jake was leaving but now Eric, the young keyboard player, had decided to move on, taking an offer for a rock band that was doing rather well. The band was no more.

Everything that Angela had tried to do to comfort him had been rebuffed. She had made his favourites for dinner, which he had merely toyed with. When she had asked if something was wrong with the meal, he had thrown the plate towards her where she stood at the counter and it shattered against the wall above the sink. A shard of the broken china had scraped her forearm but she dare not complain. On his way out the door, he threw a parting shot over his shoulder.

"This fucking mess had better be cleaned up when I get back!"

She had cleaned up and turned her attention back to the children. Once they were both bathed, she put Tyson in his crib and together she and Melissa found a story book for Mommy to read. Mother and daughter curled up in the big easy chair in the living room and Angela read nursery rhymes to her until the child's head finally nodded. She carried her to bed then returned to the living room.

Angela restlessly surfed through the TV channels but found nothing to capture her interest. She paced around the house for a time, checking the children, tidying a spotless bathroom then wiping kitchen counters that were shining and clean. Finally she returned to the living room and curled up under a blanket on the couch. In no time she was asleep.

So soundly did she sleep, that she did not hear Lucas when he came in. He put his guitars and amplifier away downstairs then went through to the bedrooms without noticing that she was on the couch in the living room. He had been drinking rather heavily and he weaved down the hallway stopping at Tyson's room. He stood watching the baby sleep awhile then turned as he heard a cry behind him. Melissa was standing in the doorway, thumb in mouth and tears in her eyes.

"Daddy." she whimpered. He went and picked her up, thinking 'Where the hell is Angie?'

"Hi sweetie," he said, "What you doing up?" He gently carried the child back to her room, patting her back rhythmically with one of his large powerful hands. He was quietly humming a lullaby as he walked and Melissa laid her head on his shoulder. He rocked her gently a while, standing beside her bed, then gently tucked her back beneath her blankets. He then went angrily in search of his wife.

He found her curled up under a blanket on the couch; still sound asleep. Driven by a combination of drink and rage, he ripped the blanket off her in one sudden wrench. Angela came awake with a startled cry. He dragged her to her feet almost before her eyes were fully open, gripping tightly to her upper arms. The force of his hold on her brought tears to those half open eyes. He brought his face just inches from hers and she could smell the liquor on his breath.

"I've been home for fifteen fucking minutes and your daughter's been up wandering round the house!" He bellowed at her. "What the hell woulda happened to her if I hadn't been here?"

She was fully awake now and trembling with fear. She was unable to form words to answer him and all that escaped her lips was a terrified whimper. Lucas didn't wait for an answer in any case. He shook her like she was a ragdoll then brought one hand back and smashed it into her face close fisted with such force that she fell away from him and sprawled, head swimming, half-on and half-off the couch. He reached for her again and pulled her back to her feet, where she stood on legs that felt like rubber. He shook her again, his voice quieter now but the tone was unmistakably furious.

"You only have one job here, looking after my kids." he seethed at her. "I would think you could get it right!" He slapped the other side of her face and this time she barely felt it, still numb and only partially conscious. He pushed her back to the couch and turned away from her. As he stalked out of the room, he shot back at her over his shoulder. "Shut up that fucking whimpering or you'll wake the kids. I'm going to bed."

Angela barely remembered leaving the living room, but found herself standing in the bathroom, gripping the counter to remain on her feet. She had at first turned on the light but couldn't stand the sight that met her in the mirror. She gingerly dabbed at her cheekbone with a dampened facecloth where Lucas's ring had split her skin and the trickle of blood had clotted all over her skin. Even the lightest touch on her cheekbone caused her dreadful pain and she was frightened that the bone was broken. Finally she gave up the effort, dropped the cloth into the laundry hamper and shuffled to the bedroom.

In the dark, she could just make out Lucas sprawled diagonally across the bed. She carefully lowered herself to the bed and rolled her small frame into a ball, curling into the small triangle of space in front of her sleeping husband. She pulled a tiny corner of the quilt over her for warmth and drifted into an uneasy sleep.

Angela woke to a strangely lopsided view of the room, made so by her left eye which was almost completely shut from the swollen and bruised cheekbone. The bed beside her was empty. Her first thought on opening her one good eye was for her children. In a near panic, she arose quickly then staggered and slid back on to the bed as a wave of dizziness overcame her. She heard Melissa's voice but it seemed to come from a great distance.

"Lissa, baby." she murmured, "Mommy's here." She slipped back into semi-consciousness.

In the living room, Lucas was playing quietly on his Gibson acoustic, while Melissa played with building blocks and Tyson lay peacefully napping in the playpen. As his fingers caressed the strings of the guitar, trying to find some focus, his mind raced panic stricken through memories old and new that brought chaos and fear rather than the peace he sought. Finally, completely frustrated, he laid the instrument aside and joined Melissa on the floor with her blocks.

Later in the afternoon, he walked quietly into the bedroom and deposited a cup of tea on the night table beside his sleeping wife. She stirred, vaguely aware of his presence, and opened her one good eye. Lucas shifted uneasily from one foot to the other as he stared down at her bruised face.

"I made you tea." he told her quietly.

She stared, almost uncomprehendingly, at the mug on the table beside her. Then she managed to mumble, "Thanks Lucas."

He nodded then backed silently to the door and disappeared, pulling it closed behind him. Angela reached towards the tea, then seemed to lose interest and closed her eyes again, pulling the blankets over her head to sleep once more.

Much later she woke again and, at first, was confused by the darkness. 'Somehow' she thought, 'I've lost a whole day, because it's night again.' The bedroom door opened and Lucas walked to the side of the bed. He noticed that her tea was untouched but made no comment. He undressed and slid under the covers beside her. He took her gently into his arms pulling her back against his chest. His lips found her shoulders and neck lightly brushing her with tiny kisses. His only words came murmured against her skin.

"My angel," he told her. "I am so very sorry."

Angela wept silently. She turned towards him, bruised face cushioned against his chest. Even as she drifted again towards sleep, she whispered, "Lucas, I love you. Please just hold me." Lucas held her and they both found the peace of sleep.

The months went by in a now familiar pattern of sameness for Angela. Her children grew day by day and she took great pleasure in them. Tyson in his turn started to discover his world through both mother's and big sister's eyes, as all three played beneath the maples at the park. Both children thrived on Angela's nurturing and gentle ways.

Belle Griffen watched her daughter with pride at the wonderful mother she had become for Melissa and Tyson. But she was troubled by the distance which Angela now maintained between herself and her own mother. Some weeks, Angela would not allow her mother to visit, always making some reasonable sounding excuse. But in light of Michael's unchanged feelings towards Lucas Reeves, the excuses and evasions were becoming increasingly frightening to Belle.

Lucas continued his job at the music store and also picked up some work in different bands around town or as an in-studio player as his reputation as a guitar man was excellent. He grew quieter than ever before, seeking solace always in the music, playing for hours at a time in the music room in the basement. The passion that drove him to play like he was possessed also fueled his anger. So, although she was lonely for his company, Angela welcomed the peace his music brought him. It was only when the music stopped that life became precarious. The maple trees in the park took them all through another season.

Endings And Beginnings

Lucas pulled up in front of Kurt's with a satisfying squeal of tires. He pulled one of the guitars and a bag of clothing out of the back seat and marched up to the front door. Not ringing the bell or waiting for Kurt to open the door, he pulled out his own spare set of keys to his brother's house and walked into the front hall.

Kurt came through from the kitchen where he had the account books for Reeves Woodworking spread all over the table. He looked with some surprise at his younger brother. He nodded towards the bag and the guitar which Lucas had already deposited on the floor.

"Lucas, what's up man?" he asked.

"I'm gonna crash here for a while." Lucas growled, "Angie's got herself in a damn knot 'cause we had a spat last night."

Kurt wondered just what his brother had done to cause the always serene Angela to at last find the capacity to stand up to him. But Lucas was his brother, though he struggled with the terrible clash of divided loyalty that had chafed at him for the better part of two years now, he shrugged. For the moment, the blood loyalty won the battle and he merely nodded at Lucas as he replied.

"I ain't rented your old room out yet man. Take your stuff in there okay."

"Thanks Kurt." Lucas said, "Don't sweat it. Stupid chick will come to her senses in no time so I won't be here long." Lucas laughed cruelly. Kurt made no further comment but returned to his task in the kitchen. Lucas moved his things into the house, then grabbed a beer out of the fridge and returned to his room. Kurt finished his accounting chores to the accompaniment of a wailing guitar.

Angela spent the rest of the day playing with the children but try as she might to distract herself, her mind kept returning to Lucas. Her resolve, so strong earlier, was fading in the face of being alone. Lucas was, at once, her strength and her weakness. She felt relief at his leaving but still longed for his return. As long as the children were up and needed her attention, she felt a sense of purpose. But later, supper done, baths taken and both of her babies tucked into bed, Angela wandered through the house, lost and frightened. Finally she turned back to the computer which, ironically, Lucas had bought her the previous Christmas to allow her to work from home and still be with her children.

She logged into the music chat room. There weren't many people online but she amazingly found WhyDoThat. She wondered what he would say when she told him that Lucas was gone. She quickly sent a simple private message.

"Hi Brian."

"Hey Angela, how r u?" he typed back.

"I'm okay." she replied then quickly added "Lucas is staying at his brother's for a while."

"Umm okay." Brian typed. "His idea or yours?" She read next.

"Mine. I decided we needed some time, you know, to work things out."

"Angela, there are places that will help. Check domestic violence sites online, check your phone book. Please find some real help."

"Brian, maybe he'll realize I'm serious. 'Cause I sent him away, you know?" she replied. But his words about help stayed with her. 'What could it hurt if she just surfed at bit?' she thought.

"I hope so Angela. Look after yourself though and your kids. Okay?"

"I will Brian. ((((((Brian))))))" she finished with a chat 'hug'.

"(((((((Angela)))))))" was his reply.

She logged off the chat but opened a search engine in her browser screen. Three hours later, with tear stains down her cheeks she was still reading through material that she had found. She had no idea that other women before her had gone through this nightmare. Somehow the knowing both comforted and frightened her.

After she turned off the computer, out of habit she went to the kitchen and made tea before bed. She drank her cup by the tiny light from the bulb in the hood over the stove and suddenly it reminded her of having tea late at night with her mother. She put her head down on her forearms and wept. 'How could she ever tell her mother what a failure her daughter was?' She thought and then. 'Daddy, I need you.'

Angela woke in the morning before the children were awake. She turned over towards Lucas's side of the bed and pulled his pillow into the circle of her arms. Her nostrils drew in the aroma of his cologne, his scent and she felt a lump rise in her throat. She snuggled deeper into the covers clinging to his pillow, her nameless fear of being without him now seemingly looming larger than her fear of his ever present anger. 'Perhaps this time apart would make him understand.' she thought.

Down the hall, she heard the children stirring and resignedly slid out of bed. Melissa and Tyson's youthful exuberance and energy was quite contagious and it was not long before Angela was feeling less melancholy. She decided both her and the children needed a day out. After breakfast, she made the necessary preparations for a visit to the park by the sea.

Mother and children spent happy morning hours exploring the beach. Both children were content and largely unconcerned by their father's absence. Angela kept a watchful eye on them, especially near the water, but she also let her mind wander, reviewing a lot of what she had read the previous evening online, realizing the parallels to her own situation.

By lunch time, they had come to a grassy field bordered by large shade trees, overlooking the strait below them where a myriad of small sailboats danced on the swells in the sunshine. Angela pulled out their picnic lunch from her bag and spread a blanket beneath a beautiful maple tree. As she gazed up through the fluttering green leaves, she heard from memory the haunting acoustic blues that Lucas loved to play, somehow the melody belonged here beneath the maple. After the children had eaten, she was loath to leave their idyllic spot under the maple's watchful boughs. She read them a story from the nursery stories book that she always carried in her bag. Then Tyson curled up beneath his mother's sweater for a nap. Angela played a happy game of I Spy with Melissa to pass the time. Angela puzzled and fretted about Lucas even as she played with her daughter. 'Had he gone to work today? Was he alright? Would she see him soon, or ever?' All these questions plagued her with uncertainty and doubt. All the pleasure she drew from having her children close to her also brought her a new trepidation as she wondered how she could think to look after her precious babies without Lucas's help.

After supper both children settled down quickly and Angela faced another long evening alone. She did some household chores, tried to sit and watch TV, then paced around the house, ending up in Lucas's music room. He'd left two guitars behind, but Angela did not touch them. She sat on the low couch and listened to the ghosts of music played there previously. 'How could he be at once so beautiful in his music and so frightening in his anger? How did she love him still so very much that it hurt to have him gone?' Frustrated with her own questions which sadly lacked any answers, she finally returned upstairs.

The only thing which seemed to comfort her was to cling to routines. She stayed up reading until it was about time for him to come in from a gig, then made tea and went to bed, the ritual, at least in part, was satisfied.

Lucas played his gig as usual but even the band sensed the extra tension in their newest member. He had a reputation around town as one of the better lead guitar players in the business but nearly everyone had heard too that the bad boy image he cultivated had a lot of basis in fact. Between sets he remained alone and aloof, sitting by himself at a back corner table.

He watched the people in the bar around him through half lidded eyes, but his mind's eye was seeing another place and time entirely. Perhaps it was the wash of sound in the bar or the very setting itself, but his mind had carried him back to his first meeting with Angela. She had been so perfect, so innocent, yet so ready to be caught up in his passion. That first meeting had been a sweet taste of the pleasure to come in discovering and unfolding this beauty whose pretty blues eyes held the promise of as much passion for life and music as he had himself. Lucas slammed the empty beer bottle in his hand to the table top and raked all ten fingers through his hair in a frustrated gesture. 'I love her,' he thought angrily, 'Damn she makes me crazy.'

Moments later, he arose and marched back to the small stage to finish the last set. Roxanne had been watching him all evening and, though she wasn't sure what was eating the handsome guitar player, she was wary of his restless look and short tempered manner this night. When the set finally ended, Lucas started packing up his guitars without even a glance at his companions. When he was packed, he headed for the door without a word to any of them. Lenny shot a wink at Roxanne from behind his drum kit.

"What's up with Mr. Reeves tonight?" He said with a chuckle.

"Dunno, Lenny." The redhead replied. "But when he's like that, the devil hisself ought to give him some space, ya know?"

"Yeah Roxy." Lenny agreed. "I'd hate to be at home waiting for that to be coming through the door."

Roxanne chuckled at Lenny's comment outwardly. But all the same she was picturing the soft spoken, timid creature who was Lucas's wife and she suddenly was very worried for her new friend.

Three days had passed without Lucas in the house. Angela went through all the motions to maintain a regular and secure routine for her children. They spent time each day down the street at the little park under the maple trees where she laughed and played with them as though nothing were out of place. Her mind and heart, however, were at odds with one another. She welcomed the peace of not worrying that he may come home in a rage but missed him terribly when it was tea time or when she climbed into their big bed, all alone.

This third afternoon, she put both children down for a nap then wandered restlessly through the rest of the house. Finally she ended up in the den and turned on the computer. She put some finishing touches on a flyer she was preparing for a local Craft market then, as she waited for a copy to print, her mind was reviewing the practical considerations of groceries which she knew she must soon restock. Angela's mind and heart again were at odds. Her practical side told her she must call Lucas and tell him she needed money to feed their children and a ride to the grocery store. Her heart rebelled; frightened of his reaction, frightened that she would seem weak in his eyes. She had a small amount of grocery money put aside and she would get a little more from this flyer. 'Perhaps,' she thought, 'I can make do a few more days and then maybe he will call.'

She had started to surf through some sites that she had discovered that offered resources and help to women left in her circumstances, when the doorbell rang. She jumped in surprise, wondering who would be calling in the afternoon. Leaving the computer on, she went through to the front door, surprised to find her mother and Michael standing on the step.

"Hi Angela," Belle said, glancing past her daughter into the house. "Hope we're not here at a bad time, but Michael had the day off, so we came to see the kids. Lucas isn't here, is he?"

Angela grimaced slightly at her mother's words but managed to keep her tone even as she replied. "Hi Mom; Michael. No he's not home. Come on in, it's nice to see you." She stepped aside to let Belle and Michael pass through the doorway. "The kids are napping but they should be up soon." she told them.

She led them into the kitchen and put the kettle on to make some tea. Belle settled at the kitchen table, resisting the urge to go through and wake her grandchildren. Michael excused himself and went down the hall to the bathroom. Just before he emerged, the kettle started to whistle and Tyson, still rubbing sleepy eyes, toddled in to the kitchen.

"Gramma." he said happily. Belle swept him up on to her lap and almost magically produced a box of animal crackers from her purse. Tyson giggled with glee.

"Great, Mom." Angela told her. "Now he'll never eat his supper."

Michael came back into the kitchen and gratefully accepted the cup of tea that Angela offered. Belle took her teacup and set it on the table, but left it there untouched as she went off with Tyson to change him. Angela smiled ruefully. A wasted cup of tea was a small price indeed for Grandma's attention. Michael was studying Angela carefully over the rim of his teacup and, when she suddenly noticed his eyes appraising her, she shifted uncomfortably in her seat.

"Angela," he said a questioning tone in his voice. She looked up at him shyly but offered no words so he continued. "How long has Lucas been gone?"

Angela swallowed hard. 'How could Michael know?' she thought. "Well he's just out." she replied vaguely.

"Angie, I'm an ex-cop." Michael told her in a gentle tone. "I notice things. How long ago did Lucas leave you?"

Angela found it impossible to meet Michael's gaze, so she talked to the teacup in front of her. "He didn't exactly leave me, Michael." she said, in a tiny frightened voice. "I asked him to go to Kurt's for a while. I needed to think and be alone."

Michael was amazed but ecstatic that the shy young woman before him had found the strength to face Lucas Reeves. But his delight at her courage was tempered by the sobering thought of how her strength could have been rewarded by her volatile hotheaded husband. He replied to the news with as much deference as possible.

"So this is temporary, you being alone?" He asked and she only nodded. "You're a wise young woman Angela, to know you need space to work things out. Is there anything your mother and I could help with though? Maybe we could take the kids for a few days?"

She did look up at him then and the frightened glaze in her eyes brought him anger. 'Lucas put that fear there, damn him!' He thought. Angela shook her head negatively and said only, "No Michael, I need my babies. Maybe just a ride to the grocery store?" She added hesitantly.

He nodded with a smile that he hoped was encouraging. "Yes we can do that for sure. But you'd better tell Belle what's going on."

Belle was surprised but to her credit, despite her well-known dislike of Lucas, she was most supportive. She agreed to watch the children while Michael took Angela to the store right away. Angela went to the counter and counted a little of the money that she kept in the recipe box. She left a small amount there, just in case she needed it. Michael watched her and felt his heart breaking as his anger at Lucas was rising.

Angela was very careful at the store, only buying things that the kids needed for sure and though she was almost out of tea, she bit her lip, and ignored the boxes as she went down that aisle. Michael could stand it no longer. He put a hand on her shoulder, stopping her tremblingly in her tracks.

"Angela, get the tea," he told her firmly. "And everything else that you really need. And some treats for the kids. I'm paying for this."

"Michael I couldn't" she told him shyly.

"Yes, you can, because I don't take rejection too well." He told her with a smile.

She looked up gratefully at him. "Thanks Michael. Lucas probably just forgot it was grocery week, you know?"

"Yeah I know," he replied. He said no more, knowing that voicing his opinions about Lucas may sever the small connection he had managed to build with Belle's girl and all his senses told him she really needed a friend right now. Angela was thrilled about Michael's offer to assist. She felt a small degree of the pressure she was under fall away. She was lighter of heart as they drove back to the house.

Kurt had seen very little of Lucas since his unannounced arrival as an uninvited houseguest. The younger man was usually still in bed when Kurt left for work and he mostly made himself scarce in his room, playing guitar, in the evenings. But on a Friday, his fourth day there, Lucas sat down for dinner with Kurt before leaving for his gig.

Kurt studied his brother surreptitiously, noting the unshaven look and real signs of exhaustion. He wondered to himself if Lucas was getting any sleep at all.

"Hey man, you look kind of tired." He commented trying to keep his tone even and light.

Lucas shrugged slightly, barely acknowledging that he had heard his brother. He took a long swallow of coffee then finally looked across the table.

"I'm fine man." he mumbled. "Just the store and gigs, ya know?"

Kurt nodded, not willing to push further. But then, thinking about Angela alone with her two small children, he ventured more anyway.

"You talked to Angie, at all?" he asked, still trying to keep his voice light.

"No man." Lucas snapped back. "The bitch needs to come to me and she will! She ain't working or nothing. She needs me! She'll come begging!"

"Geez man, didn't you leave her any money, like for groceries and stuff?" Kurt was shocked. 'Lucas couldn't be this cruel, could he?' he thought.

"'Bout time she understood who's the boss in that house, damn her!" Lucas spat the words at Kurt.

Kurt stared in shock at his brother. His mind was desperately racing, trying to come up with words to both placate the volatile man across from him and to suggest a better course of action. It was clear that Lucas was, in fact, affected deeply by the separation from Angela but, as usual Kurt thought, he was lashing out in anger to cover his hurt.

"Man, maybe all she needs is a little romance." Kurt suggested. "You guys have been married awhile. Why don't you like call her up and ask her out. Kind of like a date. Bet she'd come round."

Lucas drained his coffee mug and pushed back from the table. He didn't bother with the dirty dishes, leaving them to Kurt. Without a word, he pulled on his boots, picked up his guitar and opened the back door. Finally, with his back to his older sibling, he spoke.

"Maybe that'd work." he said, "I'll give her a call tomorrow."

Kurt was dumbstruck by his younger brother's response but merely shouted a hurried 'see you later' even as the door was closing. He cleared the table, wondering as he did so, if Lucas had finally begun to see that Angela would no longer allow herself to be treated badly. He silently applauded his shy sister-in-law for finding the strength to stand up to her hot-headed husband. 'Perhaps,' he thought, 'I should take a lesson from her example.'

Angela slept until the children woke her on Sunday morning. It had been her first really sound sleep since Lucas had left the house the previous weekend. Melissa and Tyson both needed very little encouragement from her to gleefully join her in the big bed. She smiled happily as she lavished big hugs on both her children. Melissa, sitting cross-legged beside her mother, looked up earnestly at her.

"Mommy, when's Daddy coming home?" she asked.

A small uncertain shadow passed over Angela's face, but she answered the girl as positively as she could. "Not sure about that, honey. But he is going to take us out for a picnic today."

"Yippee!" Melissa shouted, gleefully clapping her hands. Tyson was instantly caught up in his sister's enthusiasm and started to bounce on the bed.

"Be careful Ty," Angela laughed, "You'll fall sweetie."

"Picnic, picnic!" He giggled at her. She pulled him down into another big hug then hustled both children off the bed so they could all get some breakfast and get ready for Lucas's arrival.

The phone rang just after Angela had settled both children at the kitchen table with some breakfast cereal and juice. She picked up the receiver as she poured some cream into her coffee.

"Hello." she said questioningly.

"Hi Angela," replied the mature male voice on the line and she took a moment to recognize her mother's gentleman friend, Michael. "Belle and I are going to drive down the coast to White Sands Beach today. We thought you and the kids might like to join us?"

Angela hesitated a moment, touched by the offer and unsure how to turn down Michael's generosity after he had been so wonderful about the groceries the other day.

"Oh Michael, that's a wonderful invitation." she told him shyly, "But I'm afraid we can't come. Lucas is taking us all out for a picnic, isn't that great?"

There was a long silence on the other end of the line before Michael replied and Angela was momentarily very frightened she had offended him in some way. Finally, he spoke with measured caution.

"Angela, are you sure that's a good idea." He asked her and, without waiting for an answer, continued, "Has he moved back to the house with you, or what?"

Angela became a little defensive. "Michael, he is my husband." she said, her voice raised just enough for Michael to realize she was upset. "He's still living at Kurt's but these are his children and he, well we, talked and decided that we would kinda like make this a 'date' thing. We can't work out our problems if we don't ever talk."

Michael realized he'd been too quick to criticize but his concern for her safety was now his main motivation. He was surer than ever that Lucas had mistreated his timid wife and his instincts told him to protect her from further hurt.

"Okay Angela, fair enough." he said placating her. "I am concerned about you, that's all. I know we don't know each other too well, but I do know that your mother loves you and the kids very much and that's good enough for me. Take care and if you ever need anything, please come to Belle and I, okay?"

"Sure Michael," Angela said, almost bewildered by his intensity. "Thank you for the other day, the groceries. I will repay you, I promise."

Michael heard again the underlying timidity and lack of self-esteem in her voice as she spoke. He wished that he could someday have the opportunity of making Lucas Reeves feel some of the fear that he had obviously instilled in his wife. But until that opportunity arose, he knew that keeping Angela's trust was most important.

"Don't worry about it." He assured her, "My pleasure. You and the kids enjoy your day. Bye now."

Angela softly said goodbye and replaced the receiver on its cradle. As she sipped her coffee, she wondered how it was that Michael, who she barely knew, had given her such a secure feeling. She pictured Michael in her mind and the image became muddied with that of her father, Paul Griffen, standing tall under the maple tree in her childhood backyard.

Lucas picked up his family at about eleven o'clock. Angela was surprised at how nervous and shy she suddenly felt around him. He helped her with getting the kids into the big back seat and secured in car seats. Melissa clung around her father's neck and, at first, seemed loath to let go of him.

"Daddy, I missed you." she told him.

Lucas hugged her, casting a glance at Angela that let her know without words that he considered Melissa's happiness had been somehow compromised by her mother's actions. Angela could not meet his accusing eyes and busied herself with Tyson's jacket.

"Missed you too, pretty baby." he said to her. "Maybe Daddy should come home, hey?"

"Yippee!" Melissa squealed, then chanted, "Yes, yes, yes." as her tiny arms hugged Lucas's neck as tight as she could.

Angela suddenly hated the fact the he had managed in a few words to make her seem like the 'bad guy' in her daughter's eyes. But she was hesitant to confront him directly about it as; after all, he was a least trying now by taking them all for this picnic. Softly, gently, she addressed her daughter. "We'll see about Daddy coming home, maybe, Melissa. Your daddy and I need to talk about it first. Now please get in the car."

Melissa's face fell, but she did as her mother had asked. Lucas and Angela got into the front seat of the big Buick and Lucas pulled away from the curb without a word.

He drove north out of the city and up the coast to a campground and picnic site on a little sheltered cove where a noisy stream tumbled down the mountainside and into the sea. There was an almost cathedral stillness under the old growth fir trees which lined the slopes running down to the cove. The air was fresh with a salt tang and, although the day was a little chilly, the sun dappled everything with radiant warmth.

Angela had brought a bag with some toy trucks, a ball and Melissa's skipping rope to help keep the children amused. She gave those to the children first and then helped Lucas to lift out the things for a picnic. The last thing Lucas lifted from the trunk was his Gibson acoustic.

"It's beautiful here." she said almost reverently.

"Yeah, used to come up here when Kurt and I were kids." Lucas told her. Both children were occupied for a moment with a game of ball. Lucas put the guitar case down on the picnic table and took Angela in his arms. She melted against him, wrapping her arms round his waist and suddenly realizing that she missed being held.

"Baby, I've missed you." Lucas whispered huskily in her ear, his lips brushing the skin of her neck as he spoke. "'Bout time you ended all this BS, don't you think?"

She was having trouble concentrating on his words as his lips caressed her and his hands slid down to cup her buttocks.

"I've missed you too, Lucas." she murmured, then was about to continue, "But, I..."

He cut off the rest of her words by abruptly releasing her from his embrace and turning his back on her to retrieve his guitar from its case.

"Like old times," He said as though her unfinished thought had never existed. "I want to play for you."

She let the moment pass; content, for now, that they were at peace. As he got the guitar out she spread a blanket on a relatively level and grassy spot. Tyson drove his toys trucks around the area close by the blanket. Melissa settled into her mother's arms as Lucas took a seat on a nearby log and started to play. He played a slow ballad that he knew Angela loved. She cuddled Melissa close to her and rocked her gently in time to the music as Lucas sang to them both.

Lucas, as he often did when Melissa was watching Daddy play, played her an acoustic version of Pride and Joy. Melissa, with the boundless energy and enthusiasm of a five year old, stood up beside her dad and sang along with him. Tyson was more intent still on his trucks but determined to be part of the action by driving them across Angela's lap. After the last notes of Pride and Joy faded, Lucas put the guitar safely away in the trunk.

"These kids are too energetic to sit still long." he said, chuckling. "Let's take a walk down to the beach."

Angela was completely amazed by the effort he seemed to be making. She dared to hope that perhaps he was now willing to make their relationship work. Her fear that had built from the moment she had told him to leave their home was now slowly being pushed from her mind. They played on the beach, ate the wonderful picnic goodies that Lucas had brought with him, and then played ball with the kids until nearly supper time. Lucas took them all for burgers for supper, teasing Angela about how long it had been since they'd eaten 'gourmet road food'.

On the drive back home, Angela slid across the front seat to cuddle next to her husband. In the back seat, the children, tired from playing in the fresh air all day, nodded off to sleep. When they arrived at the house, Lucas pulled into the driveway, parking next to the side entrance into the kitchen. He lifted Melissa out of the car without waking her and carried her to the house. Angela followed him, with her sleepy son in her arms.

Angela carefully undressed Tyson and made him comfortable in his crib then kissed him softly on his forehead and backed quietly out of the room. She glanced in as Lucas was sitting on the edge of Melissa's bed, helping the half-awake little girl to slide into a nightie.

"Daddy, don't go." the girl pleaded with him.

"I'll stay till you're asleep, princess." he told her.

Angela turned away, suddenly dreading the morning when her daughter would look accusingly at her as she told her Daddy had gone back to Uncle Kurt's. She went to the kitchen and put the kettle on, hoping that perhaps over a cup of tea, Lucas and her may be able to talk finally.

When Lucas came out of Melissa's room, he crossed the kitchen to where she stood by the counter. Putting his arms around her from behind, he leaned down and started to kiss and nibble softly at her ear.

"Hey babe, great day!" He said happily.

She leaned back against him, putting the mugs in her hands down and wrapping her own arms over his. When she threw her head back to look up at him, his lips found hers immediately. They kissed long and deeply. Lucas pressed hard against her, almost urgently. She broke the kiss and shifted uncomfortably in his arms. He released her but gently took her shoulders and spun her to face him.

"I've missed you, Angel." He whispered. She looked up into the intense green eyes and saw herself reflected there. Her heart skipped several wild beats as she reached her arms around him and felt herself falling into his passionate gaze.

"I've missed you too, Lucas."

He needed no further encouragement. He reached past her and unplugged the kettle, then swept her up into his arms, kissing her passionately as he carried her to their bedroom.

They slowly undressed one another, lost in the familiar rituals of their love-making, comfortable in each other's arms. Even as she lost herself in his eyes and his desire, a tiny corner of her mind was still insisting they should be talking, working things out. Her own sweet passion won out as he gently laid her on their bed.

Afterwards, they lay entwined together and she gently ran her finger tips across his cheek and neck. He kissed her in return, a light friendly peck, not the deep impassioned kisses of earlier.

"Lucas, we need to talk." She murmured.

"Sure baby, plenty of time for that in the morning." He replied.

She stiffened a little at his words. "You're staying?" she asked, a quaver in her voice.

"Of course I am." he stated bluntly. "I live here. And how can we talk if I'm not here?" He softened his words a little by hugging her warmly. She relaxed in his arms. 'It sounded so reasonable,' she thought, 'How could they work this out if he wasn't here?' He started to sing softly an old lullaby they had often shared together. Glad of the comfort and peace she found in his arms, she closed her eyes and drifted into sleep. He smiled triumphantly into the darkness. 'I'm home.' he thought.

Angela awoke in Lucas's arms and snuggled closer to his warmth, not willing yet to start the day. He had been awake for some time, watching her sleep, marveling at how innocent she still could look. He gently stroked her hair now, whispering softly, "Good morning, Angel."

Her eyes fluttered open and she focused briefly on his face, then with something akin to embarrassment she shifted her gaze to the curtained window where the sun was just starting to light the world. He gently kissed her cheek, brushing his lips softly across her skin which was already flushing with emotion.

"It's a new morning, baby." he told her. "I love you."

She rolled back towards him, burying her face against his chest and planting tiny kisses all over his skin. His hands ran the length of her back in smooth massaging strokes which brought her senses awake even as she felt him harden against her.

"I love you, Lucas." she murmured, "Please be like this always."

His only answer was to find her mouth with his lips and tongue, her tongue quickly rose to play with his as they found one another. Angela's eyes closed to the sunrise as she lost herself in morning's sweet passion.

It was only moments after she had reluctantly slid from their bed and slipped on a t-shirt and jeans, that she heard both her children stirring down the hall. Before she could cross to the closed bedroom door a small hand turned the knob and Melissa stood in the doorway. Her whole face lit up when she saw Lucas in the bed.

"Daddy!" she cried, delightedly, scampering across the few short steps to clamber into his arms. Lucas, laughing deeply, gave her a big hug. Tyson followed his sister into the room and was eager to join in on the fun. Lucas obliged his son by reaching over the edge of the bed and scooping him up too, in one strong arm. Angela stood watching them and, mingled with her joy at the sight, she felt certain sadness that they could not always find this idyllic peace.

"Mommy," Melissa called to her. "Daddy's here!" Angela laughed out loud at the child's statement and Lucas winked at her lasciviously over the child's shoulder.

"Yes Lissa. I know." Angela said. "Come now, both of you, let your father get dressed. Let's go find some breakfast."

Melissa slid down reluctantly from the bed and Angela reached to take Tyson out of Lucas's arms. He relinquished his son but grasped Angela by one wrist. She tensed for a moment when his strong hand held her but he merely brushed the back of her hand with his lips, smiling up at her.

"I'm gonna take a shower." He told her. "Then we'll have our breakfast; you and me."

Lucas went out for a while that afternoon to pick up his things from Kurt's house and to get his pay cheque from the music store. While he was out, Angela played with the kids for a while, helping them to build towers from their blocks on the living room rug. When the telephone rang, she jumped with surprise.

"Hello." she said hesitantly.

Michael's strong masculine tones greeted her. "Hello Angela. Belle and I thought we might come over this evening and see the kids. That okay with you?"

Angela looked out the living room window with fear, as if she expected to see Lucas's car pulling in to the driveway as Michael spoke. She was silent, unsure what to reply.

"Angela, are you still there?" Michael asked a worried note in his voice.

"Yes, Michael." she finally replied quietly. "I'm sorry."

"No need to apologize." he told her kindly. "But about tonight, can Belle and I drop in?"

Angela hesitated again before answering. "Umm," she stuttered then added with little conviction. "Maybe not tonight."

Michael heard the hesitation and fear in Angela's voice even through the telephone lines. He was suddenly very wary about what may or may not be occurring at her end of the phone line. "Angela, answer me with a simple yes or no, okay? Is Lucas there right now?"

"No," she whispered and he wondered at her need to whisper.

"Okay," he replied. He wasn't sure he should press her further but some sixth sense seemed to be propelling him on. "Angela, you sound frightened. Is everything okay there?"

"It's okay, Michael." she murmured. "I'm sorry. It's just, well, Lucas has moved back home. So it wouldn't be good for you and Mom to come over, you know? I'm sorry."

"Angela, whose idea was it for him to move back?" he asked her, almost sharply then softened the question by adding, "I'm only worried about you, okay?"

"Well Lucas says we can't work things out when he's not here." she confessed, wondering herself how he had so easily moved back into her life, heart and bed.

Michael took a deep breath to calm himself before he said anything further. Then, he spoke gently, but firmly. "Angela, I'm getting the impression that you didn't really want him moving back just yet. No, wait, don't say anything yet," he told her, as she had started to voice a protest, "You sound frightened. And I believe I know why you are fearful. Angela, does Lucas ever hit you?"

The question hit her almost as hard as if it had been one of Lucas's hands across her face. 'How could Michael know?' she wondered fearfully. She couldn't bring herself to answer the question, to admit even to herself, that she had been beaten. Instead, she answered indirectly. "Michael, please don't tell Mom." She begged.

That heartfelt plea told the whole story to Michael and, though Angela couldn't see it, he was weeping himself as he spoke again. "I won't tell your mother, if you insist. But Angela, you've got to tell someone. If not for you; for your kid's sake."

"He would never hurt the kids, Michael!" She said adamantly. "He loves them."

Michael shook his head sadly as he heard her words. 'How could she defend this man who abused her?' He wondered. "He loves you too, right?" he asked then continued without letting her have a chance to speak. "Angela, you need to look after yourself and your children. What will happen to your kids, if he goes too far one night and kills you? You're dead and he's in jail? What then?"

Angela heard every word and they stung her mind and her heart like arrows but, though she had a brief urge to hang up the phone and listen no more, she was compelled to hear him.

"Michael, I'm scared." She admitted, breaking down in tears.

"Angela, I can't tell you what to do. This is your marriage." He told her gently. "But no one deserves to be hit, ever! Do you understand that? It doesn't matter what you have done, you don't deserve to be abused. You need to be sure he knows that, understands it and lives by it. Let him know that he cannot do that to you again. Tell him that you won't put up with it."

She heard Michael's words but the thought of confronting Lucas with an ulti-matum like that was incomprehensible to her. "I couldn't Michael. I can't talk to him sometimes. He just gets so angry." She tried to explain. "I just need to learn how not to make him mad is all, it'll be okay."

Michael listened as her fear and self-doubt won over common sense. He rea-soned he had said all that he could and, hoping that she would hear those words on reflection, he decided to push her no further. "Angela, he needs to learn that he cannot go round taking his anger out on others. He needs to learn to control his temper. You need to look after yourself and those little ones. Take care and know that Belle and I are here for you."

"Thank you, Michael." she whispered, seeing the Buick pull into the drive-way. "He's home, I've gotta go." She replaced the receiver on the hook without hearing Michael's goodbye.

"God go with you, Angela." he whispered as he hung up the phone and went in search of Belle.

Lucas came in the side door and deposited a paper grocery bag on the table, then turned to put the case of beer he was carrying in his other hand into the fridge. He had to move a few things round in the surprisingly full fridge for the beer to fit. Angela came in from the living room as he was doing so.

"Can I help, Lucas?" She said softly.

He straightened up from the fridge and turned towards her, his piercing green eyes studying her so intensely she began to shake. Finally, he winked and grinned at her. "Sure, I brought in some steaks and stuff for dinner, in the bag there." He motioned to the bag on the table with a nod of his head. "I'll go get the rest of my stuff from the car." He gave her one last long appraising look before going back out the door.

Lucas had been wonderful since his return. He had cooked dinner that evening, leaving very little for Angela to do, though he happily let her take a cloth to dry dishes with him afterwards. Then, after they had played together with the children for a while, he volunteered to get them to bed with stories, songs and all, while she took a long bath.

She lay in a tub of deliciously warm water with softly scented bubbles and shook her head at her own confusion. Michael's words rang in her mind frighten-ing her while at the same time Lucas's actions caused her to hope he had changed. She wanted so much to believe that her decision to ask him to leave had been just the message that her handsome guitar player needed. She lay back in the water trying to drown the fear and the last vestiges of images from the abuse web pages from her mind. 'Those were other women.' She thought, 'Not me because Lucas really loves me.'

When she got out of the tub and slipped into a nightie and robe, she found Lucas sitting in the living room strumming quietly on the Gibson acoustic. She sat down opposite him with her hair brush in her hand and started to slowly brush out her long dark hair.

"Feel better, my love?" he asked her, without looking up from the guitar.

"Mm hmmm." she breathed, smiling at him. "I feel relaxed again, thank you."

Neither of them spoke for long minutes. The sound of her brush pulling through the length of her tresses fell into a rhythm with his strumming. Finally, he looked up at her.

"God your hair is beautiful." he said huskily. "Long cool woman, huh? Remember?" He added, reminding her of the first night he had seen her so very long ago.

She blushed at the thought and a tiny tear came to the corner of her eye. "I do remember. I never understood why the most handsome talented man I'd ever seen was interested in me."

"Angel, you were everything that I had ever wanted." he told her, as he lay the guitar aside and crossed to her chair. He took the hair brush from her and gently started to brush her hair himself, eventually though he laid the brush aside and started to kiss the nape of her neck as his fingers parted her long tresses to reveal her soft skin. Angela trembled with excitement and, at least for the moment, let go of her fear to melt again into Lucas Reeves' passionate embrace.

Later, as they lay entwined in bed and Angela was drifting in and out of blissful sleep, Lucas asked a question.

"Did you miss me very much last week, my love?" He murmured, lips brushing against her skin, arousing her once more.

"Yes Lucas, I did." She told him honestly.

"Then you must never send me away again, do you understand?" He said, equally quietly, but his tone was much firmer.

She tensed for a moment, but his gentle hands and lips on her body reassured her. "I understand Lucas." She replied with a quaver in her voice.

He continued to caress her and, even though she was very tired, when his hand slid between her thighs she felt herself move against him with passion. In the darkness, he smiled triumphantly. "Good girl," he chuckled as he felt her arousal. "You're mine baby." He stated with satisfaction as he rolled over her again and they moved together once more.

Wednesday night was a gig night for Lucas, his first since he had moved back home from Kurt's. Angela made dinner early enough to leave him ample time to drive to the club. When he finished eating, he pushed back his chair, stretching his long legs in front of him in a relaxed and satisfied manner.

"That was great, Angie." He told her, with a grin. She smiled in response and started to reach across the table to take away his empty plate. She was brought up short by his next words. "I'm puzzled though. Perhaps you can explain where all this food came from, Angela?" His grin had vanished, replaced by an angry glare that pinned her immobile where she stood. Her hand, stretched towards him for the plate, was shaking noticeably. Before she had a chance to recover from her surprise at his words or make an answer to his question, he grasped her wrist and twisted it cruelly. She gasped with pain as he spoke again.

"Come on, damn it!" he continued in a low angry voice, "I know that you didn't have the money for all of this, even in your little recipe box stash and Kurt didn't give you anything. I already asked him. Who was it, Angie?"

"Mom and Michael came over. Michael took me shopping." She told him, her voice shaking with pain and fear. "Please Lucas, you're hurting me."

He let go of her hand and very calmly handed her his dinner plate. She took it gingerly in her hand and hesitated as his angry black eyes still bore into her. Finally his eyes left her and she felt free to move. He slid back his chair and went into the living room, kissing each of the children goodnight. Angela was at the sink when he walked back into the kitchen. He put on his boots, picked up the guitar which was leaning by the counter and reached for the door handle.

"We'll discuss this further when I get home." he shot at her. "I swear Angie if that asshole messes around here again I'll kill the son of a bitch." He slammed the door as he left and then the Buick screamed to life and roared into the evening. Angela went back to the table, sat shakily down putting her head on her arms and wept softly.

The children quickly distracted Angela from her fears so, until she read Melissa one last story and kissed her goodnight, she managed to avoid giving Lucas's harsh words much thought.

After that though, she found herself shaking with fear at the very thought that Lucas would threaten to hurt Michael. She would never be able to forgive herself if something happened to the kind hearted man whose only crime it seemed was taking her for groceries. Her hand hovered over the phone several times as she thought about warning him. 'But would he believe me?' she wondered 'And, if Lucas finds out that I warned him, what then?' In the end her fear paralyzed her once again.

She was far too full of adrenaline born of dread to sleep, so she turned on the computer to surf; the one place that Lucas could not follow her.

Her explorations were somewhat idle at first but then, on a whim, she logged into a chat server and searched for the keywords "domestic abuse". She was amazed when the server located a chat room with the name Domestic Violence Survivors. Hands shaking, tears already brimming in her eyes, she logged into the room as Lucas-Girl.

Her welcome in the chat was immediate. There were only four other chatters in the room and they all typed in greetings even though she was a newcomer. Angela returned the greetings politely. Then there was a usual exchange of basic introductions which include the chatter's age, sex and location. All four of her fellow chatters were women which made her feel somewhat more at ease. One lady whose chat nickname was DreamsHappen was a little older than the rest. Angela merely observed the ongoing chatter for a while, not feeling comfortable yet to join in, but she noticed that DreamsHappen seemed to lead the rest of the group.

One of the other women asked her if she too was a survivor of domestic abuse. Seeing the question, in print across her screen, made her wonder herself what she was, certainly not a survivor. Finally, after a long hesitation, she typed.

"I am living with abuse." She sat back and stared at the words, realizing what she had finally admitted to herself as well as the women online with her.

"Lucas-girl you don't have to live with abuse." DreamsHappen typed next.

"I love him" she replied then quickly typed, "And we have two children."

"I loved my abuser too," DreamsHappen typed again. "May I private message you?"

Angela considered the message for a long moment then she bit her lower lip and replied. "Yes Dreams, please, I need to talk."

DreamsHappen, who introduced herself as Terry, talked in a private message with Angela for nearly two hours. Angela slowly opened up to the woman as she came to trust her and hear her story. It surprised Angela a great deal to find that Terry's circumstances, though they happened years before, in many ways paralleled her own. Angela bared her soul on her computer screen that night, crying as she typed and Terry listened to every word and understood her pain, her fear and even her shame.

Angela glanced at the clock in the bottom corner of her computer screen and suddenly realized that it was nearly time for Lucas to be coming home from his gig. She quickly explained to Terry that he was expected home. Terry kept her long enough to give her some practical information. She gave her the phone number of the nearest crisis line for abuse victims who would connect Angela with her local women's shelter and she also let Angela have her own email address asking her to keep in touch. Angela thanked her new friend for listening and logged out of the chat and shut down her computer.

Twenty minutes later, she was snuggled under the covers in bed when she heard the Buick in the driveway. She heard him come through the side door into the kitchen and considered, too late, that she should have started making tea as usual.

He came straight down the hall to the bedroom without removing his boots and the sound of his heavy footfalls brought a chill of fear to her heart. The light from the corridor fell across their bed as he stepped through the door then the room went dark again as he kicked the door shut behind him.

His hands were on her, grasping the front of her nightie and pulling her to her knees on the bed, even as he spoke.

"Wake up, Angela." he growled. "I have a few things to say to you."

Her eyes, accustomed to the darkness, could clearly see the angry, glazed look in his eyes and she could clearly smell the whisky on his breath as he stood over her.

"I'm awake Lucas." she murmured timidly.

"Barely." He replied derisively. One of his hands took her by a fistful of hair, twisting her face up to his. His other hand grasped the wrist he had held her by earlier in the evening and gave it a vicious twist. Angela bit back a scream as she felt something crack in the captive wrist.

"I can't believe you went to that son of a bitch Michael for money!" he screamed at her. "Just because he's fucking your mother, that don't make him your daddy, Angie! What else does he know? What have you told him about us?"

"Nothing." she sobbed.

"I am your husband!" he bellowed at her. "You come to me for everything! Do you understand me?" He had released her wrist as he shouted and his now free hand punctuated his words by a series of backhanded slaps across both her cheeks. She instinctively raised her good hand to try and ward off the blows and that seemed to inflame him more. He took a hold of her by that upper arm and dragged her bodily off the bed, where she stood unsteadily, head hanging, sobbing quietly. "Do you understand me?" he repeated.

"Yes Lucas." she managed to say.

He pulled her face up to him once more with one hand gripping harshly at the nape of her neck. She saw him through tear filled eyes as he glared down at her, the black anger in his eyes unabated. He was silent for a long time, staring unrelentingly at her as she stood there sobbing and trembling. Finally he spoke again.

"I meant what I said earlier." he told her in a dangerously quiet voice now. "I'll kill that bastard if he interferes with you again. You are mine, baby!"

Angela, frightened and hurting as she was, heard every word that he was saying and suddenly deep inside her realized that Lucas was afraid too; afraid of losing her, afraid of losing control of her and, perhaps, even afraid of Michael. It was a startling realization that was chased quickly from her mind as Lucas suddenly stepped right against her and she felt her already wobbly legs give way. She fell backwards, half on and half off the bed. He stood for a moment staring down at her then stepped to the bedside. He pulled her back up to a sitting position with his left hand taking a vice-like grip on her shoulder. His other hand came towards her and she buried her face against his left arm. As his hand connected with the back of her head, she whimpered, "Lucas, oh God, please don't hurt me anymore."

Her words seem to stop him momentarily, but her relief was short lived because he let go of her shoulder and used both hands to pull her up in front of him once again. Lucas then put one of his strong hands round her neck just below her chin and half choked her as he shook the forefinger of his free hand in her face.

"You know maybe if you'd smarten up, I wouldn't have to smack you." he told her. "Quit your damn whining baby."

When he did let go of her she slumped to her knees at his feet. He stared disdainfully down at the crumpled figure in the darkness then leveled a booted kick at her which connected with her hip. Angela cried out in pained surprise. Lucas turned away from her and stepped towards the door. As he opened the door, he spoke once more.

"Don't you ever forget girl, you are mine."

The door slammed shut and she was left alone in blessed darkness. She slowly pulled herself back on to the bed, weeping with the pain from her wrist, hip and elsewhere. She pulled the quilt up over herself, but the peace of sleep would not come as her battered body kept her awake and aware. In the darkness she heard his guitar wailing from the basement. Angela stared at the ceiling and spoke aloud in a frightened but firm voice. "I love you Lucas. I can't let you do this anymore, not ever."

Angela realized as she opened her eyes that she must have fallen asleep at some point because the room was bathed in full daylight streaming through the curtains. Lucas was sprawled next to her still in his jeans and t-shirt, snoring and unaware. Melissa and Tyson were both awake for she could hear their voices coming from down the hall.

She slipped gingerly out of the bed cushioning her now swollen wrist against her abdomen as she shuffled down the hallway. Both children were in Tyson's room playing on the floor. Angela breathed a silent prayer of thanks that the 'little mother' in Melissa seemed to have taken over. She had brought a box of cereal from the kitchen and was filling toy bowls as quickly as Ty could empty them. Despite her pain and fear, Angela managed to smile at the sight.

She brought both children and the cereal with her through to the kitchen and settled them at the kitchen table, where they delighted in having the rest of their breakfast on Melissa's toy dishes. Angela had no appetite herself but put coffee on. When she had clumsily filled a mug using only one hand, she joined her children at the table. She was still wearing her nightie from the night before, which she realized suddenly had a tear in it from where Lucas had pulled on it. Her first thought was to get dressed, but she could not face going back to the bedroom while he was still there.

Melissa had been studying her mother with a concentrated look on her little face as she was eating her breakfast. Finally the child spoke.

"Mommy?" she asked. "Do you need a band aid?"

Angela shook her head in confusion at her daughter. "A band aid Lissa?"

"Mommy gotta sore arm." The child told her with concern.

Angela felt hot tears sting her eyes. She tried to smile reassuringly at the girl. "It's okay sweetie. Mommy, will be okay." She heard the sound of water running in the bathroom down the hall and realized that Lucas was up. Involuntarily, she began to shake with apprehension.

When Lucas walked into the kitchen, he barely looked at his family. He crossed straight to the counter and reached for a travel coffee mug out of the cupboard where Angela kept the mugs for coffee and tea. Without a word, he filled the mug, then left it on the counter and disappeared into the basement. Angela remembered that he worked today at the music store starting at noon and it was just past eleven o'clock.

When he returned to the kitchen, he was carrying the two Fender guitars. He put them down by the door, shrugged into his leather jacket and pulled on his boots. Only then did he walk over to the table where he gave each of his children a kiss then turned to Angela. He put one hand under her chin and felt her tremble as he touched her. He pulled her face up towards him and bent down, planting a kiss on her bruised left cheekbone.

"I'm having supper downtown and going straight to my gig." he told her flatly then his tone softened a little as he kissed her lightly on her lips. "Later, baby."

"Bye Lucas." she answered her soft tone quavering only a little with emotion.

He opened the door, took the guitars and the coffee and was gone, pausing on the step only long enough to pull the door shut. Angela could already feel her tears coming and she got up as quickly as her sore body would allow turning her face away from her children.

"Melissa, take your brother and go watch TV, okay?" She said, "Mommy's going to go and get dressed."

Angela washed up and pulled some clothes on which made her feel a little stronger. Then, after double checking on her children, she set about methodically packing a few articles of necessary clothing and toiletries for herself in a bag. She also added a pillow she still had from her old childhood room. She looked briefly round the bedroom wondering if she would ever come back here again.

She then took another bag and took as much as possible of the same sort of necessary items for her children from their rooms, including Melissa's favourite doll and a toy guitar that Lucas had brought home for Tyson only a couple of weeks before. She took both bags carefully across the hall into her little den.

Again she paused to check on the children and spent a few minutes with them, reading a story. Afterwards, she took the storybook with her and went back to the den. She slid the storybook into her bag. Then she sat, staring bleakly at a picture of Lucas on the desk, trying to write a letter that she somehow knew he would not understand at all.

Lucas:

I love you very much. But I fear you far more. The children and I are somewhere safe, you must believe that but believe me when I tell you that my mother and Michael do not know where we are either. Please don't look for us. You must trust that I will take very good care of our children as I have always done.

I hope that someday you and I may be able to see one another again and perhaps even find the love we once shared. But for now, we both need help. I don't want to be afraid and battered anymore. Your anger has hurt us both. I pray that you may find some help and at last some peace, my darling.

Will love you always,

Angie

She finished the letter and signed it quickly before her tears stained the paper. She folded it neatly into an envelope and wrote Lucas in her feminine script on the front. When that done she breathed a sigh of relief and went again to check on her children. It was midafternoon so she put Tyson down for a nap. Melissa was content to move to her room, across the hall from where Mommy was working and play with her dolls.

Angela stared at the telephone on the desk beside her computer for a long time, debating with herself on whether to call her mother and Michael and alert them to her actions. She decided finally that to tell them now would probably result in them arriving at her door to rescue her and the children. She was unable to take the risk that Lucas may, in anger, hurt either of them so she thought it better that they not know immediately.

Finally, after taking a very deep breath and steeling herself for what she knew she must do, she picked up the phone and carefully dialed the number of the local domestic abuse hotline.

Angela had never felt so many mixed emotions at once till now as she and her children huddled in the back of a cab on the way to an emergency shelter. The counselor she had spoken to on the phone had agreed her safest choice was to seek shelter with her children. She had cautioned Angela to make sure she brought all her personal identification with her as well as the children's birth certificates. Also, she had been advised it may be necessary to quickly seek both a temporary custody order for the children and a restraining order to discourage Lucas from coming after them or her.

Angela had told her children that they were going to live in a safe new place for a little while where there were other children with whom they could play. Tyson was content with that explanation but Melissa had wanted to know if Daddy was coming too. The question and its answer were heartbreaking for Angela but she explained as simply as possible that Daddy would not be coming and he would not see them for a while. Melissa listened attentively to her mother then said, "Poor Daddy, he will miss us."

Angela, biting back tears, had to agree with her daughter's simplistic assessment of the situation.

When they pulled up in front of the building which looked like all the others on the street, carefully hiding in anonymity for its resident's safety, Angela actually smiled. There in the front yard was a grand old maple tree guarding the pathway to the front door.

The shelter staff was very welcoming and compassionate, understanding how very strange and frightening this whole experience was for the little family. The intake officer, a slightly plump blonde lady not too much older than Angela, showed them to a small bedroom which had two twin beds and a crib in its cramped space. After they had placed their belongings in the small bureau, Cathy suggested gently that the children could go to the playroom while Angela saw the shelter's on call doctor and met with her counselor.

Angela was hesitant about letting her babies out of her sight so quickly, but Cathy was quick to reassure her. Together they went to the playroom and lingered long enough for Angela to be able to see that Melissa and Tyson were both content and well supervised.

The doctor on call was a soft spoken but matter-of-fact woman of about forty-five. She explained to Angela that she had a clinic about a block away where she practiced in partnership with two other physicians so one of them was always on call for the shelter. Her first concern was Angela's wrist which was badly swollen. She did not press her frightened patient for too many details because her trained eye could see that a bone in it had been cracked. She splinted it and fastened it immobile against Angela's chest with a bandage and sling, telling her to keep it immobile as much as possible. She carefully examined and documented all of Angela's other injuries. At first Angela had been frightened and embarrassed when the soft spoken Dr. had told her she would photograph a lot of the injuries but the older lady gently explained that Angela may need this medical evidence to apply for custody and possibly a restraining order. Blushing but determined, Angela submitted to the full examination.

Cathy had waited for her while she had seen the doctor and led her next to an office near the front of the building. Its windows looked out on the yard and the maple tree. Cathy showed her to a seat, leaving her by herself to wait for her counselor. Angela didn't have long to wait. The door opened and a tall slim woman in blue jeans and a soft peasant blouse came in.

"Angela," she said in a welcoming and familiar tone. "I'm Peggy; I talked to you on the crisis line earlier. I'm glad you've come to us." She held a hand out which Angela took timidly for a brief handshake.

"Pleased to meet you." she murmured.

Peggy moved round the desk and took a seat behind it. She smiled reassuringly at the young woman before her. "Angela I know it's all very strange and scary right now. But you've done the right thing. I glanced at the Dr.'s notes briefly. You were not safe there; your husband is a very violent man."

"I know," Angela confessed, her head bowed, staring at her hands. "He just gets so angry. I'm always disappointing him."

"The first thing you need to understand, Mrs. Reeves," Peggy told her firmly, "Is that none of this is your fault. He is responsible for his anger and controlling himself, not you. We have great group sessions with the clients here. You all learn from each other, with a counselor's help, that it's not your fault."

Angela merely nodded, not yet ready to contemplate that it was not some terrible fault of hers that had made Lucas so angry with her so often. Peggy watched the frightened woman struggle with her thoughts a moment before she spoke again.

"Right now we need to think about immediate things, Angela." She told her.

Peggy went on to explain the procedures to get a temporary custody order for Melissa and Tyson and the very real possibility that Angela would require a restraining order to deter Lucas from interfering with either her or her children. Angela heard most of what was said but was also very grateful that Peggy was able to give her some papers that explained it all again.

"Well," Peggy said finally, "For tonight, you and your children should get some rest. We have several lawyers who do volunteer consultations and help you file the necessary papers. We can arrange for you to discuss this first thing in the morning." Peggy stood and came round the desk. Angela got up from her seat, realizing that for now the session was over. Peggy stretched out a hand again to the younger woman. Angela took her hand more firmly this time.

Cathy was again waiting to show her back to the playroom to collect Melissa and Tyson. Angela took the children back to the little room that was now their home, at least temporarily. The shelter would allow them to stay only three weeks, giving sanctuary; counseling and resources to help women like her start to build a life in some safety. Angela wondered how much she could manage to do in three weeks. She put her own worries and fears aside and turned to her children.

She read to them and together they sang songs until both children climbed contentedly into bed. For Angela, sleep would not come. She lay in the darkness listening to her children breathe and worrying about Lucas. 'What will he do when he finds us gone?' she wondered. She hugged her pillow to her with her good arm and cried softly. 'This is crazy.' she thought, 'I miss him.'

Lucas turned the big Buick into the driveway about one thirty in the morning. He slid from behind the wheel and grabbed his guitars from the backseat. There were no lights on in the house, not even the porch light at the side door and he could not help but wonder about that. He let himself in to the kitchen and propped both guitars in their cases against the wall by the door to the basement. It was profoundly quiet in the house and Lucas sensed something was terribly wrong.

He went down the hall towards the bedrooms, noticing in the dark that the children's doors were both open. He looked first into Melissa's and then into Tyson's rooms, stunned to find his children gone.

"Angie!" he shouted, a panicked note coming into his voice. He opened the door to their bedroom with a feeling of dread for what he may find. The room was empty, the bed neatly made. A pale lilac envelope was lying on the bedspread with his name on it in Angela's neat script. He picked up the envelope and slumped to the bed, turning on the small lamp at the bedside as he did so. As he read her words, his whole body seemed to tense and he started to shake almost imperceptibly. His eyes grew dark with a mixture of anger and fear and he crumpled the paper in his hand, holding it in his tightly closed fist.

"NO!" he screamed. That she would do this was incomprehensible to him. 'Where would she go?' he wondered. 'She knows no one, except Kurt and me and her mother and that bastard she's living with.'

Lucas looked wildly about the bedroom as if he may find some clue there as to where Angela may have gone. He pulled open the dresser drawers and could see that some of his wife's clothing was missing. He raced back into the kitchen and opened her recipe box. The small amount of money she kept there was gone. 'How far could she get though?' he thought, 'it was only twenty or thirty dollars.' He went frantically from room to room, not even sure what he may be searching for, except he thought there must be some clue as to where she had gone.

Finally he came to the den. He checked every scrap of paper he could find on the desk then started pulling the drawers open and angrily pawing through the contents. In frustration, he threw a stapler against the wall where it knocked a picture down breaking the glass in the frame. He screamed again, this time a frustrated, hurt and angry wail which was not a word at all but a purely animal noise. He kicked the office chair across the floor so violently that when it collided with the far wall it damaged the drywall. His search of the desk did find something, or rather, it revealed something more that was missing. The file that had been stored there holding the children's birth certificates, health records, Angela's personal papers, their marriage certificate and other documents was gone.

His frustration and confusion grew as he tried to guess where she may be. He went back to the bedroom and retrieved the crumpled note, looking again for any clue and finding none. Over an hour had passed since he'd arrived home. He slumped back onto the bed and started to sob. Out of a habit developed from childhood, his thoughts turned to Kurt. He picked up the phone by the bedside and dialed his older brother's number.

Kurt Reeves surfaced out of a deep sleep as his phone jangled alarmingly beside the bed. His bleary eyes tried to focus on the clock as he reached for the receiver. 'Two forty five.' he thought. 'This better be important.'

"Hello." he snapped.

"She's gone man," Kurt barely recognized Lucas's voice, but the hurt and fear was unmistakable. "She took the kids and she's gone."

"Lucas?" Kurt asked gently. "Where man, where'd she go?"

Some of Lucas's anger came through then. "I don't fucking know! If I knew, I'd go bring her home, damn it!" he shouted.

"Okay man, calm down." Kurt replied. "You at the house now? Want me to come over there?"

Lucas broke down completely after his angry outburst. He sobbed into the phone. "I've looked man, she's gone. Taken my kids. I've looked, Kurt. She's gone."

"I'll be right there Lucas." Was all Kurt said, before he hung up.

As Kurt pulled on jeans and boots, he could not get the image of his sister-in-law out of his head; as she was on that morning years ago, beaten but refusing silently to acknowledge it and him, too scared and weak to come to her aid. A sick feeling was growing in the pit of his stomach but his heart was soaring all the same. As he strode across the front lawn towards his truck, he looked up at the star studded sky and spoke aloud.

"God speed, Angela, your courage will see you through. Take care beautiful one."

Kurt had let himself in when he arrived at the house. Lucas was sitting at the kitchen table with a glass and a bottle of rye whisky. It was plain to Kurt that his brother had been weeping and that he had already consumed a significant amount of the alcohol in a very short time.

"Wanna drink, Kurt?" Lucas slurred.

"Sure man." Kurt took a glass from the cupboard over the sink and found a can of cola in the fridge to mix with the alcohol. He sat down next to Lucas and poured himself a meager shot of the liquor with plenty of cola.

"She's gone man." Lucas told him. "She's gone and she's taken my kids." Lucas poured himself more of the straight liquor and took a long swallow.

"Hey man," Kurt said gently, "They're her kids too. Angie loves those kids, Lucas. She'll take care of them."

Lucas stared at his brother for a long minute then swallowed down more of the liquor. "I love her man. She's mine. She can't just fucking leave."

"I know you love her man." Kurt replied. "I knew you loved her the day you first told me about her. And I know she loves you. But damn it Lucas, she had to be way unhappy or hurting to leave."

"I gave her everything she needed man." Lucas said. "Everything, this house, ya know? I loved her, took care of her."

Kurt watched as Lucas continued to drink the rye like it was water. He nodded now and then as Lucas rambled drunkenly about Angela. But realizing that anything he said would be forgotten in Lucas's drunken state, he did not bother to comment further on his brother's marriage.

By five thirty, Lucas had passed out where he sat at the table. Kurt manhandled his drunken brother down the hall and none too gently tumbled him onto the bed. When he came out of the room, he stooped and picked up the crumpled piece of paper lying on the floor by the bed.

In the kitchen, he put on the kettle for a coffee and carefully flattened the paper out. As he stood at the counter waiting for the water to boil, he read his sister-in-law's note and an emotional wave wrenched at his heart. "Somewhere safe." He murmured aloud. He pondered that as he stirred the instant coffee into boiling water.

He took the mug of coffee with him and went back down the hall to the den, surveying the damage his brother had done there which he had noticed briefly when he'd helped Lucas to bed. His eyes fell on the computer and a thought occurred to him. When Lucas had bought the computer for Angela, he had considered it a toy, something else to keep her amused and at home. What Kurt realized, because he had a computer at home too, was that having a computer hooked to the internet, like Angie's was, opened the world to her without leaving home.

He pulled the chair back in front of the monitor and turned the machine on. The computer came up with a picture of Melissa and Tyson as wallpaper which made Kurt grin. He quickly browsed through her icons and selected the web browser, hoping she had not password protected it against entry.

He smiled as the browser page came up. Without any hesitation, he clicked the mouse on the bookmarks button and brought up her bookmarked pages. Kurt quickly looked through the pages she had there and nodded with admiration. The first had been a chat screen for abuse victims, the next two had been sites specifically for education, resources and support to people facing domestic violence. He looked no further and quickly closed the browser.

He returned to the kitchen feeling very much lighter of heart. Angela had clearly found an escape route that Lucas could not have comprehended. The computer he bought her as a distraction had shown the intelligent but timid woman the way to a safe place where she could rebuild her life. He now understood Angela's meaning in her note about being 'somewhere safe'. He also guessed, correctly, that she would not have told anyone even her mother; for fear that they may lead Lucas to her.

By about seven in the morning, Kurt was exhausted and was going to take a nap on the couch. But his eyes fell on the phone in the living room. 'Perhaps Belle Griffen should know what little I know.' he thought, 'At least she'd know her daughter and grandkids are safe.'

He found the number in the small personal directory lying beside the phone.

Michael looked up from the breakfast table in surprise when the phone rang so early. Belle turned from the counter as he reached for the receiver.

"Hello?" he said.

"Michael? This is Kurt Reeves."

"Kurt. What's up? My caller id says you're calling from Angela's." Michael said. Belle stepped closer to the table, a frightened look in her eyes.

"Yeah, I've been here most of the night." Kurt answered. "Lucas called me about three a.m. Angela has taken the kids and left."

"She left? But where to?" Michael demanded. Belle put one hand on Michael's forearm and he glanced up at her, trying to smile reassuringly.

"I don't know exactly where man. But her note says she and the kids are safe. I think she's gone to a women's shelter." Kurt told him. "I wanted Belle to know."

"Okay." Michael said cautiously. "Kurt, thank you. Now I've got a question for you."

Kurt took a deep breath, and then replied. "Alright, ask away."

"I'm guessing either that son-of-a-bitch Lucas ain't there right now or can't hear you." Michael stated flatly. "What the fuck did he do to her?"

"He's passed out, got loaded." Kurt answered. "I don't know what he did this time, Michael. But I do know that Angela has clearly decided he ain't going to do it again."

"This time," Michael said thoughtfully. "So you knew?"

Kurt choked on his words as he fought with loyalty to Lucas and the shame he felt at his cowardice. "Yeah man, I knew. I have no excuse here. Lucas is my brother, but I still should have stopped him. I thought he was gonna kill me too. Damn man; just tell Belle that her girl is safe. I'm so fucking sorry."

Kurt didn't wait for Michael to reply. He gently replaced the phone on the cradle, put his head in his hands and wept.

After sharing breakfast with the kids and two other women with their children in the warm, welcoming kitchen of the shelter, Angela left the children with a child assessment officer. She assured the woman that her children were fine, unaffected by Lucas's abuse of her and that her husband would never have hurt his children. The woman had, in her turn, assured Angela that they were only being cautious.

Angela, herself, made her way to Peggy's office. The counselor noticed immediately how tired and drawn the young woman looked.

"Good morning Angela." She said warmly. "How was your night?"

"Didn't sleep much." she confessed. "Maybe I'm crazy. I missed him."

Peggy motioned to a small seating area with two easy chairs and a low table in front of the window in her office. As Angela settled herself gingerly into one of the chairs, the counselor answered her.

"You're not crazy at all. You've been with this man, what, seven years? Of course you missed him. Don't beat yourself up over it, you're perfectly normal."

"Seems like I've got more worries now than before." Angela told Peggy then her words and cares tumbled out of her in a rush. "I've got two children to look after alone, I don't know how I'll find a job, these custody things and the restraining order stuff is really scary, I'm worried my Mom will call, or that Lucas will get angry with her...." as she finally paused for a breath, Peggy laid a hand on Angela's forearm and spoke gently.

"We can help you with most of that Angela. But let's deal with one thing at a time, it's easier that way. I've already passed your file on to one of our centre lawyers so, by the time you and I are done talking, we'll probably be able to see him about your court orders."

Angela smiled gratefully. "Thank you, Peggy. You're all so wonderful here. But court orders, it's so very scary."

Peggy acknowledged Angela's words with a nod and a reassuring smile. "Angela, you have to face some brutal truths. I know you have already started to face how very violent your husband can be, just because you're here." She paused long enough for her words to sink in then continued. "Unless you obtain a temporary custody order, based on the fact that Lucas is so violent, there's a very real possibility he could charge you with kidnapping your own children. When an abuser has lost control of his victim, they will often go to great lengths to regain control."

Angela stared at Peggy, already feeling the tears welling up in her eyes. She knew what the counselor was saying was quite true. She thought of the times that she had protested Lucas's treatment of her and his response had always been to threaten in some way. Peggy offered her a box of tissues. Angela took one and clutched it tightly in her good hand as she spoke. "I know," she said softly. "I remember he threatened things before. That's why I'm worried about my mother."

"Alright then," Peggy said. "We can do something about that too. The shelter has a couple of secure telephone lines that clients can use to contact family. We strongly recommend that you do not tell them where exactly you are but it's a very good idea to let them know that you are safe and warn them about the situation. Chances are Angela that if your mother already knows that you and the children are not at home, she's very worried about you."

Angela managed a weak smile through her tears. "My mother always worries about me. And she and Lucas have always hated one another."

"Alright. So we'll finish up here, then take you to see the lawyer, it's just down the street a couple of blocks." Peggy explained. "Then you can phone your Mom. The other things you mentioned are important too; a job, a place to live and how to best look after your children."

"I hardly worked at all since I met Lucas." She said, feeling ashamed to be admitting her dependence on her husband.

"Angela, you're a very intelligent young woman. Didn't you find us through the internet?" Peggy paused only long enough for Angela to nod in answer. "We have resources you can utilize here to help you search for jobs, accommodations, extended counseling, self-defense, and many other things you may find helpful in rebuilding your life. Take advantage of what we have to offer."

"I'll try Peggy." Angela told her. She seemed to steel herself a moment as she sat there, then she spoke with a determination that Peggy was thrilled to hear. "I'm ready. Let's go and see the lawyer."

When Lucas finally woke around suppertime, the profound silence in the house brought the events of the previous evening into a kind of sharp but surreal focus.

"Angie!" The half scream, half moan tore from his lips in anguished desperation, though he knew there would be no answer. He stumbled to the bathroom and splashed cold water on his face. The empty spaces in the toothbrush holder, the missing bottles of spray cologne, all conspired to magnify his loss.

In the kitchen, he found a note from Kurt and it was only then he remembered that his brother had been in the house at all.

Lucas: Gotta check a couple of things for a contract. Angie ain't at Belle's, I already called. I'll be back later. Kurt

Lucas stared at the note briefly then, in a gesture of frustration, ran all ten fingers through his hair. His eyes roamed round the room and fell on the guitars, still leaning against the wall where he'd left them the previous night.

'Damn.' he thought, 'I've got a fucking gig.'

He took the milk carton from the fridge and gulped down about a glassful straight out of it. He wiped his mouth with the back of his hand, shrugged into his leather jacket, picked up the guitars and left. As he backed the Buick out of the driveway, he spoke aloud to the empty house. "You'd better be home when I get back, girl."

Lucas walked into The Stardust Room and made his way straight to the stage. Roxanne, sitting in a corner table with Don, the keyboard player, and his wife, Sherry, watched him walk in, immediately wondering what was bothering the temperamental guitar player this night. He looked like he may not have slept at all and, Roxanne thought he had a distracted look almost like a lost boy.

After depositing the guitars on the stage, Lucas came over to their table and slid in next to Don. He ordered a beer and, when it arrived, sat nervously peeling the label off the bottle as he slowly consumed its contents. Roxanne studied his face surreptitiously as she sipped her ginger ale. She had little doubt that something was eating at him, but could think of no way to broach the subject without risking his temper.

By the time they were into the last three songs of the second set, Lucas had switched to rye whisky and, though he was playing as blisteringly as always, his fellow musicians knew he was becoming very drunk. The combination of stress, lack of food and alcohol were taking a major toll on his judgment.

Michael walked into The Stardust Room just about that time and, with the eye of a trained policeman, quickly assessed the room itself, the clientele and found himself an unobtrusive spot near the back of the room where he could still plainly see Lucas Reeves. What he intended to do by coming to the club that night, he was not sure himself.

Vic, Stardust's manager had seen Michael arrive and his keen eye for people combined with experience caused him to wonder about the man who was easily fifteen to twenty years older than the average clientele here. Curious, he made his way across the room and casually stood arms folded next to Michael. In the lull between songs, he spoke.

"Evening, never seen you round the club before." Vic offered.

"It's not my scene." Michael told him, though his eyes hardly left the stage.

"Excuse my abruptness," Vic said, cordially enough, "You a cop?"

Michael glanced up at the tall blonde man with a sheepish smile. "I used to be. Is it that obvious?" He asked as Vic grinned. "I'm just here checking up on someone."

Vic nodded casually in the direction of the stage, "My guess would be Lucas Reeves." He said flatly. "What's your beef with him man? Did he screw your daughter or beat the crap out of your son?"

Michael's eyes widened at Vic's frank characterization of Lucas.

"Neither." He told him. "He's married to my step daughter."

It was Vic's turn to be surprised. "Angie? What a sweet gal." He answered. "I only met her once and all I kept thinking was this bastard don't deserve her. Listen, if you've got a beef with him, do me a favour and take it outside, okay?"

Michael nodded his understanding of Vic's words, "Yeah, I will. You got my word on it." The two men shook hands briefly and Michael's eyes returned to the stage. The band was just finishing the final number of the set. Lucas finished with a crashing chord and a flourish of the guitar in his hands. Then he left the stage, made his way to the bar and got another whisky and soda. He leaned against a corner of the bar and surveyed the room.

Michael kept a low profile where he was near the back of the room but still kept a watchful eye on the guitar player. He would keep his word to Vic and would not start anything with Lucas until after he left the club, but he was becoming more determined than ever to confront Angela's abuser as he watched Lucas's arrogant demeanor.

Jason, the rhythm guitar player approached Lucas. As the two men talked, Lucas's eyes were still watching the room. He picked his glass up from the bar and drained it in one long swallow. Michael's keen observation could tell he was somewhat inebriated but he did seem to be in some control of himself as he spoke with his band mate.

Lucas's ever roving eye caught sight of something or someone across the room and Michael was put in mind of a cat stalking its prey, so intense was his sudden concentration. His eyes followed the same track as Lucas's and he drew in a sudden surprised breath. At the far side of the room from were Michael stood, near the hallway leading to the kitchen and washrooms, stood a girl with her back to the room. Her long dark hair and slight figure looked almost identical to Angela's; though Michael was sure it could not be her. He focused back on Lucas and realized that the guitar player was just as sure that it was his wife. He had already stepped past Jason and was taking long purposeful strides through the room towards the unsuspecting woman.

Vic came back alongside Michael at that moment and stuck his hand out to offer another handshake.

"We didn't really introduce ourselves earlier." he said, "I'm Vic."

Michael was still focused on the tableau which was unfolding across the room. He barely glanced at Vic, but acknowledged him with a hand on his forearm. "Vic, you may want to consider calling a cop right about now." He said, gesturing towards the back hall and then stepping that way himself.

Lucas had caught a hold of the girl by one arm and spun her quite violently to face him. The girl, clearly not Angie, screamed in sudden surprise at his man-handling of her. Then several things seemed to happen all at once. Michael made his way quickly across the bar, watching as the girl that Lucas had mistaken for Angela swung an open handed blow at him. Lucas, despite the liquor, fended off the blow easily and grabbed her wrist in his own iron hard grip.

"Don't ever swing at me, baby!" he snarled at her. As he spoke, one man broke out of the group of young people that the girl had been standing with and flew at Lucas. The girl was forgotten by Lucas now as he turned to face this new opponent who had come at him with fists already held menacingly. The two men parried a few blows as Michael joined the circle of patrons which had formed around them.

The girl's defender seemed to have some advantage of sobriety over Lucas, as the guitar player stumbled rather clumsily when his attacker's first blows landed. Michael was sure that Lucas would merely concede the mistaken identity, apologize and retreat. But Lucas, now surprisingly down on one knee forced there by the fury of the other man's attack, was reaching into the top edge of his ankle high boot. Too late, Michael realized what Reeves was doing. He saw the sudden flash of a silvery blade as a knife appeared in Lucas's hand.

He heard a woman's voice scream, "Oh my god, he's got a knife!" There was a sound of sirens which seemed to move Michael to some sort of action.

Lucas lunged at his opponent with the knife and grazed only the inside of his forearm. Michael started into the circle planning to try and overpower Lucas and perhaps safely wrest the knife from his grasp. A well-meaning onlooker, however, pulled him back, thinking that Michael was unaware of the danger. That delay meant Lucas had time for another thrust of his weapon and this time he caught his opponent on the side of his chest, cutting through his shirt and drawing a nasty deep cut across his ribs.

Two uniformed policemen broke through the crowd then, just as Michael did lay a hold of Lucas Reeves in a headlock from behind and reach his own viselike grip around to disable the hand that held the knife. One of the officer's quickly took over from Michael and they efficiently cuffed the guitar player and hauled him none too gently to his feet.

Lucas looked round and focused on Michael for the first time.

"You!" he spat in surprise.

"Reeves you disgust me." Michael told him. Then he turned to the officers. "Glad you guys are here. Thought I was going to have to come out of retirement and make an arrest."

Both officers chuckled and the older one shook Michael's hand. "Nice to see you Michael. We gotta take care of this then let's talk, okay?"

"Sure thing." Michael replied, and respectfully stepped back as they led Lucas past him. Michael would never forget the utterly black rage that was in Lucas Reeves' eyes as they led him away.

An hour and a half later, after two plain clothes officers, who Michael also knew from his days with the force, had taken witness statements and left to process paperwork, Vic motioned Michael to a seat beside him at the bar. Michael gratefully slid onto the stool realizing he was still shaken from the incident.

"What are you drinking, my friend?" Vic asked him.

"Vodka tonic, Vic." Michael answered. "Thanks, after that I could use one."

Vic waved the bartender over and placed Michael's order. "I owe you one. I'm glad you were here. Thanks."

"Geez man, I'm still shaking." Michael confessed as he took the glass the bartender placed in front of him. "That bastard is nastier than even I imagined."

"He's got a rep for a hot temper round the players in town." Vic told him. "But he's also the best damn guitar player I've ever seen in clubs anywhere. Too bad, he won't ever play in this club again."

The rest of Lucas's band mates had played a half-hearted third set, with Jason doing the best he could on lead guitar. But they had cut the set short and were now packing up their equipment. Roxanne approached Vic and Michael rather hesitantly.

"Hey Vic," she said as she stood next to them.

"Nasty scene Roxy." He said, but smiled reassuringly. "You guys going to be able to pick up a new guitar man pretty quick?"

"Umm yeah, I think so. Lenny says he knows of a guy." Roxanne answered then she turned towards Michael. "I'm sorry to be so forward, but I overheard you telling one of the officers that you are Angela's step dad?"

"Well yeah," Michael said, "Me and Angela's mom, Belle are together."

Roxanne nodded. "I like Angie, she's a great gal. Are you going to tell her about Lucas? I could come along if you like. She might need a woman there, you know?"

Michael liked the petite singer, her open and caring heart showed through the concerned look in her honest eyes. "I'm not really able to contact Angela right now, Roxy." He tried to explain. "She and the kids left Lucas last night. I believe they are in a women's shelter right now. But I appreciate your offer."

"Oh god, poor Angie." Roxanne gasped. "I knew something was way wrong when Lucas walked in here tonight. And I only met Angie a couple of times, but she was way scared of him. Thank god she got out."

"Amen to that." Michael said quietly.

As they had been speaking, Kurt Reeves walked into the club and headed straight up towards the stage. He was surprised to see his brother's guitars there but no sign of Lucas. Jason told him there'd been some trouble and then asked if Kurt would take Lucas's guitars and amp with him. As far as the band was concerned, he explained, they didn't want Lucas back. Kurt merely nodded tiredly and asked where Lucas was now. Jason motioned him towards where Vic, Michael and Roxanne were at the bar.

"Talk to that older guy there. He pulled your brother off of some guy here before he killed him." Jason told him.

Kurt had not noticed Michael earlier and was stunned now to see him in the club. He quickly crossed the distance to the bar, wondering what the ex-cop had been doing here at all.

"Michael, what the hell's been going on here?" Kurt demanded without any preamble.

Michael turned towards him and slipped down from his barstool at the same time. "We'd better talk alone Kurt." He answered curtly. Then he turned back to Vic and Roxanne. "Thanks for the drink Vic. It's been a pleasure meeting you despite the circumstance. And Roxanne, if and when I get a chance to see Angela, I'll give her your love."

He turned back to Kurt and both men went to a table in an empty corner of the room. Michael sat down tiredly resting his forearms in front of him. Kurt slid into the chair opposite him and stared intently at the older man.

"Kurt, your little brother got himself in a mess of trouble tonight." Michael told him. "He mistook a girl in the bar for Angela and went after her. When one of her guy friends started a fight with him, your brother pulled a knife. The guy ain't hurt too bad, but Lucas is in jail and charges have been laid."

"Damn when will he learn?" Kurt asked rhetorically. "Guess I'd better collect his stuff here then go see about bailing him out."

"Kurt, look man, I know you love your brother." Michael told him. "But maybe you want to reconsider bailing him out?"

Kurt stared at Michael for a long moment. "He ain't got anyone else, Michael. I'm like his only family."

Michael nodded his understanding but then continued. "I know that Kurt. But you're not doing him any favours when you keep helping him out of the hard spots he puts himself into. I understand why you were scared of him, man. I saw him tonight. He's vicious and unpredictable. I know you're feeling guilty about not helping Angela when you knew what he was doing to her. Here's your chance to help them both."

"How so?" Asked Kurt, as part of him wanted to defend his brother, but another part knew that Michael was right in what he was saying.

"Leaving Lucas in jail to stew in his own trouble till his hearing will be good for him. It's about time that he felt what it was like to be a prisoner in someone else's control. And, if he's in jail for a while, that gives Angela some real breathing space to try and put her life in order. You will be helping them both. Though Lucas will not see it that way."

"Damn right he won't see it that way." Kurt said, quietly. "But it makes sense Michael. It's like what they call tough love, right?"

"Yeah that's what they call it when a parent has an out of control kid and they simply let the kid face the consequences, police or jail or whatever, on their own. There comes a time when all people need to be accountable. Lucas's time has come Kurt. Help him by not helping him this time."

Kurt was silent for a few moments and Michael watched him closely as he weighed up the ex-cop's words. Finally, Kurt thrust his hand across the table and Michael took it. As they shook hands, Kurt spoke.

"It's about time I got a damn backbone." He said with a wry smile. "I think this is going to help all three of us." Michael helped Kurt to carry Lucas's gear to his truck, then the two men shook hands again and Michael headed for home. As he drove through the darkened streets, he wondered where Angela was and wished somehow that Belle and he could be there to help soften the blow that was sure to come when she learned of her husband's arrest. He was very impressed with the courage she must have had to find to leave the monster that was her husband, but knew that this latest fiasco would frighten the strongest heart. Even telling Belle was not something he looked forward to but, he sighed aloud, it must be done.

To Michael's surprise, Belle was sitting in the kitchen drinking tea when he let himself into the house. She looked relieved when he came in but it was also apparent that she had been crying. He went straight to her and pulled her up into his arms.

"Hey lady, I know that I'm late." He told her. "I'm so sorry." He had not told her where he had been going but now suspected that she had guessed at his errand's purpose.

"Michael, I've been so worried about you." she exclaimed, taking comfort in his embrace. "And then Angie called, and I just couldn't sleep." Michael was tall and broad across his muscular chest and Belle felt a sense of security nestled there.

Michael gently guided her back into her chair, then pulled up the one adjacent to hers and sat holding both her hands in his. As he settled into place, he spoke again.

"She called? Where is she?" He asked anxiously. "There any way we can get a hold of her?"

"Michael, she's okay." Belle told him. 'They're staying at a women's shelter. I begged her to come here to us. But she kept saying 'it's not safe'. Michael, I'll kill the bastard myself if I ever see him, he's made her so afraid she can't come home!"

"I know exactly how you feel, my darling." Michael agreed, squeezing her hands as reassuringly as he could. "But at least for now, Lucas Reeves isn't going to be hurting anyone. He's in a bit of trouble of his own. Did Angela give you a number where we can reach her?"

Belle stared blankly at him for a moment, trying to comprehend the meaning of what he had said. She finally shook her head negatively at his question. "No, she said she couldn't give out the number, but she promised to call tomorrow. Michael, what's happened?"

The question hung between them for a long moment. Michael straightened up a little in his seat and looked directly into Belle's eyes. "Your son-in-law has been arrested. He's in jail." He said matter-of-factly. "I didn't tell you where I was going tonight, because I didn't want to worry you."

Belle was shaking a little, but he saw her take a deep breath to steady herself, then she said softly, "You'd better tell me now."

"I went down to that club where he plays, 'cause I was going to tell him just exactly what I thought of him." To emphasize his words, Michael clenched one of his fists in the air between them. Belle swallowed hard. "He got into an altercation with a patron in the bar. The other man had him clearly beat when the cowardly son of a bitch pulled a knife."

Belle gasped at Michael's words. "Oh my God." she breathed. "Michael, he scared me right from the first time I met him. But I never dreamed he would do something like that. He could have killed my Angela! Is the other man alright?"

"His wounds were only surface." Michael assured her. "Someone pulled Reeves off before he got a good thrust in." Michael intentionally omitted the fact that he had been that someone. 'No need to worry her further.' he thought.

"Belle, I want to talk to Angela tomorrow when she calls." Michael stated flatly. "And I definitely want her and the children to come here and live with us. I've already spent a fortune on our state-of-the-art security system; might as well use it. And with Lucas in jail, we've got some breathing space, all of us."

They talked for a little while longer, but now that Belle was lighter of heart knowing that Michael was home safe, Lucas in jail and her girl and grandchildren in a safe haven, her eyes started to droop with sleepiness. Michael suggested gently that they could both use a good long cozy cuddle. He helped her to her feet and arm in arm they went down the hall to the bedroom.

Angela went down to lunch with her children the day after she had called her Mom; the conversation still on her mind. Tyson insisted on sitting on her lap and Melissa huddled as close as she could move her chair to her mother's. She looked up at Angela, her little face full of concern.

"Mommy?" She said tentatively.

"Yes Melissa, what's up sweetie?" Angie asked.

"Doesn't Daddy love us anymore? Is that why we had to go away?" She asked.

Angela felt a lump rise in her throat at Melissa's innocent but plaintive question. "Melissa, Daddy still loves you, I promise." she assured the child, "It's just that Daddy and I need to be away from each other for a while."

"Was Daddy bad?" Melissa asked.

"Sometimes Melissa, grown-ups make mistakes, just like children." Angela told the child. "Daddy made some mistakes and so did Mommy. Now I'm trying to get better."

That answer seemed to satisfy the child and she went happily back to her bowl of soup. Tyson clung to Angela still, but did eat his macaroni as she fed him between mouthfuls of her own coffee. When they had finished and Angela went to the sink to wash the dishes they had used, Tyson toddled after her and clung to the leg of her jeans. She suddenly felt overwhelmed by a sense of guilt for taking them away from their father. 'Maybe I was too hasty to get custody orders,' she thought, 'After all they're his kids too.'

As the thought went through her mind, Peggy walked into the kitchen in search of her. The counselor had an almost unreadable expression on her face, but Angela sensed something was terribly wrong.

"There you are Angela." she said smoothly. "We have to talk, right away."

Something in Peggy's tone sent a chill up Angela's spine. She wasn't sure what the counselor needed to talk to her for, but she had a sudden sense of dread.

"But Peggy, I......"

The counselor cut her off rather abruptly. "This is important Angela. Melissa and Tyson can play for a little while; we'll walk them to the playroom then go to my office."

Angela nodded resignedly. A few minutes later, Peggy ushered her into the office and motioned to the comfy easy chairs by the window. One extra chair had been moved round from the desk and Angela recognized the young lawyer, Mr. Blakely, sitting waiting for them. She felt a knot start to form in her stomach as she imagined all the possible bad news he may be bearing. She sat down and looked from Peggy to Mr. Blakely fearfully. Peggy spoke first.

"Angela, Mr. Blakely came in to let us know that the two court orders, for temporary custody of Melissa and Tyson and the restraining order have both been granted and served." She said.

"Thank you Mr. Blakely." Angela murmured, still wondering why the lawyer needed to make a personal trip to tell them this news.

"You're welcome Angela." he replied, "The orders help; at least they give limits to your husband that the courts will be able to enforce if he tries to trouble you."

Before Angela could say anything further, Peggy spoke again. "Angela, there's something else you need to know; the process server had some trouble in locating your husband to serve the orders." Angela had tensed at Peggy's words and waited now to hear the rest. "Lucas is in jail. He was arrested last night. There was some trouble at a bar where he was playing."

Angela gasped softly, bit her lower lip and tried to hold back tears which were threatening to flood. In a tiny, frightened voice, she asked. "What was he arrested for?"

Mr. Blakely answered her. "He was involved in an altercation with a patron at the bar. The fight became rather nasty and I'm afraid you husband pulled a knife and assaulted the man."

"Oh my God!" she breathed, "What have I done?" She broke down sobbing, as she thought that if she'd only been home this would never have happened.

"Angela, listen to me." Peggy said sharply, "You are not responsible for Lucas's actions. He did this, not you!"

Angela stared at the counselor through her tears. "But Peggy, he only got so mad because I wasn't there."

Peggy reached across the space between their chairs and took Angela's hands in hers. "Angela, he is a grown man, with an anger problem. You have never done anything to cause it. He needs help and perhaps some time in jail will make him realize that. But you need to worry about yourself and your children. What if he'd pulled that knife when he was angry with you? He may very well have killed you."

Angela was shaking violently as she listened to the counselor's words, knowing in her heart that Peggy was right, she did fear that Lucas would kill her. 'And what then?' she thought in despair.

"I loved him Peggy, I loved him so much." she sobbed. "But I was so scared of him. He isn't the same when he's angry, it's like he's somewhere I can't reach, can't help."

Peggy passed her some tissues and as Angela was wiping her eyes, the counselor spoke gently. "I know you loved him, Angela. But you can't help him, no one can unless he is willing to admit that he has a problem and accept some help. I know this sounds harsh, but maybe now after losing you and his children and his freedom he will realize that he needs to change." She paused and glanced up at young Mr. Blakely who had sat in silence feeling compassion for his frightened client. "Mr. Blakely, thank you for bringing this news."

"No problem, Peggy." He said, as he started to rise. "I'll leave you two now. Angela, I'm sorry this is so very difficult for you but, if it helps, you are taking the right steps to make your life peaceful, safe and happy for you and your children."

"Thank you." Angela whispered softly.

After the door had closed behind Mr. Blakely, Peggy turned back to Angela. "As bad as this all seems right now, Angela. It may turn out to be the best news for all of you. Lucas will be held, possibly without bail, until his hearing and that may be six weeks to two months. You have some time to get your own life in order."

"But I don't want to go back to that house." Angie said with conviction, "And I can't stay here. And what if there is bail? Then what?"

Peggy spoke calmly. "Now, you have options. I can understand your feelings about not going back to the house. So many bad things happened there. When we talked yesterday, you told me your mother and her partner wanted to take you and the children in to stay with them. Perhaps now, that's not such a bad idea."

"I would love to be with my mother. But what if Lucas gets out of jail?" Angela asked, still frightened.

"If the court sets bail, do you think someone may post it for him?" Peggy asked.

"His older brother, Kurt, would." Angela said, picturing all the times that Lucas got help from his older sibling. Kurt was always there for Lucas, almost like a father rather than a brother.

"Perhaps you should start by calling your mother and discussing it with them, Angela. Didn't you say her partner was a policeman?" Peggy asked.

"Well yes, Michael was a policeman; he's retired and does consulting now." She explained.

"Well I'm sure he has an understanding of these types of situations. You may find a great deal of help and good advice from him." Peggy ventured. "And, if you do decide to leave the shelter, we still offer you continued counselling and Mr. Blakely can follow through with you for the legal needs you will have. Family is important Angela. You know that or you wouldn't have tried so very hard to keep your children and yourself in the relationship with Lucas. Talk to your mother and just see what happens."

Angela nodded, still wiping the rest of her tears. She left Peggy's office, still a little shaken by the news but Peggy's words were ringing through her mind. She went first to the playroom and gave Melissa and Tyson both very big hugs. As she sat on the floor with them both, Melissa curled in her lap and Tyson driving a toy truck along her leg, she began to realize that family was the important thing to her. These children were her strength. She saw Belle's face before her and had the urge to talk to her, so clear was the image. She gently extricated herself from Melissa's hug and got back to her feet.

"I love you, my precious babies." She told them, planting a kiss on each forehead. "Mommy has to make a phone call, I'll be right back."

Kurt walked into the reception area of the City Jail where Lucas was being held. He still cringed inwardly when he recalled their telephone conversation of two days before in the early morning hours of Saturday after his arrest on Friday night. Lucas had been full of what could only be described as self-pity, but when he blamed Angela for his current situation Kurt almost lost his self-control. Kurt told him that he had brought the guitars and amplifier home because the band no longer wanted his services. 'Their loss.' Lucas had told him arrogantly.

Lucas then asked his brother to come down and bail him out and suggested that maybe Kurt's business lawyer may be able to refer them to someone for the criminal charges. Kurt told him tersely that the woodworking business did not currently have sufficient cash flow and assets to float a loan for bail and that Kurt would be unable to use Lucas and Angela's house as collateral because that would require Angela's signature and who knew where she was right now. His younger brother had been livid, even over the telephone Kurt could picture the seething anger and know that the young hothead would have swung at him for sure had they been face to face. Kurt said he'd get the lawyer lined up and come in and see Lucas on Monday. Lucas had angrily slammed down the phone, leaving Kurt shaken but convinced that this was the right thing to do.

So now, he looked around the reception area and his eyes fell on a well-dressed blonde man about forty years old, carrying a briefcase. The man eyed Kurt at the same time and seemed to recognize him, as though from a description given.

He stood and extended a hand towards Kurt. "Hi, you must be Mr. Reeves. Bill showed me your picture. I'm Jack Mercer." He said by way of introduction.

Kurt took the man's firm handshake and managed a weak smile. "Thanks for taking this on, Jack. I didn't know what to do, but I figured that Bill would steer us right."

"Well, I've taken a look at the arrest report, Mr. Reeves." the lawyer told him. "Your brother's in a lot of trouble. The courts don't like it much when people go round sticking other people with knives, and the police and bar owners in the city have been waging their own unified campaign against violence in the bars. I noticed they posted a bail amount on Saturday, you going to be paying that?"

"My brother has had trouble all his life with anger." Kurt said with a sad tone in his voice. "I know that ain't any excuse. No, I already told him I'm not putting up bail. And please call me Kurt."

The lawyer nodded then asked another question. "Lucas is married. What about the wife, she want to bail him out?"

"Angela took her children and left my brother last Thursday. As far as I know she has taken refuge in a shelter for battered women." Kurt told the lawyer.

"Nasty situation, Kurt." Jack said frankly. "The two things, criminal and family court matters should be dealt with separately but the judges and lawyers all know the angles. And her lawyer may be allowed to use this criminal action to show your brother's propensity for violent solutions. Either way, it doesn't look good."

"Yeah, no kidding." Was all Kurt could say.

"Well," Jack announced, "Shall we go and see little brother?"

Kurt nodded his head resignedly. He was not looking forward to facing his brother's wrath in person, but at least here, Lucas could not use his fists to express his anger. The two men were shown down a long hallway after passing through a double door security system. Because Jack Mercer had declared himself as Lucas's lawyer, they would be allowed to see him in an interview room, with his guard escort posted outside the door. Kurt was wholly unprepared, however, for the sight which met him when they walked in.

Lucas was sitting at the table, his once handsome face was bloody with a nasty scratch across one cheek, his left eye was swollen shut and bruised to black. He had bandages wrapped around his ribs which showed under the open front of the coverall he wore and as he turned his face towards them, Kurt saw a nasty bruise on his upper neck right behind his right ear as though he'd been kicked in the head.

"Oh my God, Lucas!" Kurt breathed.

Lucas looked up at him accusingly, then to Kurt's amazement began to weep. "Kurt, man you've gotta get me outta here. They're gonna kill me."

"What the hell happened?" Kurt demanded. Before Lucas answered, he looked suspiciously at Jack Mercer. Jack stepped to the table, put his briefcase down and introduced himself.

"I'm Jack Mercer, Mr. Reeves." he explained, "Your brother here has hired me to defend you."

Lucas nodded but did not take the lawyer's proffered handshake. Kurt sat down opposite Lucas and asked him once more to explain.

"Lucas, this happened in here, in jail?"

"Yeah." Lucas said softly. "They served that shit on me 'bout custody for the kids and an order that I'm supposed to stay away from Angie, and this other guy said 'hey man you beat your wife?' and I said 'none of your business, asshole.' But then later a couple of them jumped me man. I thought they would kill me."

Kurt shook his head in disbelief. He looked round to the lawyer.

"Jack can't we do something 'bout this. This just isn't right?" He demanded.

"Pretty hard to prove Mr. Reeves," Jack Mercer said with a shrug. "Prison justice is harsh and most times the guards look the other way. Even criminals have these standards, you see, and wife beating just isn't tolerated. If they find out, they beat you."

Kurt weighed the lawyer's words carefully as he looked again at his battered brother. Then in his mind's eye, he flashed back to a similar picture of Angela beaten black and blue. Lucas looked hopefully at Kurt, expecting that his big brother would rescue him once more. The three men were silent as the older Reeves struggled with the ultimate dilemma. Finally he spoke.

"Lucas, I'm real sorry this happened to you man." He said. "But as Jack says, justice in here is harsh. You want me to be 'big brother' again and jump in and protect you, right? But answer me this Lucas, who protected Angie from you when you beat her?" Lucas looked like he was about to protest then, but Kurt cut him off. "No, don't fucking deny it, man! I was there, I heard you batter her. Lucas you've lost your wife, your kids, the band don't want you back and you tried to kill a man, all for what? You've hit the fucking bottom Lucas, get up and be a man and get some help!"

"I never meant to hurt Angie, I loved her man." Lucas sobbed.

"Yeah, well you did hurt her didn't you, and I let you keep on doing it too!" Kurt spat at him. "Well no more. I still love you little brother, but I can't protect you anymore. Grow up and be a man. I've got you a lawyer and I'll look after your things and house, but you deal with this Lucas 'cause you put yourself here, nobody else did!" Kurt turned to Jack Mercer as he stood up. "Do whatever you can for him man. And send me all the bills, I'll look after it. Pleasure meeting you."

The lawyer stood, shook Kurt's hand and Kurt walked out of the room without looking back. Jack Mercer, inwardly applauding the older Reeves' actions, turned back to his beaten and sobbing client with a reassuring smile painted on his face.

Michael and Belle had picked up Angela and the children on Sunday morning and brought them home. At least 'home' was what Belle kept calling the house she and Michael shared. Angela was not sure that anywhere would ever feel like home again for her. The children had settled in contentedly enough as grandma lavished lots of attention and treats on them both. Michael had helped Belle to make a couple of the bedrooms in the large house as comfortable as possible for her daughter and grandchildren and Angela was grateful for that.

All day Sunday, Belle cast surreptitious glances at her daughter, not wanting to comment in front of the children, but all the same feeling horror at the visible signs of Lucas's beating. Over and over in her mind she reviewed the events of the last seven years and wondered somehow if this could have been avoided. Her mother's instincts had told her not to trust Lucas Reeves now, it seemed, her worst fears were proved true.

After dinner, Belle told Melissa and Tyson that 'grandma' would give them their baths and help them with pajamas so 'mommy' could relax. The children went gleefully off to the bathroom with her with visions of the bubble bath she had hinted at bringing a sparkle of excitement to their eyes.

In the kitchen, Angela started to wipe countertops self-consciously still feeling like an intruder in Michael's home. Michael watched her for a moment from his seat at the kitchen table, then rose and gently took the cloth from her hand. He tossed it into the sink with a grin reminiscent of a mischievous child.

"Come on Angela." he told her, conspiratorially, "Belle didn't go to bath the kids so you could clean her kitchen. Let's take a walk and watch the sunset."

"Michael," she replied hesitantly. "Maybe I shouldn't be out walking, you know?"

"Look Angie," he said firmly but gently. "You can't make yourself a prisoner for the rest of your life. Besides, Lucas is in jail, you're safe and I'm only suggesting a walk out through the back gate there." He gestured through the kitchen window. Across the yard at the edge of the property line was a chain link fence, about four feet tall with a gate in it. The gate, much like the one in Angela's childhood home, led into undeveloped land behind the house. The hillside dipped steeply down westward towards the strait below them and Angela had marveled at the spectacular view when she'd arrived that morning.

She nodded silently at Michael and followed him out across the yard. The fresh air and early evening sunshine seemed to breathe a new vitality into her being which was drained with emotions and stress over the past few days.

The pathway she and Michael followed under dark green towering fir trees reminded her of the paths she had explored as a girl. They broke out of the firs into a clearing perched on a plateau some sixty feet above the water level. The clearing was protected a little from northern winds by two large maple trees which Angela found immediately comforting. The level ground here was quite open and rocky and there were a couple of huge fir logs which had been hewn and carved into massive one piece seats. Michael gestured to one and settled into the other one himself.

"Did you make these, Michael?" Angela asked him.

"Yeah, Belle and I like to come out here sometimes and watch the sunset. It's real pretty." He grinned.

"It's spectacular." She breathed softly.

"Angie," he started tentatively. She looked across shyly at him. "I want you to know that I'm thrilled that you've come to stay with us. I don't want you to ever feel you're intruding here."

"Michael, this isn't my home, though I thank both you and Mom for letting us stay here." She said quietly. Her gaze slid away from him and out across the water as she continued. "I don't really know where my home is. I guess I don't have one right now. But this is right for my kids. I've realized lately that family is the most important thing in the world. I just need some time to get strong again is all," she explained and raised her cracked wrist a little. "Not just this kind of strong. But as soon as I get a job and can start to look after these kids by myself, I'll find a place we can call home. Just wish I didn't have to get everything all over again, like beds and stuff. But I'll find used stuff and manage."

He marveled at the strength he saw in her already and decided it was time somebody told her so. "Angela you are one of the strongest young women I've ever met. I admire you a great deal. To go through everything that you have and to be able to come out alive and ready to start again is a credit to you. You're welcome to stay with Belle and me as long as you need to and be assured I've made this house as safe as state-of-the-art security will allow."

The two of them sat silent for a while, watching the sun dip towards the sea. Michael was thinking about what she had said about furniture. An idea was forming in the back of his mind but he didn't mention it to her right then. Angela was silenced by the beauty of the view from the plateau and was watching, far below, a young couple walking hand in hand down the beach. She had a fleeting image of herself and Lucas walking down a similar beach and tears welled into her eyes. 'Oh God,' she thought, 'Will I ever get over missing him?'

As the sun slowly sank into the western ocean, Michael and Angela returned to the house. He made no comment on the tears which he could see streaming down her cheeks. With her long dark hair flowing all round her shoulders and down her back, Michael briefly had an image of a widow in a mourning shawl and wondered if, in reality, that wasn't very close to the truth.

"Thank you for sharing your sunset spot with me, Michael." Angela said with a smile in counterpoint to her tears. "It's a beautiful place."

"You're welcome, sweet lady." he replied. "Now let's go do those dishes together, okay?"

They had just finished loading the dishwasher when Belle came back into the kitchen. She announced that both children were in bed but, of course, wanted 'mommy' to tuck them in and kiss them goodnight. Angela smiled gratefully at her mother and went to see them. Both children had climbed together into one of the two twin beds in the room, though Angela noticed the covers on the other had been pulled back. 'They must need each other's company for now' she thought, worrying inwardly about the effect of all this upheaval in their lives. She perched on the edge of the bed and caressed both small foreheads with her good hand.

"My babies both ready for sleepy time?" She asked softly.

"Tyson's sleeping with me, Mommy." Melissa told her, "He's scared in bed by himself."

"That's good 'Lissa." she assured her daughter, "Thank you sweetie for looking after your brother. I love you both very very much." She bent to give them both kisses. Tyson giggled at her when her soft lips brushed his cheek. "That tickle Ty?" she asked, laughter in her voice too.

"Yup." Tyson agreed, his eyes getting heavy with sleepiness.

She stood up, pulling the covers round them snuggly and blowing more kisses to them as she stepped towards the door. "Night Night, little ones. Sleep tight. I love you."

Melissa's serious five-year-old voice brought a lump to Angela's throat, as the child said, "Night Night Mommy, you sleep tight too. It'll be okay." Tyson, already halfway to dreamland, murmured something unintelligible but the tone was full of love.

When Angela walked back into the living room, Belle was curled on the couch alone, Michael nowhere in sight. Belle patted the couch next to her and Angela went to sit beside her mother.

"Michael is in his den, says he's got some work to catch up on." Belle told her by way of explanation.

"Mom, I don't think I ever told you this, but I'm glad you and Michael found each other." She said sincerely. "He's a wonderful and gentle man."

Belle smiled, but her eyes still held a haunted look as she looked at her daughter. "Thank you Angie. I have been very lucky. But darling, it's you I'm worried about. If I had known that bastard was hurting you this way...." her voice trailed off, unsure what else to say.

"Mom, I couldn't tell you or anyone. I was afraid and, I know this sounds crazy, I loved him. Didn't want to lose him." she paused a moment, then added more softly, "Please don't call him a bastard. Lucas is still my babies' daddy."

"Like any mother, Angie," her mother explained, "I only want to protect my child, even though you are grown up. I agree, he is Melissa and Tyson's daddy, always will be, but by what he's done to you, he's lost his right to be a part of your lives for now."

"I know Mom." Angela said sadly. "I feel so bad for him. He's lost everything, even his freedom. Maybe though, he'll now be able to rebuild. It's hard to imagine Lucas going without his music for even a day. I hope he's okay and will be able to get some help, like I have."

Belle shook her head in amazement at her daughter. "I'm not as forgiving as you are, darling." She told her. "I was hoping they'd throw away the key. You see his tortured soul and I see only the soul he tortured. Let's agree to disagree, okay? I love you Angela. I'm so glad you're safe here with us now."

"I love you too Mom." Angela said accepting a hug from the older woman, "I'm so grateful you are here. Your strength is a great support." The two women sat hugging one another for a few minutes before Belle suggested they go through to the kitchen and make bedtime tea.

On Monday afternoon, Michael drove Angela to an appointment with her new counselor. She also had a meeting scheduled with her lawyer, Mr. Blakely, and so would not be done for at least two and half hours. He assured her that was no inconvenience as he had some errands to run.

As soon as she was out of the car, Michael made one call on his cellular phone. Kurt Reeves picked up the phone on the second ring.

"Hello?" he asked and Michael could hear strain and exhaustion in the one word alone.

"Kurt this is Michael." he stated simply. 'We need to talk, right away."

Kurt became concerned when he heard the urgent tone in the ex-cop's voice. "Michael have you heard from Angie? Everything's okay isn't it?"

"Angela is fine." Michael reassured him, but refrained from elaborating. "You going to be home for a while. I really need to see you?"

"Yeah, I'm here." Kurt said tersely.

"I'll be right there." Michael told him and clicked the phone off abruptly. Kurt was puzzled but did not try to second guess Michael's motives. He went to the kitchen, his mind still very much on the state his brother had been in when he had seen Lucas that morning.

When Michael walked into Kurt's house, he wasted no time on idle chatter. Kurt motioned him to a seat at the kitchen table and sat down opposite him.

"Kurt, I've got a favour to ask, but first I need to know if you bailed out your brother?" Michael asked.

"Lucas is in jail at least till his hearing." Kurt told the older man. "And, from what our lawyer tells me, he'll probably be doing some time after that."

Michael was careful to show no outward emotion, though inwardly he was elated.

"Okay, then I'm here to ask, on behalf of your sister-in-law and your niece and nephew, whether we might take some necessities from the house for them, especially the kids. Clothes and things like that, and the children's furniture, as certainly Lucas won't need it."

"Is Angela planning to get a place for her and the kids?" Kurt asked and Michael could see the genuine concern in his eyes.

"Not in the immediate future. She's got a lot on her plate, a job, continued counseling to put her own emotional health back on track, taking care of her children alone. But she is determined to make a life for herself and her children free of fear." Michael told him.

"Michael, I'm thinking that we can solve a few problems for each other." Kurt said, as he contemplated what the older man was telling him. "I now have two different houses to look after and it would be so much easier if I could rent out one of them and live in the other. But that means storing a lot of things from one of them. You're right; Lucas will have no use for the children's clothing, toys and furniture, not for a long time and Angela's entitled to it for their children. I also think Angela's personal things and clothing should be given back to her."

"Kurt, I'll need to rent a truck to move their things, so I'm not sure when we can arrange this." Michael told him with gratitude. "Thank you. Someday perhaps Angela will be able to thank you for herself."

"No problem." Kurt replied. "I know this sounds empty after I let her down for two years, but I honestly think very highly of that gal. She's about the sweetest lady I've ever met and my little brother didn't deserve her at all."

"Perhaps you should tell her that." Michael ventured.

Kurt had no answer to that. But he did have a further offer to make. "Listen, don't rent a truck. We can move everything in my truck. And one other thing, Lucas bought Angela her computer as a Christmas gift, it's hers and I insist it's going too. Lucas will never use it and I have one of my own."

Michael put his hand out and the two men solemnly shook hands. Michael was about to get up and leave when Kurt spoke again.

"I should tell you that I saw Lucas this morning."

Michael was unsure of what to say. "Well, my guess is he wasn't too happy that you left him in jail."

"Yeah well, you were right on that count though." Kurt conceded. "He needs to be held accountable by somebody. I wish I had even half the courage Angela showed when she left him and maybe none of this would have happened. But he is learning the hard way what he put her through. He got the crap beat outta him this weekend when they found out he was a wife beater."

"Kurt, I'd like to say I'm sorry that happened to him, but you and I both know I'd be a liar. But you gotta quit blaming yourself for any of this. Lucas is a grown up, it's his responsibility. Maybe you wanna talk with a counselor about it. Most of the abuse centers have counseling available for families of abusers or victims. Might help you get some perspective."

"If I hold any blame at all Michael, it's because I should have put a stop to it two years ago." Kurt explained. "But someday I'd like to be able to tell Angie how sorry I am, whether she accepts that or not, I wanna get it off my chest."

Michael stood then, shook Kurt's hand again and headed for the door. Before he opened it, he looked back at Kurt and said, "Kurt Reeves, you're a decent guy who was caught in an impossible situation. Take care. I'm sure that Angela will find it in her heart to forgive you." Before Kurt could answer, the older man was gone.

Belle and Angela were in Michael's car with two very sleepy children nodding in the back seat. At Michael's urging, they had spent the day at the zoo. Initially Angela had been very nervous about going out anywhere until Michael assured her that he had done a little inquiring on his own, discovering that Lucas had not posted bail and was still safely behind bars.

As Belle rounded the corner into their front street, Angela was wondering again why Kurt had not come to the rescue and bailed Lucas out this time. She genuinely liked her husband's brother and understood his blind loyalty to Lucas, but had always been intimidated by him and, after that awful morning when she knew that he was aware of Lucas beating her, she had been careful to avoid him as much as possible. Belle was just about to turn into the driveway when Angela looked up and saw a truck parked there. A small audible gasp escaped her lips.

"Mom, drive by." She said urgently. "Don't pull in yet."

Belle glanced briefly across at Angela, seeing her face had turned white as a ghost. She braked the car a little and pulled to the curb across from the house before turning to speak. An excited voice from the back seat cut her off.

"Uncle Kurt's here!" Melissa squealed with delight. Angela muttered something under her breath which Belle could not make out, then turned to her daughter.

"Melissa hush, you'll wake Ty." She told the girl. Belle broke in at this point.

"Angela I'm pulling in, this is our house. You can't be afraid of his brother too!" She admonished. "Besides, Michael's home and I'm sure everything's okay."

Angela stared at her mother, who was already putting the car back into gear. "Mom, he could tell Lucas." She reminded her.

Belle did not hesitate, but wheeled the car into the wide driveway alongside Kurt's truck. As soon as the vehicle came to a stop, Melissa was out and racing up the front steps in search of Uncle Kurt. Angela glared at her mother's betrayal then slid out of her door and opened the back door to take sleeping Tyson into her arms. In front of her, through the open front door, she could hear the joyful reunion between Melissa and her Uncle Kurt. 'Why had Michael let him come here?' she thought, but without a word to Belle she steeled herself and carried her sleeping son into the house.

She could hear clearly that Michael, Kurt and Melissa were in the kitchen towards the back of the house. She turned away from there and took her son down the hall towards the room he shared with Melissa. She stopped short when she walked through the door. Tyson's crib was set up and the two small dressers which had held her children's clothes at home were side by side on one wall. On the other wall were the two toy-boxes which Kurt had built when both children were born, still full of their toys no doubt. She heard Kurt's laughter floating down the hall from the kitchen and couldn't help but smile, though tears were brimming in her eyes. She laid Tyson into his crib and gently slipped off his jacket and shoes.

Angela came out of the bedroom, softly pulling the door closed behind her, then she stood leaning against the wall listening to her daughter chattering excitedly to Michael, Belle and Kurt about the zoo. She was grateful that Kurt had brought the children's things from the house, but found she was unable to take a step closer to the kitchen, to actually facing Lucas's brother.

Michael came round the corner and down the hall, stopping short when he saw Angela standing back to the wall unmoving.

"Angela, what's up?" He asked. "You okay?"

"I'm okay, Michael." She said hesitantly, "But Kurt..." she trailed off, unsure how to voice her fear and confusion.

"It's really okay Angie. Kurt helped me bring some things from the house." He told her. "Things the kids need."

"I know Michael. I saw when I laid Ty down." She told him. "But....."

"But... Angela come here with me a minute." He held out his hand to her, but she did not take it, though she did follow him to the door of her own room. He turned the knob and ushered her in. She looked quizzically at him but stepped through the doorway. Over by the window, which overlooked the backyard, her desk and computer from the house had been neatly set up. Her jaw dropped in surprise and she turned to Michael.

"Thank you!" She exclaimed. "I didn't want anything for myself, just the kids. But thank you!" She touched Michael gently on his forearm. He beamed at her, knowing that tiny touch from her was like a bear hug. But then he nodded his head somewhat humbly.

"Don't thank me," he told her. "You need to be thanking Kurt. This was his idea. He said you would need it. He also said he was glad you'd used it so wisely."

She studied Michael wordlessly for several seconds, and then her head swiveled back to the computer. 'Was it possible that Kurt knew she'd found sanctuary on the computer, that it had showed her the way to freedom and safety?' Michael was about to speak again, when she turned back to him and very quietly said, "You're right of course, Michael. I'd better do that."

Michael and Angela walked into the kitchen together and found Belle at the counter pouring coffee. Melissa was sitting on Kurt's lap happily telling him about her trip to the zoo. Kurt looked up when they walked in.

"Hi, Angie." He said softly.

"Hullo Kurt," she said shyly barely above a whisper. Belle put a coffee mug down on the table in front of Kurt and held her arms out to her granddaughter.

"Come on, Miss 'Lissa." She said. "Grandpa Michael and I are going to take you for a walk."

Angela looked from Michael to Belle with some apprehension that they were going to leave her alone with Kurt. But Michael smiled reassuringly and mouthed the words "It's okay."

Angela still stood self-consciously in the middle of the room after they had gone through the back door. Kurt tried not to stare but his eyes kept being drawn back to the arm in a sling and the bruising still very obvious on his sister-in-law's face. Finally, Angela seemed to take one deep breath and then plunged in.

"Kurt, thank you." She told him. "The things you brought from the house mean so much to me and the kids. Thank you."

"Angie, please come and sit down." he asked with a pleading note in his voice. "You don't need to thank me. These are your things, yours and the kids' and you need them. Lucas doesn't. If there's anything else you think of that you need from the house, let me know okay?"

She slipped tiredly into the chair adjacent to his. "I'm sure you've done enough already." she said. "Kurt, I know you're not going to believe this, but I'm worried about him. How is he?"

"God Angie, of course I believe you." Kurt told her vehemently. "I've never once doubted that you love my brother. He's still in jail. I refused to post bail. Perhaps if I quit bailing him out of trouble, he'll finally learn. He's not great Ange. I won't lie to you. He's lost you and the kids, his jobs and his freedom. They won't even entertain the idea that he be allowed to play guitar in there, not after the violence he's shown. Lucas has about hit the bottom. I hope now he'll realize he wants to climb back up." "I never meant for this to come out this way." she murmured sadly. "I only wanted me and the kids to be safe."

Kurt wanted to reach a hand out to her, but dare not. "This is not your fault Angela." he told her. "It's Lucas's doing and to a lesser degree mine. My God, you're the best thing that ever happened to him. You truly are a sweet angel."

"That's what the counselors keep telling me, 'this is not your fault.' she said wryly, "But I wonder sometimes. But Kurt, you can't blame yourself either."

Kurt visibly shuddered at her words. "Angela, I am truly so very sorry. I knew what he was doing to you when you were still pregnant with Tyson. I was awake that night when we came home drunk. Angie I was such a fool, I stood there like a drunken coward and let him batter you. I heard you scream and I wasn't man enough to help. This horror should have all ended for you years ago. Sweet lady, I am so very sorry."

Angela reached out for her brother-in-law then and took one of his big hands in her small one. "I lived with him, Kurt." she said firmly, "I know what he was like. I forgive you."

They sat for a long time holding hands across the table as they both wept freely. Kurt finally pulled away, wiped his tears self-consciously with the back of his big hand and spoke again.

"Angie, I still love my brother too. Though I confess, I haven't liked him much for a long time." Kurt said. "I can tell you that I have paid for his lawyer and, if he needs and asks for it, I will pay for counseling, so perhaps he can straighten himself out too. But I make a promise to you too; Lucas Reeves will never ever harm you again, because I will never be afraid to do what is right again."

"Kurt, I will always love your brother." she said. "We had two children together, he is my only love. I wish him nothing but the best. Behind his anger there is the fear of a little boy but also a heart full of deep emotion. I have something I want you to give him."

Kurt looked puzzled as Angela got up from the table and disappeared towards the hallway to the bedrooms. When she came back through the living room he was standing by the door pulling on his boots. She stood in front of him and held out her hand fist closed. As he watched, she opened her hand and he saw the heart shaped silver locket that she had always worn. She dropped it into his hand.

"It contains his heart string, Kurt." She told him. "Tell him, I think he needs it now."

Kurt closed his fist round the token, leaned down and gave her a brotherly peck on the cheek. "Take care, Angel." he said, in a voice that she thought for a moment was Lucas. She watched him walk to the truck, start it and back out of the driveway. It was only as the truck accelerated away from the house that she spoke aloud again.

"Tell him I love him, Kurt."

Made in the USA
Charleston, SC
22 February 2012